Praise for *The Art Of Keeping Secrets*

"Johns has tackled some hard-hitting topics with sensitivity and insight and she's brought one rather high-profile social issue of our times in close and made it personal."

—*Beauty and Lace* (blogger)

"Love this book! I feel like it's the perfect book to curl up with on a rainy Sunday morning. I love the friendship between Felicity, Emma and Neve. But I also liked the honest way Rachael Johns portrayed the story—it kept me hooked right until the last page!"

—Kim Brown (*Netgalley*)

"An intoxicating ride."

—*The Australian Women's Weekly*

"Bursting at the seams with secrets that range from little white lies to those that threaten and undermine your very existence, *The Art of Keeping Secrets* was an astounding read that left me reeling in the best possible way."

—Jess Fitzpatrick (*Netgalley*)

For additional books by international bestselling author
Rachael Johns, visit her website, www.rachaeljohns.com.

RACHAEL JOHNS

the art of keeping secrets

mira

mira

Recycling programs
for this product may
not exist in your area.

ISBN-13: 978-0-7783-3040-0

The Art of Keeping Secrets

This is the revised text of the work first published by
Harlequin Enterprises (Australia) Pty. Limited in 2016.

Revised text edition © 2017 by Rachael Johns

For questions and comments about the quality of this book, please contact us at
CustomerService@Harlequin.com.

www.BookClubbish.com

Printed in U.S.A.

For Kirsten—the strongest woman I know
and one I'm blessed to call a best friend.

the art of keeping secrets

1

Felicity

Felicity Bell could think of a number of places she'd rather be on a Friday night than in the pretentiously decorated living room of a house owned by her friend's no-good ex-husband. But here they were—she, Neve and Emma—for the benefit of their beloved sons, who were all dressed up like James Bond and ready to attend their grade-twelve prom.

"Do you think I should get Botox?" Neve asked, reaching a perfectly manicured hand up to her forehead and brushing her fingers across her wrinkle-free skin.

Flick laughed and took another sip of her champagne— yes, actual champagne; Max and Chanel were obviously trying to impress tonight. "You are the last person I know who needs Botox."

Beside them, Emma sighed and eyed herself in the nearby floor-to-ceiling mirrors. She flattened a hand down the front of her dress. "If you need Botox, then I need a total-body makeover. Know any good plastic surgeons who do the whole shebang?"

Flick shook her head. "Would you two listen to yourselves? You're both being ridiculous. You're beautiful."

Neve was dressed for the occasion in a knee-length gold cocktail dress only a shade or two darker than her pixie-cut hair. Her muddy brown eyes almost looked gold as well tonight. Emma, less flashy but just as gorgeous, had gone for a simple black shift that showed off her curves. Her ash-blond hair—usually tied back—cascaded in waves to just below her shoulders, indicating she'd made more effort than usual tonight. Although the gray beneath her eyes suggested she could do with a good night's sleep. Flick, in a green silk shirt and black trousers she'd had for years, felt positively drab in comparison.

Neve wrapped her arm around Emma and turned her away from the mirror. "I'm sorry. You're right. I'm being ridiculous. Maybe it's the boys. I just can't believe they're so close to graduating. I feel really old all of a sudden." She sipped her champagne and glanced through the open windows to the landscaped backyard. It could have been a resort or a set for one of those tropical reality shows.

Outside by the pool, Neve's seventeen-year-old son, Will, a tall, cheekily handsome blond, was larking with Flick's own son, Toby, Emma's son, Caleb, and a couple of other boys from Dayton Grammar School. Their partners for the dance were a few feet away fawning over each other's gowns, many of which Flick suspected cost more than her wedding dress had.

It didn't seem five minutes since Toby had been a dark-haired newborn. But now her baby was a teenager in his final year at high school and her daughter, Zoe, was only a few months away from marriage. Wasn't forty-five too young for a mother-of-the-bride outfit? Never mind the fact that these days twenty was far too young to get married. Everything was changing too fast. "You're right," Flick said. "We're too young for all of this."

"No, *she's* too young for this," Emma spit, and downed the

contents of her crystal champagne flute in one quick gulp. She pointed the empty glass at the skinny platinum blonde currently schmoozing with her other, more deserving guests. Chanel and Max had been pointedly ignoring them since they'd arrived.

None of them knew exactly how old Chanel was, but Flick guessed midtwenties at most. It was easy to see what Emma's ex-husband, Max, saw in her, and let's just say it wasn't her brains. But brains or not, if looks could kill Chanel would be lying in a pool of blood on her immaculate outdoor decking.

A waiter swooped upon the trio of women and refilled their glasses.

"Maybe you should just leave us the bottle." Emma grabbed for it but the man had superhuman reflexes and raised it out of her reach. He smiled politely and then retreated hastily, taking the champagne with him.

Flick looked around, wondering where her husband had vanished to. Maybe Seb would steal them another bottle. He'd relish the challenge of sneaking into the kitchen without getting caught. He was always the life of the party, the first to suggest some kind of silly prank or accept a stupid dare, so much more spontaneous and social than she was—one of the many things that had attracted her to him.

"Hey, did you hear about Julian?" Emma's question interrupted Flick's thoughts.

"Julian who?" she and Neve asked in unison.

"Julian Fletcher-Jones." At their blank faces, Emma elaborated. "He's that hotshot basketball player in grade twelve. Has had the Wildcats sniffing around him."

Flick racked her brain for a face. Although Dayton sometimes felt like a small country town, it had in excess of six hundred students, so she didn't know every kid in her son's year.

"Well…" Emma leaned in close, indicating she had juicy

gossip indeed. "Word is he got a girl from the local *public* high school up the duff."

"Pregnant?" Neve whispered.

Flick gasped as her hand shot to cover her mouth. "Now I remember!" She lowered her voice, hoping no one had heard her shriek. "His mom's that toffee-nosed cow who wouldn't let us join her book club all those years ago. What's her name again?"

Emma smiled victoriously and nodded. "Anouk. Apparently she's furious—'the least he could have done was choose a girl of better breeding'—and *her* parents are very religious and want them to get married the moment they are both eighteen. The baby is due smack bang in the middle of final exams. Poor kids."

"Jeez." Neve shook her head, her face turning pale. She looked out at the pool, where the boys were joking around with their friends. "I'd murder Will if he got Stacey knocked up. I've been leaving condoms in his bedside table just in case."

Emma gripped Neve's arm. "And has he been...you know... using them?"

"I haven't actually asked him. He'd probably die if I tried to talk to him about sex, but either there's a condom fairy taking them during the night or, yes, he's using them."

"*God.*" Flick groaned, feeling simultaneously sick and in need of more alcohol. Should *she* be leaving condoms for Toby? Not that he paid much attention to girls; desperate to be a pilot, he put most of his energy into his studies and whatever was left over into sports.

At that moment, Seb appeared, his broad shoulders pushed back as he swaggered toward them with a smile on his face that would make a nun think about taking off her panties. Where had he been? Flick stepped forward and kissed him, then he leaned across and gave her friends a peck on each of their cheeks.

"Looking lovely as usual this evening, ladies," he said, admiring their dresses as they batted their eyelashes at him.

Neve grinned. "Why, thank you, Sebastian."

Flick held out her empty champagne flute. "Make yourself useful and go find us another bottle. The waiter is rationing us and—"

"And I'm not going to survive this unless I'm drunk," Emma interjected, her voice louder than it should have been. Her face went pale as Max and Chanel finally made their way toward them.

Of course they'd wooed the other couples first; couples they no doubt considered much more their kind of people. Flick had never been one of the ladies who lunch—the group of moms who ran the Parents and Friends association. All those women aspired to was having the most expensive designer handbag or raising the most money at the annual P&F Art Show. They didn't work, they all had help at home and none of them seemed to have anything better to do than keep up their regular beauty salon appointments. Flick glanced down at her hands, unable to remember the last time she'd had a manicure. Besides, in her line of work, long nails were a hindrance.

Then there were the mothers with high-flying careers—lawyers, dentists, CEOs, pilots. There were even a couple of surgeons. The "professional" moms weren't as insufferable as the ladies who lunched, but Flick suspected that was more because they rarely had the time to interact with anyone than because they were actually nice.

The other group were the boarders' moms, mostly country women who were friendly and often as well dressed as the in crowd, but were always rushing about, too busy running errands while they were in the Big Smoke to stop and chat.

She, Neve and Emma worked just as hard as the professional moms, but as they didn't make the same money, they'd become their own little group of misfits. The taxidermist, the makeup artist and the travel agent—three unlikely friends who now rarely went a day without speaking to each other. Although they didn't give two hoots what the other parents thought of them, being a misfit wasn't always easy and tonight's gathering was the perfect example of why.

"Have you stopped going to the gym?" Max demanded of Emma, as if he still had any right to ask her anything. "You look…" His voice drifted off but the expression on his face made his thoughts clear.

Flick opened her mouth to ask if he still used hair dye to cover his grays, but Seb came to the rescue first. "I think she looks gorgeous."

Emma shot him a grateful smile as Max raised his eyebrows disdainfully.

The truth was Emma may have put on a few pounds in the last few months but she was by no means fat, and anyway, it was no concern of Max's. Maybe if he hadn't left her near destitute in the divorce, she wouldn't have to work so bloody much and she might have more time to do things for herself.

Five years ago, when Flick had first met Emma, Max had just left her for a legal secretary from his law firm, but she reckoned he'd always been a wanker. Obviously the only reason he and Chanel had volunteered to have the preprom get-together was so they could show off their new place. Personally, Flick didn't see the appeal—the massive house felt like a showroom, something you might admire in a magazine but not practical for normal everyday living. She could only imagine the way Chanel's nose would turn up if she came to Flick and Seb's place, where pieces of art and beautifully preserved and mounted animal specimens filled every available space.

"Nice decor," Neve said loudly, making a show of gazing around the massive entertaining area.

"Why, thank you." Chanel's eyes twinkled in obvious pride.

Neve gestured to the full-length mirrors lining one wall. "Are those from Ikea? They look exactly like some I saw on the weekend." Chanel's smile faded and she almost choked on her drink as she shot a quick glance over at the other couples to make sure they hadn't heard this absurdity. She wouldn't be seen dead in Swedish flat-pack heaven.

As she spluttered, Max patted her on the back. "We had them shipped from Milan," he explained.

"Oh! That sounds pricey. I hope you didn't get ripped off," Neve said with a saccharine smile.

Flick caught Emma's gaze, both of them trying not to laugh out loud. As the three friends and Seb smirked, awkward silence descended on the unlikely circle.

"Well." Max glanced at his watch. "The limos should be here to pick up the kids soon. Shall we get the photos started?"

That had to be one of the best ideas Max had ever had. The sooner the photos were over and the boys and their belles were on their way for their big night, the sooner Flick, Seb, Neve and Emma could make their escape.

As Max went away to fetch his camera, Seb embarked on his mission to unearth more booze and Chanel couldn't return to her other guests fast enough.

"I thought Max would have organized a professional photographer," Flick mused.

It was good to hear Emma laugh. "He doesn't always think of everything."

"Was he always that much of a dick?" Neve asked. "I honestly don't know how you tolerated being married to him for... How many years was it?"

"Too many. I actually thought he was sweet when we first

got together," Emma admitted as Seb returned with a bottle of champagne.

Neve smiled her approval. "That was quick."

"My hero." Flick took the bottle and poured a generous amount into Emma's glass, then did the same for herself and Neve. By the time she took her first sip, Emma had already downed hers and was holding her hand out for more.

Flick raised an eyebrow, but filled the glass again nevertheless. Who was she to judge? Lord knew if Seb suddenly left her for some tart almost half his age, she'd likely turn to drink as well.

Out on the pool deck, Chanel and Max were now trying to organize the promgoers. The waiter circled with a plate of arancini balls. If this gathering had been at Flick and Seb's place, they'd have made do with a couple of dips and chopped-up veggie sticks, but at least she'd have made the food herself.

Bitchy, she thought as she watched Chanel. Max's treatment of Emma had brought her claws out.

Max had an enormous camera—compensation for a smaller something else, perhaps—and the other parents snapped their own shots with their latest-model smartphones.

Flick and her friends left Seb to do the honors with their sons, choosing instead to stand back and admire the young men their boys were growing into. She watched Toby offer his hand out to his date as she navigated the rocky garden stairs they were assembling on. Brooklyn, a sweet redheaded thing who had recently emigrated with her family from America, beamed up at Toby and laughed as he whispered something in her ear. A rush of love warmed Flick's insides, making her forget her bitterness of a few moments earlier. Although not usually very emotional, she found her throat clogging up and tears prickling at the corners of her eyes. Toby might have his moments—what teenage boy didn't?—but his sunny personality and hardworking nature made her and Seb proud almost every day.

"Here." Neve conjured a tissue from her Mary Poppins handbag—she carried everything but the kitchen sink with her—and handed it to Flick.

Flick smiled her thanks as she wiped her eyes, once again grateful that she never bothered with mascara. "I reckon we've done okay with our boys."

"It's easy to see where Toby gets his great personality from," Emma said, her words slightly slurring as she pointed her champagne flute in Seb's direction. "Not to mention his gorgeous smile and impeccable manners. I just pray that Caleb doesn't turn out anything like his father."

"Yeah, Seb's great." Neve looked to Flick, a wistful expression on her face. "You're so lucky to have him—he's a wonderful husband, father and provider. I wish Will had a role model like that in his life."

"Yes, I'm very lucky." Flick smiled tightly—biting down on the impulse to remind her friends that he wasn't the only one who contributed to the household income and their children's upbringing. Honestly, sometimes she wouldn't be surprised if Neve and Emma started a Sebastian Bell fan club.

2

Emma

By the time the photos were over and the limos had arrived to collect the excited teenagers, Emma had lost count of the number of glasses of champagne she'd consumed. Thankfully Laura and Louise were at a friend's house for a sleepover so they wouldn't see her in a state when she got home. But she didn't want to embarrass Caleb in front of his friends either— or make a scene in front of Max. As she and the other parents followed their children out through the marble entrance hall to the front garden, she grabbed a glass of water from the waiter and focused all her efforts into maintaining her balance.

"You okay?" Flick whispered beside her.

She nodded, almost stumbling over the front step. Neve and Flick reached out to steady her and she offered them grateful smiles. Thank God for these two wonderful women, because no way could she have come here on her own. Without them, she'd have missed seeing her gorgeous Caleb all dressed up in his suit, missed seeing this momentous occasion in her only son's life. He looked so handsome, so grown-up; she just wanted to go over and wrap her arms around him.

"Thanks, Mr. and Mrs. McLoughlin," called the young

men and young ladies as they began climbing into the limos, their faces aglow with glee. Emma flinched and couldn't help pursing her lips. *She* was Mrs. McLoughlin, not the wispy blonde whom Max had dumped her for. She'd have changed her name back to her maiden name—Fleming, which she'd always preferred—if it wasn't for the kids. Everything she did was for Caleb and the twins, and the last thing she wanted was for them to have different surnames.

She and Max had got married in their early twenties—the old shotgun wedding—and back then Max had been a fun guy, a lot like Caleb was now: smart, funny and charismatic. But his drive to get to the top of his career and to keep up with the Joneses had changed him into someone who valued money and status above all else. They'd had Caleb, and then the twins, and though being parents had changed things in the bedroom, she'd thought him so involved with his career that he wouldn't have time for extramarital activities. But Max had proved her wrong in that department, too.

Distracted by her thoughts, Emma didn't notice Caleb until he was right in front of her. His hands landed on her shoulders and his big brown eyes looked down into hers as his slightly too-long dirty-blond hair fell across his face.

"You okay, Mom?" he asked, his voice deep and so like Max's. Thankfully, he hadn't inherited many of his father's personality traits. Caleb was one of the most caring people she knew. If he got the marks he was hoping for, he'd make a good doctor one day.

She felt a rush of emotion as she examined him. She still remembered when he had fit into the crook of her arm, and now he was a good head and a half taller than her. "Fine. I'm fine."

"I love you, you know that? Thanks for coming tonight." Then he leaned forward and gave her the hug she'd been craving. Unsaid was the fact that he knew being here wasn't easy for her.

"I love you, too," she whispered into Caleb's chest, praying she'd be able to hold her tears back until the kids were gone and she was far away from Max's place. Her ex wouldn't feel guilt or remorse that he'd turned her into a blubbering mess; he'd simply pity her. And he could shove his pity where the sun didn't shine.

One of the other boys called to Caleb from the limo and he pulled back, laughing, not at all embarrassed by their teasing.

"You go," she told him. "Have a fabulous night. I can't wait to hear all about it."

With another smile that melted her heart even more, Caleb turned and jogged back to the limo. Around her, smartphones were snapping photos as the kids settled into their seats, already sipping the nonalcoholic sparkling wine the limo company had provided for them. The chauffeur shut the door behind Caleb and walked briskly around to the driver's side, the engine starting seconds after he slid into his seat. Emma waved alongside the other parents until both limousines were no longer in view.

Now what?

As if Max could read her mind—*heaven forbid*—he made an announcement. "The night's still young, folks. You're all welcome to come inside and have a few more drinks. Why should the kids have all the fun?"

The other parents chuckled and murmured their agreement, but she thought she'd rather kill herself than spend any more time in Max and Chanel's perfect love nest. Then again, going home alone to an empty house appealed only a fraction more. She didn't even have a pet to keep her company.

"I'm not staying here," she hissed under her breath, her tears thankfully subsided now the kids were out of sight.

Neve gave her a wry smile. "We thought as much."

"As if we want to hang around either," Flick added, making no effort to keep her voice down.

Seb, one arm around his wife, made a suggestion. "How about you all go back to Emma's place and have a girls' night? Flick can drive your car back—" so lovely the way he didn't come straight out and say she was too pissed to drive it herself "—and I'll pick her up later."

Neve nodded. "Brilliant idea. But don't worry, I'll give Flick a ride back when we're finished."

"Better still," Seb suggested, "how about you leave your car at Emma's as well, and I'll pick you both up. That way you can all enjoy a few drinks while you're kid-free."

Neve's eyes sparkled. "You really are the perfect man, aren't you, Sebastian?"

He shrugged one shoulder as if to say "I can't help it if it comes naturally."

With her friends like bodyguards at her side, Emma followed the other parents as they trekked back into the near mansion, then collected her bag from where she'd left it in the living room. The others were ready to leave without saying goodbye to their hosts, but Emma's good breeding wouldn't allow it. Her mother would turn in her grave if she thought Emma would fail to thank anyone for their hospitality. And she didn't want Max and Chanel to think they could upset her.

"Going already?" Max asked, his fake smile in place once again as he nodded toward the three women with their handbags. For a moment Emma was tempted to say no, just to see the smirk fall from his face, but Neve got in first.

"Yes, sadly," she said, her friendly tone giving Max's fake smile a run for its money. "We've got somewhere better to be."

Emma had to stifle a giggle. "But thanks to you and Chanel for hosting the preprom party." With her allies on either side of her, Max didn't have as much power over her as he sometimes did.

"Yes," Neve said. "I'm sure your efforts to impress worked on *most*."

Before Max could reply, Flick grabbed hold of Emma's and Neve's hands and dragged them out the front, where Seb was waiting.

"Have a good night, girls," he said as he leaned forward to kiss them all in turn. Emma and Neve received friendly pecks on the cheek, but Seb's lips lingered longer on Flick's mouth, and instead of looking away, Emma found herself wishing she had someone to kiss good-night.

Seb jogged down the driveway and then climbed into their black SUV. Emma, assisted by Flick, settled herself in the passenger seat of her boring sedan and Neve headed over to her cute lime-green hatchback, calling over her shoulder that she'd stop at the liquor store on her way.

"You handled that well," Flick said as she shoved Emma's key into the ignition, flicked on the headlights and adjusted the rearview mirror.

Emma tossed her a cut-the-bullshit look. "If getting myself sloshed counts as handling things well, then yeah, I guess I did. Maybe I'm a better ex-wife than I was a wife."

Flick laughed. "I'd rather be Max's ex than his current wife any day."

That made Emma giggle because aside from the fact that without Max she had to work her butt off at the travel agency just to make ends meet, she agreed.

"Hey," she said, a silly idea suddenly popping into her head—she blamed the alcohol. "How much would you charge to stuff a human? Actually, make that *humans*."

Her hands still gripping the wheel, Flick turned to look at Emma and her lips broke into a grin. "Max and Chanel?"

Smiling, Emma nodded.

"For you, honey, I'd do it for free. And I'd enjoy every moment of it."

They were still laughing when Neve joined them at Emma's place. "What's so funny?" she asked, dumping a brown paper bag onto the kitchen counter. Emma took great pleasure in explaining as Flick located champagne flutes and cracked open the bubbly.

"Sorry, it's not Veuve or Moët but it's pink and I didn't need to mortgage my unit to buy it," Neve apologized over her own laughter.

As Flick handed out the glasses and the women headed into the living room to flop down on Emma's comfy couches, she said, "Is it just me or do you guys think that the cheap champagne usually tastes better than the expensive stuff?"

"It's just you," Neve said, lifting her glass to her lips. "It's the reason I'm still single—I haven't yet found a man with a big enough wallet to accommodate my champagne tastes."

Flick laughed. "That and the fact you don't actually put yourself out there and go on dates!"

Neve grimaced. "The few I went on when Will was little turned me off. Bad breath, wandering hands, tongues like lizards and dicks you could barely find with a magnifying glass. I can satisfy myself and I don't have to get dressed up or leave the house to do so."

Smiling to be in the comfort of her own home with her two closest friends, Emma sighed. "I do miss the sex, though. Max might be an arrogant ass but he knew how to make me scream."

"Are you thinking of reentering the dating game?" Flick asked from her position on the opposite couch.

Emma shook her head. "I hadn't given it any thought until tonight." Truthfully, the idea terrified her. Ever since the whole Max debacle, she'd harbored evil-stabby feelings toward the opposite sex. "I know you found a good one, Flick, but in my experience, good men are few and far between and, sadly, many of them bat for the other team. Anyway, how on earth would I find the time?"

"Um…" Neve said, her tone sarcastic. "What else do you think single mothers do on the weekends when their exes have the kids?"

"But every other Friday night is when I catch up with you guys," Emma protested. "And by the time I do all the housework and laundry and grocery shopping on Saturday—*if* I'm not working—I'm too tired to think about entertaining a man. Nope, silly idea. Sex is overrated anyway, forget I ever mentioned it."

"Mentioned what?" Flick asked, a twinkle in her eyes. "Anyway, right now I care more about food than men. Should we order some pizza or something?"

Neve agreed this was a splendid suggestion.

Max's words about the gym rang clear in Emma's ears but she pushed them aside, not wanting to give him any power over her. "Sounds good to me. I really should eat if I don't want to wake up with a hangover." Emma leaped off the couch to make the call, hoping either her friends would insist on chipping in to pay or there'd still be some money left in one of the kids' piggy banks. Barely managing to keep up with her mortgage, she'd been raiding them more often than she liked lately and always made a silent promise to herself to replenish what she took as soon as possible. It wasn't like they ever needed money—Max bought them everything their hearts could possibly desire.

She worried about this, not simply because it pained her to think of her ex buying the kids' affections when she couldn't afford to, but because she didn't want him turning them into spoiled little brats who didn't think they needed to work for anything.

"Em? You okay?"

Emma blinked out of her reverie to see Flick and Neve staring up at her, concern scrawled across both their faces.

"Sorry." She shook her head and then lifted her hand to her forehead because the action irritated her blossoming headache. Maybe it was already too late to save tomorrow's hangover with food. "Was just thinking about Max and the kids."

Neve stood. "Sit down and relax," she insisted. "I'll order the pizza."

"And I'll go get some water," Flick announced, also pushing up from her seat. "Tonight was emotional for all of us, but you had the extra stress of having to pretend you were fine and dandy about hanging out with… Well, you know what I mean."

Emma let out a half laugh and slunk back onto the couch. Flick and Neve rarely uttered Max's and Chanel's names, treating them both a little like Lord Voldemort from Harry Potter. "Thanks, guys. I don't know what I'd do without you."

"That's what friends are for," Neve said as the two of them retreated into her kitchen.

Emma took a few deep breaths in and out, not wanting her headache or bitter thoughts to ruin her night with friends. Their boys would never again head off to their grade-twelve prom, and they should be commemorating the occasion with happy memories, not by talking about her conniving ex-husband. She didn't want to turn into one of those bitter women who couldn't discuss anything but how hard done by they were. Usually she worked very hard to be positive, but being in such close proximity to Max and Chanel always threatened this resolve.

"Here you are." Flick returned a few moments later with an ice-cold glass filled with water.

Emma pressed it against her forehead as Flick sat back down. "Headache?"

Emma nodded, the simple action making her head throb more.

"Not surprising."

Emma took a long sip of water and tried to perk up. "So... how good did our boys look tonight?"

A smile crept onto Flick's face as she tucked her long straight dark hair behind her ears. "*So* good." She sniffed. "Watching Toby with Brooklyn made my heart break a little."

"I know what you mean."

"It made me realize that he won't be my little boy forever," Flick continued, swirling her glass between her fingers, staring down into it as if it held a photo of Toby. "The way he looked at Brooklyn tonight... He used to look at me like that. I don't think I'm ready for him to grow up."

"Oh, please stop," Neve said, returning to the room, picking up her glass and taking a swig as she flopped at the other end of the couch to Flick. "If you girls are going to get all sentimental on me, I'm leaving and I'll be taking the pizza with me."

Emma laughed.

"Don't even think about it." Flick shot her a glare. "I will fight to the death for my pepperoni with extra cheese."

Smiling, Neve relaxed back into the couch. "Think about it—with empty nests we can get up to so much more fun. We'll have less laundry, less cleaning, less cooking. We won't have to get up at ungodly hours on the weekend to drive the boys to rowing practice. And maybe we'll be able to go on that girls' trip we've been fantasizing about forever."

Emma didn't want to burst Neve's bubble but there was no

way she'd be able to afford any kind of vacation unless they were talking about a weekend at the trailer park down the street. Actually, even that would probably break her budget right now. "Um...in case you've forgotten, I still have two younger daughters."

"But you also have school holidays and every second weekend kid-*free*," Flick said, making it sound like *free* was a good thing.

As much as Emma loved her friends, they had no idea what it was like having to say goodbye to your babies every second weekend. She missed them. And as for alternate Christmases alone—nothing compared to that kind of misery. She'd never asked to be separated from them—sometimes it felt like she had no control over anything in her life anymore.

Deciding that humoring her friends would be easier than arguing, Emma smiled. "Okay then, where would we go?"

"Now, that is a good question." Flick's forehead furrowed as if she was in deep contemplation. "Do we want to go somewhere hot or cold?"

"Hot," Emma and Neve said together.

"Okay. Beach or rural?"

Having grown up in the wheatbelt, Emma could think of nothing worse than being stuck in the outback during the sweltering temperatures. "Beach," she declared. Neve nodded her agreement.

"Overseas or in Australia?"

"Overseas," Neve replied.

At the same time, Emma said, "In Western Australia." They all laughed.

"What about Bali?" Flick suggested. "We can lounge on the beach or by some exquisite resort pool while some buff, tanned guy brings us a never-ending supply of cocktails. And it's practically still in Western Australia!"

Emma had to admit it did sound rather appealing. And relaxing. She couldn't remember the last time she'd done such a thing. Life was one big rush, trying to work, keep house and spend quality time with the kids. She hadn't even read a book or had her hair done for…a long time.

Her fingers drifted to the dry ends of her hair as she imagined how much fun would it be vacationing with her friends.

Flick leaned forward and rubbed her hands together, more like an excited child than a responsible mother and wife. "Now, the big question is, when?"

The answer was delayed by the buzzing of Emma's doorbell and the arrival of the pizza.

3

Genevieve

Sometime around 1:00 a.m., Neve stood on the porch of her two-bedroom town house, carrying her sparkly high heels as she waved goodbye to Seb. They'd left Emma asleep on the couch with a crochet blanket thrown over her and a glass of water on the coffee table for when she woke up in a few hours with the inevitable hangover.

Flick had already been snoring against the passenger window by the time Seb reversed out of Emma's driveway. He would probably have to carry her inside to bed. As she unlocked and then opened her front door, Neve smiled wistfully at that image, fantasizing for a moment about what it would be like to have someone like Sebastian Bell in her life. Someone kind and sexy who loved and looked out for her.

Not that she *needed* someone—she had a job she adored, which brought her enough money to cover the bills and most things she or Will desired; she could even fix a clogged toilet and change a tire on her own—but sometimes she thought it would be nice to have a man around. Emma had admitted to missing sex, and the truth was Neve wouldn't have said no to a heart-stopping orgasm either, but what she craved most

was intimacy and companionship. It had been almost two decades since she'd experienced anything close. Yet the thought
of putting herself out there again—having to meet men, go
on dates and risk heartbreak all over again—left her in a cold
sweat. Sure, she could walk the walk and talk the talk, make
jokes about men and sex, but it had been eighteen years since
she'd played the dating game—not counting the few dismal
dates she'd been on when Will was little. If only she had a different job, maybe she'd meet potential suitors at work, but in
her line of business it was mostly women. The few men she
dealt with were fun to hang out with but not relationship—for
her—material. She supposed she could try the online thing.
Internet dating hadn't been an option in her pre-Will days,
but maybe it could be fun. Or terrifying!

Deciding these thoughts were too complicated for the early
hours of the morning, Neve sighed and felt along the wall for
the light switch. She turned it on, shut the front door behind
her and sauntered down the hallway to the kitchen. Although
bed beckoned, her throat felt parched and she needed water.

"Hi, Mom."

At the sound of Will's voice, she dropped her shoes and
her bag, slamming a hand against her chest. Thanks to the
moonlight shining in through the kitchen window, she could
just make out a silhouette sitting at the kitchen table. "What
are you doing home already? And why are you sitting in the
dark?" she demanded as she turned on the kitchen light. "You
almost gave me a heart attack!"

Her son looked back at her, every bit as tall, dark and handsome as his father had been, his expression thoughtful. Will
shrugged; something was bothering him.

"Are you okay? Did something happen at the prom?" If
Stacey had dumped him, she'd kill the little tart.

He shook his head and she wasn't sure if that was a no to being okay or a no to something happening.

Pulling out a chair and sitting opposite him, she leaned across to hold his hand. "I thought you were going to the after-party?"

He shrugged again and she tried a different tack. "You hungry? What was the food like at the Hyatt?"

"It wasn't bad. Stacey and I spent most of the night dancing."

Neve smiled. "That sounds like fun."

"It was all right. But yeah, I could go for a midnight snack." As she got up to raid the fridge, he said, "Where've you been?"

"We went back to Emma's place, chatted for a bit, had a few drinks."

"You didn't drive home, did you?"

"No, of course not." Neve shook her head, smiling at the way Will looked out for her. Sometimes you'd think *he* was the parent. "Toby's dad drove me. How'd *you* get home?"

"Stacey's dad dropped me off. She wasn't allowed to go to the after-party and I felt bad going without her."

"That was nice of you." Pride soared within her as she took a chocolate cake out of the fridge—her wonderful mother had dropped it off earlier in the day when she did her weekly housecleaning. Neve wouldn't have made it through the last seventeen years without her parents—being a single mother had been a lot harder than she'd anticipated, even though Will was pretty much the perfect child.

"Had things on my mind. Didn't really feel in the mood for partying," Will admitted, and Neve's heart skipped a beat. She thought of Emma's announcement about Will's classmate getting some girl pregnant and the evening's champagne swirled in her stomach.

"What's up?" She hoped her voice didn't give away her

anxiety as she sliced two pieces of cake—a large one for him and a sliver for her—and put them on plates. She laid the plates on the table and poured two glasses of milk.

In many ways Neve and Will were closer than most mothers and sons because they were all the other had ever had, but she'd learned over the years that he closed up if she pried too much.

Hoping he couldn't hear the thumping of her heart, she took a bite of her cake. If Stacey was pregnant, she'd stand by them both; none of this forcing them to get married. Granted, she didn't feel old enough to be a grandmother, but neither had she planned on being a single mom and that had turned out all right.

Finally, after he'd almost devoured the cake, Will said, "I want to meet my dad."

Neve's stomach sank as if someone had dumped a brick inside it. If she wasn't sitting down, she'd have no doubt fainted, yet her dizziness had nothing to do with alcohol intake or fatigue. She blinked. Maybe she'd imagined the announcement, finally envisaged the most alarming bombshell he could possibly drop.

"I'm sorry, can you say that again?" she asked, snatching up her glass and taking a gulp of milk like it was something much stronger.

Will chuckled nervously. "Sorry... I meant to lead up to it or something, but I didn't know how to tell you. I want to find my father. I want to meet him, hopefully get to know him."

Nope, her ears had heard perfectly well the first time. More's the pity.

"Well..." Neve summoned the chirpiest smile she could. "What's brought this on?"

"It's not something sudden," he confessed, staring down at his plate and pushing the last bit of cake around with his fork.

"I've been thinking about him for a long time now. You said I looked like him, but I want to *know* him. I want to hear his voice, sit down and share a beer."

The first thought that came into Neve's head was "You're too young for a beer." Of course, she didn't say it. Will not being the legal drinking age was the least of their problems.

"O-*kay*," she said. Panic set her heart racing and she hoped he couldn't see it on her face. "Right. Well. Lovely."

How the hell hadn't she seen this coming? Hadn't everyone always told her that boys needed their fathers? It was only natural for kids to want to know their parentage. Until thirty seconds ago, she'd disregarded this notion whenever anyone raised it. Will hadn't suffered for being raised by a single mom. She'd watched action movies with him, played with cars instead of dolls, learned to kick a soccer ball. He'd found good friends and earned a scholarship to one of the most prestigious boys' private schools in Western Australia. What exactly had he lacked?

"Truth is, Mom, I've already started looking."

"Oh?" Her heart clenched again as an icy chill washed through her—she didn't know how many more surprises it could take.

"Please don't get all funny," Will gushed, leaning over the table and this time taking her hand. "It doesn't change how I feel about you. You've always been the best mom ever, but... it's like...it's like I don't know half of who I am. Remember that time I had to do a family tree in year nine and we made up James's side because you, *we*, didn't know anything of it?"

Neve flinched at the way Will said his father's name so casually, and an almost physical pain squeezed her chest at his heartfelt words. "I remember," she whispered, and then somehow managed to ask, "So what have you found out?"

His face fell and he pushed his plate away from him with force. "Nothing. It's like he doesn't even exist."

She closed her eyes briefly, relieved that he didn't know the truth. But guilt immediately followed at the lies she'd fed him over the years. Quick on its heels came the desire to protect her little boy. The desire to turn his downturned lips into a smile again. Putting her own needs and fears aside, she asked, "What exactly have you done so far?"

He straightened. "I've searched *James Clark* on the internet. I even narrowed it down to James Clarks involved in theater but there are literally hundreds of them on LinkedIn and Facebook and none of them look remotely like me."

That's because his surname isn't Clark. It's Cooper.

"I've contacted a few and they've all been really apologetic but none fit the mold."

"I wish you'd come to me earlier," Neve said. Over the years, Will had occasionally asked her about his father—usually near Father's Day when he had to make a card for "Dad" at school—but although she'd told him snatches of the story, she'd sanitized the truth for his young mind. "I could have helped."

He shrugged. "I didn't want to hurt you. I know thinking about him makes you sad, but I think I do need your help. Have you any idea where he could be now?"

Of course she had an idea; much more than an idea, in fact. Even before Facebook she'd kept track of him through contacts and mutual acquaintances in the theater industry. A couple of years ago she learned he'd moved from Melbourne to New York and was directing musicals on Broadway. *Lucky bugger.* How she'd kill to work on Broadway. But although she'd kept tabs on him like some crazy stalker ex, she'd never once made contact. Not since walking away almost eighteen years ago.

How could she after what she'd done?

Since James's move overseas, getting information had become much trickier; her contacts were all Aussie and didn't have the same urge as she did to know his whereabouts. She'd googled of course, but Will was right—the internet gave a lot less information than most people believed. Although Neve still thought about him all the time, she'd decided this was fate's way of telling her to finally let go.

But perhaps she'd been wrong about fate.

"I'm sorry, darling, I don't have any idea." Somehow she kept her voice steady. "But if this is something you really want to do, how about you let me look into it? You shouldn't be worrying about this during the most important year of your school career."

Hopefully he'd agree, which would give her time to work out what the hell to do. And she really didn't want him wasting time that could be better spent.

Will's eyes widened and an optimistic smile spread across his face. "You'd do that for me?"

"I'd do anything for you," she said, and it was true, even if the thought of facing James churned her stomach. "But I really do want you to concentrate on your studies for the next few months, so why don't we agree to wait until your exams are over?"

His face fell. "I can't, Mom. It's all I think about."

Neve tried not to frown. "Why now, sweetheart?"

"It's not just now," he said. "I told you. I've always thought about him, but I didn't want to hurt you. I still don't. But as you said, I'm in my last year at school and soon we'll be having the graduation ceremony. Everyone else will have their dads there. I want mine, too. I want to feel normal for a while."

Normal? She didn't think there was such a thing as a normal family anymore. Besides Flick and Seb—but couples like them were few and far between. Still, she could tell Will wasn't going to be swayed on this.

"Okay. I get it," she whispered, swallowing a large gulp of air as she imagined herself and James sitting beside each other at the Dayton grade-twelve graduation night later in the year. It was such a bizarre image that she had to smother a maniacal laugh. "It's a lovely idea, wanting your father to see you graduate, but I don't want you to get your hopes up."

"I won't," he promised. "But if you mean it about helping, then you've got to keep me posted with your progress, okay? I want to know the minute you find him or any lead about where he might be. Don't treat me like a baby. Don't protect me from the truth. And please don't talk to him without me. Once you find him, can you let me handle it from there?"

He sounded so grown-up that Neve agreed without thinking, immediately regretting the promise. She noticed her hands were shaking to match the trepidation in her heart and just wanted to be alone awhile to digest this news. "Now, if you've had enough to eat, don't you think we should both be getting off to bed? We can talk more about this in the morning."

Truthfully she hoped this was a crazy dream; either that or Will would have forgotten this conversation or changed his mind by the morning. She wanted to bury her head right back in that sand. Will pushed back his chair and nodded. "I'll clean up this mess first. You look exhausted. I'll see you in the morning." Then he trekked around the table and leaned over and hugged her. He'd never been shy about showing his affection, not even in public as he'd grown into a teenager, but this hug held greater meaning than any before. It was his silent message of thanks and it made her want to cry.

As his head rested on her shoulder, she bit hard down on her lower lip. "Sweet dreams, my boy," she said, patting him on the back.

"Thanks, Mom. You, too." He pulled back and looked right into her eyes. "You're the best, you know that?" And with those words, he started collecting their plates and glasses from the table.

Neve headed down the corridor to her bedroom on shaky legs. Once there, she went inside, closed the door behind her and flopped down on the bed.

As a makeup artist, she knew the importance of cleansing her face every evening before bed. She'd never once gone to sleep without scrubbing off her makeup and applying all sorts of antiaging creams, but there was a first time for everything.

Although exhausted, she lay on top of the covers, staring at the ceiling, thinking of the promise she'd just made to Will.

How the hell was she ever going to get any sleep now?

4

Felicity

"What are you doing?" Flick woke up with a start, her face cool from the car window, as Seb attempted to lift her from the passenger seat. Somehow he'd opened the gate, driven through, parked the car in the carport and closed the gate again without disturbing her. Their border collie–black Labrador cross, aptly named Dog by a much-younger Toby, danced at his feet in his usual excited welcome.

Seb chuckled and smiled down at her. "Taking Sleeping Beauty to bed. Relax and go back to sleep, my love."

She shooed his hands away as he tried to get a grip on her. "I'm awake. I can walk myself."

Hurt flashed in Seb's eyes at her irritated tone. "Sorry. I was just trying—"

She sighed and put her hand out to touch his perfectly toned forearm. "I know. I'm sorry. It's me. I'm in a funny mood to-night. Think it's something to do with the realization my babies are growing up. That soon they won't need me anymore."

"Of course they'll need you," he reassured, offering his hand to assist her out of the vehicle. "Just because Zoe's get-ting married and Toby's almost finished school doesn't mean you'll suddenly become superfluous. If anything, they'll need you more as they navigate the highs and lows of adult life."

"I guess." Flick took his hand and Seb grabbed her bag and closed the door behind them. He beeped the car locked as they turned toward the house.

"And," he began as he took hold of her elbow so she didn't stumble over Dog or trip on the uneven garden path, "even if they don't need you, I always will."

"Thank you." She squeezed his hand, hit with a sudden rush of love for him. As much as her friends' insistence that he was some sort of Prince Charming irritated her, they were right; she *was* one of the lucky ones. "For always being my voice of reason and also for being so wonderful tonight and letting us spend some time with Emma. She's not doing so well at the moment."

"I can hardly blame her. The way Max flaunts his new life in her face... Well, it's distasteful to say the least."

"I could honestly murder him sometimes. We talked about going on a girls' trip tonight and she really needs the break, but even though she played along, I can tell she'd never go."

Seb opened the front door and Dog dashed inside. "That's really tough. Maybe even a night away to a fancy hotel would cheer her up. She's a travel agent. Perhaps she could arrange a discount through work?"

Flick slipped off her uncomfortable heels and leaned forward to kiss him. "That's a great idea."

He smiled. "And you know what else is a good idea? It's starts with *b* and ends with *ed*."

"Yes." Flick yawned. "I can't remember the last time I stayed up this late. I'm going to be paying for it for days."

"I bet Emma appreciated it, though."

The two of them—married for what seemed like forever, but was in fact twenty-two years—headed down the hallway to their bedroom at the other end of the house and began their evening rituals. Usually if Toby was out overnight at a friend's place, they'd make love and enjoy the quiet time together, but tonight Flick could barely find the energy to wash her face and get out of her outfit.

"What did you get up to this evening?" she asked as she squeezed toothpaste onto her brush.

They had a double vanity—his and hers sinks—and she recognized Seb's expression as she looked at it in the mirror. What a stupid question. As if Seb got up to anything else when *he* had the house all to himself. After more than two decades of marriage, she shouldn't have been surprised—she'd accepted him for who he was, and they'd talked openly about it, but she'd never quite got used to his clandestine hobby.

He picked up his own toothbrush. "Just messed about on the computer."

That was when she also noticed the tissues in the wastebasket—bright pink lip prints on them. She hadn't even bothered with lipstick before she left the house, had hurriedly smeared some gloss across her lips as they parked in front of Max's house.

She spit into the sink, put down her toothbrush and wiped her mouth. "Buy anything?"

He shook his head. "Just did a little window-shopping." A slow smile spread across his face. "I may have taken a wrong turn on my way to the bathroom at Max's place and somehow stumbled into Chanel's walk-in closet. Oh, my God, you should see how big it is—at least twice the size of ours—and her dresses... I simply had to check out some of the designers online."

"You went into their *bedroom*?" Flick couldn't keep the horror from her voice. Her heart slammed against her chest at the thought of someone finding him in there. How would he have explained that one?

"Relax." Seb moved to stand beside her and rubbed his hands up and down her arms as he met her gaze in the mirror. She drank in his smoky gray eyes and his long, dark lashes that matched his slightly too long, black hair. Hair that reminded her of Johnny Depp in *Pirates of the Caribbean*. He was so handsome, so hot, and she felt herself melting beneath his touch.

"I was stealthy," he told her. "And besides, Max and Chanel were too busy schmoozing outside to notice little old me."

She had to smile at that. "I bet her clothes were *amazing*."

"You have *no* idea. It was a drag queen's fantasy!"

Flick turned around to look at him properly, reaching her hand up to cup Seb's smooth cheek. He'd had a sexy five-o'clock shadow at the party, but while she'd been at Emma's he'd obviously done more than try on a new shade of lipstick. Most people would have been shocked if they knew her husband liked dresses, shoes and all things girlie, but she figured there were plenty of worse things he could get up to.

Would her friends think the same about Seb if they knew he was a cross-dresser who had a better fashion sense than she did and went by the name of Sofia when in that zone? Strictly in the privacy of their own home, of course. She was the only person in the world who knew his secret—well, aside from some other cross-dressers whom he sometimes spoke to online, but as they weren't "real" people, they didn't count. He wasn't a gambler or an alcoholic, he didn't abuse her and he'd certainly never cheat on her. Perhaps theirs was an odd relationship, one most people couldn't understand, but Seb was her best friend and her soul mate.

It had been that way almost from the beginning.

They'd met in college. She was in her first year of a fine-arts degree and he was at the tail end of his degree. She'd been reading an article about taxidermy in a journal while eating her lunch in the crowded cafeteria and he'd stopped to ask her if he could share her table. *That voice*. Even before she'd looked up to see who it belonged to her stomach had flipped at the delicious, deep, intensely masculine sound.

When her eyes had met his startling gray ones—so different, so gorgeous, so honest—she'd felt heat rush to her cheeks. Everything about him, from his luminous smile to the way his long brown hair flopped across his eyes, had her answer stumbling on her tongue.

Until then, she'd never experienced such an intense reaction to a guy. She'd had little experience of boys or men, except for the guy she used to hang out with at school, Jeremy, but he'd certainly never made her toes curl and her heart skip. The man in front of her absentmindedly reached up to brush the hair off his forehead while he waited for her reply, and she may actually have whimpered.

Okay, she'd definitely whimpered.

"What was that?" he asked, his smile cheeky as if he wasn't surprised about the effect he had on her; he probably had the same effect on every woman he asked to share a table with.

"Sure," she choked, gesturing to the seat opposite and hoping she didn't have any pumpkin soup on her face. "Sit."

Still smiling, he dumped his backpack on the ground by the table and pulled out a chair. He introduced himself as Sebastian Bell—*oh, what a lovely name*—and offered her his hand. Somehow, despite her heart galloping wildly and her inability to think straight, she managed to place her hand in his and not leap halfway to the ceiling when his warm fingers closed around hers. It appeared the jolt she'd read about in romance novels wasn't a myth after all.

"And your name is?" he asked, after a short silence in which she sat gawking at him with her tongue hanging out like a happy and contented dog.

She blinked at him, her mind a void of everything except him. And then, thank God, she pulled herself together and attempted a confident, slightly flirtatious smile. Hot guys like this didn't come along every day. "I'm Felicity," she said. "Felicity Bird, but most of my friends call me Flick."

"And what would you like me to call you?" he asked, suggesting that their acquaintance might be longer than the time it took for him to eat his sausage roll.

She almost said "Sweet stuff, you can call me anything you want to," but chickened out at the last second. Flirting had never been her forte. "Flick's fine."

"Great." He picked up the sausage roll but didn't take a bite, instead nodding toward the journal. "What are you reading?"

"Oh." Her cheeks flushed again but this time with embarrassment. She generally didn't talk about her dream career until she'd known people quite some time. The last thing she wanted was for this man to think her an oddball; then again, if her fantasies came true and he asked her on a date or something... Well, if things ever got serious, she'd have to tell him. Of course, her imagination was now running away on some tangent—as if someone like him would ever think of someone like her in that way. She doubted mousy, brown-haired, too-thin plain Janes were his type.

"Is it a secret?" He leaned forward a little and whispered, "I promise I'm good at keeping secrets."

And Flick thought, What the heck? If it scared him away then he wasn't man enough for her anyway. It would be a good test, in fact.

"It's about taxidermy actually," she said, her chin held high, although her belly flip-flopped.

He showed surprise, but not in a bad way. "Just something you randomly stumbled upon?"

"I want to be a taxidermist," she declared, holding her breath for his reaction. The very few guys who had previously shown vague interest in her had run for the hills the moment she told them about her desired career. They thought it, and therefore her, weird.

"That's…amazing." He put the sausage roll back down on its paper bag as if too fascinated—or horrified—to eat. "Where did your interest come from?"

At that point, all her nerves about talking to a hot guy evaporated. She told him about her childhood, how her mother had died in a house fire before Flick could even remember her. That her father had saved his little girl but failed—in his eyes—to save his wife and had never been the same again, not that Flick really remembered how he'd been Before Fire. The whole house had burned to the ground—pretty much nothing had been salvageable—and the happy world she'd known since birth had also gone up in smoke. No photos, no clothes, none of her toys were saved. Miraculously there'd been one brooch undamaged from her mother's jewelry stash.

"Have you ever heard of a grouse-claw brooch?" Flick asked Sebastian.

The cutest little furrow appeared between his thick, dark eyebrows as if he was flipping through all the information in his brain, looking for recognition. She was about to explain when he blurted, "They're those stuffed bird claws the Scottish used to wear on their kilts, right?"

He was so excited—as if he'd given the right answer on some TV game show in the nick of time—that she couldn't help but laugh.

"How did you know that? I'm very impressed. I feel like I should give you some kind of prize. You might be the first person I've ever met who I didn't have to explain the grouse claw to."

"That's because I'm not your average guy, Flick." He smiled at her as if she were the only person in the cafeteria and she felt its effect right down to her toes. That smile made every single cell in her body happy.

No, he wasn't average at all.

"So," she said, sitting straighter and trying to cling to some kind of composure. "A grouse claw is the only possession I had of my mother's. Dad wanted to get rid of it as he couldn't bear to look at anything that reminded him of her, but I begged and begged for him to keep it. In the end my grandparents said that it would be good for me to have something of Mom's as a keepsake, and he relented."

Whereas most five-and-a-half-year-old girls collected Barbies and My Little Pony toys, Flick's most prized possession had become this odd, slightly macabre brooch. After a while, her two grandmas worried about her obsession with it, but her mom's father taught her the Scottish tradition of the claws and how this particular one had been made by a relative who'd been a taxidermist turned jeweler. Flick had spent hours on end listening to tales of this ancestor and the animals he'd found and brought back to life, of the happiness he'd returned to people who'd lost beloved pets and found comfort in having them eternalized. Looking back, she guessed these stories and the brooch had somehow made her feel closer to her mother, but her grandmothers had been right to worry.

When most of her friends decided they wanted to become hairdressers or nurses, she'd proudly announced her determination to become one of only a few female taxidermists.

"And you need an arts degree for that?" Sebastian asked.

She nodded. "Taxidermy *is* an art form, and my father insisted that I go to university, but I'm also apprenticing with a local expert who does a lot of work for the state museum. And I'm enrolled to do a summer course with a world-renowned taxidermist in London."

"Well," Sebastian said when she'd finished explaining. "That officially makes you the most interesting girl I've ever met."

She laughed and blushed, but was secretly ecstatic. "Is that right? And are you interesting, too, Sebastian? What are you studying?"

"Architecture. Which isn't that far from what you want to do when you think about it. We're both creators, artists, and we both want to make things to last."

They'd spoken so long that by the time they realized they'd missed their next lectures, the cafeteria was empty and Flick was more than halfway to falling in love. Seb asked if she wanted to continue the conversation over a drink at the university tavern. One drink turned to two and eventually led to dinner. Flick never wanted the day to end, but neither did she want to do something stupid like sleep with him on the first date.

Not that he pressured her. He'd walked her to her little secondhand Corolla and kissed her good-night—on her hand. For some reason Sebastian Bell found her fascinating. And fun to be with. And, most surprisingly, he christened her the most beautiful girl he'd ever laid eyes on. In hindsight that line was rather cheesy, but at the time she'd swooned like Lydia Bennet over the rakish Mr. Wickham. Sebastian made her *feel* beautiful, and not at all ashamed about the person she was and the one she wanted to become.

"Flick! Felicity! Is there something on my face, or have you fallen asleep standing?"

Back in the present, she startled at Seb's slightly raised voice, wondering how long she'd been staring at him. "Sorry," she confessed, as she reached across and wiped a faint trace of lipstick off his mouth. "I was just reminiscing about the day we met."

The worry in his eyes evaporated and his lips curved into his delicious smile. "The best day of my life," he told her, scooping her up into his arms.

"Mine, too," she said as he walked her out of the en suite and into the bedroom.

Seb gently laid Flick onto the bed, tucked her under the covers and then kissed her on the forehead. "Sweet dreams, my darling," he said, before walking around to his side of the bed and climbing in beside her.

The day had been a tumultuous one emotionally, but falling asleep in his arms made her feel safe and content. The kids might be growing up, and she and her friends might be getting older, but as long as she had Seb, all was right with the world.

5

Emma

"Has everyone got everything?" Emma asked as she popped two painkillers out of their package and picked up her glass of water. "Library bags, sports shoes, homework, musical instruments, iPads? You're all ready to go?"

Her three kids—all of whom towered over her now—nodded as they picked up their schoolbags. She downed the tablets in quick succession, sighed at the absolute state they were about to leave the kitchen in and made shooing movements toward the front door.

Caleb, Laura and Louise sounded like a herd of elephants—and not baby ones at that—as they hurried down the hallway, each of them talking loudly over the others so that she couldn't make out what any of them were saying.

"One at a time," she called after them as she grabbed her handbag and keys from the kitchen counter. She really hated to leave the morning's breakfast dishes and lunch-preparation stuff all over it, but between getting everyone up, making breakfast and lunches and ironing the uniforms that she hadn't managed to get done on the weekend, she hadn't had the time.

How did other working moms do it? And make it look so

damn easy? When Max still lived at home, he hadn't helped much with the domestic duties—although he'd probably have claimed otherwise—but then she'd only worked part-time at the travel agency. She'd kept house, made sure her family ate nutritious meals, enjoyed her job and had even gone to two or three exercise classes a week. Nowadays the kids were lucky if they got vegetables with dinner, and she couldn't remember the last time she'd stepped inside the gym. Everything just felt so damn overwhelming.

The kids were waiting by the car as she shut the front door, so she pointed the key fob and beeped it unlocked. There was the usual squabble over who'd sit in the front seat but she ignored it, knowing that by the time she landed in the driver's seat, one teen would have won and the other two would be reluctantly doing up their seat belts in the back. She didn't have the energy to deal with bickering this morning, not when her head was still pounding like a heavy-metal rock band was rehearsing inside it.

"Mom," Laura—winner of the front-seat contest—said the moment Emma climbed into the car. "Can I have ten dollars?"

"Me, too," Louise piped up from the back.

Caleb chuckled. "If you're handing out money, I won't say no."

She hadn't even turned the key in the ignition, but Emma's hands tightened on the steering wheel. "What do you think I am?" she snapped. "A bloody ATM?"

Laura blinked and raised her eyebrows. "No need to swear, Mom. It's fine, we'll just starve."

Emma sighed. "Why on earth would you starve? I've filled your lunch boxes to the brim." *And all I've taken for myself is a banana and packet of Tim Tams that were on special.*

"Um…we have an extra band rehearsal this afternoon, remember, so school's putting on dinner, but it's five dollars each."

Emma didn't like Louise's tone and also wondered why they needed twice that amount, but instead of asking or reprimanding her, she said, "Since when?"

"We told you yesterday." The twins often spoke as one, something that Emma rarely noticed but other people often remarked on.

Had they? Emma couldn't remember, but then yesterday had been a blur. Saturday she'd spent in bed recovering from the excessive drinking on Friday night, and Sunday she'd had to rush around like a madwoman, doing the weekly grocery shopping, cleaning the house, washing clothes and then collecting the kids from Max's because he had something going on and couldn't drop them off himself. She sighed; this time she'd give the girls the benefit of the doubt. Truth was, it wasn't the first thing she'd forgotten lately.

Stress—it had a lot to answer for.

"I'm sorry, it slipped my mind. Grab my purse and see what I've got."

While Laura rifled through her handbag and divvied out money among her siblings, Emma started the car, not wanting the kids to be late for school or her to be late for work. Her supervisor would have her guts for garters if she was late, and the last thing she needed was to lose her job.

The heavy-metal band inside her head continued as strong as ever as she navigated the morning traffic and, thankfully, once the kids had snack money, they turned to their phones to do whatever teenagers did on those expensive devices. She should have been more vigilant about keeping an eye on their social media, email and internet use, but she hadn't even wanted them to have phones in the first place. Caleb, she understood—he was almost an adult—but the girls were barely out of primary school. Of course, Max had bought them all the latest iPhones without bothering to consult her.

Thinking of Max did not help ease her headache at all. If only there was a tablet that would eradicate *him* from her life.

"Mom, you planning on stopping?" Caleb's urgent tone jolted her thoughts and she realized she was almost past his bus stop.

She slammed on the brakes and pulled the car to the side of the road, ignoring the angry sound of horns behind her. "Sorry, sweetheart." She summoned a smile to her face and turned around to say goodbye.

He leaned forward to kiss her, then put his hand on the door but paused and looked back. "You okay, Mom? You seem kind of agitated lately."

As more horns sounded behind them, Emma swallowed the lump that formed in her throat at the fact her boy had noticed she wasn't quite herself. Both proud of him and annoyed at herself for letting her stress affect the kids, she shook her head. "I'm fine, honey, just got a bit of a headache."

"You've had a lot of headaches lately," Louise mused, proving that although she was glued to her phone, she always had one ear to the ground. "Maybe you should see a doctor?"

"I probably just need to drink more water," Emma said, thinking that maybe if she took the time to drink her two liters a day it could help. But really, who had time for that? "Now, Caleb, go, before the man behind us has a road rage tantrum."

The second Caleb slammed the door, she flicked her indicator on, pressed down on the accelerator and shot back out into the unrelenting stream of traffic. She dropped the girls off next—their school was on her way to work—but neither of them bothered with kisses goodbye. As Laura and Louise rushed toward the school entrance, Emma waved but they didn't see her, already having found friends to gossip with. Caleb was more affectionate and thoughtful than the two of *them* put together, but maybe it was just a stage they were going through.

Emma took a deep breath, enjoying the sudden silence. As she resumed her journey, she turned the radio on, hoping her favorite station would help ease her headache before she arrived at work. When the kids were in the car, they didn't listen to music because they all had very different tastes. She drove the rest of the way on autopilot, trying not to think about all the things she hadn't achieved that weekend, and by the time she parked her car she felt marginally better. Her head still hurt but she was ready to face the day. At least in the office, she couldn't see her messy house or unrelenting laundry pile; instead, she got to make people's travel dreams come true. Where most parts of her life had fallen apart over the last few years, at least she had a job she liked getting up for.

"Hey." Mandy, the youngest employee at Donoghue's Boutique Travel, looked up from her computer and waved as Emma let herself into the shop. Despite the rush, she'd managed to arrive half an hour before the doors opened to customers.

"You're here early." Emma returned a smile and then lowered her voice. "Is Darby here yet?"

Mandy shook her head and, relieved to have a few moments' reprieve before their supervisor arrived, Emma headed out to the tiny staff room to dump her bag and fire up the coffee machine.

As she flicked the switch, the rear door opened and the owner of the travel agency strode in—a bright smile on his cute face and a cardboard carrier with four steaming take-out cups inside. Tall, dark-haired, tanned and always immaculately dressed in the latest fashion, Patrick Donoghue looked like he'd just stepped off the cover of a *GQ* magazine.

Although he owned five travel agencies across the metropolitan area, including the one Emma worked at in Subiaco, he spent most of his time at the Nedlands branch, but popped in at least twice a month to the other offices. Thank God she'd scraped into work early. He was the one who wrote her paycheck, so she needed to impress him even more than she did Darby.

"Oh, hi," she said, trying not to sound rattled by his unexpected appearance. His presence always flummoxed her.

"Good morning, Emma." He smiled that delicious grin of his. "Darby's had a family emergency, so I'll be filling in for him here over the next couple of weeks."

"Is he okay?"

"He's fine, but his father suffered a stroke over the weekend and he and his wife have flown over to Queensland to spend some time with him. He's taking some family leave."

"Oh, that's awful," Emma said. "We should send them flowers or a card or something to let them know we're thinking of them."

"Good idea. Can you organize that?"

When Emma nodded, Patrick winked. "So how's my favorite employee today?" He lifted one of the take-out cups out of the carrier and handed it to her.

She raised an eyebrow as her fingers closed around the warmth. "I bet you say that to *all* your employees." She dipped her nose to inhale the tantalizing aroma, her headache already fading at the prospect of a caffeine hit. This morning she'd had time for a shower *or* coffee; the shower had won.

"You look like you need that." He nodded toward the cup as she removed the plastic lid and lifted it to her lips. "Everything okay?"

"Is that your polite way of telling me I look terrible?" she asked before taking a gulp. It was hot and burned her mouth a little, but pain was a mild inconvenience for an addict.

"Never." He shook his head and his smile faded. "You always look fabulous, Emma."

She laughed nervously at his compliment, unsure how to take it. Ever since Max had knocked her confidence by sleeping with someone half her age *and* half her weight, she'd been unable to handle admiration from men, especially men as good-looking as Patrick Donoghue. Then there was his lovely Irish accent... Oh, Lord, and now she was staring at him, probably as red as a fire engine, doing a great impression of being mute.

"Thanks." She forced the word out, remembering the advice she always gave the girls about compliments. *Accept them graciously and with thanks.* "Did you have a good weekend?"

Patrick shrugged one shoulder lazily. "Wasn't bad. We were very busy. Had one of those customers that insists she gets a window seat because she didn't want to ruin her hair."

Emma laughed—there was nothing travel agents liked better than sharing stories about silly or sometimes downright stupid customers. Her all-time favorite was a woman who insisted that she wanted to fly to Hippopotamus in America. Finally she'd worked out the woman meant Buffalo, but it had taken a while.

"What about you? Get up to anything exciting?"

Emma contemplated telling him about Caleb going to the prom—she even had photos she could show him on her phone—but thought better of it at the last moment. Patrick never discussed his private life. He was simply being polite. She'd save the photos for Jenny and Mandy when Patrick went out for lunch.

"Lovely, thanks," she said instead.

"Well then, I'd better go give these to the others," he said, indicating the remaining polystyrene cups.

Emma nodded and then took another long sip. Patrick was a good businessman—he had won Travel Agent of the Year several times and was often asked to speak at travel confer-

ences around the world—but he was also a great boss. He often
bought take-out coffees or other treats for his staff when he
dropped into the office, and he never complained if his employees needed time off for sick kids or school assemblies. Not
that she took time if she could possibly help it—she couldn't
afford the loss of income—but not all workplaces were as flex-
ible and she knew she was lucky. It would be nice to have him
around for a few weeks.

She retrieved the Tim Tams from her handbag and then
carried them and her coffee out into the office area just as
Patrick was opening the door for Jenny and turning the sign
on the window from Closed to Open.

"Sorry I'm late." Jenny, a woman who had been in the travel
industry for about a hundred years and loved it so much she
never planned to retire, rushed into the office. "You wouldn't
believe it. I got stopped at every bloody red light and then by
a party bus. Seriously! I mean *who* would be drinking at this
time on a Monday morning?"

Emma, Mandy and Patrick laughed.

"Probably more people than you'd think," Patrick said as
the first phone began to ring.

"Good morning, Donoghue Boutique Travel, Subiaco,
Mandy speaking. How may I help you today?"

Emma and Jenny headed to their desks and Patrick sat himself down in Darby's desk. Not long after that first phone call,
the first two customers walked through the door. They were
future honeymooners, children of Jenny's friends, so she took
them, which allowed Emma to go through her email. She used
to whiz through her morning inquiries, but lately everything
seemed to be taking longer than usual and she found it difficult to concentrate on more than one thing. Maybe once
women got past forty the old adage that they could do more
than one thing at once was simply no longer true.

She glanced sideways at Mandy, who was on her third—or was it fourth?—phone call of the day, chatting away on her headset while typing furiously away at the keyboard and reading a message that had just landed on her mobile. The sight made Emma's head spin. Not wanting Patrick to think she was slacking off, she took a deep breath and began reading an inquiry from a retired couple who wanted quotes for a cruise that stopped in as many places around the globe as possible.

"Cost is not a concern, we want the best," read the email.

Lucky for some, Emma thought, as she opened a file from her favored cruise company to check out their latest packages. Oh, well, the more her clients spent, the better for her.

For a few moments, she lost herself in images of a luxury cruise liner and postcard-perfect photos of exotic locations. She imagined herself sitting on that perfectly white sand, drinking a cocktail out of a real coconut and watching the clear blue waves lap against the shore. She could almost smell the sea breeze and hear the ocean. She could definitely taste the cocktail. Her mind drifted back to Friday night and the laughter she'd had with Flick and Neve as they'd planned their fantasy trip. *If only…*

"Are you all right, Emma?"

She looked up from the pictures on her screen to see Patrick leaning against her desk, looking all debonair in his dark designer suit. Donoghues was a chain of higher-end travel agencies, assisting people who wanted a more personal service than offered at the local Flight Shop, and all his employees were expected to look the part and dress for success. Patrick led by example.

"What? Sorry?" Her headache rearing its ugly head again, she pressed a couple of fingers against the side of her forehead and looked up, *way* up—the man was practically a giant—at him.

He frowned. "I asked if you were free to take a client—" he

nodded toward a young woman now sitting down at Mandy's desk "—and you didn't seem to hear me."

Oh, Lord. "I'm so sorry, Patrick," she gushed. "I have a bit of a headache this morning." His catching her in a daydream had ruined any good the caffeine had done. Her whole head throbbed once again. "I'll take the next walk-in, definitely."

"Can I get you a painkiller?" he asked, his frown transforming into an expression of concern.

What time did she take the last ones? Was it when she got up or when she was leaving the house? *Damn, why can't I remember?*

"No, thanks." She smiled, thankful he wasn't the type of boss to get angry easily. "The caffeine is doing the trick, I think."

"If it doesn't get better, don't be a martyr, go home and get some rest."

"I'll be fine." To prove her point, Emma turned back to her computer and began a reply to the cruise couple. She couldn't start taking time off for headaches; she needed to save her sick days for when the kids were unwell or if she really got ill.

"Look after yourself, Emma." Patrick reached out and rested his hand on her shoulder, squeezing gently. Her body stilled— so long since she'd felt a man's touch, it had no idea what to do with it.

He's only being friendly.

But something inside Emma tingled and her imagination switched tracks from thinking about a vacation to thinking about what it would feel like to have Patrick touch her just a little bit more.

Oh, dear. It appeared she was completely losing her head.

He turned to walk away and she forced her eyes *not* to follow him. The last thing she needed was to start having inappropriate fantasies about her boss. Life was already complicated enough.

6

Genevieve

"You're not going to make me look like a clown, are you?"

Neve, lost in a world of her own, smiled down at Sandrine Priest, the author whose makeup she was currently doing for professional photos; it took a few seconds for the comment to register, but by the time she'd opened her mouth to reply, the woman was speaking again.

"I want to look good, but natural. You probably can't tell," she said, lifting her fingers to brush against her cheeks, "but I don't wear much makeup from day to day. No point really, is there? Not when I work from home. Hardly worthwhile dressing up for the pool boy, now, is it?"

Neve smiled. "Well, that depends what the pool boy looks like."

The woman chuckled. "And I've always been told I have glowing skin anyway."

"You definitely won't look like a clown," Neve promised, not making a comment on her pasty, pale skin, which looked as if she didn't get enough meat or sunlight. Sandrine wouldn't recognize herself when Neve had finished—instead she'd be singing her praises and begging her to spill her beauty secrets.

"To be frank," Sandrine continued, talking as if she'd had lessons in how to speak the Queen's English but had never quite conquered the art, "clowns have always given me the heebie-jeebies, don't you agree? Freaky-looking things."

Neve continued to smile and make what she hoped were the right noises as the Booker-nominated author blathered on about clowns, which somehow led to her theories on Santa Claus and the Easter Bunny and how all made-up characters are a cruel deception on the part of parents and big business.

"And don't get me started on the tooth fairy!"

Neve made a mental note never to read one of Sandrine's books—if she wrote anything like she spoke, she'd probably die of boredom. Thankfully, her client appeared content to carry the conversation herself, with Neve murmuring the occasional agreement and every now and then interrupting to ask her to purse her lips or close her eyes. Under the mind-numbing tones of Sandrine's soliloquy, Neve found her mind drifting again to the one thing she'd been thinking about since Will's announcement in the early hours of Saturday morning.

James.

Her insides tightened and then twisted at the thought of him. She now lived with a permanent knot in her stomach. Eighteen years had passed since she'd left him but when she closed her eyes, she could still see him as if it had been yesterday, still smell his unique male scent and still recall exactly what it felt like to have his lips on hers. This was nothing new. She'd always thought about him—it infuriated her that she couldn't get him out of her head after so long, when he no doubt never gave a passing thought to her. That Deborah Conway song "It's Only The Beginning" reminded her of James—that bit about this being the love of a lifetime, even if it lasts a week. They'd been together longer than a week, but James had definitely been the love of her lifetime; he'd ruined her for anyone else.

Now that Will had broken his silence on his desire to meet his dad, James invaded her headspace more than ever. Will kept asking questions she either didn't know the answer to or didn't want to tell him.

Do you think Dad still lives in Melbourne? Will I have to go there to meet him?

I wonder if he ever got married. Do you think I could have brothers or sisters? It'd be fun to be a big brother, don't you reckon?

Will's enthusiasm twisted her heart, and with each question she grew more and more nauseous; she'd barely eaten since Friday night's cake. In a matter of days, her life had been totally turned upside down with a number of different scenarios rolling through her head. What if James didn't want to be found? Refused to meet Will and broke her baby's heart? What if he *did* want to be part of Will's life?

She didn't know which prospect scared her more.

"Careful!" Sandrine's shriek startled Neve and she yanked back the dark brown eyeliner in her hand.

"Oh, I'm so sorry." She had somehow drawn a dark line down Sandrine's cheek.

Sandrine peered up at Neve, her eyes narrowed. "I thought you said you knew what you were doing?"

"I do." Neve swallowed as she put down the eyeliner, grabbed a cotton ball and dipped it in a bottle of makeup remover. "That won't happen again."

Her fingers shook as she erased the line from Sandrine's face. Not only was the Will/James dilemma costing her sleep and her appetite, but now it was affecting her work. She couldn't afford to let that happen—she had a reputation to uphold, not to mention bills to pay. Teenage boys with hollow legs weren't cheap to feed, and Will often brought his friends around to raid her pantry.

As she finished Sandrine's face—gorgeous despite the mishap—Neve realized she couldn't handle this thing on her own. She needed to talk it out with someone who wasn't as intimately involved as she was. Someone who could look at her problem with a clear head and tell her what she should do.

"There," she said, putting the illuminizer brush back on the top of her enormous makeup case. "All finished." Before Sandrine could utter a word, Neve whipped a mirror out of her bag and held it up in front of the author's face. "Ta-da!"

Sandrine sucked in her cheeks and made her lips into a fish mouth as she slowly turned her head from side to side and examined her reflection. Neve glanced down at her watch, wondering if Flick could get into the city in time to meet her and Emma during Emma's lunch break.

Finally, Sandrine spoke. "I'll admit I was skeptical, but you've earned your exorbitant fee. I could almost be mistaken for Audrey Hepburn."

Neve endeavored to keep a straight face. She might be one of the best in the business, but she wasn't a miracle worker and this woman was light-years from Audrey. "Yes, I *can* see the resemblance."

Sandrine's lips transformed into a smile Neve wouldn't have thought possible when she'd met her an hour or so ago. "Thank you," she said, pushing herself to a stand. "I only hope the photographer who recommended you is as good as you are."

"I guarantee Pierre is a genius. You'll love your new shots," Neve promised and then packed up her tool kit in record time. "Good luck this afternoon," she said. "I'll ask Pierre to send me a photo from the shoot. I always love to see the finished product."

Sandrine nodded and then walked across to a bookshelf and plucked a hardback from a row of identical copies. She returned and thrust it at Neve.

"It's presigned," Sandrine explained as Neve looked down at the tome and saw it was the Booker-nominated work of supposed literary genius. Why did these books always have the most atrocious covers? Frankly, Neve preferred a good, easy beach read. Something with a bit of spice in it.

"Oh, thanks." She tried to inject enthusiasm into her voice, while picturing the tome as a rather funky doorstop. "I can't wait to read it."

"Be sure to let me know what you think," Sandrine said as she led Neve to the door.

"I promise I will," Neve lied.

The moment the front door shut behind her, Neve whipped her cell phone out of her jacket pocket and typed out a message.

Need to talk. Can you guys meet for lunch at that Italian café near the travel agency? x N. She sent the message to Flick and Emma and then continued on to her car. As she loaded her equipment into the trunk, her phone beeped twice in quick succession. Her heart sank as she read their replies.

Sorry, can't do today, swamped at work. What about tomorrow? Hugs, E.

What's up? Nothing too serious I hope—I'm wedding-dress shopping with Seb and Zoe. Yes, it IS as traumatic as it sounds. How about tomorrow? Flick.

"Dammit." Neve kicked her car tire in frustration. She'd felt better just at the prospect of talking to her friends, but that feeling was short-lived.

I'm working all day on a shoot tomorrow, she typed and then racked her brain for another solution.

Before she could think of one, Emma sent another message. What about Friday night? It's Max's mom's birthday so he's taking the kids for the night.

Sounds good to me, Flick replied.

That worked for Neve—Will had said something that morning about going to see a movie with Stacey on Friday night, but... What about date night? she typed back, knowing how much Flick hated the term. Whatever you called it, every second Friday Seb and Flick went out to dinner or a show together, and Neve didn't want to ruin their special night.

We'll do Saturday instead. Not a big deal. Seb won't care. And if either of you call it "date night" again, I will kill you.

Neve smiled at Flick's reply, grateful she had friends who were willing to change their plans when she needed them. Thankfully she had a busy week scheduled so she wouldn't have too much alone time to dwell on everything before she saw them.

Excellent. Why don't you two come to my place and I'll throw something together for dinner? Her place was safer than a restaurant or bar where their conversation might be overheard.

One could never be too careful with secrets.

7

Felicity

After the message exchange with Neve and Emma, Flick popped her phone into her handbag and turned back to Zoe, who was pirouetting in front of the massive mirrors of the bridal boutique. She'd lost count of the number of wedding dresses her daughter had modeled in the last couple of hours while she and Seb sat on the plush white leather couches and sipped sparkling wine. All the gowns were blurring into one. There'd been poofy styles, A-lines, mermaid something or others, some with ultradramatic high necklines and others so low she feared the guests would cop an eyeful of Zoe's pert, young chest. Flick herself had worn a simple A-line gown when she and Seb got married, but it appeared today's brides were all about lace, ruffles and color.

"Who were you messaging?" Seb whispered as their darling daughter stepped back into the fitting room to try on dress number one zillion and three.

"Neve and Emma." Flick frowned. "Something's going on with Neve. She wanted to meet for lunch, but Em and I couldn't so we've arranged to see her on Friday night. You don't mind, do you?"

"Not at all." Seb smiled and squeezed her hand. "We can go out Saturday instead."

"That's what I thought."

"Mom? Dad? What do you think of this one?" Zoe appeared again in a new gown, having mastered the art of the quick change.

Flick couldn't help but gasp. "Holy shit, isn't there any more of it?" Made of some kind of sheer fabric and lace, the figure-hugging number left nothing to the imagination. "Do you want the whole church to see your nipples?"

Seb, as usual, was far more diplomatic. "Honey, you always look gorgeous, but is that really the tone you want to set for your big day?"

Most dads would be mortified by the sight in front of them now—unsure where to look—but then again, most dads would rather take up scrapbooking as a hobby than go dress shopping with their wife and daughter.

Zoe turned from left to right, examining herself in the mirrors. She skimmed her hands over her hips and Flick held her breath, praying she'd see what a ghastly mistake a dress like this would be. The sales assistant beamed at Zoe. "This style is very in right now and you definitely have the body for it. All brides want to look sexy on their wedding day."

Flick couldn't help herself. "I'm not sure they want to look like prostitutes, though."

The sales assistant smiled tightly and kind of chuckled; she seemed to think Flick was joking.

"It's all right, Mom," Zoe said, grinning over at Flick. "I just had to try it. Can you imagine what Granny would say if I walked down the aisle in this?"

Flick let out a sigh of relief and Seb laughed—his mom was not only prim and proper, but extremely religious.

"So are we any closer to a decision?" Flick asked, her stomach reminding her it was nearly lunchtime.

Zoe rubbed her lips one over the other in the way she always did when she was thinking. "Can I try the third dress again?" she finally asked the sales assistant.

Flick had no idea what dress number three was but the assistant nodded, her high blond ponytail swishing behind her. "You take that gown off and I'll bring the other one in for you."

As Zoe disappeared through the fancy velvet curtains, the assistant went over to a rack on the wall that looked as if it might collapse any minute under the weight of all the gowns Zoe had tried and rejected. Within seconds she selected a dress and turned around.

"This is the one. What do you think, mother and father of the bride?" asked the sales assistant, fluttering her eyelashes in Seb's direction. The dress was a classic strapless bodice with tiny crystals embroidered across the front in the shape of flowers and a beautiful full skirt, ruffled from just below the hip to the floor. This had been Flick's favorite by far of all the gowns Zoe had tried on.

"I love it," she said, relieved her daughter had good taste after all. She glanced at Seb and saw his eyes were glistening. He'd always been far more emotional than her. She took his hand and smiled at him. "Can you believe our little girl is getting married?"

He sniffed. "Not really. I hope Beau realizes how lucky he is."

Flick opened her mouth but the sales assistant got in first. "No boy is ever good enough for Daddy's little girl. You must be very close—we don't get many men in here."

Seb nodded and smiled back, but Flick saw the pulse in his Adam's apple. He and Zoe had always been close, but supporting his daughter wasn't the only reason he was here today, and Flick knew it.

"I'm ready," Zoe called from inside the fitting room, and the assistant stepped in to give her the gown.

"Got Mr. Visa ready?" Flick asked Seb.

He grimaced. "What's the wedding tally so far? Do we need to take out a second mortgage?"

"Not yet—just be thankful we only have one daughter."

"I thought the thing these days was for the bride and groom to share the costs," Seb said. "Aren't the days of the bride's family paying for everything long gone?"

Flick shrugged. "Maybe if the bride and groom have been working and living together for a few years, but our daughter and her fiancé are practically children."

"I heard that," Zoe yelled. Seconds later the assistant peeled the curtain back and she stepped into their midst once again.

This time Flick gasped for entirely different reasons. This gown was about as far removed from the scanty piece of chiffon she'd tried on before as you could get. "Oh, my darling, you look…" Her throat choked up. So much for not being emotional.

"I think what Mom's trying to say," Seb offered, "is that you make a beautiful bride. We're speechless. That dress is quite frankly the most amazing gown I've ever seen."

Coming from Seb that was *something*, Flick thought, as she dug a tissue out of her pocket.

"Really?" Zoe whirled around like the ballerina she'd wanted to be when she was five. The ruffles flared as the skirt ballooned around her. "Do you think this is it?"

"Yes," Flick and Seb exclaimed in unison.

"It is something special," agreed the sales assistant, "and between you and me, it suits you far better than the others. Shall we discuss fittings and finance?"

"Yes, let's." Flick didn't want Zoe to change her mind. She couldn't bear the thought of going through all this again.

Zoe changed, Flick jotted down their next appointment in her calendar and Seb handed over his credit card with a bigger smile on his face than most dads in this situation would have. He'd never had a problem forking out for fashion. And then the three of them stepped outside into the busy Subiaco street.

Flick breathed in the fresh air and the alluring smells wafting from the nearby cafés. "Where shall we go for lunch?"

"Let's go to The Witches Cauldron," Zoe suggested and since this was her day, they did exactly that. As they walked in the direction of the restaurant, she linked her arm through Seb's and looked adoringly up at him.

"Thanks for coming today, Dad. I really appreciate it. It can't be easy being the only guy in a place like that. I'm so lucky to have such a supportive father." And then she stretched up and kissed him on the cheek.

"I wouldn't want to be anywhere else," Seb said, his cheeks turning crimson from his little girl's praise.

Flick couldn't help feeling a bitter jab to her heart.

What about her? Where was *her* thanks for sitting through hour after hour, dress after dress? Would Zoe be so quick to praise her dad if she knew that being in a bridal-dress shop was pretty much his idea of heaven?

Everyone thought Seb so wonderful—and he *was* a good father and loving husband—but Flick thought she was a pretty good wife, too, for putting up with what she did. And sometimes she felt as if she could burst under the pressure of not being able to share this secret with anyone.

8

Genevieve

The longer you kept a secret, the scarier it became. The bigger it grew, Neve realized as she prepared the meal for tonight's dinner with Flick and Emma. And she'd been keeping this one for close to eighteen years. Although she hoped she'd feel better after she'd confided in her friends—a problem shared is a problem solved and all—the thought of putting it out there left her cold.

She'd just poured herself a glass of wine and lifted it to her lips when the doorbell rang. Inhaling deeply, she straightened her top and hurried down the hallway.

"Hi," she said, perhaps a little too exuberantly as she peeled back the front door. She was relieved to see her friends had arrived at the same time.

"So what's going on?" Flick asked, leaning over to kiss Neve's cheek.

"Yes." Emma took her turn to greet Neve. "We're very curious." Neve opened her mouth, about to say that it was nothing serious, but that would be a blatant lie. There was nothing more serious right now, especially to Will.

"Come inside. I'll get you some drinks and then I'll tell you."

Emma paused just inside the door and pointed. "Is that a new doorstop?" she asked. "I love that it looks like a book. Where'd you get it?"

Neve shut the door behind them. "It *is* a book. A client gave it to me."

"You know you're supposed to *read* them," Flick said, her tone amused.

Neve shrugged. "So I'm told. But ain't nobody got time for *that* big a book. You can have it if you like."

Her friends laughed and Neve's anxiety eased a little as she led into the kitchen. She pointed at the wine bottles on the counter. "Red or white?"

Flick dumped her oversize handbag on the floor. "White, please."

"None for me." Emma also removed her shoulder bag as she shook her hand at the wine bottles.

Flick frowned.

"Is something wrong?" Neve asked as she poured Flick's drink. Flick looked to Emma and wriggled her eyebrows. "Oh, jeez, you're not pregnant, are you?"

"Don't be ridiculous." Emma laughed. "It would have to be an immaculate conception. I probably don't even have time for that. No, I'm just steering clear of the wine for a bit. I must be getting old, can't seem to handle my grog anymore. Whenever I drink, I end up with a headache for days."

"Can I get you something else, then? Water? Juice? Diet Coke?"

"Just water, but I'll get it myself."

Emma went to fill a glass of water while Flick pulled back a seat and sat down. "You know," she began, picking up her wine, "hangovers shouldn't last for days no matter how much you drink. I know you had a fair bit last Friday, but... Well, have you thought about seeing a doctor about these headaches? You seem to be getting them more and more."

Neve sucked in a breath. Not that she didn't care about Emma's health, but tonight was supposed to be about *her* problems.

"I'm fine," Emma replied, taking her glass of water to the table. "I'm just tired and busy. But I promise if I get any more, I'll make an appointment. Besides, we're not here to talk about me. What's going on with you, Neve?"

Suddenly Neve's bones turned to ice—maybe she *would* rather talk about Emma after all. She felt the gazes of her friends boring into her.

"Well..." She clasped the stem of the wineglass as if it was a lifeline. If it was this hard telling her friends, how on earth was she going to tell James? Or Will?

"Yes?" Flick prompted and then took another sip of wine. Neve closed her eyes, opened them again, sighed, then spoke.

"Will wants to meet his father."

"Oh," Emma said as if she was expecting something a lot more startling.

"Is this really such a big surprise?" Flick asked. "I mean, he's a normal kid. It makes sense that he wants to know where he comes from."

"I guess." Neve felt stupid and naive for not contemplating this possibility before. She'd been like an ostrich and buried her head in the sand, refusing to think about what she now realized had been a time bomb waiting to explode.

Emma, who'd always been sympathetic to other people's feelings, squeezed Neve's hand. "And how do you feel about it, hon?"

She swallowed. "To be honest, it makes me want to throw up."

"Aw, Neve." Flick reached across the table and took hold

of her other hand. "Just because he wants to get to know his father doesn't mean he'll love you any less. You and Will have a fabulous relationship."

"Yes," Emma agreed, "you really do. Mostly my kids spend all their time holed up in their bedrooms, but Will actually likes hanging out with you."

But that relationship is built on a lie.

Pain shot to Neve's forehead as if someone had stabbed her; Emma didn't have the monopoly on headaches.

"The thing is," she admitted after a long pause, "I haven't been entirely honest with him about his father. I haven't been entirely honest with anyone."

Both Emma and Flicked frowned at her. "What do you mean?" Flick asked.

Neve sucked in another breath and followed it quickly with a swig of wine. Her friends waited, but she didn't know where to start. Finally, she spoke again. "I haven't been honest about James."

"That's Will's dad?" Emma clarified.

"The scumbag bastard who didn't want to have anything to do with either of you." Flick's tone showed exactly what she thought of him.

"Yes, and no." Neve bit her lip as her friends' expressions grew even more befuddled. "James doesn't even know Will exists."

"What?" Flick and Emma said in unison, their mouths dropping open—Neve had never actually seen that happen before. She thought it was just something people wrote in books.

"Much of what you know is true," Neve began. "James and I met while we were working on a production of *Cats* in Melbourne. He was assistant director and I was part of the hair and makeup team. The moment I laid eyes on him, I knew he was the one. He was older than me, much more sophisticated than the boys I'd dated up to then. He was so tall, so handsome and so charismatic. I'd never met anyone like him and I fell hard and fast. James felt the same—we'd steal illicit kisses behind the stage and every night after the show we fell into bed. We couldn't get enough of each other—the sex, oh, the sex, you cannot imagine." Her spine tingled at the recollection and she squeezed her knees together under the table. "Anyway, although I couldn't get enough of him, I knew it was wrong." She paused. "He was married."

"What?" Flick and Emma asked again as if this was now the only word in their vocabularies. While Flick simply looked shocked, Emma's eyes narrowed and there was a bitter edge in her voice.

"I know." Neve held up her hands in surrender. "But you can't help who you fall in love with. I knew he was married before we started anything and I tried to stay away, I truly did, but...we just couldn't help ourselves. You don't understand how explosive the chemistry was."

Emma rolled her eyes. "Sex is just sex, whatever bow you wrap it up in."

"If you really think that," Neve said, "then you've either never experienced bad sex or you've never experienced out-of-this-world sex."

Emma scowled and crossed her arms.

"So what happened?" Flick asked.

"When I found out I was pregnant I left Melbourne and came home to Mom and Dad. I said I'd been in a brief relationship with a guy from the theater but that when I told him about the baby, he ended it. I told them he didn't want anything to do with it."

"And is that what happened?" Emma asked, a glimpse of compassion in her eyes. She knew what it was like to be rejected.

Neve wished she could say yes, but the time for lies was over. She needed to face up to what she'd done. And this was the first step.

"No." She shook her head. "James had two young daughters whom he adored, and although he loved me, I knew he'd never leave his wife because of them, so I…" She took a deep breath. "I didn't tell him that I was pregnant. He still doesn't know about Will. His name isn't even on the birth certificate."

At the looks of disbelief on her friends' faces, Neve tried to justify herself. "I've never said anything bad about him. I've barely told Will anything at all. As far as he knows, James just wasn't the settling-down-and-having-a-family type. Obviously he doesn't think too badly of him or he wouldn't want to meet him, would he?"

"I don't know." Flick shrugged but her words were barely audible over the top of Emma's.

"Oh, my God!" she spit, looking at Neve as if she was mud on a brand-new white carpet. "How could you lie about something like that? Having an affair with a married man was bad enough, but making out that this James character never even *wanted* Will? Not even giving him the *chance* to be a dad? That's terrible."

"For fuck's sake, Emma. I don't need you to yell at me. Don't you think I know all that? Don't you think I feel guilty enough? I was young and stupid."

"You were twenty-five."

"Exactly. And I thought I was doing the right thing. I didn't want to be a marriage wrecker." Neve felt uncharacteristic tears prickling her eyeballs.

"Maybe you should have thought of that before you slept with someone else's husband."

Emma's words hurt more than if she'd stabbed her in the neck with a chopstick. Neve closed her eyes, silently cursing her own stupidity. Of course Emma was the wrong person to tell this to.

Although it had been almost five years since Max had announced he was leaving her for a woman who was practically a child, her scars were still raw.

Now Neve had basically admitted that she was exactly like Chanel—the only difference being Chanel had got the guy. But maybe Neve could have had James, too, if she'd told him the truth. Leaving had seemed like the right thing to do back then, but now she wasn't so sure. She'd thought that in time her love for James would fade, but seeing him in Will every day was a constant reminder of what they'd shared. The years apart hadn't diluted her feelings for him.

"Emma, calm down," Flick ordered. "This isn't about you. Whatever you think about Neve's affair—" *Lord, she made it sound so seedy* "—*Will* is the issue here. There's no point berating Neve for something she did before you met her."

Neve smiled her appreciation at Flick. "Thank you," she said, her voice barely more than a whisper.

Emma's arms remained tightly crossed and her forehead creased. "So what are you going to do about this, then?"

"I'm not sure." Neve had always been so competent and independent—part and parcel of being a single mom—but now she wished someone would tell her what was best. "I don't want Will to get hurt, but I don't think he's going to give up on this. He knows James might not be overjoyed to hear from him, but I think he's imagining that it's going to be some wonderful father-son reunion."

"Maybe it will be," Emma said. "After all, Will isn't the one who has lied to James all these years."

Neve let that gibe slip, knowing it to be the truth. "I guess I have to tell James, don't I?"

Her friends nodded, then Flick asked, "Do you know how

to contact him? Have you had any communication with him at all over the years?"

"No. Nothing." Neve took a big gulp of wine. "Last I heard he and his…his wife—" she couldn't look at Emma as she said this but felt her disapproving stare "—had moved to New York. He got a job directing *Mamma Mia!* on Broadway."

"What's the wife do?" Emma asked.

"She was a journalist. She probably still is."

Flick sat forward. "Okay, so if he's still working on Broadway, it shouldn't take too long to track him down, should it?"

"I checked on Facebook. James isn't on there, but—"

Emma snorted. "I don't think this is the kind of thing you tell someone in a message on Facebook."

"Of course not," Neve snapped. "I was just saying that I'd looked. He is, however, on LinkedIn, but don't worry," she continued before Emma could object to that, "I'm not going to contact him there either. But I did learn that he's still working on *Mamma Mia!* for a few more months. The show's closing soon."

"I'd love to see *Mamma Mia!* on Broadway," Emma said, her voice dreamy as if for a moment she'd forgotten why they'd started talking about this.

"Me, too," Flick agreed.

"Watch the movie," Neve said. "After you've told me how the fuck to get out of this mess I've got myself into."

"I wonder how hard it would be to get his phone number?" Flick mused.

Neve raised an eyebrow. "What if his wife answered the phone?"

Flick shrugged one shoulder. "You could call him at the theater. Or leave a message for him to call you."

"Yes," Emma nodded as if they were both dimwits, "because what guy wouldn't like to receive a phone call from a woman he hasn't seen in almost two decades, telling him they have a child together? Personally, I think you should go to New York and tell him face-to-face."

"Ooh, yes." Flick raised her glass in approval and took a sip. "Good plan."

Neve's heart skipped a beat, and she wasn't sure if the adrenaline rush was down to fear or excitement or a weird combination of both.

She swallowed. "Maybe you're right. Maybe I owe it to Will and James to go and see him. He could hang up on me if I call."

What if he didn't even remember her? She felt sick at the thought that maybe she hadn't been all that special after all; maybe she'd been one in a string of floozies James had screwed while his wife was busy breastfeeding and changing diapers.

"More wine?" Flick asked, standing to grab the half-full bottle off the counter.

Neve put her hand over the top of her glass. "No, thanks." She had decisions to make and needed a clear head.

"You don't mind if I do?" Flick topped up her drink before Emma or Neve had a chance to object. Not that Neve would—who was she to judge her friends' decisions?

She looked at the table and realized none of them had eaten any of the canapés she'd put out. "Shall I serve up dinner?" she asked, needing to do something, despite not being hungry at all.

"What's on the menu?" Flick asked, taking it upon herself to clear the table of the untouched snacks.

"Vegetable tortilla stack." Neve stood and went across to the oven just as its timer beeped.

"Mmm...yum. You know I adore my meat and couldn't live without it," Flick said, "but...if anything could turn me veggie, it's your cooking."

"Thanks." Neve took the ceramic dish out of the oven and placed it on a wooden board, ready to slice. "Can you grab the salad out of the fridge, please?"

Flick obliged as Neve set to cutting everyone a slice. Emma usually raved about her food, but this time she remained quiet as Neve put her plate down in front of her.

"So when are you going to go to New York?" Flick asked.

"I guess the sooner the better." The dread and anticipation would kill her if she had to wait too long. "But I don't know what I'm going to tell Will."

"How about the truth?" Emma said drily.

"I don't want to get his hopes up," Neve said, telling herself this was the truth and it wasn't simply that she wanted to put off the conversation that would likely irrevocably damage their relationship.

"Can you tell him you've had some too-good-to-refuse makeup job come up in the States?" Flick suggested.

"That could work," Neve said, mentally checking her calendar for a gap long enough to take the trip. "But I'll have to renew my passport first—I haven't left the country in years. I wonder how long that will take."

"You can request priority processing. The passport office will get it back to you within two days of you handing in the form." This was Emma's one contribution to the conversation.

"We keep our passports up-to-date," Flick said, "although I don't know why. We haven't had an overseas vacation since Toby was in kindergarten. Private-school fees have seen to that."

"Tell me about it." Although Will was on a full scholarship, there were still plenty of extras Neve had to fork out for, things that wouldn't be needed if he went to the local public high school. "I can't believe you're going to the Big Apple," Flick said. "I've wanted to go ever since *Sex and the City* came out. Think of all the shopping you'll be able to do. You'll have to take a selfie on Fifth Avenue."

Neve laughed, appreciating that Flick was trying to make her feel better. "If I go anywhere near Fifth Avenue, the only shopping I'll be doing is window-shopping. The flights and accommodation alone will probably bankrupt me." She sighed, knowing that somehow she had to find the money—and find the courage to face James.

For Will. For her son, she would do absolutely anything.

"What's for dessert?" Flick asked, once she'd helped Neve stack the dinner dishes in the dishwasher.

"Actually, I'm going to have to go," Emma announced, glancing at her watch. "I'm really tired. Sorry. Thanks for dinner." She didn't look apologetic, though, and thanking Neve for dinner sounded like a real effort.

"You're welcome." Neve smiled, trying not to feel too hurt. She could tell Emma's opinion of her had changed tonight and she didn't want the dynamics of their trio to change, but she didn't know how to fix things either. "Thank you for coming. Would you like to take some chocolate tart home for the kids?"

To her surprise, Emma accepted.

Flick didn't stay long after that and Neve didn't mind. The evening had emotionally exhausted her and Will would be home from the movies soon anyway. Normally she'd wait up for him, to check he got in safely and to chat about his day, but tonight she sneaked off to bed, not up to facing him at all.

How could she when she finally understood just how badly she had let him down?

9

Felicity

Holy hell, Flick thought as she flopped into the back seat of the taxi and gave the driver her address. Neve had thrown them for a loop with her confession tonight. Flick could hardly reconcile the woman she knew with someone who'd sleep with a married man.

Whenever Emma lamented about Max, Neve had always been as caustic as they had with her thoughts on home-wrecker Chanel. Not once had she acted weirdly or given any indication that she, too, had once been in Chanel's position. Then again, maybe Flick just hadn't noticed because she hadn't been looking. She'd naively assumed her friends were open books, but she had her secrets, so why should she be surprised when she discovered others did, too? Either way, the revelations of the evening caused her to look at Neve in a new light. She wasn't angry and didn't think any less of her like Emma did. People made mistakes after all. Life was never black-and-white and she believed strongly that one shouldn't judge another unless they had walked in their shoes. Flick had never thought to stray, but she'd been lucky to find the love of her life young;

the way Neve spoke about James it sounded like he *was* the love of her life, too.

What would I have done if Seb was married when we met?

It was hard to wrap her head around such a thought. She couldn't imagine Seb sitting down to chat with her in the cafeteria that day if he'd already been in a relationship. He simply wasn't that kind of guy.

But whatever wrongs Neve had committed, she'd also done a hell of a lot right. Her intentions had been honorable when she'd ended her relationship with Will's father. She could have made life very messy for the adulterer; instead she'd chosen the hard path of single parenthood, and Will was a testament to what a bloody good job she'd done of that.

But, man...what a pickle she'd got herself into now. Flick didn't envy her one bit. Well, aside from that trip to New York. That was definitely a silver lining.

"Is this you?" asked the taxi driver, and Flick realized they'd stopped in front of her house.

"Oh, yes," she said, her hand already on the door when she remembered she still needed to pay. She glanced at the total charge—$12.75—and then grabbed a twenty-dollar bill out of her purse.

"Keep the change." Flick leaped out the car, slammed the door and hurried up the driveway to her front door. The TV blared from the living room as she let herself inside, and she followed the noise.

"Hi, Mom." Toby turned around from where he was sitting on the couch as she entered. "How was your night?"

"Good, thanks, sweet pea." She walked over and kissed him on the head. "What about yours?"

He shrugged. "Okay. Zoe and Beau came over, so Dad ordered pizza, then Beau and I played on the Xbox until Zoe got pissed off that he wasn't spending time with her, so they left."

Flick stifled a smile. "I see. And where's your dad now?" She'd thought Seb would have spent the rare evening alone with Toby.

He shrugged again and turned back to the movie on the screen in front of him—something gruesome by the looks of it. "He said he was tired and went to bed."

Damn. Seb had been working hard lately on a big development project and she didn't want to wake him if he was sleeping, but she was busting to talk about Neve and she couldn't spill her guts to Toby. He'd be straight on the phone to Will and that would be cataclysmic.

"Okay, honey. I'd sit and watch with you, but..."

"It's okay, Mom." Toby half laughed. "I know blood and gore isn't your thing." The kids had always joked that she couldn't handle it—after all, she made a living handling dead things—but she'd much rather spend her time off watching a romantic comedy, a good drama or even a documentary. "See you tomorrow."

"Good night." Trying not to show her desperation to escape, Flick ambled out of the room, and then once out of Toby's sight, she charged down the hallway toward their bedroom.

Forgetting about Seb being asleep, she flung open the bedroom door and burst in. "You'll never guess..." The words died on her tongue as she took in her husband in a fitted red dress, twirling in front of their full-length mirror, his face plastered with more makeup than she wore in a month, his favorite blond wig on, and their bed barely visible under the mountain of dresses he'd already tried on. Her jaw tensed and a hot wave of anger flushed through her as she quickly closed the door behind her.

Seb glanced at his wristwatch—the decorative gold-and-diamond one he wore when playing Sofia. "I didn't think you'd be home for a couple more hours."

"That's pretty damn obvious." She clenched her fists and shook her head, trying to control her fury. If Toby wasn't home, she would really let loose, shout the house down to ensure Seb heard exactly how she felt. Then again, if Toby wasn't home, she wouldn't be so effing furious.

Seb's chagrined expression proved he hadn't planned on getting caught.

"What the hell were you thinking?" Flick accused. Her voice was barely more than a whisper but that didn't mask her rage. She'd always tried to be accepting of Seb's other life, but they'd made certain rules when the kids were born, the most important being that he never indulged his hobby when Toby or Zoe were in the house. As far as she knew he'd never broken them. She nodded back toward the door. "Toby could have come in at any moment!" The shock of seeing him in full female getup almost rivaled the first time she'd discovered his secret. She occasionally wondered how different her life might have been if she'd chosen to be not quite so supportive; if she'd decided cross-dressing wasn't something she could put up with in a husband—there were plenty of women who wouldn't. But walking away had never been an option.

He was the first person she thought of when she woke up in the morning, her last thought when she went to sleep and the one she turned to throughout the day whenever she had something to share. She loved him too damn much.

Still, now he had the audacity to shrug at her distress, and that made her blood boil. "Flick, calm down. It's no biggie."

"*No biggie?*" She couldn't believe her ears. "Don't you think Zoe and Toby would think it kind of significant if they discovered their father spent more money on dresses, shoes and makeup than their mother?"

He shrugged again and tugged off his platinum-blond wig, tossing it behind him onto the pile on the bed. He still had the dress on, and now he looked even more ridiculous. "I've been thinking..."

Why did her heart freeze at those three weighted words? "Maybe it's time that Zoe and Toby get to know the real me? They're adults now and—"

"Toby's not eighteen yet." She interrupted, unable to believe her ears. Zoe might be twenty, but that didn't mean she'd be able to handle this any better than her brother. Did Seb really think she'd let him tell them?

"He's not far off," Seb continued, something in his eyes telling her he was prepared for a fight.

Arguing was something they rarely did, and whenever they did have a disagreement, Seb was always the first to back down.

"They need to learn that the world isn't black-and-white." Seb sighed and ran a hand through his hair. "I'm tired of living like what I do—who I *am*—is some dirty sin. You know I love you and the kids more than anything. And I want Toby and Zoe to know and accept me for me."

Flick swallowed. "But what if they don't accept you? Are you ready for that?"

He took his time answering. "I think maybe that's a risk I have to take. I know this might not be easy and it may take them time to come around, but we've raised our children to have open minds and I think they'll understand eventually."

Perhaps Seb had more faith in their children than Flick did, but either way she wasn't ready for *her* world to explode. It wasn't just him they might be angry at. What would they think of her for harboring this secret all these years? How would it affect Zoe and Beau's imminent marriage?

Worst-case scenarios flew through her head and she wondered why this had become so important to him all of sudden, but all she managed to say was "I'm sorry, Seb. This is a bit of a shock. Can you promise me one thing?"

He nodded, his expression earnest. "Anything."

"Don't do anything rash. If you're really serious about this, we need to choose the right time. It may be best to wait until Zoe is married and Seb has finished his final exams, don't you think?" Secretly, she hoped he'd get over this ridiculous desire to come clean.

"Perhaps." He stepped toward her and drew her into a hug. She tried to relax into him but couldn't help imitating a wooden soldier.

What the hell did *perhaps* mean? Did he not care at all about her feelings?

Before she had the chance to voice her questions, Seb asked one of his own. "How was your night with the girls?"

She remembered Neve's bombshell, but her desperation to tell him all about it had faded. Less than an hour ago, she'd thought Neve's world the most complicated of the three of them. Now she wasn't so sure. She inhaled slowly, calmed herself a little and then told him everything.

10

Emma

Emma surreptitiously popped another painkiller as the door of the travel agency opened. She looked up, readying herself to greet the possible new client, but her smile died on her lips.

What was *she* doing here? Their eyes met and Neve smiled tentatively as she stepped farther inside. She looked perfect as usual in a short denim skirt and a cute gypsy-style top, her short-cropped golden hair making her look sexy and feminine. Emma didn't think she could ever get away with such a cut, not that she'd have the guts to try. Right now she wished she had a hat to cover up her practical, busy-mom ponytail.

"Can I help you?" Mandy asked as she stood up, her tone as bubbly as ever.

Neve broke their gaze, looking away from Emma and over to Mandy a moment. "Thanks, but Emma and I are friends so I'd prefer to do business with her if you don't mind."

Do business? It sounded so formal. Then again, things had been strained between them since Friday night. Usually she, Neve and Flick texted or Facebooked at least once a day, but four days had gone by now. Flick had called her on Saturday to check she was okay and she'd told her she was "fine, just tired, just busy." It seemed to be her catchphrase these days. The truth was, whether she liked it or not, things had changed with Neve's confession. She felt sorry for Will but could no longer look at Neve in the same way.

Perhaps she was being naive, but she just couldn't help it. She didn't believe in accidents when it came to infidelity. When Neve had been trying to justify her affair by saying how much she'd loved James, how amazing their connection and the sex, all Emma could visualize was Chanel saying the same about Max. Just because she loved him didn't make what they'd done right. It didn't justify Emma's children growing up in a broken home.

She couldn't sit across her desk from Neve pretending everything was okay.

"I'm sorry," Emma said, forcing an apologetic grimace. "I'm in the middle of something at the moment. I'm sure Mandy will be able to help you." And before Neve could object, she put on her headset and feigned intense concentration on something on her computer screen.

"Take a seat," Mandy said, her tone still chirpy but also a little bemused. "Where is it you're looking to travel?"

Out of the corner of her eye, Emma saw Neve deliberate a moment. She wouldn't put it past her friend to call her bluff or ask her if she could make an appointment and come back at a more convenient time. Neve wasn't the type of person to let a disagreement fester. So she was a little surprised when she finally sighed and then sat down on the opposite side of Mandy's desk.

"New York."

Mandy beamed and turned around to grab some travel brochures from the wall behind them. "Now, first things first. When do you want to go and for how long?"

Emma waited a few moments until Neve and Mandy were

engrossed in conversation, and then she lowered her headset and tried not to be obvious about eavesdropping. Several times she had to bite her tongue to stop herself from making an alternative suggestion. She hadn't been to New York in years, but although the Times Square hotel Mandy booked was right near Broadway, she reckoned Neve might prefer somewhere a little quieter and less touristy. Somewhere like Hotel Giraffe in the Gramercy district, where she and Max had stayed on their last kid-free trip away. She had fond memories of that vacation, but little had she known that her supposedly devoted husband had a young lover back in Australia, a lover he'd left her for exactly three weeks after their return. These days she tried *not* to remember any vacations with Max if she could possibly help it.

"Emma, have you got a moment?"

Welcoming the distraction, she looked up to see Patrick beckoning to her from the door of the back-office staff room. He had a desk set up in the corner for when he needed to get admin work done without the interruption of clients, but there was also a comfy couch for staff and a small kitchen. "Sure."

With one last glance at Neve—who didn't look up at all—Emma put her headset down on the desk, pushed back her chair and stood. The moment she entered the staff room, he closed the door behind them. Her heart thudded in her chest. "Is something wrong?" she asked, trying to read his expression. She'd been a little late this morning—having been into school to see Laura's English teacher about her failing grades.

"I don't know. You tell me."

Emma frowned, unsure what he meant.

"Did I hear Mandy's new client mention she was a friend of yours?"

Emma nodded, but didn't meet his gaze. Why did he have to be so damn observant? In her experience, most men didn't register something unless you screamed it right into their face. "Yes, we go to book club together." Of course, that was a gross understatement, but it was also based in truth.

"I'd have thought you'd jump at the chance to take on her business?"

Emma shrugged. "I was busy."

Patrick raised one eyebrow and his shamrock-green eyes felt as if they could see right into her soul. "So I just imagined the tenseness between you two, then?" He went on before she could reply. "You've seemed distracted lately, Emma. Is there anything you'd like to talk about?"

"No, I'm fine," she answered, but inwardly she desperately wanted to say yes.

Patrick gave her a look to say he wasn't buying her bullshit at all.

She sighed. "Oh, I don't know." Part of her wished she could get it off her chest; usually when something bothered her she talked to Neve or Flick, but she didn't want to make Flick feel as if she was torn between her two friends. Not that she and Neve had had an actual fight or anything.

Just thinking about this was making her head hurt again. "How about when Mandy and Jenny get back, I take you to lunch?"

Emma's heart did a little flip. While she and Patrick would often talk in the staff room when he was at Subiaco, in her five and a half years of being in his employ, they'd never gone out alone. It almost felt like he was asking her on a date, but she inwardly shook her head at the ridiculousness of that thought. Even if she did like him a little more than she should like her boss, even if he weren't gay, a man as handsome and successful as Patrick Donoghue was unlikely to look twice at a single, semifrumpy mom like her.

But she could do with a friend. "That sounds great."

"Excellent." Patrick grinned and then walked the few steps to open the door for her.

Emma stepped past him and, trying not to inhale his lovely sandalwood cologne too deeply, she breathed a sigh of relief when she noticed that Neve had gone.

Mandy looked over at her with a curious expression. "Genevieve seems lovely."

Emma nodded, unable to recall the last time she'd heard Neve referred to by her full name. "She is." Then she clicked her mouse and looked at her computer screen, hoping Mandy would get the message that she didn't want to talk about Neve or anything else really.

"I'll bet she's going to have a fantastic time in New York. Do you know why she's going?" Neve obviously hadn't confided in her travel agent. And why would she? "I mean, I know the shopping and theater and sights are fantastic, but it seems like an odd place to visit on your own. Unless she's meeting someone there. She's single, isn't she? I bet that's it. Has she met some guy online?"

"I'm not sure," Emma said, her words clipped.

"Mandy? Jenny?" Patrick called from where he'd just sat down again at Darby's desk. "Since we're quiet in here again, why don't you two take your lunch break?"

Emma shot him a grateful smile; her ex-husband would never have been so perceptive, which only proved that gay men were so much better than straight ones.

"You don't have to ask me twice." Mandy sprang from her seat and rushed into the staff room to fetch her bag.

Jenny tapped away on her keyboard a few more moments and then followed Mandy at a more leisurely pace. Although she was almost old enough to be Mandy's grandmother, the two of them often went to lunch together. Emma rarely left the shop, making do with coffee and biscuits, which were cheap if you bought them on special. When Coles had Tim Tams on sale it was like winning the lottery.

Mandy looked from Patrick to Emma as she opened the shop door and held it for Jenny to go through, then she shook her finger at them, a gleam in her eye. "Don't do anything I wouldn't do, you two."

"We'll be back soon," Jenny said, her tone amused.

Emma felt her cheeks flush again. Was her pathetic crush that obvious?

Thankfully a couple of young women—about the age of Flick's Zoe—came in as Mandy and Jenny went out, and Emma leaped at the chance to help them.

"Hi," she said, with perhaps a tad too much enthusiasm. "How may I help you?" She'd bet the packet of Tim Tams in her drawer that they wanted to know all about Contiki Tours. Oh, youth!

The girls sat down opposite her and glanced at her name on her badge. "Hi, Emma," said the fairer of the two. "I'm Lili and this is Vanessa. We want to know everything you can tell us about Contiki Tours in North America."

Bingo!

"We've been working our butts off and saving for this," added Vanessa, almost dancing in her seat.

"How exciting." Emma smiled, relishing the opportunity to forget about her issues a few moments. "You've come to the right place."

For the next half an hour, she waxed lyrical to Lili and Vanessa about companies that specialized in tours for under thirty-fives.

The girls eventually decided on a Southern focus, thirteen days away, starting in New Orleans and ending in sunny California. They paid the deposit and were just leaving as Jenny and Mandy returned.

As Patrick was still with a client that had come in not long after the Contiki combo, Emma replied to a few emails and then messaged Max, reminding him that it was the twins' birthday in a couple of weeks. It irked her that she still had to remind him, but she couldn't help herself—he'd forget otherwise and the girls would be devastated.

"You ready?" Patrick loomed over her desk and she shoved her cell phone into her handbag. He didn't mind about messaging at work, but she didn't want him to see that she was messaging Max. She didn't want him to think of her as one of those sad women who couldn't let go of her ex-husband.

"Sure am." She smiled up at him and then stood, hitching her handbag onto her shoulder.

She expected they'd grab a sandwich from the deli on the corner and eat it in the park or at the plastic tables outside, but Patrick walked right past and led her to a fancy Indian restaurant around the block. A restaurant known for awesome food and with a price tag to match. Emma's chest tightened. How the heck could she tell Patrick that she didn't want to eat here because she couldn't afford it? The kids had raided her wallet again for lunch that morning, because somehow she'd forgotten to buy bread and they'd been unable to make sandwiches. Payday was Friday, and until then she was well and truly scraping the barrel.

"Won't they take longer than half an hour to serve us here?" she asked, thinking quickly.

He grinned. "Possibly, but I'm the boss, so we can take an extended lunch if I say."

She rubbed her lips together, her stomach churning and her head starting to ache once again. It was best to come clean. "I'm sorry, Patrick, but lunch here isn't within my budget."

If she'd blushed when Mandy had teased them, her cheeks were burning now.

Patrick frowned slightly, then reached out and palmed his hand against her arm; her skin heated beneath his warm touch, despite the cotton of her shirt between them. "Emma, when your boss asks you out to lunch, he doesn't expect you to pay."

Relief warred with embarrassment inside her, but she forced a smile and said, "Thank you," not wanting to make a thing about this.

"My pleasure." He dropped his hand from her arm as he opened the door to the restaurant and gestured for her to go in ahead of him.

They were greeted by a jovial waiter, who escorted them to a table and went through the specials enthusiastically. Everything he mentioned made Emma's mouth water and she had no idea what to choose.

"Shall we get the lunch for two?" Patrick suggested, looking to her for approval.

"Great idea." Still not entirely comfortable about him paying, she was happy for him to make the decision.

"And what wine would you like with that?" asked the waiter, collecting their menus and tucking them under his arm.

"Red or white?" Patrick asked her.

She blinked.

As if he could read her mind, his lips curled up at the edges. "One glass won't hurt, Emma."

She decided that maybe she'd relax a little if she had a drink. "Okay. I'll have a chardonnay, please."

Patrick ordered a glass of red, and when the waiter retreated, he looked intently at her across the table. "What's going on, Emma?" She remembered that was why he'd asked her to lunch—to listen to her woes—and took a deep breath. Where to start? "My friend Neve, Mandy's client, told me something the other night."

She swallowed, guilt weighing down her heart. "And I haven't been able to see her in the same light since."

"I see. Can you tell me what she said or would that be breaking a confidence?"

Emma thought a moment, working out how she could fully explain her bugbear without mentioning the Will/James issue. "She told me she had an affair years ago with a colleague and ended up pregnant." When Patrick didn't say anything, she continued, "Do you know why my ex-husband and I broke up?"

He shook his head. "I'm guessing he cheated on you?"

She nodded, her chest tightening at the admission. Everyone knew that cheated wives were naive, stupid—all those late meetings at the office, business trips away, they were dead giveaways for "bored married man has a bit on the side." Patrick would probably never respect her again. She ignored the urge to make excuses about why she'd never suspected it, because that wasn't the point right now.

"That sucks," he said, and she couldn't help but laugh because she'd never heard such a word escape his mouth before.

"It was a long time ago, but just when I think I'm over it," she confessed, "something happens to bring all the hurt and humiliation back. I've poured my heart out to Neve— she knows every nasty, intimate detail about my marriage breakup. We've been best friends for five years and she never once thought to mention that she probably related more to Chanel's situation than mine."

"I'm sorry, who's Chanel?"

"Oh, Max's new wife. I'm the stereotypical ex-wife, all frumpy and bitter and boring. She's the clichéd other woman, ridiculously skinny except for her breasts and her huge blow-job lips."

Patrick snorted and then laughed. "You're not frumpy,

Emma, and you're definitely not boring. And Max is obviously a jerk."

It was her turn to laugh. "I've called him a lot worse."

The waiter arrived with their drinks, and once they'd uttered their thanks, Patrick lifted his glass to clink hers. "I say you're better off without him, but let's get back to you and Neve. Why does something she did in the past upset you so much? Good friendships are hard to come by."

"I know that." She took a sip of her wine, savoring the fruity taste. "But I keep thinking if Neve could do something like that, then she's not at the person I've thought she is all these years. And I can't help thinking that all the sympathy she's given me was hypocritical. Know what I mean?"

"I can see how it might feel that way," Patrick said, "but this affair was how many years ago?"

"About eighteen."

"Well then, haven't you changed at all in the last couple of decades? I know I have. And if Neve's kept this secret for that long, it's probably because she's ashamed of what she did."

Emma thought about the way her friend had talked about sex with her married man the other night and wasn't so sure. Then again, Neve had left James, rather than pressuring *him* to leave his wife. "Oh, I don't know."

She sighed and for some stupid reason felt tears prickle at the back of her eyeballs. Although she tried to swallow them, one escaped, leaving a hot trail down her cheek. "I'm sorry." She swiped at her eyes, appalled that she'd almost lost it in front of her boss. What must he think of her?

"Hey." Patrick reached out and squeezed her hand across the table. "No need to apologize. You're allowed to be human."

She snorted, trying to ignore the flutter in her chest at the way his touch felt. "Tell my kids that. I think they missed the memo. They expect me to be superwoman, which involves cleaning, cooking, chauffeuring, cheerleading, counseling—all while holding down a full-time job to keep them in the manner their father has made them accustomed to."

Before he could comment on her minor explosion, Emma's cell phone started buzzing in her pocket. She used it as an excuse to retrieve her hand—Patrick holding it made her a little dizzy—and to pull herself together.

As if he'd known she'd been talking about him, it was Max. She considered ignoring him, but he'd only keep calling until she answered. "Sorry," she said, "I'd better get this."

"Go ahead." Patrick smiled at her in his easy way and took out his own phone.

"Hello, Emma speaking," she said, pretending to have no idea who'd called her.

"Em, it's Max." He sounded perplexed and she considered asking "Max, who?" but why prolong the agony?

"Yes?" she said instead.

"I'm glad you mentioned the girls' birthday, because Chanel and I've been thinking about it and I wanted to tell you our plans."

Here we go. At least they weren't old enough to get their licenses because no doubt then he'd buy them a car—each, and not secondhand ones either. At least they were past the stage of wanting ponies. *Thank God.*

"And?" she prompted.

"You can talk now?"

She glanced over at Patrick, who was pretending to be engaged with his phone. "Briefly."

"The girls want us to throw a big party at our place, but to be honest, Chanel is not all that keen."

"Really, why not?" Although Emma wasn't keen on the idea either—she didn't trust Max and Chanel not to try to win the popularity contest by providing alcohol—she wanted to make Max say it; that Chanel had been happy to entertain Will's friends because that involved showing off to their well-to-do parents, but two dozen fifteen-year-olds *without* parental supervision would probably have her coming out in hives.

At that moment, the waiter arrived with their food and she flashed a grateful smile.

"We think parties are overrated," Max said, "so Chanel and I have decided to take the twins and Caleb to Hawaii for a couple of weeks."

Emma's eyebrows shot up so fast they surprised even her. "What?" She only just managed to stop herself from adding *the fuck*, because of Patrick and where they were. A party would have been bad enough, but *Hawaii*? How the hell would she ever top that? Only this morning she'd put another installment down on a pair of quilt-cover sets she had on layaway from one of her favorite designers. Laura and Louise had been lusting after these for ages, but new bedding would pale in comparison to an overseas vacation.

She tried to keep her voice calm when inside she felt anything but. "When exactly are you planning this trip?"

"That's just the thing, I know you'd like to be with the girls on their actual birthday, but you always have them, so—"

She interrupted. "Their birthday is in two weeks' time. *And not during school holidays.*"

"Our kids are bright enough. It won't hurt them to miss a few days." Emma could almost hear him shrug.

Taking a deep breath, she said, "I thought you said a couple of weeks."

"It wouldn't be worth taking them for anything less than a week."

"No, Max. Absolutely not. You are not taking our teenagers to Hawaii. Throw the party instead. I'm sure Chanel can handle one night of children taking over her house."

"*Our* house," Max said, and she heard the irritation in his tone. He'd started all friendly, as if they were still bosom buddies, but that act was over. They were back to barely being civil.

"Whatever you like to believe," she snapped, no longer able to control her anger either. Max might make a good living, but if it wasn't for Chanel's rich parents, they'd never be able to afford a place like theirs.

"Anyway, the tickets are already booked. I messaged the kids before I called you. They're stoked."

"Already booked?" Her blood boiling, she struggled to keep her voice down. Max was lucky he wasn't here because she would have no qualms about punching him in the face. "Five seconds ago you sounded like you didn't know exactly how long you were taking them."

"Tickets can be changed. We've booked two weeks," Max admitted, "but…"

She didn't hear the rest of his sentence as she pulled the phone away from her ear and considered throwing it across the room. Whatever he said, he wouldn't commit to an exact time frame in case he and Chanel found paradise wasn't so blissful with three teenage children in tow. Max always left his options open. After a deep breath, she returned the phone to her ear—he was still rambling.

"Look, we'll talk exact arrangements later, but please, Em, think of your children here. You don't want to begrudge them the vacation of a lifetime, do you?"

"Think of our children?" She *was* thinking of their children. About how detrimental it could be to Caleb's final exams if he missed two weeks of school. And Laura's work was already suffering—Max would have known if he'd bothered to attend any of the parent-teacher interviews.

But he disconnected before she could reply and that only

made her more furious. She'd wanted the satisfaction of hanging up on *him*.

She looked to Patrick apologetically and wished to God he hadn't witnessed that ugly conversation. Her ex-wife persona wasn't her best.

He smiled back and gestured to the food. "Dig in."

"You didn't have to wait for me. And I'm sorry about that."

He shrugged one shoulder. "I promise I tried not to eavesdrop, but your side of the conversation has only confirmed my suspicions that your ex-husband is a jerk."

She puffed out a breath. "I think *jerk* is too polite a term." Then, although she'd only planned on unloading to him about Neve, she couldn't help herself. "He wants to take my kids on vacation for the girls' fifteenth-birthday celebrations. To Hawaii, no less. During school time." Simply saying these words had her temperature rising again.

"Wow," Patrick breathed. "Hard to beat that." He began to spoon rice and curry onto his plate.

"Exactly." Emma sniffed, then swallowed. "I know it sounds stupid but he makes it a competition of materialism, and on my income I can't keep up. Not that my income's bad," she rushed, not wanting to offend her boss. "It's fabulous and the fact you let me have school hours is awesome, but Max makes four times what I do and he has Chanel's family wealth on top of that. And he did some kind of trick and convinced the courts he can't afford to pay as much as he should."

"You don't have to explain anything to me. I know how hard you work." He ate a spoonful of his curry. "This is good."

She glanced down at her plate and realized he'd served her as well. He was such a lovely, lovely man, and not wanting to offend him, she forced herself to eat a little.

"You're right," she said after the first mouthful. "Never tastes the same when you make it at home, hey?"

"I don't know." Patrick's eyes sparkled. "I reckon my curry's not bad."

"You cook?" She'd always imagined him the type to grab gourmet takeout on his way home from work or the gym. Then again, she'd once imagined Max the trustworthy type. What did she know?

He chuckled. "I don't live on beans on toast, if that's what you're wondering."

Before she could think twice, she said, "I'll have to test this curry of yours one day."

He took a moment to reply and she wondered if she'd overstepped the mark, being so casual with her employer. "I'd like that."

She shoved another spoonful of curry in her mouth simply for something to do, because at the thought of another meal alone with Patrick, every organ in her body twisted inside out.

"Hang on." Concern furrowed Patrick's brow. "Can he do that?" For a second she had no idea what he was talking about.

"Just take them out of the country without your permission?" he clarified.

"Oh, right." She shook her head. "Probably not, although he is a lawyer, so he'll find some loophole, I suppose. He seems to with everything else." She'd totally lost her appetite. "And besides, if I say they can't go, then I'm going to look like the bad guy. Laura and Louise will never forgive me."

She took a sip of wine and then pursed her lips together because—*dammit*—those tears were threatening again. It was easy to be angry while on the phone to Max, but now that she knew she'd lost the battle, all she could think about was not being with her girls on their birthday.

"Look," Patrick began, "maybe you should take a few days off. You've obviously got a lot going on at the moment. Between Neve, your husband—"

"No," Emma shrieked, then covered her mouth when she realized heads in the restaurant had turned her way. She lowered her voice. "Please, Patrick, work is the only thing keeping me sane right now. I *need* it. And Max is my *ex*-husband."

"Okay," Patrick said, holding up his hands in surrender. "It was just a suggestion."

"I know. And thank you, I appreciate the thought." She racked her brain for something to talk about other than Neve or Max, but came up blank, so she tried to eat some more.

Once again Patrick proved to be far more intuitive than the majority of his gender. He nodded toward her barely touched plate. "We could ask them to box it up so you could eat the rest later. It's probably time to head back anyway."

A little while later, as they strolled down the pavement back toward the agency, Emma said, "Thank you so much for lunch and I'm sorry I was such a downer."

He shook his head. "You weren't. I dragged you out of the office because you looked like you needed a friendly ear, but I'm not sure I've helped much."

"It's not your fault my life is—" She broke off as she lost her balance and almost stumbled to the ground.

Patrick's hand shot out to save her fall. "Are you all right?"

She looked at him and blinked because he seemed kind of fuzzy. "Must have tripped on something." But when her eyesight cleared and she looked back, she couldn't see what that could possibly have been.

"Let's not take any chances. I want to get my favorite employee back to the agency in one piece."

With that, he linked his arm through hers and kept it there all the way back to work.

11

Genevieve

Novel tucked under her arm, Neve stepped inside the funky North Perth bar and glanced toward their favorite table to see if Flick or Emma had arrived yet. They hadn't, but their table was thankfully free, so she went over and slammed the book down to stake their claim.

The Classroom, with its quirky decor made to look like an actual school—encyclopedias, old-fashioned desks alongside primary-colored stools, hopscotch on the floor—seemed a fitting place for their fortnightly book club/gab fest, especially since they'd likely never have met in the first place if it weren't for their sons attending the same school. She pulled back a stool to sit, dumped her handbag by her feet and then glanced up at the cocktail specials on an actual classroom blackboard, while absentmindedly flicking the pages of the book, *We Are All Completely Beside Ourselves.*

A man stepped in front, blocking her from reading the chalk scrawl. He smiled and nodded toward the book. "Karen Joy Fowler. That's a great book. You finished it yet?"

She shook her head. "Not quite."

"If you like it, I can recommend some others that might be up your alley."

She smiled politely. "Thanks. But I'm part of a book club and don't really get the chance to read much else." Truthfully, she'd barely even started reading this one, like most of the reads they had chosen for book club lately.

The man's smile wilted a little, but she saw him take a not-so-sneaky look at her naked ring finger. "Can I buy you a drink? Seems wrong to find a beautiful woman like you sitting all on her lonesome."

Her cheeks flushed at his obvious come-on. He *was* a handsome chap. In addition to his height and pleasing attire, his salt-and-pepper hair gave him an air of sophistication. Just Neve's type if she were interested in playing the dating game again. Which she was not. Still, it was nice to be asked.

She flashed him a polite but friendly smile. "Thanks, but I'm meeting a couple of friends. They should be here any moment."

"Can't blame a man for trying." The gentleman grinned and bowed his head. "You have a good evening, won't you?"

"Thank you," she said, and he turned toward the bar.

Flick appeared seconds later. "Who was that?" she asked.

Neve shrugged one shoulder and grinned. "Just a handsome stranger who wanted to buy me a drink."

"Ooh, go, girl." Flick punched her arm jokingly. "Did you give him your number?"

"No!"

"Why not? He's good-looking," she said, turning her head toward the bar where he now stood. "Although he does look a little like a lawyer, and after Em's experience, I think it best you stay clear of them."

At the mention of Emma, Neve's heart grew heavy. "Have you spoken to her this week?"

Flick shook her head. "I've been busy with Zoe's wedding preparations and work is crazy."

"How's all that going?" Talking about a happy occasion like a wedding appealed far more than thinking about her approaching trip or the chasm that had appeared between her and Emma.

Flick leaned forward and spoke with her hands. "I'm working on this gorgeous family of quokkas for an art exhibition on Rottnest Island in a couple of months. And I've put in a bid for a Tasmanian devil from Adelaide Zoo that has been frozen for fifteen years. I have all sorts of ideas about what I'm going to do should I get lucky."

Neve laughed. When they'd first met, she'd felt nauseous every time Flick spoke about taxidermy. To be honest, stuffed dead things gave her the creeps. Their glossy eyes were eerie and they always smelled musty. As a child, she'd hated going to museums for this one reason. But Flick's work was more like art than specimen preservation, and she'd come to admire the beauty in taxidermy, to understand why so many wealthy people commissioned her to create pieces for their homes. "That sounds great, but I was actually asking about the wedding preparation."

"Oh." Flick's smile dulled. "I've been doing my best to be enthusiastic and supportive—and I *am* happy for her. But I can't help thinking back to our wedding—would you believe I wore Doc Martens?—and I just can't get all that excited about fancy white dresses and flowers."

"You're lucky you have a daughter to do all that girlie stuff with," Neve chastised. She loved Will and wouldn't swap him for anything, but she could admit to a stab of jealousy whenever Flick or Emma talked about going clothes shopping or out to the movies with their girls.

"I know, it's just—"

The simultaneous beeping of their phones interrupted Flick's sentence. They dived for their handbags, guessing it would be Emma. They were right.

Really sorry but I'm going to have to bail. Been a full week and I think I need to make the most of Max having the kids to catch up on some house stuff and get some rest.

"House stuff?" Neve turned her nose up in distaste. "She's ditching us for housework?"

"Do you think something's wrong with her?" asked Flick.

"What do you mean?"

"Well, she's always tired or has a headache lately. I can't help wondering if she's a bit depressed."

Neve thought about it a moment. "I don't know, but I think her absence tonight could have more to do with her feelings toward me."

"Why do you think that?"

Neve sighed. "Let me get us a couple of cocktails and I'll fill you in."

Nodding, Flick swiveled around to check out the cocktail board. "I'll have a Flamin' Galah," she said, choosing one of the specials.

Neve shuddered. She could never drink something that reminded her of Alf Stewart from *Home and Away*. "Okay. And I'll get us something to eat, too." Between doing makeup for a couple of shoots and trying to organize a rush on a new passport, she'd barely had time to eat anything all day.

"I'll never say no to food. I'll text Emma while you order."

"Thanks." As Flick began tapping on her phone, Neve crossed to the bar. The guy who'd tried to chat her up earlier was now sitting at a table with three women and looked to be smooth talking all of them. So, maybe she wasn't so special. Disheartened by this and also by Emma bailing on them, she tapped her nails against the counter as she waited for a bartender.

"Hey, there." A young redheaded guy grinned at her from behind the bar. "What can I get for you this evening, madam?"

She placed her order, watched him create their cocktails and then carried the elaborate drinks back to the table.

"Now," Flick said when she sat down again, "why do you think Emma isn't coming because of you?"

Neve exhaled deeply and stared into her bright green drink, wishing it held the answers to all of life's problems. "You saw how she reacted the other night when I told you guys about James."

Flick shook her head in dismissal. "She was shocked—we both were—but she's not the type to hold a grudge. And if she was pissed off at you, then surely she'd only have messaged me."

Neve raised her eyebrows, took a sip of her cocktail. "Maybe, but she barely even said hello to me when I went into the travel agency the other day. She's always going on about being pushed for cash, so I thought she'd be happy to get my business."

"You went to book your trip to New York?"

Neve nodded. "But Emma refused to deal with me and I ended up being helped by the young girl, Mandy. Not that she wasn't brilliant. In fact, she's been really helpful, telling me how to get my passport renewed quickly and everything."

"Maybe she really was busy?" Flick suggested—always the type to see the best in people.

"Whatever." Neve tried to sound like Emma's standoffishness didn't hurt. "But if she's angry at me, then so be it. I really don't have time for high school theatrics right now. It wasn't like I slept with *her* husband."

Flick half laughed, half grimaced. "Who would want to?" She took another sip of her drink as a waiter arrived with their Teachers' Grazing Board, a share plate that changed daily but never failed to arouse their taste buds.

"Enjoy, ladies."

Flick plucked a stuffed olive from the plate and popped it into her mouth, but Neve's appetite had all but vanished, the thought of New York making her stomach turn.

"Seriously, try not to worry about Emma," Flick said once she'd finished her mouthful. "She'll come around. So, New York. You're actually going? How are you feeling about it?"

"I'm terrified," Neve admitted. "What if I can't find James? What if I do and he refuses to talk to me? What if he's so angry he turns Will against me?"

She'd imagined every possible scenario over the last week, and the majority of them weren't good. Would James still look at her the same way after all these years? Would he still make her spine tingle and her body crave for his touch? Would *he* still be attracted to *her*? This last thought caused a little panic. Yes, she looked after herself and had aged well, but perhaps her appeal to James had been that she'd been young, her body lithe and unsullied by pregnancy and birth. She immediately chastised herself for thinking such a thing. It didn't matter what James thought of her or her body.

"It's natural to be nervous, but you're doing this for Will. Remember that."

Neve nodded, swallowing. "What if I can't even get off the plane?"

Flick rolled her eyes and grinned. "You know the advice they give to people who are scared of public speaking? Just imagine everyone naked."

"Trust me, imagining James naked is not going to help in this situation."

Flick snorted. "That is *not* what I was going to say. When you board the plane, think of it as just a well-deserved vacation. When you get off, think about staying in a hotel room by yourself for... How long are you going?"

"A week." Neve panicked at the thought. "Do you think that's long enough?"

"Think of all the good things," Flick said, ignoring the question. "Room service, shopping, art galleries, strolls in Central Park, food—I've heard the food in New York is out of this world." She pointed at her drink. "Cocktails! Carrie and her friends were always drinking cocktails."

"Okay, okay, I get it. I'm lucky to have good reason to go to New York." So why did she feel like anything but lucky? "I just wish you were coming with me."

"Hmm...now, *that* would be fun. When do you leave?"

"Two weeks from today."

For the next half hour, Neve filled Flick in on all the details. She wasn't sure if talking about her imminent trip made her feel better or worse. "I finally told Mom and Dad the whole story. I had to because they're going to keep an eye on Will when I go to New York. They reprimanded me for not telling them years ago and then told me to stop beating myself up—water under the bridge." She sighed again, wishing she could forgive herself as easily as her parents had. "Do you think he'll believe that I'm going over for work?"

Flick tugged on her earring and looked blankly at Neve. "Who? Will?"

"Who else?"

"Sorry." Flick smiled half-heartedly and swished her straw around her empty glass.

"I'm so sick of secrets, you know? But it's strange. No matter how terrified I am about facing James, and then Will, there's also a weird lightness inside me now I've started telling people."

Flick made another noncommittal sound and Neve was suddenly conscious of the fact she'd been talking nonstop about herself.

"I'm sorry. Am I boring you with all this New York talk?" She nodded toward Flick's glass. "Shall I get you another drink?"

"No, thanks. But I'll buy yours if you want one."

Neve shook her head. It was no fun drinking alone. "Is something wrong?"

Flick didn't answer immediately, instead picking a serviette off the table and twisting in her fingers. Fidgeting was *very* un-Flick-like.

"Wrong?" Flick dropped the serviette like it was burning her and blinked at Neve. "What could possibly be wrong? Maybe we *should* have another drink. My treat."

12

Emma

At ten o'clock on Saturday morning, Flick turned up on Emma's doorstep. Emma had been expecting a visit. In their nearly five years of friendship, she could count on one hand the number of times any of them had missed their fortnightly Friday-night rendezvous.

"Good morning," Emma said, smiling sheepishly as her friend handed her a take-out coffee from the local café. She could do with a drink—her throat was thick with guilt after bailing on her friends last night, but she just couldn't let go of her irritation at Neve.

Not waiting for an invitation, Flick stepped into the house. "Did you get a good night's sleep?"

Emma's instinct was to say yes, but Flick had a lie detector like a psychic cop, so she didn't bother. "Not really. I never sleep well in an empty house. You'd think I'd be used to it after all these years."

Flick squeezed Emma's shoulder. "I doubt you ever get used to being separated from your kids."

Emma walked through to the kitchen and gestured to the bar stools that were nestled under the counter. "Take a seat.

Can I get you something to eat? I've got Tim Tams or two-minute noodles."

"No, thanks." Flick smiled. "While part of me believes it's never too early for chocolate, I'm trying to be good. I over-indulged a bit last night."

Although Emma had decided not to go out the night before for a number of reasons—one being that she didn't want to be a wet blanket about the Max/Hawaii thing—she couldn't wait a second longer to get it off her chest. "You'll never guess what my ex-husband has done now."

Flick clasped her hands together and leaned forward. "This should be good."

"Oh, he's really excelled himself this time." Emma paused to build suspense. "He's taking everyone to Hawaii for Laura and Louise's birthday."

Flick's eyes bulged as she almost choked on her last mouthful of coffee. When she recovered, she said, "Everyone? As in *you* as well?"

"Hell, no! Can you imagine? I can't think of anything worse than going on a vacation with Max and Chanel. I'd have to bunk in with the kids or sleep on a sofa bed." Although horrified, she couldn't help but laugh.

Flick rubbed a hand down the side of her face. "So he just landed this on you as a done deal?"

"Pretty much. I don't know why I'm surprised. That's his style after all."

She recalled the day he'd told her he was leaving her for Chanel. She'd been folding laundry at the kitchen table after a long day volunteering in the scorer's tent at the twins' school sports carnival. Max had been there, too, cheering his girls on and going off to buy coffees and snacks whenever Emma needed them. She and the girls had come straight home when the carnival finished and collapsed in front of the television to watch *Tangled*, but he'd gone into work, claiming he had some things to deal with that couldn't wait. When Caleb had come home after band practice, she'd been too exhausted to cook and the kids were stoked when she suggested they order pizza. Max was late as usual, but they were getting used to eating without him and saving him leftovers, which he never ate anyway.

But that night he'd come in even later than usual. It was almost midnight when she heard his key turn in the front door. He strode down the hallway, whistling to himself like the happy dwarf in *Snow White* and did a double take when he walked into the room and saw her.

"I didn't think you'd still be awake," he stated in an almost accusatory tone.

She shrugged. "The laundry won't fold itself and I have work tomorrow." In those days, she'd worked part-time—the perfect home/work balance.

"I guess." He went through into the kitchen. She heard the fridge door open and he returned a moment later with a bottle of beer.

"You didn't think I might like one, too?" She nodded toward the bottle as he lifted it to his lips.

"Listen, Em," he said as he took a seat at the table. "You're the mother of my children and you'll always be special to me, but I've fallen in love...with someone else."

Before she had the time to get her head around the shocking snippet of information, he landed the next blow. "I want a divorce."

"What?" Her grip tightened on the underwear she'd been about to fold. His underwear. Tight black boxers, the only type he ever wore. She blinked and shook her head. Perhaps this was a nightmare and she'd fallen asleep in the never-ending pile of laundry. But the bitter cold that was spreading throughout her body suggested otherwise.

"Look, these things happen." Max shrugged and took another sip of his beer. "We both know we only got married because of Caleb."

She raised her eyebrows and dropped his boxers back into the basket. "Oh, we do, do we? Because I recall that even before we found out I was pregnant, you were declaring that I was the love of your life."

And she'd sure as hell thought he was hers!

"And perhaps you were, but things change. People move on."

Emma felt heat rush to her cheeks. "So how long since you...moved on?"

"It doesn't matter."

"It does to me," she said through gritted teeth, wanting to scream and shout but not wanting to wake her children.

"A couple of months. I thought it was just sex at first, but then I realized I wanted more with Chanel. We're going to get married."

Funny how the mention of marriage hadn't even registered at the time. Instead, her stomach had revolted at the thought of her husband making love with someone before coming home to have sex with her. Although when she'd analyzed it from every which way later, their sex life had diminished over those last few months. Like the dumb, trusting wife she was, she'd stupidly put it down to him being tired and busy at work.

"I guess I don't need to ask how you feel about this?" Flick said, and Emma, lost in her reverie, took a moment to work out what they'd been talking about.

"Oh, right," she said, coming back to the present. *Hawaii.* "I want to murder him and bury him in that corner of the backyard where next door's cat always does her business."

Flick smirked. "That's my girl. If you need any help, you know Neve and I are always available for the disposal of dead bodies."

She tried to smile but at the mention of Neve, Emma's jaw tightened.

Flick, being her annoyingly observant self, noticed. "So it's true, then?"

"What?"

"I thought maybe you didn't come last night because you were depressed, but Neve reckoned it might have been because of her."

Emma glanced down and studied the marble pattern on her countertop. "Maybe that was a small part of it."

"Emma." Flick sighed. "I know you're angry because of your situation, and to be honest, I feel a little upset that she never trusted us enough to say something before, but we can't let this ruin our friendship. You and Neve mean the world to me. I've never had such good friends before. Please try to get over this."

"I will. I know you're right. Patrick said the same thing."

"Who's Patrick?"

"My boss." Emma tried to sound nonchalant. She didn't want Flick to suspect she had a stupid crush on him or she'd never hear the end of it.

"Ah, right."

"I guess Neve told you she came into the travel agency?" When Flick nodded, Emma continued, "Well, she mentioned we were friends and then Patrick wanted to know why I didn't serve her. He's very perceptive."

"She was really hurt that you didn't," Flick said, her tone not judgmental, simply direct.

"I know." Emma's stomach felt heavy at the thought. "It

was just too soon. And I know her situation is different to mine. I'll get over it."

"I hope so." Never one to lament things for too long, Flick moved on. "When exactly is Max taking the kids away?"

"In thirteen days."

And three hours and about thirty-two minutes, not that Emma was counting.

"I know those days will fly by and then the time they're actually away will drag. I'm going to ask Patrick if I can work Saturdays as well while they're gone."

"Hey!" Flick eyes lit up. "That's when Neve is going to New York. You should go with her. Better than sitting at home and sulking. That'll show Max."

"Oh, *yeah.*" Even if things were right between her and Neve, it would be impossible. "If I could afford to flit over to New York at the drop of a hat, I could afford to play Max's game of Who Can Buy the Best Birthday Presents."

Flick tossed her a look of reproof. "Now, that would be stupid and you know it. You give your kids everything they need and put more thought into gifts than he ever does. They'll realize heart trumps materialism eventually."

"I hope so." Emma sighed, her heart heavy again. She dreaded the day one of them would tell her they wanted to move in with their dad and Chanel. That would break her heart even more than Max had when he'd told her it was over.

13

Felicity

Flick looked at the baby quokka on her workbench and sighed. She'd been so excited when she'd been commissioned to create this display with the marsupial and glad of the opportunity to give this little creature whose life had been cut tragically short another chance to shine, but today she simply couldn't concentrate.

She glanced at the clock on her studio wall, disgusted at how little she'd achieved. Usually when she stepped inside this space, the rest of the world disappeared and she lost herself in her work, but thoughts of Seb kept encroaching. Over the last week, things had been growing more tense between them. Being a guy, he probably hadn't even noticed, but the knowledge he wanted to tell their children about his cross-dressing left her uneasy.

He'd kept it a secret for so long; why did he suddenly want to let it out now?

This question, along with her speculation over what such an announcement might do to her kids—and, if she was honest, herself—had her insides in knots all weekend. She'd almost decided to tell Emma and Neve on Friday night, but when Emma hadn't shown, she'd chickened out.

Part of her desperately needed to talk her worries over with someone, but another part simply wasn't ready to admit to the intricacies of her married life. Confessing you didn't have the blemish-free relationship that everyone believed wasn't easy. And as much as it irked her sometimes that everyone thought Seb so bloody marvelous, the alternative appealed even less. It wouldn't simply be him coming out, but her, too. What would people think? Besides, with Neve full of New York nerves and Emma dealing with moron Max, she didn't feel right dumping her issues on them as well.

Maybe she should confront Seb—have it properly out with him—but the fear that this might speed things up held her back. If she acted as if everything was normal, then maybe he'd just forget about it.

Footsteps approached from outside and she picked up her scalpel and feigned intense concentration on her work just as the door was flung open.

"Hey, Mom."

"Hi, honey." She put down her tool, glad of the interruption. "How was your day?"

"Yeah, okay." Toby took a seat in the comfy old leather armchair she called her "pondering" chair. She noticed he'd collected the mail from the mailbox. "I got ninety-eight percent on my physics test."

"Wow." She cracked a smile in genuine pride and delight. He wanted to be a pilot and studying physics was a requirement to get in. It didn't come easy to him and she knew how hard he'd been working. "That's awesome news."

He beamed, exactly the way he'd done when he was just a little boy and excited over something.

"I think we should celebrate," she said. "I know it's almost dinner time, but how do you feel about ice-cream sundaes?"

She half expected him to turn down her offer—after all, ice cream with your mom was something you did in primary school, right? But to her relief and joy, he nodded.

"Sounds great, Mom."

Relieved to have an excuse to stop flogging a dead horse and in dire need of some ice-cream therapy herself, she followed Toby outside, switching off the lights as she left.

"Here you go," he said, thrusting the bundle of letters at her as they headed for the house.

"Thanks." She flicked through them. As usual, they were mostly bills, but a plain white envelope addressed to Seb caught her attention. She turned it over but there was no return address.

"I'll get the ice cream," Toby volunteered as they entered the kitchen.

"Okay," she replied, staring the envelope. After all Neve and Emma's talk of extramarital affairs, it unsettled her. She dumped the windowed envelopes on the kitchen counter and then stared a little longer at the plain white one. Her index finger hovered over the opening—should she? Shouldn't she?—but when Toby arrived beside her with the ice cream, she tossed it back on top of the pile and reached into the overhead cupboard to grab two bowls instead.

Toby scooped ice cream into the bowls, all but drowned his with chocolate sauce and then loaded it up with an array of candy they kept in the cupboard for special occasions. Flick followed suit, although she went a little lighter on the toppings—she didn't have his youthful metabolism—and then they sat down at the table.

She dug her spoon into the ice cream and then lifted it into the air. "To you acing your test."

"Thanks, Mom," Toby said before shoving his first spoonful into his mouth.

"So how's everything else going at school?" Flick asked, taking this rare moment of alone time with her son.

Before he could reply, the front door opened, then slammed shut and footsteps hurried down the hallway. "Mom? You home? Can I borrow your computer?" Zoe finished this question as she appeared in the doorway. "Hey, guys."

"Hi, sis," Toby said through another mouthful.

Flick smiled at her daughter. "Hey, sweetheart."

"Ooh, ice-cream sundaes." Zoe's face lit up as she surveyed the table. "Are we celebrating something?"

Toby blushed as Flick said proudly, "Your brother aced his physics test."

"On ya, little brother." Zoe held up her hand and Toby high-fived it, making Flick feel all warm inside. Since Zoe moved out there'd been less bickering between the two of them, but also fewer moments like this when they showed their sibling love.

"Can I get you some ice cream?" she asked her daughter.

Zoe hesitated a moment and Flick knew she was thinking of her wedding dress—not that she needed to worry about such things as putting on weight at her age. "Yes, please."

Flick made another sundae, put it down in front of Zoe and then asked, "So why do you need to use my computer?"

"For an assignment. My laptop died and Beau's using his."

Flick nodded.

"So what's new? Anything exciting happening here?" Zoe asked, looking from Flick to Toby between mouthfuls.

"Well…"

Where do I start? One of my best friends had an affair with a married man. The other one can't seem to forgive her for it. Oh, and did I ever mention your dad is a cross-dresser?

"Nope, nothing much," Flick said.

"Lucky you've got my wedding to bring some excitement to your life, then," Zoe said, her spoon scraping against her bowl.

At the mention of the wedding, Toby shoved back his seat, stood and picked up his bowl. "Thanks for the ice cream, Mom," he said, dumping the bowl in the sink. He couldn't leave the room fast enough.

"What's up with him?" Zoe asked.

Flick shrugged; her daughter would never understand that not everyone was as enthusiastic about wedding planning as she was. "Oh, well, I can't stop to chat anyway. Things to do, people to see." Zoe stood, then leaned down and kissed Flick on the cheek. "Thanks for the laptop, Mom," she said, before leaving the kitchen, presumably to do whatever needed to be done on the computer.

Flick sighed. Left with the dishes and the prospect of making dinner, her gaze traveled once again to the pile of letters, in particular that mysterious white one sitting on top. Before she knew what she was doing, the envelope was in her hand and she was sliding it open with her finger. Her heart raced as she drew out the piece of paper from inside. No good ever came from snooping.

Then again, husbands and wives weren't supposed to have secrets, so Seb's mail was her mail, right?

As she registered the letterhead and business details on the top of the page, she gasped, unable to hide her shock. Her knees buckled and she reached out to steady herself on the kitchen counter.

"Mom? What is it? You okay?"

Flick looked up to see Zoe had reentered the kitchen, laptop tucked under her arm. Her chest tightening as if she might go into cardiac arrest at any second, it took Flick a moment to gather the wherewithal to speak. She summoned everything she'd ever learned in school drama classes and commanded her lips into a smile.

"'Course I am," she said, hearing the strain in her own voice. She folded the paper back up, shoved it into the pocket of her ancient work shirt and then stuffed the envelope in, too.

Zoe looked at her funnily a moment, then shook her head and crossed to the fridge, where she pulled out a cola. She cracked it open, took a sip and then left again without question. Flick let out a long, slow puff of air. Her heart and hands still quaking, she needed something a lot stronger than Diet Coke.

14

Genevieve

Neve frowned at the sound of knocking on her front door. It was half past nine on Monday night—too late for salesmen or religious callers, she hoped—and she wasn't expecting anyone.

"You want me to get that?" Will called from his bedroom next door.

She surveyed her open suitcase on the floor and the mess on her bed and sighed. "No," she called back. "I'll go." Responsible mothers didn't let their children open the door to strangers late at night. Even though Will now towered over her at well over six foot, he was still a child in the eyes of the law.

As she hurried down the hallway, the knocking grew louder, more persistent. She switched on the light that flooded the porch outside and recognized the familiar silhouette on the other side of the frosted glass.

"What are you doing here?" she asked as she yanked open the door to find Flick standing there looking disheveled—her shirt done up unevenly and her hair frizzy as if she hadn't brushed it at all today. "Are you okay?"

"I'm fine."

She didn't look it, though, thought Neve as Flick stepped past to get inside.

"And a very good evening to you. Why aren't you answering your phone?"

"It's charging in the kitchen and I've been in my bedroom trying to sort things out for New York."

"I see." Flick glanced down the hallway and peered around the living room door as if casing the joint, then asked in a whisper, "Is Will here?"

"Of course. Where else would he be? It's a school night. He's in his room."

Flick nodded but didn't say anything else.

"Are you sure you're okay?" Neve asked. The Flick in front of her looked like her friend, but her behavior suggested otherwise.

"Huh?" Flick met her gaze as if she'd only just seen her. "You got any wine?"

Flick usually didn't drink during the week—this night was getting weirder and weirder. "Sure. I'll grab a couple of glasses and we can go into my bedroom and talk."

"Talk?"

"I assume you came here because you had something to say?" When Flick just stared at her blankly, Neve shrugged. "Whatever. It's good to see you. Come help me work out what to pack for New York."

Half an hour later, Flick had knocked back two glasses of wine but still hadn't mentioned the reason for her visit. Neve gave up trying to pry after being shut down a couple more times. If there was something wrong, Flick would talk when she was ready. Neve had now succeeded in packing the things she didn't need to think about—socks, panties and bras—but was still no closer to deciding the important things.

Like "What do you wear to tell a man you haven't seen for eighteen years that he has a seventeen-year-old son?"

Flick leaned back against the pillows on Neve's bed, where she was now half-buried under a pile of discarded outfits. "Eff knows. I think I was in pj's both times I told Sebastian we were pregnant."

Neve arched an eyebrow; she could count on one hand the number of times Flick had called her husband by his full name. "I hardly think I can turn up to the theater in my nightie."

Flick, staring off out the window again, said, "I can't see why not. Plenty of people go shopping in their pajamas these days. Besides, what you wear to bed is probably nicer than most people's day wear."

"True." Neve did pride herself on her appearance, even if she didn't have the fortune to spend on clothes that most of the mothers at Dayton did. But no, when she saw James again she wanted to look fabulous because inside she'd be a quivering mess.

"Why don't we just shop when we get there?" Flick suggested, and Neve thought she must have heard wrong.

"We?" she asked, her hands halting in the action of removing a slinky silver cocktail dress from its hanger.

"Oh, that's what I came around to tell you." Flick grinned— the first time she'd truly smiled all night. "I'm coming to New York with you. That's if you don't mind the company."

Neve gasped and tossed the dress on the bed. "Are you serious?"

Flick's smile spread wider. "I wouldn't joke about something like this. I've been fantasizing about going since you first told us about James, and then this afternoon, I suddenly thought, why the hell shouldn't I go with you?"

Neve thought Flick would have a number of reasons— leaving Seb and Toby, Zoe's upcoming wedding already costing them a small fortune—but she wasn't about to mention either of these. She felt giddy at the thought of a trip across the other side of the world with one of her best friends. They'd have so much fun—shopping, dining and exploring the city that never slept—and if her meeting with James was as awful as she imagined it could be, well then at least she'd have Flick to help her drown her sorrows.

"Why the hell not, indeed?" She squealed like an excited little girl and rushed forward to grab her friend in a hug, forgetting her weirdness of a few minutes ago.

"And," Flick said, when Neve finally stopped squeezing, "I think we should take Emma as well."

Neve could just imagine the mischief the three of them could get up to together in New York, but a little voice reminded her that Emma was barely speaking to her. "While that would be great," she agreed, "I don't like your chances of convincing her. Even if the trip wasn't to hunt down my married ex-lover, there's no way Emma would flit across the world on a whim. This is a person who takes a year to decide whether to buy a new pair of shoes or not."

Flick held up her empty wineglass as if to toast. "That, my friend, is why we're not going to tell her."

15

Emma

"Want to buy some of my chocolates?"

Emma looked sideways at the box of fund-raising chocolates Mandy was holding and her mouth watered so badly she almost drooled. Since she'd cut back on wine due to her headaches, chocolate was one of her few pleasures, and she'd shared her last packet of Tim Tams with the others yesterday. Unfortunately, the kids had emptied her purse again that morning and she'd grabbed a packet of crackers that was near its use-by date from the pantry for herself.

Not wanting her colleagues to know how dire her financial situation was, she shook her head and smiled apologetically. "Maybe tomorrow?" Which was—thankfully—payday.

"You're not on one of those new diets, are you?" Jenny butted in from across the office, her voice tinged with disapproval. "My daughters-in-law are both eating nothing but protein at the moment and it's turned them into monsters."

Emma glanced over at Patrick's desk, relieved to see he appeared to be engrossed in something on his computer screen, then looked back to Jenny. "No, I'm just not in the mood for chocolate today."

Jenny and Mandy raised their eyebrows and looked at each other as if they couldn't believe their ears. Emma wasn't known as the office chocoholic for nothing. She covertly slid her hands down to her stomach, which was squishier than she remembered. Or liked. Max's comment from a couple of weekends ago came back to haunt her.

Have you stopped going to the gym? You look...

She could only imagine what he might have said if Seb hadn't cut him off. The truth was she had let herself go over the last couple of years. Somewhere along the line she'd gone from being barely able to eat anything due to the shock, disappointment and embarrassment of her broken marriage, to consoling herself with chocolate, ice cream and whatever other sweet things she could get her hands on. And that had remained a habit long after the wounds Max had left started to heal.

"Earth to Emma, earth to Emma!"

She blinked at the sound of Mandy's voice. "What?" she snapped, wishing to God someone would come into the agency to distract them.

Undeterred by her grumpiness, Mandy flashed her a full, perfectly white-toothed grin that might have worked if Emma was a twentysomething male. "You could buy some for your kids as an after-school snack? It's for a good cause."

"Your netball club is a *good cause*?" Emma asked, her voice rising with her body temperature. Why couldn't Mandy just leave it? "Excuse *me* if I'd rather give my money to starving children in third-world countries, research for terminal illness or animals that are near extinction!"

Mandy's smile transformed into an O and she snatched the chocolates up to her chest, holding them as if they were a puppy Emma had just kicked. The office went silent and Emma could feel Jenny's and even Patrick's eyes trained on her now as well. They probably thought she was going through early menopause. Hell, maybe she was—that could account for her headaches and irritable mood swings, for her snapping at poor Mandy over something so trivial.

She took a deep breath, praying for a natural disaster or something that would take the limelight off her. Unfortunately no earthquakes shook the floor but the telephone did start to ring, and she'd never been so pleased to hear the sound. Hoping her colleagues would forget about her uncharacteristic outburst, she dived for her headset and snatched it up before any of the others could.

"Good morning, Donoghue's Boutique Travel, Subiaco, Emma speaking. How may I help you?"

"Ooh, hello," said a high-pitched Irish-accented female voice. "Top of the morning to you. May I speak with Patrick Donoghue?"

There was something familiar about the voice but Emma couldn't quite work out what. "May I ask who's speaking?"

The caller took a moment to reply, then began, "Um… I'd prefer to surprise him, thank you. You can tell him it's an old friend."

An old friend? Irritated, and then irritated by her irritation, Emma put the woman on hold, then looked over to Patrick, who, she found, was still looking at her with his brow furrowed. She smiled at him. "I've got an old friend of yours on the line."

His expression changed to one of confusion. "Who is he?"

"*She* wouldn't tell me her name. But she's on line one."

Patrick picked up his receiver. "Good morning, Patrick Donoghue."

Emma forced her eyes away from him and looked over to Mandy. "I'm sorry about the chocolates," she said. "I'll buy some later in the week, okay?"

"Whatever." Sounding like one of Emma's teenage children, Mandy shrugged and then looked over to Patrick, making no secret of the fact she was as curious as Emma about the mystery caller.

Emma opened her email, pretending to work while keeping one ear on his side of the conversation. Ever since their lunch together last week, she'd been entertaining late-night fantasies that maybe Patrick wanted more than friendship from her. She kept reminding herself that was impossible, but every time she recalled the way he'd caught her when she'd stumbled, her whole body heated with pleasure. Those feelings had been absent from her life for so long she'd almost forgotten the buzz they brought. Reliving their lunch together was better than any painkiller she could pop and also helped keep her mind off the Hawaii trip, which appeared to be the only thing Caleb, Laura and Louise were now capable of talking about.

"No, no, it's wonderful to hear from you," Patrick said, his grin stretching across his face as he leaned back into his chair. He made brief eye contact with Emma but then looked away again, giving all his attention to the woman on the other end of the line.

She felt a stab of jealousy and wished she'd told the caller Patrick was unavailable. Part of her didn't want to hear his conversation, but the masochistic side of her couldn't help eavesdropping. Whoever the *old friend* was on the other end of the line, Patrick was more than happy to hear from them. So happy in fact, he agreed to meet them for lunch. Emma felt like a first grader, jealous because someone else was playing with her new best friend.

Berating herself for her foolishness, she set to answering some inquiries, throwing herself into work like she hadn't done in days and barely noticing when Patrick finally hung up the phone.

Half an hour later, he stood up at his desk and announced, "I'll be going out for lunch today."

"Have fun," Emma said, cursing her faux-chirpy tone and

the way her hand lifted of its own accord, her fingers giving him some silly wave.

He smiled oddly at her and then slipped his arms into his blazer, which only enhanced his sexiness. She'd always preferred Max in his around-the-house casual clothes, but Patrick wore a suit better than any guy she'd ever known. A wave of heat came over her. Her first hot flash no doubt, giving weight to the theory she was menopausal and crazy.

The moment the agency door shut behind them, Mandy turned to Emma. "So who's this *old friend* he's gone out with? They sounded awfully chummy. The dark horse! I thought he was gay," she exclaimed, shaking her head in amusement. She'd obviously forgiven their earlier altercation.

Emma summoned a laugh that sounded not unlike a cat being strangled, and once again wished for a natural disaster. Were they close enough to the ocean for tsunamis to be a threat?

Jenny was ensconced with a client and Mandy didn't appear to notice her discomfort. "Hey, maybe one of us should follow him? I had this spy book when I was a kid and I used to love sneaking around the house, wearing Mom's long black coat and shadowing my brothers. I was pretty good."

"Go ahead, be my guest." Emma gestured to the door, resisting the urge to jump up, grab her jacket and do exactly that. A vision popped into her head; herself alone in some fancy restaurant, sipping tap water and holding the menu up to her face to disguise herself.

Mandy bit her lip as if seriously contemplating the idea. "Nah, I'd better not. What would I say if he saw me?"

Emma shrugged, forced a smile and eyed the box of fundraiser chocolates on Mandy's desk.

Right now, she'd kill for a Caramello Koala. Would Mandy accept an IOU?

16

Felicity

Every Thursday night Flick made dinner for her family and Beau, who'd been a regular visitor since he and Zoe started dating at sixteen. Growing up in a silent house with no mother and a mentally absent father, there'd never been such traditions in her household and she'd been firm right from when the kids were little that they should sit down to dinner every night and talk. It was her favorite time of the day—she'd always loved hearing about the kids' shenanigans at school and Seb's latest design project at work. Thursday was the only evening now when none of them had a regular commitment. So Thursday nights were sacred, like Friday-night book club with her friends. To everyone else sitting around the table munching on homemade pasties this was just another normal family dinner, but tonight Flick felt as if her world was closing in around her. First Seb's casual comment about telling Zoe and Toby his secret and then…then the letter, which had been burning a hole in her pocket since Monday afternoon. She'd looked at it so many times, hoping she'd been wrong, that it now looked a few decades old. Unable to think about anything *but* the letter, she was finding it hard to concentrate on the conversation.

"That was delicious, Mrs. Bell," Beau said, leaning back in his seat and stretching an arm around Zoe's shoulder.

"Thank you." Flick smiled at her future son-in-law. He was tall and muscular; she could see what attracted Zoe. She couldn't imagine *him* ever flitting around the marital bedroom in a frock. Then again, when she'd first met Seb, it was the last thing she'd expected of him as well.

"Don't you think it's time you started calling her Flick, like everybody else?" Seb suggested. "Or even *Mom*. Flick started calling my parents Mom and Dad not long after we met."

Beau's cheeks flushed red, highlighting the dimple that Zoe was always waxing lyrical about.

"It's all right, Beau," Flick said, not even glancing at her husband. "You call me whatever you're comfortable with." While she'd love Beau to call her Mom—she already thought of him as a second son—something irked her that Seb had been the one to suggest the idea. When had he taken it upon himself to make all their decisions without consulting her? Well, two could play at that game.

"Hey, Mom," Zoe said, looking from Flick to her father and back again as if she detected something uncomfortable in the air. "I heard from the bridal shop. My dress has come in earlier than they thought and they can do a fitting next Friday. You'll come with me, right?"

Flick hesitated a moment; she'd been waiting for the right time to tell everyone. "Actually, sorry, Zoe, but I can't. I'm going to be on my way to New York that day. Maybe your father will be able to go." She wanted to look at Seb and smile as she landed this announcement but found she couldn't bring herself to do so.

Everyone was quiet a few seconds and then, "New York?" Zoe exclaimed. "Since when?"

"Are you going with Will's mom?" Toby asked.

"I hope you get to watch a baseball game." This from Beau.

"Yes, with Neve," Flick said, and then she looked to Beau. "I doubt we'll have time to fit in anything like that." Considering she didn't even like watching *Aussie* sports, a baseball game wasn't high on her list of priorities. Besides, this trip was more about getting away for a while than seeing the sights.

"They'll be too busy shopping." Zoe scoffed, bouncing in her seat as if she were the one going away. "I'd give *anything* to come with you."

Seb sat silently across the table while the others expressed their excitement and Toby put in orders for things he *needed* her to bring back.

"I wish you could bring home a pizza. I've heard they're better in New York than in Italy."

Zoe glared at her little brother. "How's she going to bring you a pizza, goofhead? Even if they did let her bring it through customs, it'd be cold and gross by the time she gave it to you."

"Duh. I know that." Toby shrugged, his sister's name-calling like water off a duck's back. He'd probably be shocked if she called him by his actual name. "Can you get me a pair of Nikes? I hear they're like totally cheap in New York. And I'd love a Yankees snapback."

"A Yankees what?" Flick had no idea what he was talking about.

"It's a type of baseball cap," Beau explained. "Everyone's wearing them these days."

"Right." She nodded and braved a look at Seb, who raised an eyebrow at her.

"What about you, honey?" she asked, smiling sweetly. "Any requests?"

Seb shook his head and stood. She'd possibly taken things a little too far.

"Can you get me some earrings from Tiffany's?" Zoe touched her fingers to her ears as Seb left the dining room and headed into the kitchen. "They can be my 'something new' on the wedding day."

"I think your dress is something new." Flick stood and picked up the near-empty baking dishes. "Why don't you guys make a list, and I'll see what I can do," she promised. Normally she'd insist the kids do the washing up, but she could hear Seb already running the water. He cleaned whenever he was grumpy, angry or upset—tonight he might be all three. She took a deep breath and went to face the music.

"New York, hey?" Seb said as she came up beside him and put the dishes on the counter.

"Yep. I've always wanted to go."

He yanked his hands out of the soapy water, dried them on his sweater and turned to look at her. "And it's a done deal? You've booked your tickets?"

Flick nodded, keeping her chin high as she looked him right in the eye. She'd wanted to shock him like he'd shocked her, to show him how it felt to have your spouse keep you in the dark.

"An overseas trip is going to cost us a bit," he said, his tone dry. "Don't you think it might have been a good idea to tell me before you made the decision?"

She half laughed at the irony of this. "What? Like you tell me everything, Sebastian?"

Never in their twenty-two years together had she gone behind his back to do anything, but she'd felt no remorse as she'd handed over her credit card to Patrick Donoghue the other day. *Therapeutic* had been the word. But the satisfaction of spending such a large portion of their life savings had only lasted a short while, and although part of her couldn't wait to go to New York, she'd give it up in an instant if she could turn back time. If she could go back to the way things had been before The Letter. If only…

Seb's brow furrowed in confusion, and before he could ask her what the hell she meant, she pulled the crumpled piece of paper out of her pocket and thrust it at him. "This came for you the other day."

He took the letter and as he glanced down, all color drained from his face. She wondered if he'd have a go at her for opening his mail, but when he finally looked up, she saw no fight in his eyes.

"Shall we take this into the bedroom?"

Flick nodded—she had no idea what would occur as a result of this conversation, but it was not one she wanted her offspring and soon-to-be son-in-law privy to. Leaving the dishes, they trekked down the hallway, past the moose head hanging on the wall, not a word spoken between them. All Flick could hear was the pounding of her own heart, which felt like it had relocated to between her ears.

Was this it? The end of her relationship? The evening's dinner churned in her stomach.

She walked into the bedroom first and Seb closed the door behind them. What had always been like a sanctuary to her now felt confined and almost claustrophobic. The man she thought she knew better than anyone else stood before her like a stranger. Had she ever really known him at all?

"Do you want to sit down?" he asked as he gestured to their bed. Without replying, she walked the few steps and perched herself on the edge. It didn't feel right to sprawl back on the pillows as she often did at night while they talked about their days. This wasn't going to be one of those conversations.

Seb leaned back against the dresser and let out a loud puff of breath. Although he was leaning back, his posture was rigid.

Silence filled the small space between them; it appeared neither of them quite knew how to start.

Flick's jaw clenched and she wished he'd just say something. But she wasn't going to make this easy for him. The recollection of opening that envelope—the shock that had filled her so completely—had been unlike anything she'd ever experienced before. She'd felt so *stupid*.

Finally, he cleared his throat and held up the letter. "So this is why you've been a little cold the last few days."

Cold? She'd been cold? Heat whooshed into her body at this accusation. She'd wanted to discuss this calmly like two adults, which was why she'd put it off for so long, but now her heart had other ideas. Clenching her fists so as not to grab the nearest thing and hurl it at him, she said, "This isn't about me, Sebastian. Don't try to make it about me. I want to know about that letter."

Seb nodded, his shoulders slumping as he let out another sigh. "I… It's just…" He stuttered before he finally managed a sentence. "All I wanted to do was get a little information. See how much it costs, what the process is, how long it takes."

With each word he spoke, she felt the gap between them growing wider and her heart rate picking up speed. When *she* spoke, her chest heaved. "Forgive me if I'm wrong, but that there is confirmation of an appointment with a gender-reassignment clinic."

He nodded, but didn't meet her gaze. "Yes, but only to discuss things. To talk about my options."

"Things?" The word left a bad taste in her mouth. "And *your* options? What about *my* options? What happens after that? What if you decide this is something you want to do?"

When he didn't answer, she spit another question, "And when exactly were you planning on telling me, Seb?"

He had the audacity to shrug, as if they were talking about

something normal, something mundane. *When were you planning on telling me you broke my favorite vase?* The conversation felt surreal, almost as if she was watching it from outside her own body. She was saying the words, but she couldn't believe them.

"I didn't want to tell you until I was absolutely certain this was something I wanted to do. I didn't want to cause you undue stress." He looked close to tears, but she wasn't feeling very charitable.

"How very thoughtful of you!"

He ignored her sarcasm, wiped his eyes with his index finger and continued, "Telling you I wanted to tell Zoe and Toby about the cross-dressing was me testing the waters."

She swallowed the bile that rose in the back of her throat. At the time *that* had seemed like an outrageous idea—she couldn't understand why he would even think of doing something that could destroy his relationship with his kids—but telling them their dad sometimes liked to wear women's clothes was nothing compared to this.

This was a whole other level. Was she stupid never to have contemplated the possibility?

Flick opened her mouth, but struggled to ask the big question in all of this. "Have you... How long... Have you always thought it might come to this?"

Seb's expression was pained and he couldn't meet her gaze. "It's never been far from my mind, but I guess times are changing in the world, and it suddenly feels like what was once impossible might actually not be."

"You lied to me." There was so much hurt inside her right now, she didn't know what was worse—the lies or the truth.

"It's more complicated than that, Felicity."

He never called her Felicity. Her stomach churned and it was all she could do to remain upright.

"I'm sorry."

He took a step toward her but she held up her hand. "Don't."

He stopped, as if she was a dangerous creature and he realized the need to back off. "I never wanted to hurt you."

Yet he had. A tear slipped down her cheek. He had hurt her more than anyone ever had before, more than she'd ever thought it was possible to be hurt.

"Why don't you come to the appointment with me?" Seb suggested. "We can talk to the counselors together. Learn more about the actual process."

She shook her head, unable to bear the thought of going into such a place. Did he think that talking about this would help her understand? That in turn she would accept it?

"What happens to us if you go ahead with this?" she asked, the words blurting out of her mouth before she could think them through.

"I guess that would be up to you," Seb said, taking another tentative step toward her.

"You *guess*?"

"It's me I want to change, not you. I'd like to think we could go through this together and come out the other side."

Flick couldn't believe her ears. "Are you insane? Did you really think I'd just have a little panic attack and then move on? This is huge."

A vision of them walking down the street came into her head, both of them in women's clothes, holding hands as they went to meet their kids for lunch or something. What if they had grandchildren? Would Seb want to be the granny as well? She grimaced at the thought. And what about Mother's Day? Would she have to share that with him also? Then there were the other mothers at Dayton—she could just imagine what they'd make of this.

Who needed daytime television when her life was turning into a soap opera?

"I know it is." Seb reached out and took her hand; she didn't have the mental energy to snatch it away. "But I don't want to lose you."

She looked into his gorgeous gray eyes. "This isn't a shock to you, but I can't even begin to describe what it is to me. It feels like the worst kind of betrayal. I think I'd prefer if you told me you were gay or had an affair behind my back. I'm not a lesbian, Seb. I didn't sign on to have a wife."

Flick liked him because he had a penis—well, among other things, but the penis was definitely important. She didn't even realize she was still crying until a drop of salt water trickled over her lips and her tongue darted out to catch it.

"I know this isn't fair to you," he whispered again, looking as sad and confused as she felt, "but I'm tired of living a lie. I'm tired of pretending to be someone I'm not. I've never felt right inside this body of mine."

"But you've never said." That was the kicker.

She blamed Caitlyn Jenner for this—until she exploded onto the pages of *Vanity Fair* as a woman, telling the world about her transition from living as a man, this wasn't the kind of thing people she knew contemplated. Caitlyn had given so many mere mortals the courage to do something they'd never have felt able to do before.

While such a thing had only been something she'd read about in magazines or watched on TV, she'd always been politically correct in her thinking—or so she thought. Happy for these people she didn't know. She hated the idea that some individuals were so desperately unhappy about gender issues that they committed suicide, and she'd always supported a person's right to be whoever they wanted to be.

But that was before it got so incredibly close to home. Now she didn't know what she thought. About anything.

"I'm sorry," Seb said, squeezing her hand.

Flick glanced down at their adjoined hands as if hers wasn't actually a part of her. She didn't know her husband anymore, and that meant she didn't even know herself.

"I was scared," he continued. "I love you so much, Flick—always have, always will—and I was scared that if I ever told you, it would be over. But I'm not sure I can continue living a lie."

Love her? How could he truly love her and do this?

"Do you hate me?"

She took her time answering as she slowly pulled her hand from his grasp. She shivered and wrapped her arms around her body, her initial rage cooling as reality washed over her. This wasn't some kind of practical joke—Seb was serious. She wanted to tell him that she didn't hate him, but right now she wasn't even sure she wanted to look at him. Part of her wanted him to pull her into his arms and comfort her, but the other half—equally as strong—wanted to push him away.

To punish him in the way it felt like he was punishing her.

"I don't know," she said. "This is too new. I need time. I don't know what I think or how I feel. About you, about me, about any of this. That's why I decided to go to New York. I need some time away."

She had so many questions: What did he see as her role in this? Did he expect her to give up her heterosexual identity? How long had he been contemplating this? Would he go ahead even if she didn't want him to? But she couldn't bring herself to ask any of them. Not just yet.

He nodded. "I understand. Are you going to tell Emma and Neve?"

She raised her eyebrows. "Do you want me to?"

"I'm not ashamed of who I am, and if you need to talk to your closest friends about this then I understand. My only worry is that they might mention it to Caleb or Will. I wouldn't want Toby or Zoe finding out about this secondhand."

"I agree." At least he was still thinking of their children. Maybe if he thought some more, he'd realize this was all a big mistake. That them finding out at all would be a disaster and the only way to prevent that was to give up this ridiculous idea. If only there was some switch she could press to turn back time.

The question was, how far would she go? Knowing what she did now, would she even have married him at all?

"When do you leave?" Seb asked.

For a moment she thought he was asking her when she was leaving the marriage, then she remembered New York. "A week today."

And right now those seven days couldn't go fast enough.

17

Emma

"Mom!" Laura hollered down the hallway from the direction of the bathroom. "Have you seen our hair straightener?" The day she'd dreaded had finally arrived, and Emma could barely bring herself to drag her body out of bed. With a groan, Emma rolled over to the edge of the bed, which hadn't seemed so massive when she'd shared it with Max, and grabbed her water bottle and the box of painkillers that now lived permanently on her bedside table. She popped two from the packet and swallowed them with a few gulps of water before forcing herself upright.

She frowned at her scary reflection in the mirror—she'd have to plaster her face with makeup before Max and Chanel arrived—and vowed to finally make an appointment with the doctor. Her headaches and dizziness were getting beyond a joke and if she was going through early menopause; there had to be something stronger she could take for it.

"Mom?" Laura screamed again, this time from Emma's bedroom doorway, and she realized she hadn't got around to screaming back yet.

"Have you looked in the bathroom cupboard?"

"Yes." Laura rolled her eyes and flounced her shoulders in a manner both twins had perfected in the last few months. "I *cannot* go to Hawaii without it."

Emma stifled a smile. If she'd known that was all it would take she'd have hidden the damn thing somewhere even she couldn't find it. Of course, Max would just buy them another one duty-free. "Let me have a look," she said as she walked past her daughter and almost ran smack bang into Caleb.

"Oh, hey, Mom. Can you believe this? We're going to Ha-*wa*-ii!" He pretended to surf down the hallway and she forced enthusiasm into her reply.

"I know. You kids are very lucky."

Caleb dropped his arms to his side and a serious expression came over his face. "I wish you could come with us. Will you be okay here all on your own?"

He made her sound like such a sad case. She'd been trying not to let her feelings be known to her children, because she didn't want to dampen their excitement.

"I'll be fine. I'll probably be so busy out partying every night that I'll hardly miss you." *Ha!* The closest she'd get to a party would be ordering her favorite Chinese takeout and eating it in front of the TV.

Caleb laughed, a smile returning to his face. It kind of hurt that he didn't believe her.

"Um, *mother.*" Laura perched her hands on her hips. "My hair straightener?"

"I don't know why you bother with it," Caleb said, nodding toward his sister's head before Emma could reply. "You'd look better if you just put a paper bag over your head."

Laura gave him the finger, but Emma ignored it, not wanting to be any kind of grouch during their last minutes together.

"I'll find it," she said and headed for the bathroom. Find

it, she did. Exactly where she'd said it would be—sometimes she wondered if her children were blind.

The next hour passed in a blur of breakfast, excited conversation and last-minute reshuffling of things in suitcases. Caleb had a medium-size backpack, but the twins had a large suitcase each, so overstuffed with clothes that Caleb had had to sit on them in order to zip them up. Emma didn't say a word. If they were over the weight limit, that was Max's problem.

And then the doorbell rang—her heart slammed into her chest—and she had no more time to dread saying goodbye to her babies because it was time to actually do so. Part of her had wanted to go to the airport, but Max had made it clear she wasn't needed.

"Morning!" Max boomed as Caleb opened the front door. "Caleb, my main man!" He high-fived his son and then leaned forward, peering inside and glancing around him as if assessing whether or not Emma was taking care of the house. She didn't invite him in.

"Hello," she said, smiling through tight lips as she looked past him for Chanel. She saw the other woman sitting in the front seat of the car and lifted her hand to wave.

Hey, she could be civil when she wanted to.

Chanel hesitated a moment and then waved back.

"She's not coming in?" Emma asked, turning back to look at Max, smiling as though her heart wasn't about to shatter into a million pieces.

He looked sheepish. "We want to get to the airport and get checked in. Got anything exciting planned for your kid-free fortnight?"

Before she could admit that she had nothing to look forward to besides eating too much, missing the kids and feeling sorry for herself, the twins came charging out of their bedroom, ran down the hallway and hurled themselves at Max. "Daddy," they both shrieked, as if they were five years old, not almost fifteen. For a few months after the split they'd refused to talk to him, but when he started buying them everything they wanted, they'd quickly forgiven his sins. Sometimes they even made an effort with Chanel; although to Emma's secret joy, they mostly hated that a woman barely older than them had the power to twist their father around her little finger.

"Sweethearts," Max said, in a voice that had once made Emma's insides liquidize but now sounded like nails down a blackboard. "Are you all ready to go?"

"Born ready." Caleb bent over and hitched his backpack up off the floor and onto his shoulder.

"Dad, we might need some help with our luggage," Louise said, gesturing to the suitcases lined up on the front porch.

Laura nodded. "They're a little bit heavy."

Max looked back to Emma and frowned. "You didn't tell them there was a weight limit?"

She shrugged and summoned the most innocent expression she could. "I figured you'd just pay for extra baggage."

Max looked like he had something to say about this, but he opened his mouth and then closed it again; he'd never admit to anything that could be seen as a weakness in front of the kids. "Say goodbye to your mother then," he said eventually.

Caleb swamped her in his embrace. "We'll miss you, Mom. Have fun without us."

She swallowed a snort as he pulled away again.

Laura and Louise were next—hugging her as one, their conflicting body sprays wafting together to create a sickly aroma. Emma didn't care; it was the closest they'd got to her in months and having them in her arms was almost worth the disappointment of them going away.

When Louise said, "Mom, we've got to go," Emma realized she was clasping them a little tightly, but she didn't ever want to let go.

As her hands dropped to her sides and the girls sprang away, panic rose within her; not because she was worried anything would happen to them in Hawaii—she was a travel agent for goodness' sake—but because she couldn't help stressing that after two weeks of the high life the kids might decide they wanted to live with their dad permanently. However much they drove her insane on a daily basis, that would really push her over the edge.

She tried to banish this thought from her head as she watched Max go back and forth to his car with the suitcases. He had one of those flashy four-wheel drives that city people bought because bigger was better. And her heart had a moment of happiness as he struggled to lift the bags off the ground.

"I'll help, Dad." Before Max could object, Caleb had lifted them into the trunk.

Emma stood a few feet away as they all climbed into the vehicle, every bit of her focused on not crying. Somehow she held on to her composure as Max reversed out the driveway and slowly drove out of sight.

Only then did she finally let out her breath and a great big sob.

The couple of weeks since Max had announced the trip had gone by in a flash, but she knew their time away would drag like months rather than days. Especially because their vacation coincided with Neve and Flick's trip to New York. Keeping herself busy with work was the only way she'd ever get through it, but right now she couldn't summon any enthusiasm for heading into the travel agency. Patrick had given her the morning off to farewell the kids, but now she wished she'd taken the whole day.

She thought of the tub of chocolate-chip ice cream she'd

bought on special last week, then buried at the back of the deep freeze so the children wouldn't find it. She'd been saving it for a rainy day, and sending her children halfway across the world with her wanker of an ex-husband and his infuriatingly perfect wife definitely qualified as stormy weather.

18

Genevieve

Passport. Check. US dollars. Check. Power adaptor. Check. Sexy lingerie? Perhaps not. Her bare necessities makeup kit. Check. Picture of Will to show James. Well, she'd have her phone with her, and that had plenty.

At the thought of James, Neve's fingers shook as she tried to zip up her suitcase. She could manage her anxiety perfectly well as long as she pretended this was a girls' trip overseas with her two closest friends, but whenever she remembered the real reason, her usually competent self turned into a bundle of nerves. She'd even caught herself biting her nails, which was unforgivable in her profession.

"Here, let me help," Will said as he wandered into her bedroom, smartly dressed in his school uniform and so much like how she remembered James her heart hurt.

The first time she'd laid eyes on James Cooper had been at a cast party, following the successful opening night of *Cats*. It was one of the few times the production crew, the cast and the head honchos like the directors and the producers got together. Everyone in the theater was on a high, drinking, dancing, laughing and schmoozing with the key sponsors who liked to be praised and acknowledged for their commitment to the arts. Fancy caterers had been hired in for the occasion, the expensive wine flowed freely and everyone had dressed up to the nines.

It wasn't that Neve didn't like parties, but as a mere entry-level makeup artist, the only people who ever seemed to pay attention to her were some of the young male actors. They *were* unbelievably good-looking, but their egos—which she'd experienced firsthand when doing their makeup—turned her off. But James was different. Although just as good-looking—more so in her opinion—his flirtations had been much more subtle.

"What are you doing hiding over here in the corner?" he'd said by way of greeting as he arrived beside her with a sparkling flute of champagne.

Her fingers instinctively reached out to take it as she replied, "Just people-watching." *Biding time until I can go home to bed* probably wasn't the right answer.

He nodded and leaned back against the wall beside her. "I like a bit of people-watching myself." Then he offered her his hand. "I'm James."

"I know," she replied, trying not to blush at the reaction his hand touching hers caused inside her body. Of course she knew who he was; everyone knew the directors.

"And you are…?" he asked with a grin, taking longer than necessary to let go of her hand.

She smiled back. "Genevieve Taylor. I'm a makeup artist."

"No wonder our cast looked so fabulous on stage tonight. How long have you been working in the theater?"

She'd given him her answer—a year, but this was her first major production—and he'd delved deeper with his questions. Instead of talking about himself, he wanted to know about her. How she'd got into the theater side of makeup artistry.

Whether it was her dream job or merely a stepping stone on the way to something else.

His interest had been intoxicating, as was his smile, his masculine woody scent and the way he looked at her as they chatted—like he might lean forward and kiss her at any moment. And when he had, she'd reassessed her whole thoughts on kissing. A simple four-letter word didn't seem enough to describe the way James's mouth—his lips and tongue—had made her feel. No one had ever kissed her like that. Not before. Not since.

"Mom? Are you coming?" Will's voice jolted Neve back to the present. She sucked in a quick breath and smiled at him standing before her carrying her suitcase. "Thanks, hon. Are you all packed to stay with Nan and Pop? I'll drop your stuff at their house after I take you to school."

"Yep." Will started toward the door but paused as he reached it. "Mom, I know you've been preoccupied with this big job but have you had any more luck trying to track Dad down?"

The word *dad* sounded alien coming from his lips, but she made a concerted effort not to flinch. "Well, I've sent emails to everyone I know who might have an idea of where James is now. I've had a few leads and I promise I'm following them through. Try to be patient. You've got to trust me on this, sweetheart, and concentrate on your school work."

"Yeah, yeah. I will," promised Will, his tone petulant as he stalked out of her bedroom with the suitcase.

Neve sighed—although she'd heard plenty of horror stories of moody teenagers, hers had never been one. She guessed it was his right to be sulky and bad-tempered when things didn't happen immediately. She herself hadn't possessed an ounce of patience until she'd had a toddler who refused to be rushed in anything. But that toddler had been her world and she'd learned to adapt, and as he'd grown, they'd become closer. She hated the way this thing about James had changed the dynamics of their relationship.

Where they used to hang out together in the evenings— talk about their days over dinner—for the last couple of weeks every conversation had been strained. She'd been constantly on edge, terrified that Will would demand to know more about his father. She'd had the feeling he'd been trying not to say too much, so as not to upset her. But his reference to "Dad" showed that James had been on his mind as much as he'd been on hers. And that was unlikely to change until he knew the truth.

As Neve followed her son toward the front door, she told herself that holding certain things back was for the best, for his own good. She hated lying to him, but the thought of telling him the truth terrified her. What if her quest to find James went terribly, terribly wrong? She didn't want to get Will's hopes up for an outcome that might not happen. Or worse, have him begging her to take him along as well.

Meeting James alone first was imperative. Without a doubt the man would be shocked. At best he'd be angry; at worst he'd want nothing to do with either of them.

"Right." Neve injected chirpy enthusiasm into her voice. "I think we're ready. I can take my suitcase. You grab your bags and remind me again what presents you'd like me to bring back from New York."

Flick had said that her two hadn't held back with their requests and Neve hoped the prospect would cheer Will up, but so far he'd shown little enthusiasm.

He picked up his school bag and overnight bag from the floor by the front door. "You *are* going for work, aren't you?" It sounded like an accusation, as if he didn't believe her.

"Yes, but I'll have some time to explore. That's why Flick's coming along." Will didn't know that Emma would also be joining them. No one did but her, Flick and Emma's boss, Patrick.

Will made some kind of grunting noise in reply and Neve chose not to reprimand him as they locked the house and headed to her car. Usually they had their best conversations in the car, but today they passed the trip to school in silence.

Just as she stopped in the drop-off zone, she had a sudden urge to tell him the truth—the real reason why she was going to New York.

His hand on the door handle, his body poised to exit the car, Neve cried out, "Will!"

He turned back to look at her, his steel blue eyes meeting hers, and all she could think about was how innocent and young he looked. A boy in a man's body. And with that, she chickened out. "Have a good day, darling," she said, leaning across to kiss him on the cheek. "I'll call you the moment I land. Be good for Nan and Pop. Love you."

He sighed the deep sigh of a man four times his age. "I will. Love you, too, Mom." And then he opened the door, climbed out of the car and joined a couple of other boys as they headed into the school.

She watched him go, recalling the first time he'd ever said those three magic words to her. He'd been twenty months old and she'd thought her heart would explode with the love she felt for him. Time hadn't dulled that feeling at all. However much trepidation she felt at the thought of facing James, of telling him the truth, Neve vowed to do whatever it took to make Will's dream come true.

19

Felicity

Her suitcase packed and waiting by the front door, Flick sat at the breakfast bar sipping her second coffee of the day and counting down the hours until Neve arrived and their adventure began. She'd kissed Toby goodbye when he left for the bus, making him promise to be good for Dad while she was away. He hadn't appeared to notice the tension between his parents, but that could be because Seb had been acting as if nothing had changed.

"You sure you don't want me to drive you girls to the airport?" Seb asked now as he loaded the dishwasher like he always did.

"No, thanks," she said tersely. "I've called us a car."

Straightening again, he leaned back against the counter and smiled at her in a manner that until recently had always made every bone in her body turn to jelly. "You must be super excited. I must admit I'm a tiny bit jealous. I always hoped the first time you went to America it would be with me."

Well, we don't always get what we hope for in life, do we? Her hands tightened around the mug as she bit back the words. Instead she shrugged and downed the final dregs of her coffee.

"I'll buy you a T-shirt," she promised as she went to put her mug in the dishwasher. "Shouldn't you be getting off to work?"

He glanced at his watch. "No rush. Thought I might say hello to Neve and wave you off."

Dear God, no! She couldn't stand another half an hour of him acting as if he hadn't recently dropped a hand grenade into their marriage. Even though she strongly suspected his attempt at normality was for her, it made her blood boil. When he'd suggested they go to counseling, she'd told him she wasn't ready to talk to him yet, never mind a professional, and she'd meant it. But not talking, instead letting it fester between them, was just as horrible. Last night he'd tried to cuddle her in bed and his hands on her skin had felt like ants crawling all over her. She hated him for making her feel like that. Hated that he couldn't *be* what she needed.

"Please don't." She held up her hand and met his gaze properly for the first time.

"Don't what?" His voice cracked a little, and he recoiled as if she'd slapped him.

Flick closed her eyes and let out a long slow breath. "Pretend everything's okay!" she yelled. "You haven't said a word about the letter since I showed it to you."

"But I thought you didn't want to talk about all that yet?"

"You know what I want, Seb?" She thrust her finger at him like she was telling off a naughty child. "I want all *that* to go away. I want a *normal* husband." Tears threatened as the emotions that had been building up inside her bubbled to the surface, pushing to break free.

"I'm sorry, Flick." He looked close to tears as well. They *never* fought.

"I know. But I can't do this anymore. I can't pretend our marriage is what everyone thinks it is when inside my heart is breaking. I told you I need time and I promise I'll send you a message to say we got there safely but I need you to admit that your decision will change us in one way or another." She took a quick breath. "So please just go to work and let me pull myself together before Neve gets here."

"Okay." He nodded, his voice barely a whisper as he backed away.

She could tell he wanted to hug her but was glad he resisted. He'd always been a touchy-feely, expressive type. Other women had often commented on his public displays of affection, but right now she wished he was a straightforward guy who liked beer after work, football on the weekends and who forgot to put the rubbish out when she asked him.

"Have a good a trip then," Seb said, his voice tinged with sadness as he tightened the knot on his pale pink tie. Against his charcoal shirt and black pants, it looked stylish and not at all irregular. Real mean wore pink, or so the slogan went. She would never smile at that sentiment again.

"Thank you," she said. "We'll talk when I get back. Okay?" Hopefully a week away from him, away from their home—where she was constantly reminded about the life they'd built together and the lie that lay beneath it all—would help her work out what she wanted.

He nodded and then left the kitchen. A couple of minutes later she heard the front door shut and the car start.

Flick glanced at her watch and was contemplating another coffee when her cell phone rang. She looked around for the sound, located it near the microwave and frowned when she saw it was Emma's boss. What was he calling for?

"'Morning, Patrick." She hoped he wasn't calling with bad news.

They'd been planning to sneak into Emma's house using the spare key she'd given Flick in case of an emergency, pack

a suitcase for her and then drive by the travel agency to pick
her up. But a wrench had been thrown into their plans when
Patrick called to say she'd phoned in sick.

"What if she's really sick?" Neve said once Flick had filled
her in on the situation. "Nothing worse than flying when
you feel like shit."

"She won't be. It'll all be down to Max taking the kids
away, but I'm sure our arrival will cheer her up."

Neve tilted her head to one side, the sun glinting against
her golden hair. "I wish I had your confidence. I think she
might kill us."

Flick laughed, glad to be focusing on something other than
Seb. "She doesn't have it in her. She's been threatening to kill
Max for how long? And he's still thieving valuable oxygen
from the world."

"That's true."

Flick nodded toward the street as a black stretch limousine
pulled into her driveway. "Looks like our ride is here."

Neve's hand flew to her chest as she stared at the black
beast. Flick couldn't help grinning at her friend's incredulous
expression.

After a few seconds, Neve recovered enough to speak. "Are
you serious? I thought Seb was driving us."

Flick shook her head as their driver—wearing an actual
chauffeur's cap—emerged from the vehicle and strode toward
them. "He has to work."

The driver tipped his cap and smiled. "Ladies. I'm Gideon
Blake. Pleased to be of service." He sounded so damn masculine and looked pretty fine in that uniform as well. Heck,
even his name was hot. "Are you ready to go?"

"We certainly are," Flick said as she gestured to their luggage on the front veranda.

"Excellent." Gideon strode up the few steps and lifted Neve's suitcase in one hand and Flick's in the other.

Flick tried to imagine this man in a dress. Nope, impossible. She silently cursed.

It had crossed her mind this last week that if she and Seb were to break up, then she might one day venture again into that long-forgotten world of dating. That idea alone terrified her enough, but the worry that she'd never be able to look at another man without visualizing him in a short skirt and F-me boots amplified her anxiety.

"I can't believe we're actually doing this," Neve said as they followed Gideon with their carry-on luggage. "I can't thank you enough for coming with me."

Flick shrugged. "That's what friends do. You need our support. Em needs a vacation." *And I need to escape!* She decided not to bring up the recent awkwardness between Neve and Emma, nor her hope that some quality time together would help heal the cracks in their friendship.

"Yes, shopping therapy!" Neve's eyes sparkled at the thought. "I can't wait to see her face when we arrive."

As Emma lived nearby, they didn't have to wait long. The limo had barely stopped in front of her house when Flick and Neve leaped out like a couple of excited teenagers, promising the driver they would be as quick as possible.

"Take your time," Gideon said. "You don't need to be at the airport for another four hours."

"Maybe not, but there's a champagne bottle with our names on it waiting at the bar," Neve called over her shoulder.

Flick grinned as they stopped at the front door. Yes, champagne was definitely on the agenda. "Do we knock or use my key, really surprise her?"

"Let's knock. We don't want to give her a heart attack. She's going to be shocked enough."

"Good point." Flick raised her hand and rapped on the door. They waited, both silent as they listened for sounds of Emma approaching. Nothing. They frowned at each other and Flick was about to knock again when the door finally opened a fraction.

Emma peered around it, her eyes bloodshot and her lids puffy. "What are you two doing here?" she asked.

20

Emma

"Surprise!" Flick and Neve sang in unison. The sound grated on Emma's headache—one she attributed to the two liters of ice cream she'd inhaled in about fifteen minutes. All she could think about was that her friends should be on their way to New York. She opened the door fully.

Her confusion must have shown in her face because they exchanged glances, and then Neve, looking as if she were about to wet her very fashionable pants, said, "You tell her."

Grinning as if nothing could wipe the smile from her face, Flick reached into her jacket pocket and pulled out a piece of paper. She unfolded it and thrust it toward Emma. "Time to get ready, sunshine. You're coming to New York with us!"

Neve clapped her hands as Emma stared down at the paper. "What?"

"Not quite the reaction we were hoping for," Flick said, "but you can get used to the idea while we pack your bags." Before Emma could work out what was going on, her friends barged past her into the house and down the corridor toward her bedroom.

Too bamboozled to worry about the state of her bedroom,

she looked properly at the piece of paper, which appeared to be an eticket with her name on it. Plane departing four hours from now. Her fingers trembled and she shook her head.

"No, no, no, no, no," she called as her legs unfroze and she hurried after Flick and Neve. "I can't just up and go to New York."

"Yes, you can," Flick said with conviction as she and Neve disappeared into the walk-in closet.

"Do you have an empty suitcase?" Neve asked. "We can't dillydally or we won't be able to enjoy our preflight champagne."

Ignoring Neve's question, Emma crossed her arms and stood at the entrance to the walk-in closet. "I can't just take time off work."

"Actually, you can," Flick said, barely looking up from where she was rifling through clothes. "We've cleared everything with your lovely boss. He thinks you deserve a break as much as we do."

At the mention of Patrick, her chest tightened. "Patrick is in on this?"

"Yep," said Neve.

Flick nodded and smiled. "He even booked the flights for me. You can call him and check if you like but he told us to tell you to have fun and not to worry about anything. He's got a temp filling in for you from one of the other agencies. Oh, and he'll pay you as if you were still at work, so you don't lose your vacation days. He's quite a sweetie."

"What?"

"He sounds like a great boss," Neve said. "Is he single?"

Emma's head was spinning. Having to say goodbye to the kids, and then these two showing up out of the blue had almost made her forget her recent annoyance with Neve, but this comment brought it right back. She was about to tell her that she didn't think she was his type when Flick cut in.

"Look, I don't mean to interrupt the chitchat, but we really need to get on to this."

It took Emma a moment to understand, and then her confusion and shock returned in full. "You've really cleared this with Patrick? And what about my visa? You can't go to the US without an ESTA."

"Relax," Neve said. "Flick's organized everything. She's the only person I know who could organize another person's global travel without that person getting even a teensy bit suspicious."

Emma opened her mouth to say something but found she had no idea what she wanted to say. She stepped back a few feet and flopped into the cute armchair she'd found at a garage sale and reupholstered herself back when she'd had time to do such things. She stared ahead at her unmade bed, too stunned to feel embarrassed by the discarded tissues scattered across it and the empty ice cream carton on her bedside table.

"I can't afford this."

"But I can." Flick smiled. "Consider it a present for putting up with me for so long."

Emma rolled her eyes. "As if that's a hardship. But seriously, I can't let you do that. What does Seb think about you spending this money on me?"

Flick shrugged one shoulder. "He doesn't know. Anyway, I've worked hard for our savings as well. I can splurge when I want to." There was a defensive edge in her voice, and for a moment Emma wondered whether something wasn't quite right between Flick and Seb. But she pushed that thought aside almost immediately—it was like imagining that bread and butter no longer went together. She didn't know another couple as perfect as Flick and Seb.

"I know this is a lot to take in." Flick crossed over and perched on the arm of the chair and patted Emma's knee. "But why don't you take a shower, freshen up and Neve and I will handle the packing?"

"I can't believe this," Emma whispered, her senses slowly beginning to recover. "Are we *really* going to New York?"

"You betcha," Neve called from where she was selecting clothes.

"Call it serendipity," Flick said. "Neve going away at the same time you're kid-free, just when we'd been talking about how much fun it would be to have a vacation together. Who are we to ignore such blatant signs?"

Emma shrugged. She was starting to come around to the idea. "When you put it like that…" A rush of adrenaline zipped through her and the first real smile she'd felt in a long time lifted her lips. "Okay then, New York, here we come!"

The others cheered and ushered her into the bathroom before she could change her mind. As the door shut behind her, she stared into the mirror. *Is this some kind of wonderful dream?*

No. If this were a dream, she wouldn't be looking this tragic. She put her fingers to her puffy eyes and then glared at her red, blotchy face and her hair, which was doing a good imitation of a bird's nest. And was that dried ice cream on her chin?

Ugh. She shuddered. Perhaps this was exactly what she needed—some time out with her friends. A week of shopping, cocktails and sightseeing to destress from the grind of everyday life. To remind her she wasn't just a mom, ex-wife and employee, but a woman who needed to take better care of herself.

She opened the medicine cabinet and retrieved a couple of painkillers. She swallowed them dry, then stripped naked and jumped into the shower.

21

Felicity

After standing next to the luggage carousels at JFK airport for what felt like an inordinate period of time, Flick and the girls finally emerged from the building into the hustle and bustle of people and traffic. Every second vehicle seemed to be beeping its horn and there were sirens in the distance in all directions.

"Cabs are that way." Emma dragged her sunglasses down over her eyes and pointed across to their right, reminding Flick that she was the only one of them who'd been to New York before.

"Whose idea was it to travel all this way without a layover?" Neve groaned as they navigated through the throng of other passengers toward the taxi line. "I feel like a walking corpse."

"Yes, I'd definitely have recommended a stopover in LA," Emma said. "Or I'd have gone via Dubai, it's much shorter."

"If I recall correctly, you were too busy to help me," Neve replied snippily.

"Girls, *please*, enough already." Flick pressed the heel of her hand against her forehead as they joined the back of the line. Drinking the lion's share of a bottle of champagne at Perth airport had seemed like a good idea at the time, as had accepting the complimentary wine with her in-flight meals, but her body was punishing her now. The last thing she needed was Emma and Neve bickering like a couple of schoolgirls. After more than thirty hours in transit with next to no proper sleep, her patience was wearing thin. She had hoped they'd make an effort to be civil and that Emma would chill out and get over her disappointment with Neve's affair.

"What should we have for dinner?" Neve said after a while.

"Know anywhere good?" Flick asked Emma.

"Around Times Square?" She shrugged. "I've heard John's Pizzeria is good, although to be honest, I'm so shattered I'd rather get room service and eat it in bed."

Neve inclined her head. "I'm all for that idea. We can eat, shower and then hopefully fall asleep at a reasonable New York hour."

Flick's stomach rumbled; it didn't care what she ate as long as she washed it down with water instead of wine. "Sounds perfect. And if John's is good, maybe we can go there tomorrow before *Mamma Mia!*?"

The color drained from Neve's face and she visibly shuddered as they shuffled closer to the front of the line. "Actually I'm not really that hungry anymore."

Just as Flick had been trying to push her problems with Seb to the back of her mind, she guessed Neve was trying not to think about the main reason they were in New York.

"Have you worked out what you're going to say to him yet?" Emma asked.

Neve's complexion went from pale to green in a matter of seconds. "Can we talk about something else? *Anything* else?"

"How about those cute firemen over there?" Flick pointed to an enormous fire truck parked about ten meters up the road; three buff guys in black-and-yellow uniforms were leaning against it, seemingly in no rush to go anywhere. Masculinity oozed from their stances. She would bet none of *them* had a fetish for female fashion.

Emma chuckled slightly. "I think we're a little old to ogle firemen."

"Speak for yourself." Neve grabbed her phone and snapped a couple of photos.

One of the firemen waved and, as Neve and Flick waved back, Emma mused, "I don't think that one's much older than Will, Caleb and Toby."

"Jeez, way to spoil a girl's fun." Neve tucked her phone back in her handbag. "Look, it's almost our turn."

Sure enough, while they'd been scoping out the local talent, they'd made it to the front of the cab line. The elderly couple in front of them stepped forward to await their yellow cab, and a man that seemed to be in charge of everything smiled. "Where you lovely ladies from?"

"Australia," Flick volunteered.

He made a face. "Heard you have some big mother-effing spiders down there. Where are you all going?"

"The Marriott Marquis in Times Square," Neve supplied. The man punched something into a little machine, then tore off some kind of receipt and gave it to them.

Emma took it. "Thanks." She explained to the others that it had their taxi driver's details and the price of the trip on it. Then she pointed to a yellow car as it crawled to a stop at the curb and a driver who looked like he lived and breathed McDonald's stepped out to greet them.

"Hey, girls," he said, grinning as he ran a hand through his greasy red hair and gave the three of them a pervy once-over. "Looks like it's my lucky day."

Flick couldn't hide her distaste.

"Let's not get excited," Neve said drily. "But you *can* help us with our bags."

While Ronald McDonald's overweight twin struggled with their cases, the women squashed into the back seat. The cab smelled like take-out food and had TV screens blaring on the back of both the passenger and driver seats.

"Oh, my God," Emma squealed, snapping Flick's attention away from the TVs. "I can't believe we're actually here. It's like a dream. I can't believe you guys kidnapped me and whisked me away to New York."

"You know," Neve began with a smile, "we really didn't have to twist your arm too much."

Flick laughed. "But that look on your face when we told you… That was priceless."

"We should have taken a photo," Neve agreed.

Emma sighed and leaned her head against the back seat as their driver climbed into the front. "Thank you, guys. I think I really needed this. I was dreading this week at home without the kids."

"I'm glad you're coming with us," Neve said as Flick took Emma's hand and squeezed it.

"We're gonna be so busy living it up, you'll barely have a chance to think of them, never mind miss them," she said.

"That sounds good, but I should send them a message to let them know where I am. Just in case there's an emergency or something. Call me childish, but I wish I could see Max's face when he finds out I'm not sitting at home alone feeling sorry for myself."

They laughed and then Neve said, "Yeah, I'm going to give Will a call and make sure he's up for rowing practice. Don't want Mom having to nag him."

Flick decided she, too, should probably message her family. She dug her cell phone out of her handbag and switched it back on. Once it had located a network, she punched out a group message for Zoe, Toby and Seb. Arrived safe, heading to hotel now.

While Neve chatted to Will and then her mother, and Emma sent a thank-you message to Patrick, Flick watched the city that never sleeps roll by through the taxi window. They were on some sort of big highway, with huge American cars flying past them, many with their windows down and music blaring. She couldn't help but notice the number of dents on the vehicles. Seb would be appalled—he treated his Jeep like a fifth member of their family.

Not wanting to think about Seb, she shook her head and instead turned her attention to the television in front of her. It took her two seconds to realize her mistake. It was screening a series about Caitlyn Jenner and her transformation. Good God! Was there no escape? On the plane, she'd opened the in-flight magazine straight to an article about a group of Sydney teens lobbying to change their school's uniform policy so that boys could wear the girls' uniform if they wanted to.

It was like when you wanted to get pregnant and suddenly started seeing glowing moms-to-be with their burgeoning bumps everywhere you went.

"Excuse me?" she called to the driver. "Can you turn these TVs off?"

He didn't seem to hear but Emma looked up from her cell phone. "You okay?"

Flick forced a smile. "Fine. Just getting a little carsick."

"It is a bit stuffy in here," Neve said, rolling down her window a little.

Exhausted from their journey, the friends took in the passing sights in relative silence—with only the occasional remark when they saw something familiar like the *New York Times* building and Grand Central Station. Flick might never have been to New York before, but you'd have to have been living on another planet not to recognize the massive billboards of Times Square, flashing advertisements for shows and brands like Coca-Cola. It wasn't quite six o'clock at night, but there were people and vehicles everywhere when they finally arrived at their hotel.

"This is *my* kind of place," Neve said, her head almost out the window as she looked on in awe.

Flick wasn't sure she agreed—it was all a little too neon and flashy for her liking—but all the glitz and glamour was about as far away from her life in Western Australia as she could get and that was all that mattered right now.

"There's the sign for *Mamma Mia!*" Emma noted as she pointed past Neve out the window. "It's so close to our hotel."

Neve groaned.

"Marriot Marquis Times Square," announced the driver.

Flick glanced up at the massive hotel as the cab slowed to turn into the drop-off zone. She couldn't wait to get out of her traveling clothes into comfy pajamas, climb into a big fluffy hotel bed and order room service.

Usually the most reticent of all of them, Emma took control when it came to tipping the driver.

Flick and Neve were grateful. "The whole idea of tipping makes me nervous," Flick admitted as they climbed out of the taxi.

"Me, too," Neve agreed.

"It's easy when you get the hang of it," Emma said, smiling her thanks at the driver as he lifted the last of their bags from the trunk. A smartly dressed African American porter rushed over to assist. "How y'all doing, ladies?" he asked, dipping his hat to greet them. He had the most adorable accent. Flick could have listened to him for days.

"We're dead on our feet," Neve said.

"Australians?" He cocked his head to one side and gave them a wide grin.

They nodded.

"That's a long trip. Let's get you inside."

The lovely man took their luggage and their names, and then directed them up eight floors to reception. Now that they were actually here, the jet lag hit them with a vengeance. Somehow they checked in and found the way to the thirty-sixth floor without really registering anything except how fast the elevator was and how high up they were.

"Lucky none of us are scared of heights," Emma mused, looking out their window when they finally let themselves into their room. Neve joined her to admire the view but Flick flopped down onto one of the two double beds and toed off her shoes. There'd be enough time later to check out the view.

"I'll take the sofa bed," Emma said, turning around to inspect their room.

From her position on the bed, Flick had to admit it'd be a nice place to spend the week. The beds were comfy, the sheets soft and, even with three of them sharing, there'd be ample room.

She forced herself into a sitting position. "We thought we could take turns sleeping on the sofa bed."

Emma gave her a dirty look. "Don't be silly. Since I'm not contributing financially, the sofa bed is all mine." She perched down on the edge of it and bounced a little. "It actually feels comfier than my bed back home."

Before they could argue over the arrangements, a knock on the door announced the arrival of the porter. Neve let him in, and once he'd deposited their luggage, Emma gave him a tip and Flick raised her hand in a wave of thanks as he departed.

"Ready to order room service?" Neve asked. She picked up the menu and leaned back against the desk.

"Definitely." Flick needed food, a shower and bed, and right now her body didn't care in what order.

Standing beside Neve, Emma looked over her shoulder. "Ooh, look, you can create your own salad, burgers, pizza or pasta."

"What's the point in that?" Neve said. "If I'm paying for food, I want someone else to do *all* the work."

"Fair point," Emma agreed. "I think I'll have the halibut with a side of sweet potato fries, then."

"The grilled-chicken Cobb salad sounds good."

Flick screwed up her nose. "I'm not going to waste my vacation eating salad."

"But it's got bacon and blue cheese in it," Neve countered.

"Anything with the word *salad* in it is rabbit food," Flick said. "Here, let me have a look."

Emma passed the menu to Flick and decided on a burger with potato chips, which would hopefully satisfy her hangover/ jet lag craving.

Neve called down to order, thanked the person on the other end of the line and disconnected. "Food will be here in half an hour. Do you mind if I have the first shower?"

Flick lay back against the pillows. "If I fall asleep, wake me up when the meals arrive," she told Emma as Neve disappeared into the bathroom.

"No worries." Emma went over to her handbag and retrieved a packet of painkillers.

Flick frowned, trying to recall how many Emma had already taken since they'd left Perth. "Are you still getting those headaches?" she asked, as Emma downed two without water. "Did you end up seeing a doctor?"

"I was going to book an appointment this week, but then two crazy women abducted me and now here I am." Smiling, she gestured around the room as if she were a real estate agent delivering her sales spiel. "Which happens to be better than winning the lottery. Thank you again."

"Thank *you* for coming," Flick said, still concerned about her friend's persistent headaches. "How long have you been having them now?"

Emma shrugged as she flopped down onto the sofa bed. "Maybe a month or so. I think I might be going through early menopause."

"Really?"

"Yes. As well as the headaches, I've been so damn moody. I remember my mom experienced the change younger than most and she was hell to live with at the time."

Flick thought about this a moment. "I suppose there are advantages. You'll never have to worry about contraception again."

Emma laughed and hugged a pillow to her chest. "That's the least of my concerns. I'd have to find a man first."

"What about Patrick?"

Emma's eyes widened. "My boss?"

When Flick nodded, Emma blushed. "Plenty of people hook up with their bosses. And Patrick seems like a really great guy."

"How do you know?"

"We met to discuss secret New York business, remember? And he spoke *very* highly of you." Flick grinned. "I didn't notice a wedding band."

Emma sighed. "That's because he's gay."

Flick shook her head, unable to hide her shock. "No way. Are you sure? He didn't give off that vibe at all."

Emma nodded. "That's what everyone says, and I've never seen anything to the contrary. Besides, aren't all the good men already taken or gay?"

Flick ignored this question, much more intrigued by the

gleam in Emma's eye when Patrick's name was mentioned. "But what if he's not? Would you be interested, then?"

Emma hesitated and for a second Flick saw the truth in her eyes, but then she shook her head. "I wouldn't want to jeopardize my job."

Before Flick could grill her any further, the bathroom door opened and Neve emerged.

"Shower's all free," she said, raking her hands through her short wet hair.

"You want to go next?" Flick asked Emma.

"No, you go."

In dire need of a hot shower, Flick didn't argue, and by the time she'd finished, their room service had arrived.

"Sorry, we didn't wait for you," Emma said, gesturing to her half-eaten dinner, "but I thought it best I eat mine so I can shower and then we can all get some rest."

"Good plan," Flick said as she crossed over to the room-service cart, picked up the remaining silver dish and lifted the lid. "Is it any good?"

Neve moaned through a mouthful of food. "My salad is to die for."

"Yep." Emma nodded. "The halibut's great, too."

"They gave me crisps," Flick exclaimed, staring down at her dinner as if it were road kill. "I wanted hot bloody chips, not crisps." Neve and Emma thought this was hilarious, but Flick felt like crying. Granted, it was a ridiculous thing to cry about, but after the few weeks she'd had and so little sleep in the last forty hours, her emotions were all over the place. *Maybe I'm going through early menopause, too.*

"Oh, well," she said, hoping her voice didn't give away how close she was to tears. "At least the burger smells good."

They devoured their meals in record time and Flick had already climbed into bed by the time Emma headed into the bathroom for her shower. She snuggled down under the lovely clean covers, inhaling the fresh smell of the sheets, and hoped that she would feel more like herself after a good night's sleep.

"'Night, Neve," she said, turning over to face the wall. "Sleep well."

"I'll be lucky if I get any sleep at all."

Although Flick knew the right thing to do would be to roll over again and try to soothe her friend's nerves, she pretended not to hear, pretended she was already asleep. She *was* far too exhausted for such a conversation.

Yet despite her body beginning to shut down now that she was finally horizontal, she wasn't sure she'd get much rest either. She couldn't remember the last time she'd gone to sleep without Seb beside her. She shivered and pulled the covers tighter. Was this something she would have to get used to?

22

Genevieve

Neve woke up in a strange bed in a strange place. It took five seconds to orientate herself. She was in Manhattan, and the flashing lights from Times Square had crept in through the curtains, interrupting her sleep for half the night.

Then she remembered the other reason her slumber had been restless, the reason she and her two best friends had come to New York in the first place, and her heart threatened to leap out of her body and toss itself out the window.

She sat up in bed, clutching the covers to her chest as she looked over at Emma sleeping peacefully on the sofa bed and Flick dead to the world in the other bed. Daylight blared through those gaps in the curtains, but she had no idea what time it was. Trying to be quiet so as not to wake the others, Neve stretched over to grab her cell phone from the bedside table.

Eight o'clock. The time most normal people would be rousing for breakfast, but she didn't have any appetite. Her stomach had been churning nonstop ever since they'd left Perth and she doubted she'd be able to keep any food down.

It was D-day, or rather J-day, and she suddenly wondered

why the hell she'd listened to Flick and Emma when they'd suggested going to confront him in person.

"Neve? You okay?" Emma's sleep-soaked voice jolted her from her thoughts and she looked back to her friend.

She opened her mouth to lie—to tell Emma she was fine, excited even about a day of shopping and exploring the Empire State Building—but the truth spilled out instead. "Not really. I need a drink."

Emma chuckled sleepily. "I think it's a little early."

"I meant water." Neve reached a hand up to her throat. "My mouth is so dry I feel like my throat is closing up."

Emma threw back her covers and climbed out of bed. She crossed to the minibar and retrieved a bottle of Evian. "Classic symptoms of anxiety," she said, unscrewing the lid and offering the bottle to Neve. "Have a drink and then take a few deep breaths. It's going to be okay."

Neve slurped a couple of desperate gulps and then wiped her mouth. "Thanks. For the water. And for coming. I know you don't—"

Emma cut her off before she could finish her sentence. "I'm sorry I've been a bit of a cow about your…your situation. I'm not trying to make excuses but I haven't exactly been myself lately. As I told Flick last night, I think I might be going through The Change. You know? Early menopause."

Neve shuddered, forgetting her own worries for a moment. "Oh, God, I'm so sorry."

Emma snorted. "Flick thought it could be a good thing."

"How so?"

There was an odd groaning sound from Flick's bed. "What did I think?" she asked, her words slurred.

"That there were benefits to early menopause."

"Oh, right." Slowly, she sat up and rubbed her eyes. "Is it really morning already?"

"Yep," Emma said. "Rise and shine, princess. If we're going to get through that shopping list from Zoe and Toby, we can't lounge around all day in bed. Do you want to have breakfast in the hotel or find a café somewhere?"

Flick glared at Emma. "Are you always this cheery in the morning?"

"Only when I wake up in a luxurious hotel with no kids and no ex-husband in sight. In fact, I reckon I could get used to this."

"How are you feeling about tonight?" Flick looked to Neve, ignoring Emma's question about breakfast.

Neve's insides quivered again. "Can we talk about something else?"

She saw Flick and Emma exchange an anxious glance and then Flick finally answered Emma. "I think hotel breakfasts are pretty much the same worldwide. I reckon we go out and start exploring and find somewhere to eat along the way."

"Good idea," Neve said, hoping she sounded more enthusiastic than she felt. She grabbed her toiletries bag and escaped into the bathroom. Maybe if her friends stopped reminding her about tonight, she'd get through the day without hyperventilating.

Yet Neve could think of nothing else as they navigated the grid-like streets on foot, although Flick and Emma made a concerted effort to avoid talking about the main reason for their trip. Why couldn't James have lived and worked somewhere else? He was spoiling New York for her. They stopped to eat breakfast at the Magnolia Bakery on Sixth Avenue and then walked on to explore the designer stores on Fifth Avenue, but no matter how hard she tried, she simply couldn't relax and enjoy the experience.

Strolling in and out of Prada, Louis Vuitton and Swarovski should have been one of the highlights of Neve's life, but as the others oohed and aahed over handbags with price tags three times their weekly paychecks, it was all she could do to stop herself from throwing up her minuscule breakfast onto the sidewalk.

"Oh, my God," Emma exclaimed, pointing to a simple but elegant pale blue travel tote in a store window. "I wonder how much that is? Bet my first car cost less."

"I think one of the moms at Dayton has that one in pink," Flick said, "but you know what? I picked one up in Target that looks exactly the same."

Neve tried to contribute to the conversation, but she simply couldn't get excited about handbags—designer, bargain or otherwise.

"You're very quiet," Emma said, turning away from the window.

"Yes," Flick agreed. "Are you sure you still don't want to talk about it?"

Perhaps expressing how terrified she was about seeing James again would be better than keeping it all bundled up inside her. "I *don't* want to talk about it, but maybe I should."

"Come on." Emma wrapped an arm around Neve's shoulder. "Let's go to Macy's for lunch—when I messaged Patrick yesterday, he said we should go there. Apparently it's got a really good restaurant, so we'll blame him if it's not."

"Good idea." Flick linked her arm through Neve's. "You can have a glass of wine to calm your nerves and tell us exactly how you're feeling and then we can look at stuff we might actually be able to afford."

They ate lunch at Stella 34, which was amazingly good for a restaurant inside a department store. Somehow Neve managed to eat half her *di verdure* salad and sip a glass of prosecco as she confessed to thoughts of chickening out. She couldn't even find the right word to describe her level of panic.

"This is the scariest thing I've ever done in my life. I barely slept last night imagining scenarios about what might happen. What James might say or do when I tell him he has a son." Her mouth went dry again but this time she reached for the sparkling water. She took a long drink and then continued, "What if he's so angry he wants to sue me or something? Is that possible?"

"I could ask Max, I suppose," Emma offered, although she didn't sound enthused by the idea.

"I've never heard of anything like that," Flick said. "You're not the first person who hasn't told a man she's pregnant. And you had good reason not to."

"You think?" At the time, James being married with a young family had seemed like reason enough, but now she wasn't so sure. If the tables were somehow turned, would she see that as an acceptable excuse? Could *she* ever forgive someone for keeping her away from her son?

"Anyway, we'll be there tonight for the show, and if it makes you feel better, we can stay with you while you talk to James," Flick offered.

Emma nodded her agreement.

"Thanks, guys, but I think this is something I need to do by myself." Hopefully she wouldn't run for the hills the moment she saw him. "Now all I need to do is work out what to wear."

They spent the rest of lunch going through Neve's options, but she wasn't excited by any of the outfits she'd packed. Although she didn't admit it to her friends, she wanted to look good—*better* than good—when James laid eyes on her for the first time in eighteen years. It might make her a bad person, but she wanted to see that flicker of interest in his eyes that had always been there in the past.

"I guess there's only one thing to do then," Flick said, after they'd tipped their waiter and were on their way out of the restaurant. "Let's go shopping."

They felt much more at home at Macy's. Even Flick, who generally wasn't a huge fan of shopping, couldn't resist the bargains in the handbag department. And Emma tried on a pair of shoes that looked like they were made especially for her.

"They're much higher than I usually wear and I really can't afford any luxuries at the moment, but..." She eyed the sparkly black high-heeled sandals, pointing and flexing her toes as she did so.

"That's what Mr. Visa is for," Neve finished. Only while encouraging her friends to shop did the crazy fluttering in her belly ease a little. She almost forgot why they were there until they turned their attentions to the clothing department with the specific goal of finding her an outfit for that evening.

Then all her apprehension and anxiety returned. She could barely bring herself to flick through the racks.

"You always look good in pink," Flick said, plucking a dress off a rail and hanging it over her arm along with others she'd already selected.

Emma nodded. "Yes, you do. It makes you look really feminine. Not that you necessarily want that," she added, her smile turning into a frown. "And it might be a little revealing."

"But," Flick reasoned, "if she looks *good*, James is less likely to want to kill her."

Bile crept up Neve's throat. "Can we please not talk about killing. Pink is fine," she snapped, feeling as if the small amount of lunch she'd managed to eat might not stay down after all. She snatched the pile of dresses from Flick and spun around, charging off in the direction of the fitting rooms.

A sales assistant nodded toward the pink dress at the top of the pile as she approached. "Ooh, that's a pretty color. I bet it'll look fabulous on you."

Neve glared at her and disappeared into the change rooms. She yanked off her sundress and almost tore the first dress from its hanger. As the silky material slithered over her bare skin, she shivered and then reached around to pull up the zip. The sundress hadn't required a bra and neither did this dress. Puffing out a breath to try to regulate her breathing, she eyed herself in the full-length mirror. The color did suit her skin tones. The material glistened under the fluorescent lights, and she had to admit that she'd always had a penchant for sparkly clothing. The dress's only downfall was that it was perhaps a little too short and hugged her figure in a way that might be considered inappropriate for the objective of her evening.

Yet, despite common sense telling her to try on something a little more staid—okay, a *lot* more staid—she'd fallen in love with this dress. It made her feel like herself. It made her feel confident and sexy, and if she felt good tonight, then she'd be more able to deliver her announcement without floundering or losing the plot. "Neve? Are you in here?" Flick called from outside the fitting room.

"Yep," she replied. "And I think I'm going to go with that pink dress you spotted."

"Show us," Emma demanded.

"Not yet." Neve shook her head even though they couldn't see, then unzipped the dress and was more careful as she took it off than when she'd put it on. She hung it on the hanger—knowing she didn't need to try any of the others—and then put on her own dress again. She hadn't even looked at the price, but she didn't care; money was the least of her worries right now. "You'll see it tonight."

"Spoilsport," said her friends, and then they laughed. "Jinx!"

"What do you want to do now?" Flick asked when Neve came out of the fitting rooms. "Shall we keep wandering and exploring, or do you want to go back to the hotel and rest a bit?"

Emma sighed as if she was tired, but there were still a few hours until they were due at the theater and Neve didn't want to spend them bouncing around their hotel room, watching the clock and trying to stop herself from having a nervous breakdown. Finding the right dress had calmed her a little, but if she had too much time to think, she'd start questioning herself again. Not simply about her outfit, but about coming to New York in the first place. And even about whether or not she'd made the right decision all those years ago to keep James in the dark. *Argh!*

"Why don't we go do something touristy?" she suggested, kicking her thoughts to the curb. No good had ever come from playing the what-if game.

23

Emma

Looking down from Top of the Rock, Emma had to summon everything she'd ever learned about acting—which was minimal—to keep her agony from the others. It wasn't just her splitting headache, but that the place held too many memories. The other time she'd been here, she'd been with Max; the last vacation before he'd left.

When Flick had suggested going to the Rockefeller Center, Emma had contemplated suggesting something else, anything else, but then decided that it would be good for her to go somewhere she'd been with Max and create new memories, better ones. But now all she could remember were the lies he'd fed her as they explored the exhibits together. Thinking about it made her feel like such a fool.

"This view is pretty amazing," Flick said, looking out over Central Park. "Is that the Statue of Liberty in the distance?"

"Yes," Neve mused, "but you've gotta admit the view from our hotel room is pretty damn special as well, and we don't have to pay to see it."

Flick laughed. "I didn't know we were getting the accommodation free!"

While her friends walked around the observatory deck, snapping photos and exclaiming over the skyscrapers, Emma looked longingly into the indoor area and the comfy couch-like seats. How she longed to lie down and close her eyes, even for a few seconds. She should have told the others she'd rather go back to the hotel and rest before tonight, but not wanting them to know she had *another* headache, she'd soldiered on through the day, shopping and sightseeing.

"I'd kill for a coffee," Flick said after she and Neve had forced Emma into a selfie.

"Good idea." Neve glanced at her watch. "And then I guess we'd better head back to the hotel and start getting ready." She went a little green as she said this and looked a lot like Emma felt.

Back on street level, they went into the first café they found. The decor was very modern—lots of bright furniture with sharp angles—and the food smelled divine, but when Emma's friends lifted their coffees to their lips, they both frowned and spluttered. "What is *this*?" Neve exclaimed, holding her take-out cup away from her and glaring at it like it contained poison.

"Welcome to New York." Emma lifted her own cup and took a sip, immediately making a face. She'd forgotten how terrible the coffee was here. There might be a Starbucks in every hotel and on every street corner, but like fast food, fast coffee did little, if anything, to deliver her desperately needed caffeine hit. In addition to her premenopausal headaches, she could now add caffeine withdrawal to the mix.

"I suppose caffeine is caffeine," Flick said with a sigh.

Neve shook her head. "No, it's not, but right now it'll have to do."

They sipped their coffees as they walked back to the hotel. With just over two hours until they were due at the Broadhurst Theatre, they could tell Neve was a basket of nerves. Emma still didn't approve of her affair, but it was impossible not to sympathize with her friend's tricky situation, and both she and Flick wanted to do everything they could to help.

This began with a bottle of wine in their room, but as much as Emma wanted to have a drink, she steered clear so as not to make her headache any worse.

Finally, when Neve and Flick disappeared into the bathroom to get ready, Emma sneaked over to her handbag and popped a couple of acetaminophen tablets, chasing them down with a couple of ibuprofen pills. Didn't doctors say it was okay to take both together? Maybe they meant a few hours apart, but drastic times and all. Her head felt as if it might explode at any moment, so waiting wasn't an option. Collapsing onto the sofa bed for a few seconds of rest, she held her cool water bottle against her head and took a deep breath.

"Emma?" She awoke to Flick gently shaking her shoulder. "It's almost time to go."

Emma looked up and blinked, disorientated for a moment. "How long was I asleep?"

"We let you nap as long as we could," Flick apologized.

Embarrassed, Emma shot up and glanced down at her dress, now crumpled. *Dammit.* "Thanks. Guess the jet lag is getting to me."

Flick patted her hand to her mouth and feigned a yawn. "Me, too. But I'm sure we'll wake up once we get to Broadway."

Emma glanced at her watch. They needed to leave ASAP. "I'll just go do my makeup." This consisted of a bit of foundation, some powder over the top, a few swipes of blush on her cheeks, a little mascara and, as it was an evening event, some experimentation with eye shadow. Oh, and lipstick—the same brand and color she'd been buying since her early twenties.

Usually Neve would fix Emma's makeup as well, but it was a testament to her anxiety that she didn't even bat an eyelid when Emma emerged from the bathroom. "I guess it's time." She looked as if she was about to throw up or wet her pants. Maybe both.

"You'll be fine." Emma crossed over to her and gave her a hug, showing the support she perhaps hadn't showed properly until now.

"We're here for you," Flick added, joining them in a group hug. "Now, let's go break a leg."

Neve made a sound something between a laugh and a sob. "I think that only applies to the actors."

Then, their arms linked, they left the room. They weren't even at the elevators when Neve freaked out.

"I can't do this," she said, breaking free. "I'll just tell Will I found out James died or something."

"Don't be ridiculous," Flick said tersely. "I never thought you a coward, Neve. The worst thing that can happen is James is furious with you and doesn't want to meet Will. Then you tell Will the truth and ask him for his forgiveness."

"That's easy for you to say. You've had everything easy your whole life," Neve snapped.

"Really?" Flick recoiled, her voice not more than a whisper but her tone incensed. "You don't know everything about me. I'd hardly say losing my mother to a fire when I was a kid was *easy.*"

Emma opened her mouth to try to calm the sudden storm, but Neve got in first. "I'm so sorry," she said, her eyes watering. "That was uncalled-for. I'm just so...petrified."

"I know." Flick reached out and pulled her close again. "And because you're not yourself, I'm going to forgive you. But remember why we're all here—to get you through tonight. And whatever James's reaction, we'll be here for you."

"Besides," Emma said, attempting to lighten the mood, "worst-case scenario is we get to watch *Mamma Mia!*"

Neve nodded, but despite her acquiescence, they had to keep a firm hold on her all the way to the theater *and* as they lined up out the front, waiting in line for the doors to open.

When they were finally inside, Neve darted her head from side to side as if expecting to see James in the crowd.

"Won't he be backstage?" Emma whispered, squeezing Neve's arm.

Neve couldn't even manage a reply; she just shuffled forward between them like a robot.

"We should get some drinks and snacks," Flick suggested as they came near the bar.

"My treat." It was the least Emma could do after Flick had paid for everything else.

"Okay, thanks." Flick nodded toward Neve, who looked like dementors had sucked out her soul, leaving only a human shell. "I'll get her settled. Here's your ticket."

Emma took the ticket. "See you soon."

She waited at the bar with what felt like a hundred other people, hoping she wouldn't miss the start of the show, until a barman who looked about half her age asked, "What can I get you, babe?"

Emma blinked and then looked past him at the menu, ordering three champagnes and an assortment of chocolates.

"Single or double drinks?"

She blinked again, having never been asked such a question in relation to champagne. He grinned and held up a plastic tumbler with Broadway pictures and logos all over it. "Doubles means you won't need a refill till intermission."

"Double then, please."

He named an exorbitant amount and her heart clenched as

she counted out the notes and handed over half the US money she'd converted at Perth airport. *Holy hell.*

"I was beginning to wonder if you got lost," Flick said when Emma finally arrived at the seats. She handed over two of the drinks and rescued the chocolate bars from where they'd been wedged under her arm.

"How is she?"

"Not good." Flick thrust a glass of champagne at their silent friend. Neve's fingers closed around it but the expression on her face didn't change at all as she lifted it to her mouth.

Emma wondered if it had been a mistake getting Neve an alcoholic drink—she was already in a trance state.

"What is this?" Flick hissed, scrutinizing the cup.

"The most expensive cheap champagne you'll ever drink. Cherish that cup. I paid gold for it."

Flick laughed and took a sip as Emma got comfy in her seat. "Check out the playbill," Flick whispered, handing it across Neve to Emma. "There's a picture of James on page six."

Emma couldn't flick through the pages fast enough, and when her eyes found him, she whistled quietly in appreciation.

"I know, right?" Flick smiled, wriggling her eyebrows as she nudged Neve. "If he looks that good at fifty, imagine what he looked like in his prime. You can see why this one fell for him."

Indeed Emma could, but how many other women in the industry had fallen for him over the years? Will could have siblings all over the world. She pushed that thought aside and nodded. "And at least we know her sources led her to the right place."

"Would you two stop talking about me as if I'm not even here?" Neve snapped.

"*Oh, my!*" Flick palmed one hand over her open mouth theatrically. "It speaks."

Neve shook her head, grabbed the playbill from Emma and then looked down. "Oh, God." She let out a long breath. "He *is* still gorgeous. Can you see Will in him at all?"

Emma found it hard to look past all that dark curly hair and chiseled jawline to see if the boy who hung out with her son bore any resemblance, but she had to concede he did.

"Yep," she and Flick said at the same time.

"He's got the same unruly hair and distinguished chin," Flick added.

"So you think if I show him a picture of Will, he'll be able to see the likeness?" Neve asked, her tone anxious.

"Unless he's blind," Flick replied just as the lights dimmed above them and an instrumental medley of ABBA's hit songs blasted the theater.

Even if Neve wanted to ask for further reassurance, she wouldn't have been heard over the orchestra or the audience's enthusiasm. It was impossible not to grin and dance in their seats along with the rest of the buzzing crowd—impossible for everyone but Neve, that was. While Emma and Flick bopped their heads and swayed along to the music, their friend barely paid any attention to the stage. Instead, her eyes remained glued to the photo of her lover in her lap. Emma reached over and squeezed her hand.

"Try to relax," she whispered as the curtains peeled open. After that, although she never let go of Neve's hand, Emma lost her thoughts in the action and music in front of them, smiling through every second of the high-energy production. She even managed to forget the constant pain in her head for a couple of hours.

Occasionally, she tore her eyes from the stage and glanced at Neve, wishing she could do something to help her relax.

While others around them hurried off to the bathroom or the bar during intermission, Emma, Flick and Neve stayed in their seats. The second half of the show enthralled everyone as much as the first and there were sighs of satisfaction and disappointment when the actors danced and sung their final encore.

"Wow, that was awesome," Emma said as people around them started to stand and stagger up the aisles toward the exit. "I think I'll have an ABBA earworm for days."

"Me, too," Flick agreed. "We should get matching *Mamma Mia!* T-shirts."

"Can you two stop talking as if this is a normal night out at the theater?" Neve's voice cracked on the last word and Emma noticed her whole body shaking.

"Sorry," Emma said. "Do you know how we can find… him?"

"I could probably sneak backstage, but there's the risk someone might throw me out before I've seen him. I think I'll ask at the box office."

"Good plan."

Flick and Emma stood but Neve didn't make a move.

"Or maybe one of you guys could find him and tell him for me?" she asked.

Emma glared at her. Did she really think that was an option? "Come on." Flick grabbed Neve and dragged her to her feet.

"We've come a long way for you to do this and we'd be shit friends if we didn't make you follow through."

Following Flick's lead, Emma took Neve's other hand and started toward the aisle, pulling her along behind with Flick bringing up the rear. The audience had thinned out with only themselves and a few other stragglers lingering. Just as they exited the theater, the woman behind the little window in the box office switched off the light.

"Excuse me," Emma called loudly, soliciting the attention of everyone who remained.

The woman looked up and frowned as they approached. "Can I help you?"

Emma and Flick looked to Neve but she remained mute. Flick finally spoke for her. "We're hoping to catch James Cooper." When Ticket Girl stared blankly at them, she elaborated, "He's one of the directors."

"I know who he is." The girl rolled her eyes. "Who wants to see him?"

Neve thrust her shoulders back, held her chin high and found her voice. "I do. My name is Genevieve Turner. James and I were colleagues in Australia and he said to look him up if I was ever in town."

The lie rolled from Neve's tongue and Emma found herself impressed rather than appalled.

"*Did* he?" The woman spoke only to Neve now, still sounding skeptical.

"Yes. He did."

"Well, I'm sorry, but today is James's night off. He'll be here tomorrow night if you want to come back."

"Oh." Neve's face fell, her bravado exiting stage right.

Emma and Flick exchanged twin expressions of disappointment. How on earth were they going to get through another day of Neve in mental meltdown mode?

Ticket Girl sighed. "Look, I can give you guys cheap tickets for tomorrow night if you like. Crap seats, though."

"We'll take them." Flick's hand shot to her handbag.

"No." Neve held a hand up as she shook her head. "You guys don't have to sit through all this again." She looked to the woman behind the window. "Just one ticket please."

"You sure?" Flick asked.

"Yes?" Emma added. She'd happily watch *Mamma Mia!* on Broadway a hundred more times in the name of friendship and support.

Neve nodded, retrieving her purse and handing over her credit card. "Tonight was stressful enough. And no offense, guys, but I think you being here only magnifies my panic."

The young woman cleared her throat, eyeing them warily. "Is there a problem?"

"No, no problem at all." Neve snatched the ticket and credit card back and shoved them in her bag, all the while glaring a warning at Emma and Flick. They'd been friends long enough that they could communicate without actual conversation, and they got the message loud and clear: *zip your lips if you don't want me to lose this chance.* They thanked the woman for her help and then escaped onto the street—still abuzz with people. Neve half sighed, half laughed. "What a letdown."

Flick pointed a finger at her. "You realize if you chicken out tomorrow, we'll make you follow through the next night."

"I won't," Neve promised. "I reckon James not being here tonight is a blessing."

"How so?" Emma asked.

"Well, you may have noticed I've been a bit of a nervous wreck…"

"No way!" Flick exclaimed. "Have you?"

Neve smiled, looking more relaxed than she had since they'd landed at JFK. "I think this is fate's way of getting all my nerves out of the way before we actually meet. I know I've been anxious, but I've also been terribly excited at the prospect of making things right for Will. Finding out that wasn't going to happen tonight was such a huge disappointment that now there's only room for anticipation."

Emma couldn't tell if Neve truly felt this way or simply wanted to get them off her back. But she didn't want to stand out here on the sidewalk all night arguing over it. The pain-killers were wearing off and she just wanted to crawl into bed, go to sleep and dream of *Mamma Mia!*

"Okay, if you're sure," Flick said. "I guess Emma and I will find *something* to occupy ourselves."

Emma nodded. "This is New York after all."

"Thanks guys." Neve smiled and pulled them both into a group hug. "You two are the best, you know that? I don't know what I'd do without you."

"Get a room," yelled some guys staggering past.

"We have one," Flick retorted.

The women laughed.

"Shall we go to the bar for a nightcap?" Neve suggested as they began walking in the direction of the hotel.

Emma groaned inwardly, but she didn't want to be a killjoy. "Okay, maybe just *one* drink," she agreed.

24

Felicity

The moment the elevator doors opened onto the lobby level, Flick and her friends were hit with the loud buzz of many people chattering. They followed the noise to the hotel bar to find it full of businessmen, with only a few power-dressed women to be seen in the sea of dark suits.

"Must be some sort of conference," she observed.

Emma gaped at the crowd like it was a school of piranhas and took a step backward. "Maybe we should just order room service."

Neve pulled a face. "You don't drink cocktails in a hotel room!"

"She's right." Flick grabbed hold of Emma's hand. "Come on. We're not going to let a few tipsy guys ruin our fun."

With Neve leading the way and Flick still holding on to Emma, they wound their way through the bodies toward the bar, catching snatches of conversation.

Emma squealed and Flick stopped to glance behind her. "What's wrong?"

Her eyes were wide in horror. "I think I just got groped," she hissed.

Flick laughed. "It might be your lucky night."

Emma scowled but there was a sparkle in her eyes that made Flick's heart sing. Despite the headaches that were plaguing her friend, Emma had smiled more today than she had in the last few months. Flick could already feel this trip working its magic on her, and she hoped it would help give her some clarity of mind as well. Seb had sent her another text this morning, but she wasn't quite sure what she wanted to say to him yet.

At the bar, Neve pushed between two men to place their order. "Shuffle over, guys," she said to the men on either side of her. "Make room for my friends."

Grinning, the men did as they were told—Neve had that kind of effect—and Flick and Emma settled themselves, leaning against the bar. No chance of scoring a seat in this crowd, but at least they'd have somewhere to stand while they drank their drinks.

"I ordered three cosmopolitans," Neve told them. "We can do manhattans next."

"Sounds good, but are you sure you're okay? You know… after tonight?" Flick felt as if Neve had undergone a personality transplant in the last half hour—she'd gone from nervous wreck to wanting to party in a matter of minutes.

Neve's smile was wide but perhaps a little forced. "Of course I am. Life doesn't always go according to plan," she said as three pink-filled martini glasses landed on the bar in front of them, "but I'm adaptable." She picked up a glass and took a sip. "Mmm, it's good. Drink up, ladies."

As this wasn't the place for a deep and meaningful conversation, Flick decided the supportive thing would be to do as Neve asked. "What shall we do tomorrow?"

"Let's go to Central Park," Emma suggested, rubbing her forehead as Flick took the first sip of her cosmo.

"Have you got another headache?" Flick asked, twirling the straw between her fingers.

Emma shrugged. "Just a little one. Think it's the noise and the jet lag."

"Do you need a painkiller or something?" Neve popped her drink on the bar and put her hand on her shoulder bag. "I'm sure I have a packet in here somewhere."

"It's fine, I've already had one."

One? Flick had lost count of the number of pills Emma had popped since they'd left Perth—and that was only the ones she'd seen. Could Emma have some sort of addiction? She was genuinely worried but didn't know how to broach the subject.

"Well, let me know if you need any," Neve said, picking up her drink again. "Now, where were we? Central Park. Can we go on one of those horse-and-carriage rides?"

Flick laughed.

"What?" Neve exclaimed. "I've always wanted to be driven around in a horse and carriage, ever since Mom read me *Cinderella* when I was little."

"It's a good way to see the park," Emma said, glass in hand even though she hadn't yet taken a sip. "And Flick wanted to see the Metropolitan Museum of Art, which is close by."

Flick clapped her hands together. "Sounds like a plan, then."

"I love a plan." Neve lifted her empty glass; the contents had vanished quickly. Maybe she wasn't as chilled out about the nonevent of the evening as she wanted them to believe. "How will we get there?"

"Subway is our easiest bet," Emma said.

Neve frowned. "Carrie never took the subway. Isn't it… *dangerous?*"

Emma raised an eyebrow. "Carrie and her friends are *fictional.* You can't come to New York and not take the subway. It's part of the experience."

"If you say so." She didn't look convinced at all.

"I'm sorry," Emma said, putting her glass back on the bar. "But I'm exhausted. Hope you don't mind but I'm going to hit the sack."

"We *do* mind," Neve objected. "The night's still young and you haven't even finished your drink!"

Flick resisted the urge to point out that Emma hadn't even started it. "Go and get some rest," she said, reaching out to pat Emma's arm. "We won't be long, but we'll be quiet when we come in." Someone had to stay and supervise Neve, who seemed intent on enjoying herself.

"Thanks." Emma smiled her appreciation. "And don't worry about disturbing me. Once my head hits the pillow I'm out for the count. Here, you have my drink."

Emma thrust her cocktail toward Neve, and although she cocked her head to one side as if about to object, her fingers closed around the glass and she took a sip.

Emma kissed them both on the cheek. "Be good. Don't do anything I wouldn't do."

"That really limits our fun." Neve pouted, watching as Emma turned and started through the mob of people.

Flick was about to voice her concern about Emma when she felt a tap on her shoulder. Frowning, she turned slowly and came face-to-face with a man in a navy suit. A man she hadn't seen since she was a teenager.

"Jeremy?"

At least he *looked* like her old school friend, but like good wine he'd vastly improved with age. His undeniably handsome face grinned back at her, his dirty-blond hair slightly too long, as if he was overdue for an appointment at the barber, but on him it worked.

"Felicity!" he exclaimed, in the same stunned tone she had used. "I thought I saw you when you came in but then I thought my mind must be playing tricks on me. I'm here at the conference and we've had a few drinks, if you know what I mean. But I kept glancing over, and then when you turned your head a minute ago, I just knew it was you." He chuckled. "How the hell are you?"

"I'm great," Flick lied.

"You certainly look fabulous," Jeremy said, his gaze sweeping appreciatively down her body and back up again. She would usually have been appalled at such attention, but tonight she felt flattered. Lately Seb was more likely to appreciate his own reflection in the mirror than her.

Neve peered at him like he was some kind of creepy stalker. "You've been *watching* us?"

"Oh, relax, Neve." Flick elbowed her in the side. "This is an old friend. Jeremy Smythe. We went to high school together." Later she'd tell Neve that they had only been friends because they didn't have much choice if they didn't want to be loners in the schoolyard at lunchtime. "Jeremy, this is one of my best friends, Neve. God, how long has it been?"

When they were teenagers, they'd been the geeks that nobody else wanted to hang out with—if they'd even noticed the odd duo existed. But Jeremy had definitely grown into his looks. His acne had gone and his lanky body had filled out—he obviously spent plenty of his spare time at the gym.

"Pleased to meet you." Jeremy smiled and offered his hand.

Neve took it reluctantly. She obviously still wasn't sure whether he was a psycho serial killer or not.

"Would you like to come over and sit with me and some friends? We've got a table."

"Oh, we were just about to leave." Neve smiled tightly.

"That would be lovely," Flick said at the same time. Then she looked to Neve and gestured to Emma's drink in her hand. "You've still got to finish that."

It wasn't every day a blast from the past showed up, and she didn't want to say goodbye to her old friend just yet. Neve narrowed her eyes and then lifted the straw to take a sip.

"Excellent. We're over in the corner. Come this way." Jeremy gestured for them to go ahead of him.

Drinking as she walked, Neve went first and Flick followed, something low inside her tightening when Jeremy brushed his hand against the small of her back. An unfamiliar tingle weaved its way up her spine.

It felt like centuries had gone by since anyone besides Seb had touched her, and although this wasn't exactly an intimate caress she was glad neither Neve nor Jeremy could see the heat rush to her face. She took a sip of her cosmo, hoping the cool liquid would lower her body temperature.

"Blake, Robbie," Jeremy said when they arrived at a table covered in a multitude of empty glasses. The men had obviously been busy. "This is my old school friend Felicity, and her friend Neve. I invited them to come sit with us."

The men—one a redhead with a goatee, the other dark haired and close shaven—grinned up at the girls.

"Hallelujah," said the redhead. "If I had to listen to any more of Blake's babble, I was going to kill him. Take a seat." Robbie smiled at Neve and gestured to the seat between him and Blake.

With a reluctant sigh, she sat and both men focused on her. "So what brings you to New York?" Blake asked.

Flick didn't hear Neve's answer. Taking the chair Jeremy held back for her, she quickly got lost in his conversation.

"You still living in WA?" he asked.

"Yep—still in Mount Lawley, actually."

"What brings you to New York?"

Not about to explain that she'd run away to the other side of the world because she didn't know if she could ever look at her husband the same way again, she leaned a little closer so Neve couldn't hear. "My other friend Emma and I—she's in our hotel room—have come to support Neve in a tricky situation. She's come to reconnect with an old friend and tell him something she should have told him years ago."

"Sounds intriguing," Jeremy said, his voice low and his head close enough that Flick got a whiff of some earthy-scented cologne.

She ignored the urge to inhale deeply. "What about you? You still in Perth?"

"No. I call Dubai home now. I've been there for five years."

"Wow. I've heard some great things about Dubai. Wonderful climate, good shopping..."

"And it's all true. You should come visit one day."

It was probably an innocent invitation, but Flick found her eyes wandering to Jeremy's hand, checking for a wedding band. She was out of practice interacting with men and her gaze was far too obvious. He caught her glance, laughed and answered the question she'd been pondering.

"Not married. Tried it once but the missus got bored of me working away from home so much that she worked her way through the neighbors, trying them on for size. She finally decided on the policeman across the road, and that's when she asked me for a divorce."

Ouch! Flick didn't know what to say to that. Jeremy didn't sound too cut up, but betrayal—in whatever form—always hurt.

She gave him a sympathetic smile. "Sounds like you're better off without her."

He smiled in a way that made her both uneasy and a little bit aroused. At least that was what she thought the fluttery feeling in her belly signified. "What about you?"

She blinked. "What about me?"

He laughed and glanced down at her hand. "You're married, then?"

She suddenly wished she'd taken off her wedding ring this week, just to experience what it felt like to no longer be one half of the perfect couple. With a sigh, she rolled the ring around her finger as she stared at it. "It's...complicated."

Why the hell did she say that? She wasn't about to spill her and Seb's secrets to Jeremy. He might have been a friend over twenty years ago but he was practically a stranger now.

He let out a half laugh. "You don't have to tell me about complicated. That describes my whole relationship history."

She smiled at him, thankful he wasn't going to pry. "So what conference are you here for?"

"A global mining summit."

"You're in mining?" She didn't know why she sounded surprised. He'd had the smarts to do whatever he'd wanted and he'd always been a mad keen rock collector. Needless to say, his obsession with rocks and minerals and hers with dead animals had not been embraced by their fellow students.

"Is that so hard to believe?" He grinned as if he'd noticed her shock.

"No. Not at all, actually." She shook her head and smiled. "Never mind. What is it you do in mining?"

"I'm chief growth and innovation director of GDM."

When she looked blankly at him, he explained, "I'm accountable for all major growth projects, life-of-mine strategy and innovation for the company. In addition to the business in Dubai, we have operations all over the world and we're constantly looking for ways to innovate. I'm actually a keynote speaker at the conference, and tomorrow I'll be talking about our latest projects."

"Sounds impressive."

"It's a job." Jeremy stretched out his long legs. She'd no-

THE ART OF KEEPING SECRETS   201

ticed his height before, but now she couldn't help but see how
nicely he filled his expensive trousers. Her throat went dry
and she took another sip of her drink.

"Can I get you another?" Jeremy nodded toward the near-
empty glass.

She glanced over at Neve, who looked bored out of her
brain, with Blake and Robbie both vying for her attention.
The right answer would be no, but it wasn't the word that
came out of her mouth.

"Thank you."

"Excellent." Jeremy stood, towering above her a moment
before he turned and strode toward the bar.

"We off, then?" Neve looked to Flick, interrupting Robbie—
or was it Blake?—talking about who knows what.

But Flick shook her head. "Jeremy's getting more drinks."
Neve scowled.

"You can go up if you want," Flick said, but Neve sighed
and leaned back into her seat.

Well, if she was determined to play the martyr, so be it.
Flick hadn't seen Jeremy in decades and was enjoying catching
up with an old friend. She wasn't about to feel guilty about
it, considering she'd come halfway across the world to support Neve.

Jeremy returned with two more cosmopolitans.

"What about you?" Flick asked as he handed one to her
and one to Neve.

"And what about us?" Blake, or Robbie, demanded.

"I only have two hands. You idiots can get your own."
Jeremy grinned and sat back down. Flick swore his seat felt
even closer than it had five minutes ago; so close she felt the
warmth emanating off his thigh.

Or was the warmth coming from inside her?

"Thanks," she said, not able to meet his eye as she took a sip.

"I've bored you enough about my work—time to talk about you. Did you end up becoming a taxidermist like you always wanted?" Strangely, he hadn't bored her at all. His passion for his industry had made her want to know more. Would she be feeling this attraction to him if he'd told her he was a hairdresser? Or were her alien feelings simply because her life was such a mess?

"Felicity?" he prompted and she realized she'd been lost in her thoughts.

"Sorry." She blinked and held on to her glass like a crutch. "Yes, I am a taxidermist."

"That's wonderful. Have you got any pictures of your work?"

Blushing, Flick dug her phone out of her bag and opened the photos app. She kept a photographic record of every piece she completed from receiving the lifeless animal to the final true-to-life mount, with every stage in between. Some of them were quite graphic but Jeremy didn't squirm like some people did when they saw the process.

"These are awesome," he said as he flicked through her photos. "Oh, I love this one of the otter. When I think of taxidermy, I've got to admit I usually think of faded stuffed beasts in museums or weird antiques shops, but these are works of art."

She bit her lower lip to stop from grinning at his compliment. "Thank you. I actually do more taxi-art than commissions for museums or pet owners, although I still do that as well. But I love the creative side of my work. I love making something beautiful out of something that would otherwise be tossed away or buried and forgotten."

"I can tell." He smiled, looking right into her eyes, making her heart beat so she could almost hear it. "I'm guessing people pay quite a hefty price for some of your creations?"

"It's not a bad living," she admitted, dropping her gaze to

linger on his lips. Something fluttered in her chest, but she forced the feeling into a metaphorical box. "When I began, I had to subsidize it with a part-time job teaching art classes at night, but now that my reputation has grown, I'm sought after enough that I more than make ends meet."

"That's wonderful. There's nothing better in life than being successful at a job that you actually love doing. Well, *almost* nothing."

She swallowed at the insinuation in his last three words, whispered as he leaned even closer so that she could feel his warm breath against her skin. He smelled delicious, and she had a crazy urge to turn her head and find out if he tasted as good as well. Being close to Jeremy made her feel like a woman, rather than simply a mother or someone's wife. Until this moment, she hadn't realized how much she'd missed that pleasure. How much she'd let her needs be lost in her efforts to keep everyone else happy.

"Okay." Neve's loud voice broke the moment and Flick puffed out a breath as her friend stood and glared at her. "It's getting late. We have a busy day tomorrow and we should go check on Emma."

Disappointment flooded Flick's body, making her chest cramp, but what had she been expecting? That Neve would let her kiss a near stranger in public? The last thing she needed to be contemplating when her personal life was such a shambles was kissing some guy and complicating things even more. And Neve was right. They should check on Emma. She nodded across the low table, stood up and turned to Jeremy. "It was great catching up. Enjoy the rest of your conference."

Ignoring the urge to drop into his lap and give him a proper farewell, she smiled her goodbyes at his friends, then started walking toward the elevators, Neve's high heels click-clacking on the tiles as she hurried after her.

25

Emma

"I feel like a princess," Flick said, a contented smile on her face as they were drawn around Central Park in a beautiful carriage by two snow-white horses. She ran her hand over the luxurious leather seat. "This is divine."

"Says she who mocked the idea when I first suggested it," snapped Neve.

"I didn't *mock* it, I just laughed."

In lieu of a reply, Neve turned her body so she wasn't looking at Flick and lifted her cell phone to snap a few photos.

Emma, who was squished between her friends on the seat that would comfortably fit a couple but wasn't quite big enough for three, looked from one to the other. Was she imagining Neve's snarkiness? Or had something happened between her and Flick last night?

Dead to the world, she hadn't heard them come in, but she got the impression they'd stayed out late, and when she'd asked they'd been cagey. Perhaps jet lag had finally hit and tiredness combined with a hangover was making Neve grumpy. Aside from a couple of snide remarks from Neve about Flick's food choice, neither of them had said much at breakfast. When

Emma had asked if anything was wrong, Neve had almost bitten her head off; she'd put it down to nerves building up again for her second attempt at meeting James. And maybe that *was* all it was.

Lord help them all if she didn't make contact tonight!

Emma leaned back in her seat and tried not to worry about her friends, instead focusing on the beautiful surrounds. Although she'd been to Central Park with Max, theirs had only been a brief visit; he'd been far more interested in going to see a Yankees or Mets game and touring Madison Square Garden than spending time exploring. She'd been right that you could spend a day here, strolling through the gorgeous gardens with their tall oaks, elms and maple trees or simply sitting back on a bench, watching the joggers, skaters and cyclists that zoomed by.

She noticed a young mother trying to wrangle her three children outside one of the many playgrounds and let out a satisfied sigh.

"You sound better today," Neve said, lowering her phone into her lap.

"Just thinking how wonderful it is to be away from the family for a few days." Realizing how awful that sounded, she quickly added, "Not that I don't love the kids with everything I have, it's just…"

Neve squeezed her knee. "Relax. I know what you mean. Will is my world, but it's nice to have some adult time once in a while. Good to have more than rowing and computer games dominating the conversation."

The horses clopped along past one of the lakes and Emma marveled at the beauty. "It blows my mind to think this place is essentially man-made."

"What do you mean?" Flick asked.

"Well, the gardens are so established, the lakes so natural

looking—they make me feel close to nature, even though we're in one of the busiest cities in the world. I feel more relaxed than I have in a long time."

Flick chuckled and wrapped an arm around Emma, leaning against her shoulder. "How's your head today?"

Emma was puzzled. She'd taken painkillers upon waking up in the morning but it was almost lunchtime now and she hadn't felt that familiar stab of pain in hours. "Good, actually. Oh, look over there."

Flick followed her finger to a nearby grassy area where a group of young men were playing some kind of ball game with their shirts off. "Ooh, yeah, look, Neve, there's something worth taking photos of."

"What would Seb think of the way you ogle strange men in public?" Neve's caustic tone matched her expression.

"Seb wouldn't give two hoots."

Neve snorted her disgust.

Emma looked from one friend to the other. "What's going on between you two?"

"Beats me." Flick crossed her arms over her chest. "I think someone got out of bed on the wrong side."

"I'm hungry," Neve announced, ignoring Flick's comment. "Where shall we go for lunch?"

So much for being kid-free. Neve and Flick were acting like a pair of adolescents, and if they didn't snap out of it soon, Emma would tell them so. "I was thinking the Boathouse. There's also the Tavern on the Green, but I reckon you guys will love the Boathouse and it's not far from here."

All agreed with her choice, so once they took the obligatory selfie with their horses and driver in the background, they walked the short distance to the restaurant. They were seated at a table outside, overlooking the lake, which sparkled with the warm sun shining down on it. New York in winter might be magical, but New York in summer made Emma happy in her heart. If the merry chatter and smiling faces at the tables around them were anything to go by, she wasn't the only one feeling this way.

A waiter brought them sparkling water and the menus, and Emma's mouth watered as she read through the options. In the end she chose a starter of roasted beets with dandelion greens, sunflower seeds and poblano vinaigrette and for her main she went with the Scottish salmon. Neve ordered some kind of nectarine dish and the roasted Cornish game hen, and Flick asked for the black sea bass, followed by celery-root ravioli. Emma smirked as she imagined what the twins would make of this eclectic menu. There were definite perks to being child-free.

As their waiter retreated, Emma took a sip of her sparkling water and Flick's phone beeped. She glanced down at where it sat beside them on the table, then sucked in a breath. Her cheeks flared red.

"What it is?" Emma asked.

"Nothing. Just an old friend I met last night requesting friendship on Facebook."

"*Jeremy?*" Neve exclaimed. "You're not going to accept, are you?" Emma had no idea who they were talking about.

Flick shrugged. "Why wouldn't I? It was nice to see him again."

"*Nice?* The way you two were behaving it looked a lot more than nice."

"Could someone fill me in?" Emma asked, wondering what exactly she'd missed by going to bed early.

"Flick met an old boyfriend in the bar last night and things got pretty damn cozy."

"What?" Flick spluttered, her eyes wide. "For one, he was

never my boyfriend, and for two, things weren't cozy. We were just catching up."

Neve raised her eyebrows. "And would your catching up have been any different if your husband had been there?"

Neve had to be overreacting—she'd had an emotional night and drank a fair bit. There was no way Flick would do anything to jeopardize her relationship with Seb. Emma scrutinized her friend's face as they waited for her answer.

"That's none of your business," Flick said finally.

Worry lodged itself in Emma's throat. Where was Flick's defense that of course she'd act the same if Seb had been there?

"I beg to differ." Neve leaned across the table into Flick's personal space. "You're a good friend, Flick, but so is Seb. He dotes on you and the kids, he's a great father and the best darn husband I've ever known. Not many men would stay up so they could pick up their wife from a drunken night out with her friends, you know. I don't like to think of you—"

Flick slammed her hand against the tabletop, rattling the silver cutlery. "Can you just *stop* going on and on about how bloody wonderful Seb is? Sometimes I think the two of you are more in love with him than I am, but things on the inside aren't always as they look on the outside. You don't have the monopoly on secrets, Neve."

Neve blinked and asked the question Emma desperately wanted to, "What exactly do you mean by that?"

A pregnant pause followed, the noise around them ceasing as they both stared at Flick. Her eyes glistened and Emma realized she was close to tears. She couldn't remember ever seeing her strong friend cry. Flick was the one who always held her and Neve together through their dramas, all their ups and downs and highs and lows. Emma's heart stilled as she waited for her to speak, hoping the truth wasn't as bad as she imagined.

Had Seb cheated on Flick like Max had on her?

Or worse, had he…abused her? The mere possibility left her cold.

"I don't know where to start." Flick sniffed. Then she buried her face in her hands and burst into tears.

Emma and Neve looked at each other in horror, the dynamics of their friendship totally out of whack now that Flick had fallen apart. Emma had never felt so helpless in her life.

"What shall we do?" she mouthed at Neve.

Neve shrugged, and then both at once, they shuffled their chairs close to Flick and hugged her. She sobbed in their arms until finally their entrees arrived. The waiter looked at their huddle—a cocktail of confusion and distress on his face—and then left in a hurry when Emma told him to leave the meals on the table. Like drivers passing a car accident, other guests at the restaurant stared at the scene with bleak curiosity.

Emma didn't care. Nothing but Flick mattered. Both her and Neve's clothes were soaked by the time Flick finally pulled away. "Do you want to go back to the hotel?"

Flick shook her head and drank some water. "You must be wondering what the hell is going on."

26

Felicity

Flick could only imagine what a mess she looked like. Thank God no one in this Central Park restaurant knew her, so her confession wouldn't be heard and turned into idle gossip. That was, if she could even work out how and *what* to tell them. What if telling her friends changed things between them? Could she risk the fact that they might tell their sons? She opened and closed her mouth a couple of times before she finally managed to speak. Risk or not, she needed to get this off her chest before she suffocated under the pressure.

"Seb told me he wants to become a woman."

Her blow was so startling that Emma and Neve gasped, their hands rushing up to cover their mouths in unified shock, confusion and horror.

For a few long moments her friends sat still as statues, only their eyes giving any indication of anything happening inside their heads. Empty of tears, Flick heaved out a long breath as she waited for them to digest this crazy morsel of information.

Neve was first to speak. "What... I... Um... What do you mean exactly?"

Emma simply stared at her with wide-open eyes.

Flick had lived with Seb's cross-dressing for over twenty years, and yet his latest announcement still felt like it had come out of nowhere. How could she explain it to her closest friends? How could she expect them to even *begin* to comprehend it?

"I'm going to go back a few years," she said eventually, her voice not much more than a whisper.

Her friends nodded and she continued, "About eight months after Seb and I met—when we were engaged and living together—I came home early from classes one day and Seb seemed on edge. Later that night, when I was getting ready for bed, I found a pair of panties and a lacy bra that weren't mine." She swallowed, finding it almost impossible to speak past the ball of sandpaper in her throat. The terror sparked by that discovery was etched so deeply in her mind she would never forget it.

"I jumped to the obvious conclusion that he had another woman on the side, but when I confronted him about it, he... What he said stunned me almost more than that would have." She took another breath.

"He told me he liked wearing women's clothes and that when I wasn't there, he'd try on my stuff and use my makeup. I must admit, I had noticed some of my clothes were stretched a little, but I just put it down to me losing weight or something. This bra and panties were his, though. He'd bought them specially."

Neither Neve nor Emma said anything, but their eyebrows crept up to their hairlines in perfect synchronization. Flick's stomach churned as she tried to continue.

"He fought back tears as he confessed that he was a crossdresser and that perhaps he should have told me when we'd first met, but he'd known I was different, known I was the one, and he'd been frightened that if he told me he would scare me off. He told me he'd purged his women's wardrobe just after we met—he'd tried to stop—but that he'd recently slipped again. To be honest, I didn't really know what to think."

Neve shook her head.

Emma reached across the table and squeezed her hand.

"I was furious," Flick continued. "Of course, I was relieved that he wasn't having an affair, but there was definitely an element of betrayal. Part of me wondered if I should leave him, but I just couldn't bring myself to do it. I mean, where was the harm in dressing up? I asked him a hundred questions—how long it had been going on, how often he did it, whether he was really gay and only marrying me because he didn't want to come out of the closest—and he answered them all with patience and what I thought was honesty.

"The first time he remembered wearing women's clothes was when his two older sisters used to dress him up in their old stuff. He liked the soft fabrics and the pretty colors, the styles of dresses much more than he liked his boring boys' clothes. Apparently he used to spend hours going through the family dress-up box, which consisted mostly of his mom's castoffs. He told me that as he grew older he felt jealous when his mom took them shopping and his sisters got gorgeous new outfits when all he got were play clothes." The more she said, the faster the words spilled from her lips—she was scared if she even took a breath, she might find herself unable to continue.

"But he assured me that he wasn't gay—that he definitely liked women and he loved me. He said that over the years, coming from a strong Catholic family, he'd struggled with guilt that what he was doing was somehow wrong. Many times he tried to stop, to shut down what he knew people would think were strange and kinky feelings, but doing so only made him miserable. He had never had a long-term relationship until me, because he didn't see how his habit could coexist with marriage. He'd even sought counseling. I was the first woman he'd ever told.

"I could see the shame he felt and how conflicted he was. He was terrified that it would be the end of us. And it did take me a while to come to terms with his habit—his 'hobby' he called it. But once I got past the shock, the love still burned as strongly. I still wanted to marry him and have a family. He's the only man who ever truly understood me."

She took a quick breath and sniffed, because talking about her feelings for Seb made emotions well up in her throat again and she didn't want to cry before she'd finished. "We made ground rules that day. He wouldn't wear my clothes again— that was too weird. In time, I encouraged him to buy his own wardrobe and we even budgeted for his dress habit. You'd die if you saw his closet—he has way better fashion sense than I ever had."

Neve let out a nervous laugh.

"We also made the decision that if we had kids, which we both very much wanted, we wouldn't *ever* tell them. They were my ground rules and until recently, he never broke them. As far as I know."

"So the kids still don't know?" Neve asked.

Flick shook her head. "Just the thought of them finding out…" She couldn't verbalize how it made her feel.

"You said he wants to become a woman now. What happened? Did something happen to bring this on all of a sudden?" Emma asked.

Flick shrugged. "To be honest, I don't know. I found a letter that made me realize he was thinking about transitioning, but I haven't been able to bring myself to properly discuss it with him yet. I just feel so betrayed. I can't help thinking that he lied all those years ago when he said a desire to wear women's clothes was the end of his feelings. Surely you don't just wake up one day and decide you want to be a woman?"

When she finished, Neve and Emma stared at her.

"Please say something," she pleaded, her whole body trembling from the knowledge she'd finally revealed her biggest, darkest secret. Everything had changed between them now. There was no going back. She was no longer the perfect Flick, one half of the perfect couple, as she'd always worked so hard to be. All those memories of being the outcast in the playground came rushing back. What if Emma and Neve no longer wanted to be friends with her? Panic made her heart race as she imagined Caleb and Will shunning poor Toby as well.

"This is almost too hard to comprehend. I never imagined…" Emma's voice trailed off.

"I can't believe you never told us," Neve said.

Flick wanted to flee or maybe grin and say "Just kidding. Had you there a moment, didn't I?" But it was too late for that.

"I'm sorry," she began. "It was just—"

"Don't apologize." Neve patted her hand and then closed her fingers around it. A touch from a friend had never felt so reassuring. "I'm only sorry I've been going on and on about my own problems these last few weeks when you've had this massive thing to deal with all on your own."

"No. Don't think like that. How could you know what was happening when I was too scared to tell you?"

"Oh, Flick."

Again her friends' arms closed around her, and although being in that spot felt damn good, it also made the tears well in her eyes again and she'd done enough crying for one day. She pulled back as their waiter returned to their table.

"Is something wrong with the food?" he asked, his brow creased in bewilderment.

"No, nothing," Flick reassured him. "It's just…"

Neve continued what Flick hadn't been able to finish. "We're sure it's lovely, but we've had an emotional crisis and had other things on our mind."

The poor guy had no idea how to respond to that. He looked terrified by the idea of three women and emotions.

Neve looked to Flick. "Shall we get them to bring out the mains? Are you still hungry?"

Flick felt terrible, but the truth was her appetite for fancy cuisine had abated. "Not really," she confessed.

Neve smiled at their waiter. "We'll just have the bill, thanks."

Once they'd paid, tipped their bewildered waiter and escaped back into the park, Flick's friends looked to her.

"What do you want to do now?" Emma asked, her voice a little shaky, as if she didn't quite know what to say.

"Um…" Flick frowned and glanced around. "I know we haven't really had lunch but I kind of feel like ice cream."

Neve and Emma smiled. "Comfort food it is then," said Neve.

They walked a short distance and found a little kiosk that sold drinks and ice creams. Emma insisted on paying, and then they took their cones over to a shady spot under a grand old maple tree, secluded enough that they wouldn't be bothered by passersby. Sitting on the soft grass in this beautiful place, the warm summer sun sneaking through the branches above them, Flick could almost forget her recent confession. Almost but not quite—the heaviness in her stomach and the pitying expressions on her friends' faces made it far too real.

"What do you want to know?" she asked before licking her ice cream.

"Oh, nothing," Emma rushed. "You don't have to talk about it if you don't want to."

At the same time, Neve said, "What's the sex like?"

"Neve!" exclaimed Emma, but Flick laughed, Neve's blunt question strangely making her feel better.

Maybe talking about it would be cathartic. Maybe it would help her to understand it a little herself.

"This probably sounds strange, but the sex has always been good. Not that I had a string of sexual partners before Seb to compare it with, but I've had no complaints."

"But how do you, you know…get in the mood?"

Flick laughed. "Probably the same way you do, Neve. But if you mean how do I get aroused when I know he likes wearing women's clothes, then the truth is I usually don't even think about it. We've been together for over twenty years, I think he's the sexiest guy on the planet, and very rarely has he indulged in his habit when I've been around. It sounds weird to say, but cross-dressing isn't a sexual thing for him. He talks to like-minded people in internet chat rooms and he buys his clothes online. He dresses up when he's home alone, and the rest of the time, he's always been my Seb."

Her eyes prickled at these last words. "But that was before. We haven't slept together since he finally told me the truth. That he identifies as a woman, always has and wants to take things to the next step. I'm not sure… I don't think… I can't…" She sighed deeply, unable to finish her sentence.

Emma offered a sympathetic smile. "That's understandable. What a massive shock this must have been. I don't confess to know much about this, but I've seen a bit in the media lately—"

Flick rolled her eyes. "Haven't we all. It's everywhere I look."

"And," Emma continued, "I understood the majority of cross-dressers were just that—people who liked wearing the opposite sex's clothing. I thought being transgender was a totally different thing."

Flick had done her research—at various times over the last

two decades and a lot more in the last week. Emma was right. She nodded. "Apparently only a very small percentage of male cross-dressers do actually identify as female. Lucky for me, it looks like Seb falls in that small fraction."

"There must be other women in your situation," Neve said after another period of contemplative silence. "Maybe getting some counseling for yourself would help. Is there someone you can talk to?"

Flick swallowed. "Probably. But that would also make everything more real. And I'm just... I don't think I'm ready for that. I'm so angry at Seb right now. I can barely stand to be in the same room as him. That's why I had to go away."

"Totally understandable." Emma reached across and patted her knee. "Husbands and wives aren't supposed to keep secrets from each other, and this one is as about as big as they come. He's had a long time to work up to his announcement, and you also need time to get your head around it. I know you haven't lost Seb, but you've found out he's not the person you always thought he was, and that is tough. I'm not saying our situation is the same, but it felt like I'd married a stranger when I discovered Max was cheating on me. You'll probably go through all the stages of grief as you mourn the man you thought you were married to."

"That makes a lot of sense," Flick said. Betrayal was betrayal, whatever form it came in.

"I'd kill him if he was my husband," Neve said.

Her straight face and serious tone made Flick smile. She loved her friends—between them, they offered everything she needed.

Emma shot Neve a look of reproof.

Neve shrugged. "*What?* I would. I'd dress him in the most hideous dress I could find and bury him somewhere far, far away. I'd need your help of course, because he's a tall, strapping guy."

Flick laughed so hard tears poured down her cheeks, and even Emma, who'd been doing her best to keep a straight face, finally succumbed to giggles.

"Of course, I'd actually have to have a husband for this plan to work," Neve mused.

"Trust me, I'm beginning to think they're overrated."

"Amen." Emma lifted the remains of her cone as if in a toast.

"I must admit I've thought it might be easier if he'd died." Flick gasped, unable to believe she'd actually admitted this. "I didn't mean that," she rushed. "Of course I don't want him dead." At least, she didn't think she did.

She knew there was an appalling suicide rate among the transgender community, but right now the sympathy she'd receive as a widow seemed more appealing than the attention she'd inevitably get if Seb went ahead with the transition. Then there wouldn't just be pity; people would laugh and gossip about her family like they were on some TV drama.

"It's just that I'm so angry," she confessed. "I can't even begin to think about the future, because I'm so consumed with rage. I feel like he hasn't thought of the kids in any of this. He was always so careful about only cross-dressing when they were out, but the other night I found him doing it while Toby was home. He broke our promise. How the hell would Toby have felt if he'd walked in and found his dad all dolled up like Priscilla, Queen of the Desert?"

"Are you sure the kids have no idea?" Neve asked. "How did you hide Seb's wardrobe? You and he aren't exactly the same size and shape."

"He kept a couple of items with my clothes, but the majority of his female wardrobe is hidden in a locked trunk in the shed."

Emma raised an eyebrow. "And the kids never wondered what was in it?"

Flick thought back. "I think Zoe asked once, but she bought the story that he used it for storing old blueprints and designs and the like."

Funny, she'd never thought much about this before, but now she knew what a believable liar Seb was. He'd said there was work stuff in the trunk and they'd never questioned it, just like she'd never questioned a lot of things that perhaps she should have.

They finished their ice creams but stayed under the tree hanging out. Conversation flitted from topic to topic but always came back to Seb.

If he went ahead with gender-reassignment surgery and everything else that entailed, would that make him a lesbian? What about her? Did being in costume arouse him? Were his internet endeavors of a sexual nature? Had he ever cross-dressed in public? Flick had always thought the answer to that question was no, but now she didn't know. Her friends had more questions, many of which she didn't have answers for, but they helped her work out the things she needed to discuss with him. She wasn't looking forward to that conversation, but she owed it to herself and to her kids to have it. And the sooner, the better.

"Will you get a divorce?" Emma made a face at the question, possibly recalling her own ordeal.

The word *divorce* sent a shot of icy cold down Flick's spine. Both she and Seb had been raised to believe that marriage was for life. The possibility of divorce had never entered her mind before but surely these were extenuating circumstances. She tried to imagine her life without Seb—a near-impossible feat. Of course, because of the kids, they would always be connected.

"I haven't got that far in my thought processes," she confessed.

"Does Seb want you to stay with him?" Neve asked.

Flick rubbed her lips together a moment, thinking back over the brief conversations they'd had this past week. "I *think* that's what he wants, but could I honestly stay if he does become a woman?"

"Certainly no one would blame you if you didn't," Emma said.

"And, to be honest, being a single woman has its advantages," Neve added. "And it's not just having the bed to yourself and being able to choose the channel on the TV. Anyway, how is he planning to pay for his…you know? Aren't these gender-reassignment things pretty damn pricey?"

"Who knows?" It was another thing that had barely crossed Flick's mind, but now that Neve mentioned it, it was a damn good question. "Maybe this is why he waited till Toby was almost finished school. Maybe he thinks we can put the money we'll save on school fees toward it." *Like hell*, she thought silently. There were numerous other ways she'd prefer to spend her hard-earned cash. She had her eye on a baby elephant that had been in deep freeze for twenty years, and the zoo was now considering selling.

"He could always set up a crowd-funding account," Emma pondered. "It seems to be the thing to do now."

Flick shuddered at the thought of their private life being splashed all over the web, friends—if any stuck by him—and well-meaning strangers sharing Seb's plea for money on Facebook, Twitter and Instagram. "No way! I *will* kill him before that happens."

"So if the kids don't know yet, how are you going to break it to them?"

She shook her head at Emma's question, her chest tightening. Although what other people would think worried her, her biggest fear was what Seb's announcement would do to the kids.

"You know, their reactions might surprise you," Neve said. "Will told me there'd been a lot of discussion at school about gender issues lately."

Emma nodded. "The girls even had a unit on it in their health class. I guess it's just the way the world is going these days. Things that would have been outrageous in our childhood are things our kids are much more open about. By the time our children have grandchildren, they probably won't even have a reference to gender on birth certificates."

Her friends might have valid points, but this wasn't the future, this was now, and this was *her* life. Toby's and Zoe's lives.

"Anyway," she said, pushing herself up off the ground; she was done wasting their vacation talking about this. "Shall we keep walking? You've got another big night tonight, Neve. Maybe we should head back so you can get ready?"

Neve let out a loud sigh. "Let's hope tonight I have more success than last night."

She and Emma stood and dusted off the dirt and leaves their clothes had collected while sitting under the tree. As they walked in silence through the Mall and Literary Walk to the closest park exit, the cathedral-like canopy of elms took Flick's breath away. She might not have seen much of New York yet but she already knew this would be her favorite place.

It felt like a fictional world, comforting and safe—a little like the one she'd shared with Seb.

27

Genevieve

Neve pressed a hand to her stomach, trying to quell the butterflies—no, make that blackbirds—that were churning there again. The people nearby probably pitied her being a single woman alone at the theater, but they didn't know the half of it. Looking like a loner was the least of her worries.

As the curtain closed on the final act of *Mamma Mia!* she wished she'd allowed Flick and Emma to come with her again, but after the day they'd had, she hadn't wanted to admit she'd changed her mind and wanted some moral support after all.

Flick was emotionally exhausted after her revelation—Neve still couldn't quite believe it either. That confession in Central Park could so easily have been a dream, or a nightmare. She'd always thought Seb and Flick's relationship was so strong, but this just went to show that you never truly knew what was going on inside the head of another person. No matter *how* close you thought you were to them. Poor Flick. With all the drama between them, it wasn't surprising that Emma's headache had returned, and because of this her friends had opted for a quiet night in at the hotel.

"But you must promise to wake us when you return,"

Emma had said, a cold cloth pressed against her forehead as Neve walked out. "We want to know all the details."

Wondering what there would be to tell, Neve took a sip of her water and then followed it with some deep breathing, concentrating on inhaling and exhaling, not hyperventilating. The urge to run almost overcame her. Only the thought of Will's disappointment if she didn't find him some answers gave her the courage to rise from her seat and head for the foyer. Hopefully the girl from last night would be in the ticket box and she wouldn't have to explain herself again.

Halfway out of the theater she was almost knocked off her feet by a woman who'd had a little too much to drink.

"Sorry," the woman slurred, giggling as if she thought the whole world hilarious.

"*Really* sorry," echoed the man with her as he pulled her close to him again.

"It's fine." Neve envied them their carefree attitudes, not to mention their drinks. She'd kept to water only, wanting to be fully compos mentis when she spoke to James, but maybe a little Dutch courage would have been a good idea after all. She continued along in the wave of people, psyching herself up to ask the first theater-type person she saw for direction to James. In the foyer as the hordes flocked toward the exit, she sneaked off to one side, took another deep breath and smoothed down her dress.

"Oh. My. Fucking. God!"

Her heart stilled as she looked up. She didn't need to see the face to recognize the voice and every last little organ in her body quivered. Her brown eyes met James's piercing blue ones and something told her everything was going to be okay. He might be angry to start with, but—sunny natured and fun loving—he'd never been able to hold a grudge. He still had the same warm, mischievous smile that had won her over all those years ago.

Will looked even more like him than she'd imagined. "Gennie!" he exclaimed after a few moments in which they stared dumbfounded at each other.

She blinked as heat radiated through her body. No one else had ever called her Gennie; she suspected if anyone else ever had, she'd have put them on a hit list. But James said it in such an intimate voice, making her feel warm, cherished and sexy.

She couldn't help but smile. "Hi, James."

If Neve's voice sounded huskier than she meant it to, he either didn't care or didn't notice. He stepped forward and she sucked in a breath as he drew her into a tight hug.

"I've been wondering all afternoon who my mystery guest could be, but…" He pulled back and held her at arm's length as his gaze raked over her. "*Wow.* Look at you. Still the sexiest woman alive." Although he likely said this to all his former flings, her nipples tingled and tightened at the compliment uttered in his delicious voice; a slight American accent only intensifying his appeal. Oh, dear God, she was going to have to be very careful not to lose her head. Or anything else.

"Thanks," she said as her senses went into overload. "You don't look so bad yourself."

Total understatement! Age had done him no harm. Still a tower of hard, lean muscle with a face that made her want to drop to her knees and praise God for this beautiful creation, he looked barely five years older than when they'd last met.

They stood staring at each other for another few moments— no awkwardness, simply a couple of seconds to catch their breath.

"I'm so glad you found me," James said, breaking the silence. "Would you like to go get a drink?"

"You're sure Lydia won't mind?"

"I don't think Lydia has cared what I do for quite some time. We're divorced."

The air whooshed from Neve's lungs and her eyes opened wide. She had no hope of hiding her shock.

Why hadn't she ever considered this a possibility? If they'd been happy all those years ago, he'd never have strayed. Then, another awful thought struck her. "Was it because...? Did you...have another affair?" she whispered, feeling sick at the thought of being just one in a long line of someone elses.

"I'm wounded you would think such a thing." His warm hands, still on her arms, slid lower and he took her fingers in his and brought them up to his chest. She could feel his heart beating beneath them. "The only time I ever broke my wedding vows was with you."

His words made her head spin. And she believed him. She nodded, but couldn't speak.

He smiled again. "Is that a yes to a drink?"

"Uh-huh." She couldn't say no even if she wanted to, because they had the most important thing in the world to discuss. That and the fact that she seemed to have lost the ability to form actual words.

"Great. Just let me check everything's okay backstage and I'll be right with you. Don't run away."

She whimpered a little as he strode away, the snug fit of his dark jeans making her mouth water. Her heart pounded as she waited for him to return. The woman from last night—closing up the ticket box—eyed her curiously, obviously having witnessed James's effusive greeting. If Neve didn't feel so nervous she'd have offered the woman a smug I-told-you-so smile but she tapped her heel against the floor instead, fighting the urge to do exactly what he'd told her not to and run.

She dug her phone out of her bag and looked down at the

screen backdrop—a recent photo of Will, taken when he was all scrubbed up for the grade-twelve prom.

My beautiful boy.

He was the reason she was here, seeing James again after all these years. She couldn't mess this up.

As promised, James returned quickly, and then with another heart-stopping, libido-teasing smile, he offered Neve his arm and led her out into the night. She barely noticed the passersby or the sounds of New York after dark, so consumed was she with the smell and feel of James again.

They headed toward a bar he knew. "It's so tiny, it's easy to miss. But this is a hidden gem frequented by locals," he told her as he pushed open a door for her.

She stepped inside and immediately fell in love with the trendy but cozy establishment. Flickering candles were the only lighting inside and artwork lined the walls, giving it a special charm. In the corner a singer was crooning something sad and romantic.

"This place is gorgeous." She spoke loudly so James could hear her above the din of music and chatter.

"I'm glad you like it," he said, stepping close and placing his hand on her back as he ushered them toward the bar.

She closed her eyes briefly, relishing the pleasure that rocketed through her at this simple but oh-so-sexy touch. There was something seductive about a man touching his hand lightly to the small of a woman's back—something chivalrous and yet vaguely predatory, like a signal to other guys that this girl was taken. James's touch breathed life back into those old but not forgotten feelings. "What can I get you to drink?" he asked as they commandeered two stools at the bar.

A voice inside her head said she should buy her *own* drink to set the tone of the evening, but she didn't want to offend him before they had a chance to talk. "I'll have a white wine, thanks."

James ordered her drink and a beer for himself. He chatted to the friendly barman as if they knew each other well. This felt like a small neighborhood hangout rather than a hip bar near bustling Broadway. Once their drinks were placed on the bar in front of them, James turned all his attention back to her.

"I can't believe you're here, sitting right next to me." He took a drag of his beer. She admired the thick column of his neck and his stubbled jawline as he lifted the glass to his mouth. "What are you doing in New York?"

This was her chance—the perfect time to tell him she'd come for the sole purpose of catching up with him. To tell him about Will.

Instead, she took a sip of wine and said, "I've come with my two best friends, Emma and Flick. They're both going through some stuff at home and we decided an overseas shopping and cocktails vacation would be the perfect medicine."

He chuckled. "And is it working?"

She pursed her lips together, thinking about Emma's constant headaches and Flick's startling announcement of this afternoon. "I'm not sure yet, but there's still time. We're here for another five days."

That voice inside her head told her that according to the rules of conversation, it was her turn to ask him a question now. The things she wanted to ask him were a little personal, so she went with the safety of work. "How long have you been working on *Mamma Mia!*?"

"Three years." Of course, she already knew this answer. "And I've loved every minute of it. But we've only got a few months to go until we close."

"Oh, that's right. I read that in the playbill. What are you planning on doing next?"

He shrugged those lovely big shoulders and she squeezed her legs together as a shot of pure lust rushed to her core. "I've put some feelers out. Who knows, I might even head back Down Under, but there is a certain allure to being on Broadway."

"I can imagine."

"What about you? Still working in theater?"

"No." She shook her head. "These days I'm a freelance hair and makeup artist. I do a lot of work for magazines, indie films, advertising, that sort of thing. Keeps me busy, but I do miss the buzz of being backstage."

"Why leave, then?"

She swallowed. *Why leave the theater, or why did I leave you?*

It was another perfect opportunity to bring Will into the conversation, but something held her back. "I moved back to Perth to be nearer Mom and Dad, and there weren't as many in-theater jobs there. The longer I've been out of the industry, the harder it would be to get back in."

"So you didn't move back for a man?" he asked. They were sitting very close—ostensibly so they could hear each other better—but it also meant she could hear the interest in his voice.

"No."

"What about now? Do you have a boyfriend? Husband?"

After so many years apart, she shouldn't find so much joy in this question. But she couldn't help it. "Not at the moment."

"You've been married, then?"

"No. The right guy never came along." So why did it feel like she was looking into his eyes right this very second?

He stared intently at her for a few long moments, his gaze so hot her lips felt like they were on fire. For a second she felt positive he was going to kiss her, and then he looked down at his drink and took another gulp instead.

Neve's heart sank, but she tried not to show her disappointment. It was ridiculous. She wasn't here to jump the man's bones, she was here to tell him about her son. His son. *Their* son. Nerves once again replaced her desire, and she spoke to distract herself. "How are your daughters these days? They must be adults by now."

His lips stretched into a proud fatherly smile and he spoke with such love and delight, which, dammit, only made him more attractive. "Just awesome. They're all back in Melbourne now, so I don't see them as much as I'd like, but we talk lots. Hannah did two years of teaching but has accepted a place at WAAPA in their musical-theater program for next year. She wants to be a director. I guess she's a chip off the old block. Jolie is much more like Lydia—she's just finished her master's in English literature and is talking about going on to do a PhD. No weddings or babies yet."

Neve didn't register those last few sentences. "WAAPA? As in the *Western Australian* Academy of Performing Arts?"

"That's the one." He winked playfully. "Maybe if I visit Hannah, we'll have to catch up."

At the way he said *catch up* her insides caught fire. "Maybe," she all but squeaked. Will had a half sister in the same city and neither even knew the other existed. Gee whiz, when had her life got so convoluted?

James leaned even closer and whispered in her ear, "Because I'm really enjoying catching up right now."

She shivered, the hairs on her arms and the back of her neck rising as she drank in the intoxicating smell of *him*—far more dangerous than any wine could ever be. "Me, too," she admitted, her voice hardly more than a whisper.

And then they were kissing. All logical thoughts and well-meaning plans darted out the window. This wasn't the kiss of two people who'd only just met but the heated, demanding, salacious kiss of two people who had a scorching sexual history and wanted to repeat it.

James slid off the stool, his hands capturing her face as he slid his thigh between her legs. Thanks to her flimsy dress, she felt his hard muscle pressing against the lace of her panties, desperate need gathering there.

He broke the kiss and looked right into her eyes. "Want to have the next drink at my place?"

The voice inside her head was still trying to be heard, but it was getting softer. While her brain told her to pull away and tell him what she needed to tell him, her traitorous body had other ideas. This hadn't been in her plans, but she didn't have the good sense to scratch it off his agenda. She wanted to feel his lovely big hands on her bare skin again, she wanted his tongue exploring all her intimate places and, most urgently, she wanted his cock pulsing inside her. It had been so long since she'd had an honest-to-God real-life orgasm. What harm would one more time do before she told him the truth?

"Yes, please," she all but panted.

He downed the last dregs of his beer and then they ran outside to hail a cab.

"Drive fast," James commanded their driver, after sliding into the back seat beside her and giving him his address.

The driver swerved out into the street and shot up his middle finger at the horns that beeped behind them.

James moved so he was right next to Neve and put his hand on her thigh.

She had her first orgasm in the taxi, the second in the elevator shooting up to his apartment. By the time he'd unlocked the door and they'd collapsed inside, she could have exploded with unadulterated need. Her hands were on the buckle of his jeans even before the door had slammed shut behind them. She sank her fingers into his underwear and pressed her palm against his hot, pulsing erection. Her mouth watered at the thought of tasting him again.

Although he groaned, he didn't forget her needs, whipping

her dress over her head in one swift movement and then sucking in his breath as he gazed down at her near-naked body. "God, you're delicious," he hissed and then bent his head and took one nipple in his mouth.

Her knees almost buckled as his tongue swirled around her nipple. His other hand ventured between her legs, his fingers sneaking inside the lace of her panties to find out how hot she was for him. "And *wet*."

She hadn't been this wet for as long as she could remember. The few guys she'd slept with since James had never turned her on the way he had. And judging by the sensations flooding her body, he still had that particular talent.

"I need you. Now." She yanked her hand out of his jeans and started tugging them down his legs.

"You don't have to ask me twice." He stepped out of his jeans, then yanked her panties down her legs, before lifting her up and carrying her over to the kitchen. He perched her on the counter, and she squealed as her bare bum landed on the cool surface, but that was nothing compared to the noise she made when he thrust inside her.

She bit down hard on his shoulder to stop herself from waking the whole apartment building as he increased his pace. His hands cupped her buttocks and her legs wrapped tightly around his waist, both of them giving everything they had as the tension grew inside her until it was unbearable. They came together magnificently at exactly the same moment. Another feat that had never happened with anyone else. And afterward she planted her hands on the countertop as she caught her breath, and he dropped his head to nuzzle between her breasts.

It felt oh-so-right…and yet it was oh-so-wrong.

As Neve's heart rate recovered, she thought of Will. What kind of mother was she to put her libido ahead of the needs of her son?

28

Felicity

Flick's cell phone beeped and she shot out her hand to grab it off the bedside table. Neve had only been gone a couple of hours but she was desperate for news of how her night was going. Emma, still headachy and also upset because tomorrow would be the first time she wouldn't be with the twins for their birthday, had fallen asleep within five minutes of finishing her room-service dinner. Flick couldn't help worrying that something was seriously wrong with her friend and didn't want to wake her by turning on the television; this left her alone with nothing but her own thoughts and the internet, neither of which gave her any comfort her at all. Google was not your friend when your life was in a shambles.

She glanced down at the screen, expecting to see a message from Neve, but was shocked to find a Facebook message alert instead. It wasn't Neve. It wasn't Seb. Or one of the kids. It was *Jeremy*.

She pressed the phone against her racing heart and closed her eyes as she recalled their unexpected encounter last night. Her lips twisted into a smile at the memory of how he'd looked and how he'd made her laugh. Conversation had been easy and she'd been more pleased than she'd let on when he'd requested her friendship earlier in the day, but she'd imagined that would be it. Maybe they'd check out each other's profiles every now and then, like a few statuses here and there and perhaps even write a post for each other's birthdays, but she hadn't expected Jeremy to contact her again so soon.

Taking a quick breath, she swiped a shaky finger across the screen so she could read the message in its entirety.

Hey, Flick, hope you had a great day exploring New York. This may be presumptuous of me, but I was wondering, if you're not too busy, if you'd like to have another drink tonight? I enjoyed your company so much yesterday and thought it would be a pity not to make the most of being in the same city. Jeremy.

She read the message three times, rubbing her lips together and trying to read between the lines or second-guess meaning as she did so. While she was excited by the thought of seeing Jeremy again, her chest squeezed a little. Meeting another man on her own at night would feel like a betrayal to Seb.

Her finger hovered over the screen as she silently debated the ethics of accepting Jeremy's invitation. What harm could there be in meeting him for a drink at the hotel bar—a public place? If she stayed in this room reading more stories on online forums, she'd give herself a migraine and have to raid Emma's painkiller supply. Without allowing herself any more time to deliberate, she replied.

That would be lovely. I'll meet you in the lobby in half an hour.

Then she crept out of bed and sneaked into the bathroom to get ready. Unlike Neve, Flick didn't have a never-ending supply of dresses to choose from—in fact, she'd only brought one and it was a sundress, perfect for strolling the streets in the summer sun, but not an evening outfit. Perhaps she should have packed something from Sofia's wardrobe. Then again, none of his/her stuff would fit her. And wearing a dress might give Jeremy the wrong idea anyway. Whatever that was! She was too muddled up inside to know.

If someone had told her a month ago that she'd be in New York, without Seb, contemplating what to wear to go meet one of her oldest male friends alone at night, she'd have laughed in their face.

Life really could change in an instant.

Eventually, she decided on a pair of black capri pants and a floaty top that Emma and Neve had encouraged her to buy at Macy's. Its soft pink sheer fabric shivered over her skin and would be quite indecent if she didn't wear a camisole underneath. The silver beading on the front and the batwing sleeves made it far dressier than anything she'd have picked herself.

When she'd dressed, applied a tad more makeup than she normally would and untied her perpetual ponytail, Flick took a step back and checked herself in the mirror. She ran a brush through her hair and then smiled at her reflection. Not bad for someone whose life was falling apart. Another deep breath and she sneaked back into the room to grab her bag and room card before she could chicken out of this rendezvous.

Her heart thumped heavily as she hurried down the corridor, but she smiled at a family as she stepped into the elevator. The couple, in their thirties she'd guess, had a boy and a girl who looked remarkably like Zoe and Toby when they were little. The thought of her children almost had her exiting the elevator at the next floor down—it didn't seem right to be meeting a man who wasn't their dad—but a little voice inside reminded her that if their family unit did crumble, it wouldn't be down to her.

"Have a nice night," said the male half of the couple as the elevator doors opened to the lobby.

Flick forced a smile. "Thanks. You, too."

"We're going out for late-night sundaes," the little girl exclaimed, her eyes sparkling at the thought and her hand swinging her mom's arm as she held it.

The woman rolled her eyes. "First day of our vacation and these two are too excited to sleep."

"Enjoy," Flick said, a tear forming in her eye as she wondered what would become of this innocent, full-of-life little girl. Would she grow up to meet the man of her dreams and then discover it was all a lie?

Melodramatic, much? She shook her head and followed the family out of the elevator, jitters jangling inside her as she glanced around for Jeremy. The moment she spotted him, standing only a few feet away and looking just as anxious as her, all her nerves melted away. Her smile relaxed as his eyes met hers, and then they started toward each other.

"Good evening, Flick." Jeremy leaned forward and kissed her on the cheek, his hand brushing against her arm as he did so. Flutters of an entirely different nature danced in her belly.

"Hey, there," she replied, her voice barely more than a whisper.

"You look stunning," he said, ushering her out of the hallway.

"And so do you." It wasn't a lie. He looked more casual than last night—wearing smart dark jeans and a light blue polo shirt instead of a business suit—but he was no less attractive.

Jeremy grinned at her compliment. "Thanks for agreeing to meet me. I couldn't stand the thought of going home without seeing you again."

"Me neither," she confessed, her tongue darting out to moisten her lower lip.

"Shall we get a drink here or would you like to go out?"

"Here will be great." Going out would make it seem more like a date and she wasn't sure that was what she wanted this to be. Far more simple if this was just two old friends catching up.

"Let's go, then." He casually linked his arm through hers as they walked in the direction of the bar, which wasn't as crowded as last night. "Our conference ended today. Most of the delegates left this afternoon but I decided to stay another few days."

Was that a last-minute decision? Had he done so because of her? She wasn't sure she wanted to know the answers.

"Oh, how was your speech today?" she asked, pushing aside the niggling worry that she was heading into dangerous territory.

"I think it went well, but I don't want to bore you with all that," he said. "What can I get you to drink? More cosmopolitans tonight?"

"Just a glass of white wine, please."

Jeremy gestured to the table area. "Take a seat and I'll get one." As he strode to the bar, Flick looked around for a table. There were plenty to choose from, and she didn't know whether to go with a quiet one in the corner, or somewhere in the middle where they wouldn't be so isolated. So alone.

You're overthinking things again.

Jeremy, being a man, would no doubt laugh himself silly if he could read all the thoughts whirling through her head. To him, this was likely nothing more than a drink between old friends, but here she was reading meaning and implication into every word, every gesture, every smile. She pulled out a seat at the nearest table and plonked herself down, planting her elbows on the tabletop as she waited for his return.

It felt like hours and at the same time only a few seconds before he arrived with a pint of beer and a glass of wine.

"Here you are." Their eyes met and held for a fraction longer than necessary. He did have *lovely* eyes. They were large pools of brown, with tiny gold flecks that matched the natural highlights in his hair.

"Thank you." She took the glass and lifted it to her lips, relishing the cool liquid as it flowed down her throat.

Jeremy sat opposite her and his knees brushed against hers as he did so. "Sorry," he smiled apologetically. "One of the negatives of being tall is you can't sit politely under a table."

She laughed, her apprehension settling again at the thought of him hiding under the table. "I don't remember you being so tall in high school."

He laughed and shook his head. "I had a late growth spurt. Probably a good thing because if I'd been taller, they'd have made me join the basketball team, and I'm far too uncoordinated for ball sports."

He had such a confident aura about him that she couldn't imagine him being bad at anything. "You must do some kind of physical activity to keep yourself in such good shape." She realized seconds after the words left her mouth how they might be interpreted.

Jeremy took a long, slow sip of beer and then raised his eyebrows. "You think I'm in good shape?"

Every bone in her body right down to the tiny ones in her ears thought he was in good shape, *and then some*, but would it be perilous to admit that? She shrugged. "You're not bad for a man of our age."

"Our age?" he exclaimed. "You make it sound like we've got one foot in the bloody grave."

The last few weeks she'd felt that ancient. "You know what I mean."

"I'm going to ignore the bit about our age and concentrate

on the bit about you liking my shape. For the record, I like your shape very much as well."

It wasn't so much his words but the way he looked at her when he spoke that had heat rushing to Flick's cheeks. She took a gulp of wine. This felt so weird, sitting here, semi-flirting with Jeremy, but also exciting, a lovely distraction from the madness that was currently her life.

"Sorry," he said. "I can see I'm making you uncomfortable and I don't mean to. I guess I'm still in shock at the good fortune of bumping into you again and, if truth be told, I'm also a little nervous. I say silly things when I'm nervous. I never was that good at talking to girls."

"No need to apologize." She couldn't deny she liked the way he looked at her—as if she was sexy, desirable. Seb's announcement hadn't only made her question how well she'd ever actually known him, but also fundamental things about herself. Being here with Jeremy made her feel normal again. "I'm enjoying your company very much. I always did."

"Well, phew." Jeremy theatrically wiped his hand against his brow. "Let's start again, shall we? What were you doing before I messaged you tonight?"

She took another sip of wine, buying time as she decided how to reply. The truth? She'd been scouring the internet, unable to stop herself clicking through the stories of others like herself—wives and partners of those who had decided to go through gender transition. Those chat rooms and forums that Emma and Neve had suggested were both comforting and terrifying.

It surprised her how many others she found who were in similar situations. There were even a few men whose wives wanted to be male. She sympathized with the people who'd had no clue their spouse had any such tendencies until suddenly one day they'd announced they identified as the opposite sex. At least she'd had Seb's cross-dressing as a sign. But did that make her even more stupid?

What kind of woman stayed with a man who was more comfortable in a dress and high heels than she was? Was there something wrong with her?

She'd been intimate with her husband thousands of times, for crying out loud—shouldn't she have *known* something wasn't quite right? Problem was she'd been with only one guy before Seb, and it had been the first time for both of them. What a fumbling, awkward mess that had been. No surprises they'd broken up before ever doing it again.

Some of the women on the sites were surprisingly supportive of their husbands, others were understandably bitter but couldn't wait to move on and then some were so utterly judgmental and self-righteous that Flick had almost thrown her iPad across the room in disgust. But what she hated most about the horrible women spouting that gender dysphoria was unnatural, a mortal sin, blah-blah-blah, was that deep down she agreed with them. And she hated herself for it. She wanted to shake some sense into Seb—to tell him to stop being so selfish and take a reality check. How could he have male genitalia and identify as a woman?

It simply didn't make any sense to her at all, and she liked her life making sense. Perhaps she was more conventional than she'd always imagined.

"Flick?" Jeremy's concerned voice jutted into her self-assessment. "Are you okay?"

She blinked, remembering that he'd asked her a question but having no recollection of what that question was. "I'm sorry, what did you say?"

"I asked, what have you been up to tonight?"

"Oh, right." Could she bring herself to tell Jeremy that her life had all the ingredients for an episode of *Jerry Springer*? What would he say? Deciding not to hijack a pleasant evening with her marital woes, she told him about Neve instead. "Emma and I have been hanging out in our hotel room waiting for Neve, my friend who you met last night, to come back."

"Where is she?"

"Remember how I told you last night we were helping her through a tricky situation? She's gone to tell the father of her seventeen-year-old son that he has a child."

Jeremy's eyes widened and his mouth opened in a surprised expression. He leaned closer. "Now, this sounds like a fascinating story."

Smiling, she began to tell him how she'd met Neve when their sons had started high school and because they weren't pretentious and stuck-up like many of the other moms, they'd instantly clicked. She'd known Neve was a single mom, that Will's father wasn't on the scene, but she'd never known the whole truth. It was so much easier to talk about Neve's problems than dwell on her own.

"So now that Will wants to meet his father, Neve has had to face up to her past—tonight she's going to tell him he's a dad."

"Jeepers." Jeremy exhaled and ran a hand through his mussed-up hair. "I'd be livid if I found out some woman had kept my child from me for that long. This guy is going to be furious."

"How furious?" Flick said, her tummy twisting at the thought that Neve might be in some kind of physical danger.

"Pretty damn mad, but I wouldn't hurt her, if that's what you're inferring. I'd want to meet the boy, but then again, that's just me."

"Maybe I should have insisted on going with her? Do you think I should call her?"

Jeremy reached across the table and took hold of Flick's hand. Every organ in her body froze at the connection. She glanced down, looking at the way his long fingers wrapped around her more petite ones. "Call her if it will make you feel better. I'll wait."

"Thanks," she said, reluctantly slipping her hand out from his and reaching for her phone in her bag. When she tried Neve's number, it went straight to voice mail. She left a message. "Hey, it's me. Just wondering how your evening is going. I'm here if you need me."

She sighed and put her phone on the table.

"What's your other friend up to tonight?" Jeremy asked. "I should have asked if you wanted to bring her along."

"Emma?" Flick shook her head. "She's sleeping. She's having these shocking headaches lately and is feeling down because it's her twin daughters' birthday tomorrow and she's not going to be with them." She suddenly realized she knew about Jeremy's marital status but not if he'd ever had a family. "Do you have any kids?"

He shook his head. "Not that I know of." She chuckled at his subtle reference to Neve. "You obviously do," he said.

"Yes, two. Zoe is twenty and getting married to her high school sweetheart in a few months, and Toby is in his final year at school."

"Wow, twenty's young to get married. How do you feel about that?"

"When she first told me, I told her she was being ridiculous and that I forbade her to tie herself to one guy so young, but she rightly told me that she was old enough to do whatever she wanted and would do so with or without my blessing."

Jeremy's mouth quirked at the corners and she noticed smile lines around his eyes. "Sounds like a feisty, independent young woman."

"Yes, she is. Which is why we were so surprised by her

engagement. I thought kids these days were happy to live in sin together."

He let out a half laugh. "When you say *we*, you mean you and your husband?"

Flick's stomach tightened at the thought of Seb, who was more into all the wedding preparations than she was. Seb, who'd probably rather wear a mother-of-the-bride outfit than a suit. "Yes."

Jeremy's expression turned serious. "You can tell me if it's none of my business, but when you mentioned your marriage was complicated... What exactly did you mean?"

Him knowing the truth would be mortifying, but the little flutters that sparked within her at his close proximity made her want to tell him part of it. "We've got some problems. I'm pretty sure we're going to get divorced."

Right now she couldn't see any alternative.

"I'm so sorry." Jeremy reached across and took hold of her hand again. This time he moved his thumb in ever-so-soft circles against her skin. The feeling rippled from that one spot right through her body.

"Divorce is never fun," he admitted, "but I found it was easier to accept when I looked at it as an opportunity for new adventures."

New adventures? Like dating? Like sleeping with other men? The thought of dating didn't fill her with huge excitement, but her nipples tingled at the thought of rediscovering her sexuality. She'd never felt a need for sex the way Neve and Emma spoke about it; was that because she and Seb weren't doing it properly?

"That sounds both scary and exciting," she said, looking right into Jeremy's eyes as the tingling feeling moved lower.

He nodded and then spoke in a low voice. "You know...

at the risk of embarrassing myself, I always had a crush on you at school."

"No!" She couldn't hide her shock. "You didn't?"

"I did. Truth is, I still do. You're a beautiful woman, Felicity, and any man in his right mind would want you."

His words were a much-needed boost of confidence and warmth spread throughout her body. She stared at the handsome face in front of her and imagined how his five-o'clock shadow might feel against her thighs.

"I'm not in the right state of mind to be starting a relationship right now," she said, the words coming not from her head but somewhere else. Somewhere that craved intimacy with a real man, somewhere that wanted to feel desired and normal. Could Jeremy give her a little taste of that right now?

"And long-distance relationships never work anyway, but I'm not asking for you to move in with me."

Every hair on the back of her neck quivered with awareness at his suggestive tone. "But you are asking something?" she whispered.

"That depends on what your answer would be. I wouldn't want to make things awkward when we've only reconnected again after all these years."

She licked her lips and swallowed, her mouth suddenly parched. "My answer depends on what your question is."

"Felicity Bird," he began, using her maiden name, "would you like to come up to my room and have an adventure?"

Nothing had ever sounded so enticing. Flick pushed aside the thought that maybe she was being hasty, that maybe she was doing this to upset Seb, and followed the cravings of her body instead of the cautions of her head. "Yes, please."

29

Emma

Emma awoke to a dark room—only the flashing lights from Times Square sneaking through the gaps in the curtains. With a groan, she felt around on her bedside table for her cell phone. The screen read 11:15 p.m. Hallelujah; she'd managed about four hours of sleep before her pounding skull had woken her.

But hang on, shouldn't Neve be back by now?

She must have been exhausted not to have woken up when Neve returned, because surely the others wouldn't have been able to keep their voices down when discussing the evening's events. Frowning, Emma angled her phone to cast light over the room. She was surprised to see both beds empty. Had Neve and Flick gone down to the bar so as not to disturb her? With no fear of waking her absent friends, she sat up, turned on the bedside light and sent a message. Where the hell are you? How did James react?

While waiting for a response, she popped two painkillers from the packet by her bed and swallowed; not that drugs were doing any good. She blamed Max for putting her under added stress by taking her babies away on their fifteenth birthday. What had she ever seen in the bastard? There should be a warning for innocent young women across the foreheads of all hot, young guys: "Beware—outer package does not necessarily reflect what is inside!"

Irritated when neither of her friends replied, she logged in to Facebook and posted happy-birthday messages on Louise's and Laura's walls, glad to be the first to do so. If it were up to her, the girls wouldn't have Facebook accounts yet, but Max had given them permission two years ago without consulting her. When she'd confronted him about it, he'd accused her of being an old stick-in-the-mud and told her to get with the times.

She spent the next few minutes torturing herself by scrolling through the kids' profiles and staring at all the happy family snaps they'd posted in Hawaii. Chanel, who didn't look much older than the girls, was all skin and bones in a skimpy gold bikini. Onlookers probably assumed she was Max's eldest daughter, but Emma worried about the influence she might have on the girls. And was that beer Caleb and Max were sharing? She felt like throwing up. Discarding her phone on the bedside table in disgust, she climbed out of bed and headed into the bathroom, switching on the light as she entered.

Her gaze caught on her image in the mirror. *Why do hotels have to have such huge mirrors?*

As if she wasn't depressed enough, her reflection threatened to send her over the edge. If she couldn't love herself, how could she ever expect anyone else to? No wonder Max had left her. No wonder the kids preferred spending time with him.

And where the hell are Flick and Neve? She tapped her fingers against the vanity.

If she weren't looking so dire, she'd drag on some clothes and go downstairs to look for her friends; anything would be better than sitting here feeling sorry for herself.

As she turned toward the toilet and pulled down her pajama pants, a sharp pain shot to her head, stronger and more intense than usual.

What happened next was a blur.

One moment she was lowering herself onto the toilet seat, the next she awoke on the cold tiles—her head aching worse than ever. She reached up to touch her forehead and gasped when she looked at her fingers and saw blood. She scrambled up, pulling herself to her feet with the aid of the toilet, and realized blood wasn't the only liquid on the floor. Her pj's were soaked, and a giveaway smell had her screwing up her nose.

Oh, my God!

Self-loathing washed over her.

She came face-to-face with herself in the mirror and gasped again. If she'd thought her appearance was bad before, now she looked like she'd painted her face for Halloween and sprayed a pungent aroma all over her to make the costume more authentic. In an effort to pull herself together, Emma yanked tissues from the box on the counter and pressed them against the blood seeping out the top of her head. She applied as much pressure as she could stand to try to stop the flow.

Had she tripped on her pajama bottoms and stumbled? It was the only logical possibility.

She pulled back the tissues to check her wound, but the flow of blood hadn't eased up at all. So many times she'd tended to cuts and scrapes on the kids and had instinctively always known what to do, but right now she had nothing.

An ice pack, she thought, after a few moments. That might do the trick and also reduce the chances of her spending the rest of her time in New York wandering around with an egg-size bump on her head. Makeup might be able to hide the gray beneath her eyes, but nothing could hide a mountain with a Harry Potter scar on her forehead. There was no ice in the minibar, but there was an ice machine down the corridor. She could wrap a few cubes in a facecloth. Feeling marginally better, Emma grabbed a few clean tissues to replace the bloodied ones and then, with the heel of her hand pressed against her forehead, she opened the bathroom door.

Thank God her friends weren't back yet.

She removed her wet pajamas and shoved them in a plastic bag to deal with later, then went back into the bathroom to clean herself up and put on fresh clothes. Doing so wasn't easy while keeping one hand pressed against her seeping wound, but somehow she managed. Then, deciding against shoes, she grabbed the ice bucket and located her key card, but the door opened before she got to it.

Flick took one look at her and shrieked. "Oh, my goodness, what have you done?" She marched inside and flung her handbag onto the bed. She stared at Emma's head, her eyes wide in horror at the new tissues already soaked in blood.

"Where've you been? Where's Neve?" Emma asked, feeling a little dizzy again.

"Sit down," Flick instructed, ignoring Emma's question and taking hold of her arm to usher her onto the bed. "What happened?"

Emma swallowed, her throat dry. "I'm not exactly sure. I woke up and went to the toilet. I think I must have tripped on my pj's and hit my head on the edge of the shower."

"Let me have a look." Flick gently drew the tissues away from Emma's head. "Good Lord, you've done a good job." She rushed into the bathroom and returned a moment later with the tissues, whipping out another wad and replacing the bloodied ones.

"Do you think you could go get some ice for me?" Emma asked, trying not to wince at the pain.

Flick raised an eyebrow. "Honey, that needs more than ice. You're going to need stitches."

"No. *Way.*" Emma shook her head, which only aggravated the agony. "I hate hospitals."

"I'm putting my foot down on this one." And before Emma could object further, Flick had picked up the hotel phone. A moment later she was speaking. "It's Felicity Bell from Room 4012. Is there a doctor on call in the building? No, I don't think we can wait that long. Can you make sure there's a taxi, I mean cab, for us downstairs right away and let me know your nearest twenty-four-hour medical facility?"

Ten minutes later, Emma found herself sitting beside Flick in a yellow cab on her way to the hospital. A late-night emergency room in one of the world's busiest cities was not what she'd envisaged for her kid-free vacation.

Could things get any worse?

"Where's Neve?" she finally asked, trying to distract herself from the pain and melancholy thoughts.

Flick shrugged. "I don't know. I haven't heard from her since she left. Do you think we should be worried?"

Emma didn't have the brain space to worry about anything besides her head right now, but she made an effort. "By Neve's standards, it's not that late. Maybe they're talking about Will. James probably has lots of questions for her."

"I suppose you're right. It just feels like so much time has passed since she went to the theater. Do you need more tissues?"

"Yes, please." They did the switch and Emma couldn't help notice Flick seemed out of sorts. "Are you okay? Where were *you*?"

She took a few seconds to reply. "I got bored waiting for Neve, so I went to the bar for a drink. I'll tell you about it later."

Although that sounded inauspicious, Emma didn't press for further information; she needed all her energy to press the tissues against her head. They sat in silence for the rest of the trip—Emma praying that the blood would miraculously stop flowing and they could return to the hotel. But there were no miracles on 114th Street by the time they arrived. Flick worked out the tip for the first time since they'd been in New York. Good thing, because Emma didn't think her brain was capable of math right now.

"Good luck, ladies," said the driver before Flick slammed the back door, and he drove off to search for his next job.

Emma took a step toward the entrance and almost stumbled. Flick reached out to steady her and didn't let go again until they were inside the ER and she'd deposited Emma on a hard plastic chair.

"You wait here. I'll go talk to someone."

Thankful that she had her friend to take care of her, Emma held her head and prayed they wouldn't have to wait hours in this cold, sterile place. For some reason she'd expected something a little more sophisticated in New York, but it appeared hospitals were the same around the world. Beige walls with rows of uncomfortable seats, a smell of disinfectant and, if you were lucky, magazines to read while you waited and a TV hanging in a corner, the volume not high enough to hear.

Having watched plenty of American medical dramas where patients waited for hours on end, Emma couldn't believe it when Flick returned not long after with a tall, beefy guy dressed in navy blue scrubs and wearing a bandana on his head. Tattoos covered his thick neck and he was pushing a wheelchair.

"Blood spurting from the head must be high on the priority scale around here. They're going to assess you right away," Flick informed her.

"You must be Emma," said the giant, not meeting her eyes as he scribbled something down on a clipboard. "Come on through." Without another word, he all but heaved her up and deposited her into the wheelchair.

"I can walk," she objected, but ignoring her, he sped off as if he were in training for a wheelchair-pushing race. She gripped the sides of the chair and the bloodied tissues fell into her lap. "Flick?"

"Your friend can wait out here while we fix you up," boomed the man, who she assumed was some kind of nurse. When she'd thought tall and beefy, she'd been thinking Hagrid rather than Thor. This guy might be able to lift heavy things, but he had little bedside manner and she wasn't sure she'd trust him with a needle and surgical thread either. Where were the hot, sexy medical types she drooled over on the likes of *Grey's Anatomy* and *House*? She hoped Hagrid would soon be handing her over to Dr. McDreamy.

No. Such. Luck.

He wheeled her to a room where a matronly woman almost the size of him waited, her arms folded and a stethoscope around her neck. She gave Emma a curt nod as Hagrid lifted her out of the wheelchair and onto an assessment table. He pushed the wheelchair outside and then stepped back into the room and drew the curtain. Emma gulped as the woman came close and scrutinized her.

"I'm Doctor Chiarelli," the woman said after a few moments of peering at Emma's head like it was a newly discovered insect. "I see you have a nasty head wound. You'll need stitches."

No kidding.

As Dr. Chiarelli began firing questions, the giant nurse, who remained nameless, started to tend Emma's gash. He cleaned it with saline solution and then laid out some scary-looking instruments on a tray.

"How did you injure yourself?" The doctor spoke as if addressing a naughty child who'd fallen and split her head to get attention.

Wanting to get out of there as fast as possible, Emma answered each question as best she could. "I was asleep and I got up to go to the bathroom and must have fallen and knocked my head on the tiled shower edge."

"*Must have?* Did anyone witness this fall?"

"No."

"Do you live in New York?"

Emma shook her head. And then remembered that it hurt. *Ouch!*

Hagrid wasn't impressed either. "Hold still," he grunted.

"I'm here on vacation."

"From Australia." The doctor smiled victoriously for the first time. Did she want Emma to compliment her on cleverly picking the accent?

"Yes."

"On your own?"

"No, I'm here with two friends."

"And neither of them saw your fall?" It sounded like the bloody Spanish Inquisition.

"No. They were out." What did any of this have to do with her need for stitches?

A frown formed on Doctor Chiarelli's face. "Had you been drinking?"

"No."

"Did you bite your tongue?"

"Uh-uh." She shook her head. Although the gash on her head hurt so badly that she may not have noticed a little tongue abrasion.

"Did you lose continence of bladder or bowel?"

Her cheeks heating in humiliation, Emma confessed that, yes, she had lost control of her bladder when she'd fallen.

"I see," said the doctor, her tone ominous. "Do you know how long you were on the floor?"

She wanted to say something sarcastic about not having her egg timer with her, but she didn't think Dr. Chiarelli would find this amusing. She wasn't sure Dr. Chiarelli found anything amusing. "I guess a few seconds."

"You *guess*, but you don't *know*?" The doctor didn't wait for a reply. "Do you have any sore muscles?"

"Only my head, but that's been giving me grief for weeks."

This caused an expression of concern to cross the doctor's face. "You've been having headaches for a while?"

Jeez! Why on earth had she admitted this? But somehow she didn't have the wherewithal to lie. "Yes, a few."

"For how long?"

Emma tried to shrug, but lying down made it difficult to do so. "I don't know. Maybe a couple of months."

"And have you seen anyone? A doctor in Australia?"

"No." Emma prepared herself for the older woman's disapproval.

"I see." These two words sounded prophetic. Emma wanted to ask what exactly *she saw*, but the doctor spoke again before she could.

"I'm going to stitch you up now, and then we'll run some tests."

"Tests?" Emma's heart shot up to her throat. Stitches were bad enough, but she didn't want to be poked and prodded by this terrifying pair. She suddenly felt terribly homesick. Tears pooled in her eyes.

Dr. Chiarelli pursed her lips. "It's merely a precaution to make sure your fall was simply a trip or a faint and not the result of something more worrying, like a seizure."

Seizure? Emma gulped. She didn't remember falling and couldn't say exactly how long she'd been on the floor, but surely she'd have known if she'd convulsed? "What...kind of tests?"

"We'll run some blood tests—" *Eek, needles!* "—and do a full neurological and physical examination and a scan of your head to start with."

Before Emma could ask any further questions—like exactly what a "full neurological and physical examination" entailed— Dr. Chiarelli announced, "Right, let's get these stitches done." She had a gleam in her eyes as if she quite liked this part of her job.

Sadist!

30

Genevieve

Her head resting against his chest, Neve listened to James's heartbeat as he slept, his legs entwined with hers and his arms holding her close. They'd had sex in the kitchen and then in the shower, before moving into his bedroom and doing it all over again. No doubt muscles all over her body would ache tomorrow. Even in her younger years, she couldn't remember doing it more than once in a night. When she and James were together all those years ago, they'd had to steal moments here and there, and he'd always gone home to his wife afterward, so she'd never spent the whole night in his arms.

She had fond recollections of lying in his arms, happy and satiated, as he played with her hair and they talked about everything under the sun. It wasn't just an amazing sexual attraction they'd shared. They were also both passionate about musicals and movies, eating out and hundreds of other little things. Letting him go after making love, watching him as he'd climbed out of her bed and dressed, knowing that he was going home to *her* had broken Neve's heart every single time. So many times she'd told herself she should end it—everyone knew married men never left their wives for their mistresses—but she hadn't been able to do so until she'd found herself pregnant. That had been the catalyst.

The thought of Will intruded on her nostalgia. Reality shattered her postcoital bliss as guilt and self-loathing warred with the joy of reconnecting with the only man she'd ever truly loved. A lump formed in her throat and she blinked back tears. She had lied to the two most important people in her world. What a mess she'd got herself into. Yet although her head was scolding her selfishness, her body had far fewer scruples. Her body loved the feeling of his naked skin against hers and urged her to wake him—to slide down his body and rouse him from slumber by taking him into her mouth.

But no! Four times in one night would be greedy, especially when she'd yet to tell him her real reason for tracking him down. A reason so much bigger than simply wanting to catch up with an old lover. A voice in her head said she should wake him to talk, but there were certain rules and certain things you couldn't do after sex. Breaking up with someone was one; telling the man who'd just given you the best orgasm of your life that he was the father of your seventeen-year-old son was definitely another. At least that was what Neve wanted to believe as she gently extracted herself from a sleeping James and slid out of his bed.

She'd find some paper and leave a note with her phone number saying she needed to tell him something and asking if they could meet again. Next time she wouldn't chicken out.

As if she were a naked burglar, she crept across his bedroom toward the door—her clothes and purse were somewhere in the kitchen, discarded in the act.

The bedside light flashed on as James's sleep-soaked and satisfied voice called to her. "Gennie? Where are you going?"

She closed her eyes, schooling her emotions before she turned around to face him. "Sorry, I was trying not to wake you."

He sat up, the sheet falling down to reveal a chest far too chiseled and sexy for a man of fifty who spent his working days—and nights—indoors. "You mean you were sneaking out like this was a one-night stand you wish never happened?"

"No." She shook her head adamantly. What they'd shared was so magical that even if she should wish it never happened, she couldn't. Whatever happened next, she would always treasure this night together. "Not at all. I…"

But her voice drifted off as he climbed out of bed and crossed the room toward her. Looking at him buck naked, so confident, made her knees weak and her mouth dry.

"Come back to bed. No more hanky-panky. I promise to keep my hands off you, at least until morning, but I'm not ready to say goodbye just yet."

"It is morning," she said, feeling her resolve wavering.

He grinned as he reached out and pulled her to him, his body pressed against hers, his erection jutting into her tummy. "Till first light, then."

Her chest squeezed as the urge to climb back into bed with him almost overwhelmed her, but she had to be strong. How would she ever be able to let go again, to mend her heart, if she didn't put some distance between them?

"As tempting as your offer is, I need to get back to my hotel or my friends will start to worry."

"Call them." He had an answer for everything. His confidence had always been part of his appeal.

But Neve shook her head and palmed her hands against his chest. "They'll both be asleep. I don't want to wake them."

He sighed. "I must be losing my power of persuasion. If I let you go now, will you promise to have dinner with me before you go? I know a fabulous restaurant in Hell's Kitchen and I'm not working Thursday night."

Her stomach flipped. That was four days away. She should

have told him tonight, but doing so in a restaurant seemed far safer than telling him now, when he was trying to seduce her back into bed. "Deal," she said, stretching up to give him the most chaste kiss on the lips she could possibly manage.

He chuckled and slapped her on the bum teasingly. "I'm looking forward to it. Now, let's get you dressed and into a cab."

James helped her locate her clothes, offered to make her a coffee—which she declined—got her number so he could call to arrange their date and then escorted her downstairs to see her safely into a cab. He insisted on waiting with her, and then opened the back door and leaned inside to kiss her good-night. Him being so attentive and gentlemanly didn't make her feel any less conflicted.

"See you soon," he said, his voice full of promise and anticipation.

She swallowed and nodded as he retreated and then shut the door.

"Marriot Marquis Times Square, please," she told the driver as he edged away from the curb.

Neve whipped out her phone to find a number of missed calls and messages from Emma and Flick. She'd forgotten to take the phone off Silent after the theater. She scrolled through the messages quickly. The first few were as she would have predicted: How's it going? Have you told him yet?

But at the last message, her heart iced over.

Emma in the hospital. Call me ASAP.

"Shit!" Neve went to her recent calls and pressed Flick's number, her heart thudding as she waited what seemed like forever for her friend to pick up.

"Thank God," Flick said by way of a greeting. "Where the hell have you been?"

"With James, you know that. I'm in a cab now." She ignored the stab of self-disgust. "What happened to Emma?"

"She fell in the bathroom, split her forehead and needed stitches, but now the doctor is thinking she might've had some kind of seizure. They've moved her to a ward so they can do some tests first thing in the morning."

"Oh. My. God. Did you see her convulsing?"

"No. I told you, they don't know if she had a seizure for sure. I was grabbing a drink at the bar."

"Right." Neve nodded even though Flick couldn't see. "Driver, can you take me to—" She paused, realizing she didn't know what hospital they were in. "Flick, where's the hospital? I'm on my way."

"No, don't worry about it. Emma is settled for the night and I'm heading back to the hotel now myself to get some rest. We'll take her a change of clothes and stuff in the morning. I'll see you back there."

"Okay. Bye." Neve disconnected and closed her eyes as her head flopped back against the seat. If she'd felt guilty before, now she felt even worse. While she'd been having sex she shouldn't have been having in the first place, it sounded like Emma and Flick had been going through hell. They'd come to New York simply to support her, and she hadn't kept her half of the bargain whatsoever.

A beep announced another message on her phone. She glanced down to read it. Thanks for tonight. Can't wait to see you again. J.

Oh, Lord, she thought, if there was one thing she was talented at, it was complicating life.

Neve arrived back at the hotel first and paced the room as she waited for Flick to return. It might have been three o'clock in the morning, but any fatigue had evaporated with the news that her friend wasn't well.

Poor Emma. Nothing ever seemed to go well for her. First there'd been Max's infidelity; then, because he was a lawyer and "knew people," he'd somehow engineered it so that Emma had to buy him out of their mortgage. As this was something she couldn't afford on her part-time wage, she'd had to start working more hours, and without Max doing half the parenting, she'd had more responsibility. Single parenting one child was hard enough, but three… Neve shuddered at the thought. No wonder Emma always looked as if she'd run a marathon on no sleep. And now this. One more thing on her already stress-filled plate. A possible medical condition discovered during what was supposed to be a vacation to help her relax. Neve hoped the doctors were simply being cautious.

She stopped pacing a moment and then stared out the window down over Times Square. As she was wondering if anyone ever really got any sleep in this place, she heard the key card beep and she turned as the door opened. Flick entered, looking as drained as Neve felt but without the afterglow of intimacy that she feared might currently be surrounding her.

"How is she?"

Flick shrugged, sighed and then collapsed onto her bed, kicking off her shoes as she did so. "I don't know any more than I told you on the phone, but I'm worried. Something hasn't been quite right about Emma for a while. She thought she was going through menopause but I don't think that's it."

"Me either." Neve sat on the other bed.

"You've noticed something, too?"

Neve nodded and listed the little things that possibly added up to something big. "Emma seems to have a headache all the time. I've also noticed her limbs jerk every now and then, and she's almost tripped a couple of times when we've been out together. Oh, and I know infidelity is a sore spot for her, but I felt her reaction to my confession about James and Will was a tad over-the-top. She's been moody lately, and that's unlike Emma. Or is that just me being paranoid?"

"I don't know." Flick hugged a pillow to her chest. "Maybe she *did* overreact a little. After all, you had the affair almost twenty years ago. We all did stupid things we regret in our youth."

Neve now wondered if Flick considered marrying Seb one of those stupid things, but didn't think it was the right time to ask.

"So what could be wrong with her?" she said instead. "I wonder if she had an epileptic fit. Pity neither of us were here when it happened. Maybe we'd be able to shed some light."

"Mmm." Flick was quiet a moment, then sat up straight on the bed. "Oh, my God, how was your night anyway? What did James say about Will?"

Neve's throat constricted, her breathing suddenly difficult. For a second she considered lying, but all the secrets and lies in her life were becoming exhausting, and this was Flick, one of her best friends. "I haven't told him yet," she confessed.

Flick's brow furrowed as she stared at Neve a few long moments. "But…you were with him until three a.m.?"

She nodded slowly.

Neve saw the realization dawn in Flick's eyes as her mouth burst open, letting out a little shriek. "You didn't!"

She rushed to explain, "He's not married anymore. He's divorced."

Her heart stilled as she waited for Flick to say something else. But when her mouth remained the perfect O, Neve said, "I know. I'm a horrible, selfish person, not to mention a terrible mother." Her eyes brimmed with tears. "But I couldn't help myself. Seeing James again was like nothing I can explain.

It felt like I'd finally found a part of me I'd lost years ago. And he was so excited to see me. I think I knew the moment he hugged me that, where James is concerned, I'm a lost cause. We went to this bar…ordered drinks…but they'd barely arrived before we were in a cab crawling all over each other."

She shuddered now at the things they'd done with the driver less than a meter in front of them, but it had been like nothing else mattered except her and him.

"Wow," Flick breathed. "How long has he been divorced?"

Neve shrugged. "Awhile." But right now her concerns lay with Emma. "Anyway, now I can add bad friend to my list of faults, because if I'd told James right away, I'd have been back at the hotel when Emma fell. I could have supported you both at the hospital, but—"

"You don't know that. Even if you had told James, he'd have had questions. You may have been out even later answering them."

Neve attempted a smile—it was nice of Flick to try to make her feel better. "You're a good friend. I don't deserve you."

"Don't beat yourself up too much," Flick said. "Do you know what *I* was doing when Emma fell?"

"Getting a drink at the bar."

Flick shook her head and glanced down at the bed. "I was with Jeremy."

The look on her friend's face told Neve that when she said "with Jeremy," she didn't just mean chatting to him over a late-night drink. And Neve's own actions mirrored Flick's shock of a few moments earlier. "Oh, my God, did you—" she lowered her voice "—*sleep* with him?"

"No. Almost, but I stopped myself just in time."

"I wish *I* had stopped myself." *If wishes were fishes, we'd all swim in riches.* Neve's mom had said that a lot when she was a child; she'd never quite understood what it meant. But she knew now that wishing the past hadn't happened was futile.

"Was it that bad?" Flick asked.

Bad? That almost made Neve laugh. "No. It was…" There were no words colossal enough to explain the breathtaking, mind-blowing wonderfulness that was making love with James.

"We're a right pair, aren't we?" Flick said, half laughing, half crying.

Neve nodded, slumping back against the pillows, but rolling over so she could still look at Flick. "Are you going to tell me what happened with Jeremy?"

She groaned and covered her face with her hands. "I don't know really. I was so excited to see him again. We were such good friends in high school, and he's grown into a very good-looking man."

"I'll give you that," Neve said. Not as good-looking as James, but then again, she couldn't think of many men who were.

"I've never even *looked* at another man in my life until last night, but everything I've built over the last twenty years has just crumbled all around me. I'm not sure if I thought sleeping with Jeremy might make me feel better because it would hurt Seb, or because I hoped it would make me realize that there could be life after Seb. That if we do separate, my life won't be over and I may one day find another person I want to get close to."

Neve stayed quiet, waiting for Flick to continue, but when she didn't, she asked, "And how did *almost* going there make you feel?"

"At first it was really good. I haven't kissed anyone with such intensity since… Well, you know, I'm not sure I ever have. It was like we were teenagers, and I could have kissed him for hours, but when he started to take things to the next logical step, my body froze and my heart went cold. I wondered what on earth I was doing in the arms of another man, about to take my clothes off and cross a line I never thought I would. When he slid his hand under my top and cupped my breast, instead of feeling pleasure, I freaked. I yanked myself away from him and all but ran off. The poor man. I thought it would be liberating to have another man's touch, but all I could think of was Seb, and how despite all his years of internal struggle, he's never once cheated on me."

"Perhaps not technically," Neve said. "He may not have cheated on you with another person, but he kept his real self a secret. He could hardly blame you for doing something a little crazy in response. But maybe trying to go the whole way with someone was a little too soon, even if Jeremy wasn't quite a stranger. You need time to mourn the loss of your marriage and the husband you thought you knew before you go looking for something new."

Flick smiled at her. "When did you get so wise?"

She snorted. Being wise was easier when it involved someone else's issues. Before Neve could remind her friend just how unwise and foolish she'd been, Flick's cell phone rang. She sat up and leaned over the edge of the bed to grab it from her bag. "It's Seb. I sent him a message to call me when I was at the hospital."

Unsure whether Flick was happy or anxious about this call, Neve simply nodded.

"Hi." Flick answered the call as she slid out of bed, then headed into the bathroom and shut the door.

If Neve didn't know about the transgender thing, then a call from Seb would be the most normal thing in the world. Of course, Flick would want his comfort and support after such a hellish night, but the way she'd spoken yesterday it sounded as if she and Seb were barely talking right now. As muted conversation drifted through the wall, Neve switched off her bedside lamp, climbed under the covers and tried to get comfortable. It was almost four in the morning, and *bone weary* didn't begin to describe how she felt, but her brain refused to switch off. Worry about Emma and confusion about Flick and Seb, combined with thoughts of James and how much worse her confession would be now that she'd slept with him again, swirled together to make some kind of emotional whirlpool.

By the time she finally fell asleep, the first signs of light were beginning to creep in through the curtains and Flick still hadn't emerged from the bathroom.

31

Felicity

She hadn't cried when she'd fled from Jeremy's room and she hadn't cried in the hospital, but when Flick heard Seb on the other end of the phone line, she had to bite back the tears.

"It's so good to hear your voice," she whispered as she closed the bathroom door behind her. She'd been wanting to talk to him for hours. For over twenty years he'd been the first person she turned to when anything went wrong, and it was hard to break the habit of a lifetime.

"You, too." He puffed out a breath. "What time is it there?"

She glanced at her watch. "Almost four a.m. Thanks for calling me back."

"No worries. Sorry I didn't answer earlier. I was in a meeting." With no mention of their recent issues, Seb got straight to the point. "I got your voice mail. What happened? Is Emma okay? Are *you* okay?"

She leaned back and rested her head against the tiled wall, her eyelids drooping as she went through the events of the evening, leaving out a few key points for obvious reasons.

"God," he said when she'd finished. "Sounds like you're

having an exciting vacation, but not the kind of excitement you were hoping for."

What would he think if she told him about her other excitement that night? Flick continued, "I've been worried about Emma for a while. It's why I paid for her to come to New York with us—"

"*You* paid for her plane ticket?"

"That's beside the point right now. Please, I don't want to fight. Anyway, I looked up reasons for persistent headaches in the cab on the way back to the hotel and there aren't many positive explanations."

"Oh, Flick," Seb groaned. "How many times have I told you not to consult Dr. Google?"

"I know…but you didn't answer the phone. I had to do something. You should read what—"

"Flick, stop! You said they weren't sure what exactly had caused her fall and that the tests were just a precaution."

"Yes, but the doctors must be concerned to run all the tests they're doing."

"You don't know that. I'm sure they'd run tests for any nasty head wound, in case the bump had caused internal damage. Look, it's late there. Try to get some rest and hold off your panic until you have some answers. You won't be any good to Emma if you're exhausted."

"Rest?" Flick sighed—her body might be fatigued, but how could she rest in their lovely hotel room with Emma in the hospital? "I don't think I can."

"Then how about you tell me what you've been up to the last couple of days, before all this drama?"

Unable to think about anything except the debacle with Jeremy, her chest tightened. She didn't know yet whether she wanted to tell Seb about her old friend, so she thought hard to think of something else. Central Park felt like years ago now. "We've done a little shopping. We visited some boutiques on Fifth Ave."

"Ooh, I bet they were fancy." It sounded more like a question than a statement, but she moved on quickly, not wanting to talk to Seb about fashion. "And then we did the tourist thing and took photos from Top of the Rock. I'll post them on Facebook later. We also went to Central Park, which was even more beautiful than I imagined."

They talked some more about New York and then she asked him about home. "How are the kids? We've talked on the phone. Zoe sounds busy with university and wedding stuff but you know what Toby's like—one-word answers if I'm lucky."

Seb chuckled. "They're both great. Zoe had her next dress fitting and looks amazing. I took a couple of photos for you. I'll send them."

"Thanks," she said, wondering if he'd really taken them for her or so he could look back on them later and fawn over the gown. "And is Toby doing all his homework, eating properly, changing his socks daily?"

"Yes. I haven't had to remind him about any of those things so far. Maybe we're doing okay at this parenthood gig."

"Maybe." Although Flick couldn't help but wonder if that would be the assessment once Seb came out of the closet. Was that even the expression when someone came out to the world as transgender?

They talked some more, this time about Seb's work, until he said, "I'm sorry, sweetheart, but I have to go. I promised Toby I'd pick him up from soccer practice."

Flick flinched a little at the endearment, but found herself reluctant to let her husband go. His voice had calmed her in a way nothing else could.

"Okay." She took a deep breath, psyching herself up to disconnect. "I'll call you when I have news about Emma. If it's late your time, I'll send a text."

"Call me whatever time it is," Seb said. "I'm here for you and Emma and Neve, whatever the outcome."

"Thanks." Flick felt her throat closing over and had to disconnect before she broke down. "Talk to you tomorrow."

She went to the toilet and brushed her teeth before heading back into the bedroom. Light was starting to creep in through the curtains but Neve was dead to the world. Flick needed to try to get a little sleep as well or she'd never get through the day ahead. She set her alarm for a few hours' time and then climbed into bed and closed her eyes.

According to the hotel's concierge, they could take the subway to the hospital, but not wanting the stress of having to work out tickets and decipher maps, they grabbed a yellow cab instead.

"I feel like the walking dead," Neve said, dark sunglasses covering her eyes as the two of them settled into the back seat.

"Tell me about it." Flick took a sip of the coffee they'd just bought from Starbucks—when in Rome. Her taste buds hated her but the rest of her body needed caffeine almost as much as it needed sleep.

When her alarm had woken them at nine o'clock, Neve and Flick had moaned and groaned as they'd dragged themselves out of bed, feeling as if they hadn't slept at all. Barely any words had been spoken as they took turns using the bathroom, dressed and then headed downstairs to the hotel restaurant for a quick bite to eat.

"You were on the phone to Seb quite a while," Neve said now as they traversed the streets of Manhattan.

It sounded like an innocent enough comment, but Flick knew it to be anything but. How could she explain that although Seb had detonated a bomb in her life, she couldn't just switch off her feelings for him? She hated *Sofia* right now, but Seb... Her feelings for him were so complicated even *she* didn't understand them.

"I wanted to check how the kids were doing."

"I see," Neve said, her tone suggesting that she didn't buy that excuse for one second. "So that was all you talked about?"

Flick nodded tersely. "Yep, the kids and Emma. Emma is his friend as well and I knew he'd be concerned."

"You don't have to justify your phone calls to me. I just want you to know that I'm here if there's anything you want to talk about."

"Thanks, but I just want to concentrate on Emma. Hopefully we'll be able to break her out and continue with our vacation." That reminded her of the reason they'd come to New York in the first place. "And what are you going to do about James?"

Neve sighed. "I'm going to ask him to meet me in a public place. I'm not going to shower first, I won't wear makeup or brush my hair and I'll put on the ugliest underwear I have. That way he won't be tempted to jump my bones again and even if by some miracle he is, I'll remember what I'm wearing underneath." Flick laughed at her friend's logic. She was highly doubtful that Neve even owned ugly underwear. "Do you want me to come with you this time?"

"Maybe. Let's see what's happening with Emma. She's our priority right now."

Flick couldn't disagree with that. "Do you think we should have taken the subway?" she asked as she glanced at the gridlock of traffic ahead of them. "I would have thought rush hour was over."

"I get the feeling it's always rush hour in New York."

It took a lot longer to get to the hospital than it had when

Flick had taken Emma the night before, and when they finally found their way to the ward, Emma wasn't there.

"You her friends?" asked a dark-skinned nurse with gorgeous curly hair tied back and a bright smile on her face. "She's listed a Felicity Bell and Genevieve Turner as next of kin."

They nodded at this news. "That's us."

"Mrs. McLoughlin is currently having some tests. Maybe go grab yourselves some coffee. Have a snack or something."

"How long will she be?" Neve asked.

The nurse shrugged. "Sorry, I couldn't tell you. All depends on what they find."

"So the sooner she returns the better?" Flick asked.

"I didn't say that." Without another word, the nurse crossed over to the bony-faced old man in the bed next to Emma's.

"She meant it, though," Neve whispered. "What shall we do?"

"I don't want to leave in case she comes back and we're not here."

Neve agreed and sat down on the plastic chair next to Emma's bed. Flick dropped her bag onto the floor and climbed onto the bed. The nurse raised her eyebrows when she went across to the two patients on the other side of the room, but she left soon after without saying a word.

Before long they were both asleep, Neve slumped in the chair with her legs resting up on the bed. They awoke a few hours later to the noise of Emma being wheeled back into the room.

"Sorry." Flick sprang from the bed, wiping her mouth in case of drool as an orderly assisted Emma out of the wheelchair.

"Hey." Emma lifted a hand to wave, but her face was pale and her eyes red. "I'm fine," she snapped at the orderly as she shook herself free from his grasp and then perched on the very edge of the bed. "Whole load of fuss for nothing, I'm sure."

Without a word, the orderly took his wheelchair and left. "Did you manage to get any rest in here last night?" Flick asked.

"Crazily enough, I had the best night's sleep I've had in an age—they have better painkillers here and I slept like a baby." Emma smiled as if some of the drugs might still be in her system, then sighed. "I'm sorry I've ruined your vacation."

Neve snorted, glanced at Flick and then looked back to Emma. "Don't worry. We're doing a good enough job of that on our own. You're not the only one who had an eventful night."

Emma frowned and looked from one of them to the next. "What do you mean?"

Flick twisted a lock of hair around her finger, unsure whether to say anything about the Jeremy debacle. "You go first," she told Neve.

Neve sighed but as she opened her mouth, two men entered. One of them didn't look much older than Toby, but if the stethoscope around his neck was anything to go by, he was a doctor.

"I'm Doctor Radcliffe and this is Doctor Samuels," said the older of the two. He had short blond hair and three-day stubble, where the other man had red hair and looked as if he didn't need to shave yet.

"You guys were quick," Flick said without thinking.

"I had to wait for a while before someone could bring me back," Emma said.

Dr. Samuels smiled at her, but it wasn't a happy smile, more an apologetic, sympathetic smile. Flick held her breath as she waited for him to talk.

"Good afternoon, Mrs. McLoughlin, I presume?" When Emma nodded, he continued, "We have the results of your initial testing. Would you like your friends to stay while we discuss them?"

Flick's stomach went rock hard. Doctors always asked you to bring someone with you when they wanted to deliver bad news. She looked to Neve and they exchanged a worried glance.

"Yes." Emma's voice was barely a whisper but she nodded. "I want them both here."

"Okay," Dr. Samuels said as Flick and Neve positioned themselves on either side of Emma's bed, each taking hold of one of her hands.

32

Emma

Emma knew the moment the doctors entered the room that they weren't there to bring good news. In a hospital as large and busy as this one, if her results had been all clear, they'd probably have let the orderly tell her. She gripped her friends' hands tightly as Dr. Radcliffe closed the cubicle's curtain and they both stepped closer to the bed.

"I see you're on vacation from Australia," Dr. Samuels said, glancing down at his clipboard. "I've always wanted to visit there." He didn't look very old, so he couldn't have wished this for very long, but Emma didn't want to make small talk about places to sightsee right now. When she didn't take his bait, he cleared his throat and continued.

"As you're aware, we ran some tests because we were concerned about why you fell last night. We're fairly certain now that you did have a seizure. You told the ER doctor that you've never had one before, is that correct?"

"Yes. That's right." She nodded impatiently. Did he have to go over everything she already knew?

"I'm sorry to have to tell you but the results of our tests so far have indicated that you have a mass on your brain. This is likely what caused the seizure."

Dr. Samuels may as well have punched Emma in the head, so great was her shock and the ringing in her ears. *No, it can't be true.* Maybe she hadn't heard him correctly. She glanced at Flick and then at Neve—both of them looked close to tears as they clutched her hands tightly. Her skin tingled as if a thousand ants were crawling all over her. Slowly, she turned back to face the solemn-looking men.

"You mean...I have...brain cancer or something?"

Dr. Radcliffe took over. "Initial results show that you have a tumor in your brain, but we won't know whether it's benign or cancerous until we do further testing."

Emma couldn't decide whether to cry or laugh. This had to be some kind of sick joke. Wasn't it bad enough that she was missing the twins' fifteenth birthday? What more did the gods want to throw at her? "What are the chances that this... this mass thing *is* cancerous?"

"There's no point speculating," said Dr. Radcliffe, which Emma felt certain was code for "highly likely but we don't want to stress you any further."

As the possibility she might have a serious illness descended, her bones went numb. She heard words come out of her mouth, but it was like someone else was speaking them. "And if it's benign? What happens, then? You take it out?" Her heart picked up speed. "How long will that take? I have to get back to Australia, back to my kids, my job. My mortgage. My *life*. And any kind of brain surgery is dangerous, right?"

"Shh, Em, it'll be all right, I'm sure."

At Flick's attempt to placate her, she snatched her hands back and clutched them to her chest. "You don't know that. Oh, God, who is going to look after the kids if I die?" The idea of Chanel taking her place...

She shuddered, so full of sudden rage she didn't anticipate the tear that sneaked up on her and trickled down her cheek. She swiped at it. What an utter nightmare!

"We're going to take this one step at a time, Mrs. Mc-Loughlin," said one of the doctors—she'd forgotten which one was which. "I'd like you to have an MRI scan this afternoon. This scan uses a magnetic field and radio waves to take pictures inside your head. From the MRI we should get a clearer picture of the lesion—its size, location and if it is extending into any critical areas—which will in turn help us to determine how we treat it."

"How long will all this take? I told you, I've got to go back to Australia."

"The MRI itself will take about an hour, but the results may be a few days, although I'll try to put a rush on it considering your circumstances," promised the doctor. "We can discharge you once the examination is complete, but we don't recommend you travel home until we know exactly what we are dealing with. Do you have any questions?"

Emma stared blankly at the men. Questions? Oh, she had plenty. *Why me? Was it something I ate as a child? Or something that happened to me? How long has it been up there, invading my body?*

She tried to count back, to remember when she'd started getting the headaches. Surely it couldn't be too long or she'd have seen someone about them before now. Another awful thought struck—if she *had* gone to a doctor right away, could she have prevented this from happening?

Her stomach churned with regret and self-reproach, and she vowed never to ignore a health matter again; that was, if she recovered from this one. And jeez, how long would recovery take? Even if her tumor wasn't malignant, she guessed there'd be brain surgery or some kind of treatment. She'd need to take time off work—time she could ill afford. At the thought of the mortgage, worry entered Emma's head. Back

home in Australia, she had health insurance—something she
always resented paying because they'd never needed it—but
that policy wouldn't cover her here, would it?

She looked to Flick, who'd organized her flight and visa.
"Do we have travel insurance?" How many horror stories had
she heard in the business about clients who decided against
taking out insurance and then had an accident or got sick
when they went away and ended up having to shell out tens
of thousands of dollars? Why hadn't she checked before she'd
blindly followed her friends onto a plane?

"Relax." Flick reached out to take her hand again. "Of
course we do. Patrick was very thorough when I booked our
tickets. He refused to give me your passport number unless I
agreed to full cover for the both of us."

Bless Patrick. He was such a kindhearted, lovely man—why
couldn't she have married someone like him?

"Please don't worry about money right now," Flick said,
bringing Emma back to the issue at hand.

"Okay. I'll try." But worrying about money had become a
habit, and in some ways it was less scary than worrying about
her health.

One of the doctors clapped his hands together. "Right, if
you don't have any further questions, we'll be off. Someone
will be down shortly to take you for the scan, and we'll be in
touch as soon as we get the results. In the meantime, try not
to worry too much, don't overexert yourself but try to enjoy
your vacation." Was this guy a comedian in his spare time?
How was she supposed to relax and have fun, taking happy
snaps of the Statue of Liberty and the Brooklyn Bridge, when
she was possibly giving the big C free rent inside her head?

Cancer—it had taken her mother from her. Was it coming
for her now?

When she just stared blankly at the doctors, they smiled uncomfortably and then retreated. Neither Emma nor either of her friends thanked them for their visit. Medicine, she guessed, could be a fairly thankless job.

The small disinfectant-smelling room, with its beige curtains and uncomfortable bed, remained silent for a few long moments. When Emma couldn't stand the thoughts inside her head anymore, she broke the silence. "Well, sorry about this. Way to ruin a fun girls' trip, hey? Bet you're wishing you didn't drag me along now." There was a lump in her throat that felt the size of a basketball, but she didn't want to fall apart. These were her closest friends in the world, but if she started crying, she wasn't sure she'd be able to stop. She wanted to feel the snuggly embrace of her babies; she wished Caleb and the twins were here, yet also thanked God that they were not.

"Don't be ridiculous," Flick said, bending over to envelop her in her arms. "We don't care about anything but you getting well."

"Yes." Neve wrapped her arms around the two of them. "Is there anything we can get for you before your MRI?"

"No, I'm fine." Ha—what a ridiculous choice of word! Emma maneuvered herself free, and her friends stood awkwardly on either side of the bed, their solemn faces staring down at her. "Seriously, cheer up, you two, I'm not dead yet." But the word *dead* caught in her throat. She had a sudden impulse to grab her phone and google brain tumors. The internet wouldn't pussyfoot like those doctors; the internet would tell her the worst-case scenario. Call her morbid, but that was what she wanted to know.

"Don't make jokes like that." Neve looked shocked, and nothing much shocked Neve.

Emma raised her eyebrows at her. "It's my *mass*—" she made air quotes with her fingers "—which means I can make all the bad-taste jokes that I want."

"Okay." Neve nodded. "Just don't expect me to laugh."

Flick placed a hand on Emma's arm. "Do you want me to tell the kids for you?"

"No! It's the girls' birthday, and bad news is the last thing I want them to hear on their special day. And Caleb is probably finding it hard enough to study with Hawaii as a distraction." She still couldn't believe Max thought it was okay to whisk him away mere months before his final exams. "I don't want to make things even harder for him. You heard the doctors. We won't know what exactly is going on for a few days. I don't want to worry them for no reason. Promise me this is our secret."

Flick and Neve glanced at each other, a look of concern passing between them, but they eventually nodded their heads.

"Fair enough. We promise," Flick said.

"But let us know if there's anything you want us to do," added Neve.

"I do need to wish the girls a happy birthday, though. Can one of you find my phone for me? I think it might be in that cupboard." She nodded toward the small bedside cupboard, and a few moments later Flick handed her the phone.

"I'm just going to pop to the bathroom," Neve said, already turning toward the curtain.

"I'll come with you," Flick added. "Back soon."

As her friends left, Emma found Laura in her recent-calls list. Laura had been born seven and a half minutes before Louise, so she called her first. This was one of many reasons why Emma wanted to be with them; then she could drag them both into a massive hug as she'd done every year before on their birthday—not putting one before the other. She pressed Call before she had the chance to chicken out; not because she didn't want to talk to her daughters, but because she feared hearing their young chirpy voices would unravel her.

Laura answered after a few rings. "Hey, Mom."

Emma suddenly remembered the time difference between Hawaii and New York. "Happy birthday, darling. I hope I didn't wake you."

"No, you didn't. We're at this fabulous café having breakfast and I've got the best pancakes ever. Seriously, you cannot imagine how good they are. Dad and Chanel gave us these diamond key necklaces. From Tiffany's. And they said they've got another surprise for us later. Oh, and thanks so much for the gift certificates—we can't wait to choose some new stuff for our beds. How're things in New York? Hawaii is totes epic. The beaches are amazeballs and you should see our tans…"

Emma tried to smile as she listened to her daughter prattle on. This was how it was with the girls. It was often hard to get them talking these days, but occasionally they forgot their cool, distant act, and once they started talking, she couldn't get a word in. Today she was happy not to have to say much. She couldn't believe Max, splashing out on those expensive necklaces. Wasn't *Hawaii* supposed to be the twins' birthday present? She supposed she should be glad that the kids were having fun with Max and Chanel—if she died, they'd have to live with them full-time.

That thought made her nauseous and she pressed a hand against her stomach.

"Mom? You still there?"

"Sorry." Emma sucked in a quick breath. "I couldn't hear you a moment over the busy New York traffic."

"It doesn't *sound* very busy."

"I've just slipped into a shop. Is Louise near you or should I call her phone?"

"She's here. I'll pass you on. Love ya, Mom."

"Love you, too," Emma whispered as the tears she'd been trying so hard to repress grew stronger.

"Hi, Mom. Thanks for the gift certificates."

"You're welcome, sweetheart." They paled in significance to what *daddy dearest* had given them, but trying to compete with Max was futile. All it achieved was stress, and it had taken an enemy setting up camp inside her head for Emma to realize that. As with her sister, Louise's conversation skills were one-sided and Emma barely had to say a word. She told her about the hot lifeguards on the beach, and described everything they'd eaten so far in minute detail. "I'll just pass you on to Caleb. Oh, and Dad says hi and he hopes you're having a good time in New York. See ya."

She'd gone before Emma had the chance to say goodbye or warn her not to be *too* friendly to those lifeguards.

Caleb didn't sound quite as enthusiastic, but he admitted he was having a good time and making sure to squeeze in an hour of schoolwork each day. Her heart swelled with pride, and she felt satisfied that even if she did have cancer—even if she didn't survive it—Caleb was sensible and independent enough to make good. The twins, she was more concerned about, but then again, what fifteen-year-old girl wasn't obsessed with boys?

She managed to hold back her tears and hopefully sound normal until Caleb had hung up. The phone dropped into her lap as she grabbed some cheap hospital tissues from the bedside table. The thought of not living long enough to see her children grow up tore at her heart much more than her divorce or even the death of her mother ever had. The thought that they might go through hard times and disappointments and she wouldn't be there to comfort and support them made her chest so tight she feared she was having a heart attack.

Of course, that was when Flick and Neve chose to return.

They took one look at her and rushed back to the bed. This time as they wrapped their arms around her, she stopped trying to pretend she was okay and let herself sob on her friends' shoulders until her tears were spent. They didn't say anything—they didn't have to—but their soothing noises and the gentle massage on her back helped immensely.

Finally, Emma blew her nose one more time and said, "Right, I'm tired of talking about this. Let's talk about something else." She looked to Neve, remembering why they were here in New York. "Oh, my God, what happened with James last night? Did he explode?"

Flick snorted, a sudden smile appearing on her face. "Oh, he exploded all right. But not in the way you're thinking."

Neve glared at her. "Not funny."

"What's going on?" Emma asked.

"I don't want to worry you with it."

It was Emma's turn to glare. "*Please*, I need to think about something other than my stupid head."

Neve sighed. "Your head is not stupid, but okay. If you promise not to hate me, I'll tell you."

"Right now the only thing I hate is that I'm in the hospital with a brain tumor or some thingamajig. Everything else pales in comparison."

Neve nodded, but her lips remained pursed a few moments as if she were summoning courage. "I did see James last night but…" As Neve talked, Emma tried to make the appropriate noises in the appropriate places. Under any other circumstances, the news that Neve had slept with James instead of telling him anything would have riled her and she'd have berated Neve for her stupidity and selfishness, but for some reason she couldn't bring herself to worry. The truth was she couldn't concentrate on anything except the uninvited lump inside her head.

Strangely, for the first time in a long while, she didn't have a headache. Whatever they'd drugged her with last night, she hoped they'd give her a doggie bag to take back to the hotel when she was discharged.

"What do you think I should do?" Neve asked.

Well, that much was obvious. "You need to tell James the truth. ASAP. You need to think with your head rather than your hormones, and you need to face the consequences. You're here for Will, remember. He needs to know his father. You never know when something might happen to you."

"You're right. I know." Neve closed her eyes a moment, a flush creeping across her cheeks. "I'll text him now and see if he can meet me again later tonight."

"He'll probably think you're after a repeat of last night," Flick said.

Neve raised an eyebrow at her. "While I message James, why don't you tell Emma about *your* evening?" She met Emma's gaze as she dug her cell phone out of her handbag. "You and I weren't the only ones having an eventful night."

"Oh?" Emma looked to Flick, who scowled and then nodded.

"You know that old friend I met in the bar the other night?"

Before Flick had the chance to elaborate, the curtain peeled back and an orderly stood there grinning at them. She nodded at the wheelchair in her grasp. "Cab for Mrs. McLoughlin."

Emma found herself relieved to have a reason to escape. It wasn't that she wasn't interested in her friend's stories but she was bone tired. She attempted a smile at the cheery woman as she climbed out of bed and into the wheelchair. Surely there were other patients who needed the wheelchair more than she did—people who actually couldn't walk, perhaps?—but less than twenty-four hours in this depressing place and already Emma had learned the futility of trying to argue.

"Thanks," she said as she settled into the chair and then glanced up at her friends. "Back soon, I guess."

They nodded and spoke in unison. "We'll be right here."

33

Felicity

"Where the heck is she getting her energy from?" Flick hissed to Neve as Emma slipped into the bathroom.

"No idea." Neve groaned, taking a sip of the hotel room coffee and not even grimacing. After next to no sleep in the last forty-eight hours, their standards had dropped when it came to caffeine. "But I'm almost looking forward to seeing James again tomorrow. At least I'll have five minutes' reprieve from the sightseeing junkie in there."

Flick only had the energy for a half nod.

When Emma had been discharged the day before after her MRI, the doctors reiterated that she should take it easy over the next few days. The young man had suggested finding a day spa somewhere and enjoying a facial or massage. Neve's expression had brightened at this idea and Flick was willing to get behind *anything* that involved sitting or lying down, but Emma had glared at the poor boy as if he'd suggested naked busking in Times Square.

Flick knew then that making Emma adhere to the doctor's orders wouldn't be easy. Neither of them had dealt with anything like this before. Until yesterday, none of their friends or family had ever been diagnosed with anything potentially life threatening. Emma's brain mass had thrown them for a loop. Even Flick's marriage woes didn't seem as awful anymore. At least she, Seb and the kids had their health.

Emma was the only one who'd been close to terrible illness before—she'd lost her mother to cancer about six years ago—but she refused to talk about that now. From the moment they left the hospital, she'd refused to talk about her fall, the bang on her head or the mass inside it.

"Late lunch, anyone?" had been her precise words. "Hospital food is crap worldwide. I feel like a massive hamburger with loads of greasy fries on the side. And I know just the place. Follow me, ladies."

As Emma had strode toward the taxi line, Neve and Flick had exchanged a look. They knew her well enough to realize that this overly chipper attitude was a mask for the shock, terror and fear that would be taking over inside. Without a word to each other, they decided to follow her lead. If Emma didn't want to talk about it, then neither would they. But they'd be there with tissues and shoulders to lean on if and when she cracked.

By the time they'd got to the sidewalk, Emma was already in a cab chatting to the driver as if they were simply three carefree women on vacation from the day-to-day mundanity of their lives. He drove them to a hamburger joint not far from their hotel that Emma admitted having been to with Max. Normally she steered clear of such places, but she promised them the hamburgers were worth it. And she was right. They'd practically inhaled those burgers. And the fries... Well, they were crisp and golden and everything else you wanted in a fry. Exactly what the doctor ordered.

They'd all but licked their plates clean, and then Neve had tried to steer them back to the hotel for a few hours of R & R, but Emma wouldn't hear of it. Instead, she'd lured them out to Bloomingdale's and shopped like they'd never seen her do before. For someone who usually watched her money carefully, she'd splashed out with Mr. Visa as if she'd just won the lottery. All her purchases were for the kids—everything from tacky tourist T-shirts to expensive sneakers, jewelry and bags. When she'd finally had enough, Flick and Neve could have dropped down on the sidewalk and fallen asleep right there.

Emma had bought so much that they needed to return to the hotel to dump her purchases, and once there, Flick and Neve had tried to get her to rest. Flick wanted to wrap her in blankets or tie her to the bed and force rest upon her, but Emma wasn't having any of it. She'd dragged them to the restaurant at the top of the hotel, ordered the most expensive thing on the menu and then ordered cocktails for them all.

Only after she'd drunk so much that she tried to dance on the tabletop, only when they'd promised to open the expensive bottle of sparkling wine in the minibar, had they finally been able to coerce Emma into heading down to their room. Despite her talk of partying until the sun came up, she'd taken a few steps inside and collapsed facedown on the first bed, giving Flick and Neve their first moment of reprieve since the MRI.

They'd looked at each other, mutual expressions of relief and exhaustion on their faces. Although Flick wanted to discuss Emma's worrying coping mechanisms, she'd been so exhausted she could barely find the energy to take off her shoes or brush her teeth. Instead she'd glanced at Emma lying prostrate on the bed and silently prayed that her friend would live to pay back all the debt she'd made today. Then she'd looked to Neve, whose eyes were glistening. Neve never cried. She got angry, she got scared, she lost her shit occasionally, but in five years of friendship, Flick couldn't remember her once succumbing to tears. There were no words. Instead, they'd solemnly readied themselves for bed on autopilot. Flick had taken her turn on the sofa bed and Neve climbed into the other double, both of them hoping they'd wake up in the morning and find that it had all been an awful nightmare.

After the amount Emma drank, they'd expected her to sleep late and then wake up with a hangover to rival the headaches she'd been having for weeks, but there was no rhyme or reason to miracles. While Neve and Flick would have happily stayed in bed till noon or even later, Emma had peeled back the curtains and woken them with faux cheerfulness, insisting they "Arise, so we don't waste another beautiful day."

Well, Flick and Neve had *risen* and they'd both thrown on some clothes, but Flick wasn't sure she could handle another day of Emma on I'm-scared-I-have-cancer-but-refuse-to-admit-it adrenaline mode. It would almost have been easier if she'd fallen into bed and refused to leave, drowning in vulnerability and fear. At least then they'd have been able to ply her with alcohol and ice cream and commiserate. But this high-energy, pretending-everything-was-okay Emma was exhausting.

The door of the bathroom opened again and she appeared. For one brief moment, Flick thought she saw a glimpse of anxiety, but Emma quickly pasted on a wide grin. She clapped her hands together as if trying to excite a bunch of toddlers. "Come on, ladies. Hurry up."

Flick swallowed a groan and pushed herself up off the chair, wondering if Emma was acting like this because she was trying to keep her mind occupied with something other than her MRI results *or* because she expected the worst and wanted to live life to the fullest while she still could.

"Where are we off to first?" she asked, adopting a similar faux-chirpy tone to the one Emma had been using since the hospital.

"I thought we could walk the Brooklyn Bridge."

Flick looked at Neve. How *long* exactly was the bridge? That *definitely* didn't sound anything like the rest the doctor had ordered, but Emma would probably bite her head off if she mentioned it.

"I'm a little tired after yesterday," Neve admitted, obviously thinking similar thoughts. "Could we do something that doesn't require so much...uh, exercise?"

"You shouldn't have drank so much last night," Emma chastised.

Flick didn't know whether to laugh or not as Neve almost choked on the dregs of her coffee. It was a testament to Emma's current situation that Neve didn't snap, but rather said, "Maybe we can do that tomorrow. Got any other suggestions?"

Emma sighed and rattled off a number of ideas, including a trip to Liberty Island to see the famous monument, an authentic Mexican restaurant, the New York Public Library and the Museum of Sex. Normally Emma would never have considered entering a place like the Museum of Sex.

Flick looked to Neve—they were getting good at speaking with their eyes. Surely a museum wouldn't require too much physical exertion? And she had to admit this one piqued her interest. They could grab some lunch afterward and stretch the eating out as long as possible.

"I'm up for the Museum of Sex," Neve said.

"Me, too." Flick forced a smile. Right now she'd do pretty much anything Emma asked.

They slipped on their shoes, grabbed their bags and headed downstairs via the elevators. As they emerged from the revolving doors that led out of the hotel, Flick saw a man with a laptop bag and a medium-size suitcase waiting in the line for a cab. Her stomach turned, but not in the way it had when she'd first laid eyes on him again the other night.

RACHAEL JOHNS

"Hey, guys." She turned to Neve and Emma. "Can you give me a moment? I want to go say goodbye to Jeremy."

"Is that him?" she heard Emma ask as she walked the short distance to her old friend.

She tapped him on the shoulder and he swung around, eyes widening in surprise. "Flick? Didn't think I'd ever see you again after the other night."

Her cheeks heated as she remembered how she'd fled from his room without any sort of explanation. The poor man probably thought his kissing had turned her off. "You are a very good kisser," she blurted, and then mentally smacked herself upside the head.

"Huh?" His brow furrowed in confusion.

She pressed the heel of her hand on her forehead, wishing she was the type who thought before she spoke. "What I mean is…I'm sorry about running off on you like that." Although they'd still been fully clothed, she'd felt his erection pressing against her, and it wasn't nice to leave a man in such a state. "It was nothing you did. You were lovely and I really enjoyed chatting and catching up with you, but…but I'm not ready for more with anyone else yet. I'm still in love with my husband and, well, we might split up, I don't know, but… I… It wasn't fair to lead you on like that. You have every right to be angry."

Jeremy listened patiently, then nodded and placed his hand reassuringly on her arm. It felt warm, but in the light of day her skin no longer sparked at his touch.

"I understand," he said. "I've been through a separation myself, remember? It's confusing and depressing and we all cope in whatever way we can. I can't lie… I'd have loved to take things further with you the other night, but I'd rather you stopped like you did than regret it later."

"Thank you," she whispered, kind of happy that her brief

moment of insanity happened with someone like Jeremy, not some random guy in a bar who might not have taken her rejection so well.

He dropped his hand to his side and smiled warmly. "It was great seeing you again, Felicity. Look after yourself. If your situation changes and you feel like looking me up when you're ready...I'm on Facebook."

"Thank God for Facebook, hey?" She forced a chuckle.

"Indeed. Good luck." And with that he turned and climbed into the next cab.

Flick waved as the car drove off and then walked back to her friends, who looked to have been watching the interaction with interest.

"He's quite good-looking," Emma conceded. "I can see why you were tempted. Now, Museum of Sex?"

34

Genevieve

"Inhale, exhale," Neve whispered to herself as she followed the directions on her phone's map app to a little café not far from the theater district where she'd arranged to meet James for breakfast. He'd been busy yesterday but had sounded as eager to see her again as she'd professed to being.

Thing was, her eagerness was a big fat lie.

The cement sidewalk beneath her feet may as well have been an ocean the way her stomach lurched right now. Concentrating on her breathing, she placed a hand against her belly. If only there were some kind of pill she could take to eradicate this sensation, this feeling as if she were about to jump off one of the many skyscrapers that surrounded her. She hadn't slept all night, her thoughts alternating between worrying about what to wear for this important rendezvous and rehearsing her speech—not that she had any idea what to actually say. Despite all this, a tiny part of her had been glad to say goodbye to Flick and Emma and escape for a while.

All yesterday Emma had been hell-bent on exploring as much of New York as they possibly could. In theory, Neve agreed with this sentiment—keeping busy to keep their minds off the crap—but they weren't teenagers anymore, and her feet ached from sightseeing all day.

Granted, the Museum of Sex had been eye-opening and they'd learned a number of useless but interesting facts, such as that a duck's penis grew to twenty centimeters long when erect. They'd giggled like schoolgirls at this and professed thankfulness that none of them had been born a duck. Neve hadn't laughed so much in a long time, and Flick and Emma had needed this release as much as she had.

Between the duck's penis, the sepia photographs of carnal acts in the 1800s and the "interactive floor" that was more freaky than entertaining, they'd almost forgotten their worries for a few hours. At least that was how Neve *had* felt. But nothing could put off the inevitable—no matter what alarming secrets Flick divulged or scary illnesses Emma might have, she needed to face her own demons.

Neve took a long, deep breath and pushed open the door of the hip café James had recommended. Aromas of coffee, sugar and cinnamon filled the air as she stepped inside. Usually these smells would be welcome, but she could only think of James and the conversation that must be had. The scariest, most important conversation of her life. And there was Will to think of—if she messed this up, she could ruin her son's biggest dream as well.

The thought of Will was the only thing that made her step farther into the café and scan the tables for James. He wasn't here yet. Her chest tightened and she sucked in another breath.

"Looking for me?" came a voice from behind her, followed by the heat of a warm, hard body against her own. The woody, masculine scent of him annihilated every other smell in the café. Her resolve wavered as he whispered seductively into her ear. "I've been thinking of nothing but you the past couple of days."

Oh, shit, she thought as he spun her around and pulled her against him, planting his lips on hers and kissing her in the way every woman should be kissed every single day. Pleasure flooded her body, her limbs loosening as desire curled inside her. Heedless of their audience, James slid his hands down her back and cupped her buttocks, pressing their bodies closer together so that she'd have to have been dead not to notice how happy he was to see her. Her lips parted, inviting his tongue into her mouth and deepening their kiss. If they'd not been in a public place she had no doubt where this would end.

But no! Will's anxious, eager face appeared in her head. *This cannot happen.* She could not let it happen again.

She slid her hands up onto his chest, tore her mouth from his and pushed firmly against him. Their eyes met, a frown furrowing his brow and confusion in his gaze.

"We need to talk," she whispered.

"O-*kay*." He sounded uncertain. "Shall I order us coffee?"

She nodded. "Thanks, that would be great. I'll grab a table."

As James spoke to a waitress at the counter, Neve slid into a booth, her knees knocking together as she did so. When he returned, his smile was no longer as wide as it had been when he'd first arrived. He hesitated a moment, as if deciding whether to sit beside her in the booth or across from her. She breathed a sigh of relief when he chose to sit opposite.

"So," he said, planting his elbows on the table and looking at her as if they were the strangers they'd been for years. "You lied about not being married? Is that it?"

She shook her head—how ironic that would have been. "No, of course not."

Although I have lied. But was lying by omission technically lying? Feeling as if she might faint or vomit or have a heart attack—possibly all three—she glanced toward the door, counting the tables between herself and the exit, much like the flight attendants told you to do on an airplane. *In the event of an emergency...*

"What do you want to talk about, then?" he asked, and she'd almost have preferred to be in a plane crash than tell him.

"Our son," she blurted.

The color drained from his face, his stance grew rigid and his eyes bulged.

Neve froze—so much for running—and cursed herself for her appalling delivery of this news. But then again, was there *any* good way to tell a man he had a teenage son? It was a little late to show him the positive pregnancy test.

The silence dragged until finally James shook his head. "I'm sorry, did you just say *our son*?"

She nodded. "Yes. He's seventeen. His name's Will. Well, William—William James actually—but everyone calls him Will. It suits him. He's tall and good-looking, the girls all think he's adorable. He's doing really well at school—he's almost finished—although he's unsure what he wants to do next year. He's a rower and plays soccer and tennis as well, but rowing is his absolute passion. I've never been sporty so he must get that from you."

James's mouth hung open. He looked at her as if she were speaking a foreign language, but she couldn't seem to shut up.

"He's kind of got a girlfriend. Stacey. She's a sweetie, but you know boys at that age, I think sports and food rank higher on his priority list. His favorite subjects are math and science but he did media studies for a few years and loved the whole film-and-TV angle. I guess—"

"Stop. Just stop!" James held up his hand, glaring at her.

She shut her mouth, her heart hammering as she waited for him to say something. She watched as color climbed up his neck and painted his face a terrifying shade of red. His eyes narrowed and tiny beads of sweat pooled on his forehead.

She'd never seen him look so furious and guessed that meant he wouldn't be jumping her bones again anytime soon. Why the heck had she wasted time worrying about what to wear? James wasn't thinking about her clothes after the bolt from the blue she'd just thrown him.

Finally, he broke the silence. "Are you fucking kidding me? Is this some kind of sick joke? It's not April bloody Fools' Day, is it?"

Although he didn't shout, the curse words that punctuated his speech and his barely clipped tone gave away his fury.

"I'm not kidding," she breathed. "I'm sorry."

He leaned toward her, his height suddenly more threatening than appealing. "You're sorry? You're *fucking* sorry? You waltz back into my life, tell me I have a son who is practically an adult and this is the first I've ever heard of him, and you're *sorry*?"

As James's voice rose, Neve flinched, her heart rate accelerating even more and tears prickling in her eyes. But she refused to cry. She deserved whatever he threw at her and she didn't want him to think she was trying to manipulate him with tears.

"I know it's not enough, but…what more can I say?"

"Are you sure he's mine?"

She nodded. There'd never been any question of that—James had owned her heart and soul as well as her body. Back then, no other guy stood a chance.

Sadly, nothing much had changed.

"So that's why you disappeared? Why didn't you tell me? What's happened to suddenly make you come clean? Is he… Is Will sick? Do you need money?"

James fired questions at her like gunshots but every time she tried to answer, he barreled over the top of her with more. A waitress arrived at their table and put down their coffees. She glanced from Neve to James and then crept backward as if they were savage beasts. All other eyes in the café were glued on them, but James appeared oblivious.

"And what the hell was the other night about? You came to tell me about our son and instead you—" He stopped abruptly and glared at her as if she was dog shit on his best Italian shoes.

"That was—" She started to say that sleeping with him wasn't intentional, but he stood and shook his head as if he couldn't bear to look at her, couldn't even bear to breathe the same air. For a second she thought maybe he might hit her, but instead he slid from the booth and stormed out of the café, the door slamming shut behind him.

Of course he wouldn't get physical. She was the villain in this story, not him.

Silence surrounded her as strangers stared, expressions of repulsion on their faces. They'd heard everything. The awful secret she hadn't even shared with her closest friends until recently would now be the subject of gossip over the photocopier in offices all over New York. The two steaming mugs of coffee sat untouched on the table in front of her. All she wanted to do was stand and flee, but her legs wouldn't cooperate.

And then the door opened and James stormed right back in and sat himself down opposite her again. Her mouth opened in shock and she blinked back the tears that were so close she could taste them.

"Do you have a photo of our boy?"

Shock paralyzed her for a few moments, then she swallowed and nodded, digging her cell phone out of her bag. She opened her photos app and handed him the phone. "Aside from a few work photos of clients, they're mostly of Will. A lot are from his grade-twelve prom, which was only a few weeks ago. He usually looks a lot more casual."

Without a word he took the phone and started swiping. She

watched—fascinated, guilt struck and heartsick—as he took long moments over each photo. The expressions on James's face changed frequently—sometimes he smiled, other times he frowned—but when a tear slid down his cheek, she felt like the cruelest, most despicable woman on the planet. Eighteen years ago she'd been so certain leaving was the right thing to do. Now she was even more certain that it was not.

"Do you have any of when he was little? When he was a baby, a toddler, first day at school, that kind of thing?" James's voice swam with emotion and she cursed her stupidity and lack of forethought.

"I'm sorry, I didn't think to bring any, but I can scan some when I get home and email them to you."

"I can never forgive you for this," he said after another long silence.

She nodded, expecting nothing less. How could he forgive her when she now knew she'd never be able to forgive herself? This knowledge didn't stop her heart shattering.

"So what now?"

Neve blinked. "What do you mean?"

He hissed out a breath. "What made you suddenly decide to tell me? Does Will know about me? Because I sure as hell want to meet him as soon as possible."

She nodded, grateful at least that Will's dream would be fulfilled. "He wants to meet you. He's always known about you…"

"But?" he asked, when her voice drifted off.

Her stomach twisted. "But he believes you never wanted anything to do with him."

Fury flashed in James's steel blue eyes. He slammed his fist against the table, sloshing the now-cold coffee over the rims of the mugs. "You really are a piece of work, Gennie. You not only stole a son I would have loved and looked after, but you told him I didn't want him? And to think, two days ago, I thought I was falling in love with you again."

Neve winced. The tiny joy and hope his last words brought was short-lived. She'd suspected for years that she'd never stopped loving him, and having him sitting in front of her now, staring at her with such utter revulsion, only confirmed her fears. She'd been nothing but a coward running away all those years ago, and now she was going to pay the price. The man she loved—the man she'd *always* loved—could hardly bear to look at her.

Nothing could excuse what she'd done, so she sat there numbly, mute, prepared to take whatever he gave.

James ran a hand through his permanently mussed-up hair. He opened his mouth and then closed it again as if he, too, couldn't find the words to express his feelings. He sighed an angry breath and relaxed his fists only slightly on the table.

Finally he spoke. "I'm finding this hard to digest. I need to think it all through and work out when I can get to Australia. I need to tell my girls they have a little brother. I need…" He shook his head and changed tack. "You'll have to tell Will the truth as soon as you get home."

"Tell him?" Almost hyperventilating at the thought, she could barely get the words out. Of course that was the next step, but she'd never allowed herself to think that far ahead. Finding James, seeing him again, had been enough to deal with, but the terror of that paled in comparison to telling Will the truth.

James nodded, determination in his stare. "Yes. Because if you don't, I will. I won't have *my son* thinking his father didn't want him."

Even in the face of James's wrath, her heart swelled at the way he said *my son*. He may only have seen photos but she could tell he already loved Will with everything he had. Why had she ever doubted this would be the case? His marriage may have been on the rocks years ago, but she'd never heard anything but love and pride in his voice when he'd spoken about his daughters. The tears she'd been wrestling to keep inside sprang to the surface, spurted from her eyes and she started to ugly cry. The harder she tried to stop, the more the tears came. She swiped at her eyes and saw black streaks across her fingers. Mascara. What a sight she must be.

She hated herself. For crying. For not being able to stop. For making terrible decisions. For the way James was looking at her now with pity, hatred and disgust.

He shoved the napkin holder toward her. "When do you fly home?"

"Saturday morning," she managed as she reached out and took one.

He nodded once. "I'll be in touch before then."

And this time when he stood and marched out of the café, he didn't come back.

35

Emma

Emma sat on the edge of the sofa bed, flicking through the channels on the hotel TV. The United States might have more choices than Australia but she still couldn't find anything she wanted to watch. Being confined in their room gave her too much time to think, which was why she'd insisted on spending as much time as possible out exploring New York. Flick and Neve kept trying to make her *talk* about her situation, but she'd become an expert at dodging their questions and redirecting the conversation. Although keeping up her positive act exhausted her, she couldn't deal with discussing the news of her brain mass just yet. And talking about her fears wouldn't change the outcome.

In her heart of hearts she knew she had cancer, and she just wanted to enjoy the few last days before the diagnosis crashed into her life and changed everything. Watching her mother get sicker and sicker until she'd become little more than a shell of the woman she'd once been had broken Emma's heart and crushed her spirit. She'd seen the horror of chemotherapy and radiation treatment and the pain her mom suffered in the end, and couldn't bear to think that would be her future. And her children's future. While she was an adult when her mom had been dying, her own kids were still teenagers. They didn't deserve to go through any of this.

She glanced over at Flick, who was reading on her iPad, and sighed loudly, wondering when Neve would return. For a few moments her mind drifted from the one thing that had occupied it for the last forty-eight hours to Neve's meeting with James. How would he react? She hoped for Will's sake he would be able to get over Neve's deception and that he'd want to meet his son. Picking up her cell phone, she was about to shoot her friend a quick message of encouragement when the door of their room burst open.

Neve marched in looking as if she'd been mugged in a thunderstorm. Her cheeks were red, blotchy and streaked with mascara. Emma had never seen her with so much as a hair out of place or a smudge of lipstick on her face. The evidence suggested that James's reaction had been bad.

Without a word, Neve stalked across to the minibar, took out a tiny bottle of bourbon, unscrewed the lid and poured the whole lot down her throat. Emma glanced at Flick and raised her eyebrows.

"I guess things didn't go well, then," Flick said, putting her iPad down on the bedside table. She'd never been the type to mince words. "Do you want to talk about it?"

In reply, Neve opened a tiny bottle of vodka, unscrewed the lid and took a gulp of that as well.

"Can I get you some Coke with that?" Emma asked, concerned about the effect of drinking straight alcohol so quickly. The last thing they needed was Neve ending up in ER as well.

Their questions went unanswered. Instead Neve walked the few steps to the armchair by the window and collapsed into it.

Emma's phone rang. She glanced down at the unknown

American number on the screen and her concerns for Neve evaporated as her heart froze. "I think it's the hospital."

Flick and Neve both sat forward. "Answer it," they said in unison.

Emma's hand shook and her stomach turned as she slid her finger across the screen, then lifted the phone to her ear. "Hello?" While her friends stared at her expectantly, a woman on the other end of the line announced herself as Dr. Radcliffe's secretary, asking if Emma could come to the hospital today for the results of her MRI.

"He can't tell me over the phone?" She didn't want to go back to that place, but even as she asked, she knew the answer. Doctors didn't tell folks they were dying over the telephone.

"I'm afraid that's against hospital policy. Can you come in this afternoon?"

Emma nodded and then realized the woman couldn't see her. "Yes," she whispered. "What time?"

"Can you get here by one?"

Emma glanced at the time on her watch. It was 11:00 a.m. "Yep. That should be fine."

Somehow she took in the woman's directions to Dr. Radcliffe's offices and then disconnected the phone. "I've got a one-o'clock appointment with the doctor," she told her friends, and then rushed into the bathroom to throw up. The comfort food she'd eaten that morning while waiting for Neve spurted into the toilet bowl, and she wished stress turned her off food instead of onto it.

Shadows appeared in the doorway, but neither Flick nor Neve said anything.

Finally, when Emma didn't think she had anything left to expel from her body, she straightened and then washed her face in the sink.

"Can I get you a drink?" Neve asked, holding up her half-empty bottle of vodka.

"Of water," Flick said, glaring at Neve.

"You can be such a spoilsport sometimes, Flick. For crying out loud, our lives are crumbling around our feet. If there's ever been a good time to drink, it's right now." Neve took another swig of the bottle as if to prove her point.

"No." Emma shook her head and gestured for them to step out of the bathroom. "I'm fine. Well, probably I'm not fine, but unless vodka is the new cure for cancer, I'll pass."

Flick frowned. "You don't know you have cancer."

"Don't tell me you haven't googled brain tumors in the last two days."

Her friends looked sheepish. Just as Emma had suspected. She couldn't blame them; she'd killed time in the hospital reading articles about transgender husbands, of which there were plenty. Neve was right—their lives were a shambles. Someone could write a book about them.

The others sighed as if they could read her mind, and that made her laugh.

"What?" they asked.

Emma walked out and sat down on the sofa bed, Flick and Neve following behind. "Nothing. Now, before we were rudely interrupted by that phone call—" she shuddered at the memory and looked to Neve "—I do believe Flick and I were about to interrogate you about James. What happened?"

Neve grimaced, but Emma knew she'd talk. No one refused a woman with a possible cancer diagnosis in her imminent future. "He exploded again, but not in the way he did last time."

"So you told him?" Flick asked.

"I did." Neve took another nip of vodka—at least she was slowing down. "He was speechless for a while and then got really angry. It was awful. I've never felt so utterly dejected in my life. And there were so many people watching, not that I care about any of them. All I care about is Will and James— one already hates me and the other soon will."

Emma reached for the tissue box and passed it over. "Thanks." Neve sniffed as she pulled one out.

"I'm sure James will calm down eventually," Flick said. "And Will might be angry when he finds out, but maybe he doesn't have to know the whole truth."

Neve shook her head. "James made it clear he wants me to tell Will that I've lied to them both all these years." She paused and blew her nose. "I'm so scared I'm going to lose him. Everything I've done, every breath I've taken the past seventeen years has been because of him. I don't know what I'll do if…"

She couldn't finish her sentence. Instead she buried her face in the tissue, her whole body shuddering as she sobbed.

Emma looked to Flick. She shrugged back; obviously no clue either. Then she nodded toward the minibar and mouthed, "More booze?"

"I'm sorry." Neve stopped sniveling for a moment and looked to Emma. "Here I am blubbering about something I've brought upon myself, when you have a terrifying health issue to deal with. I promise I'll pull myself together before we have to go to the hospital."

"You guys don't have to come. And my stomach quivers less when I'm focused on something else, so talk all you like about James and Will."

"For one," Neve said, "we are coming. That's non-negotiable." Flick nodded.

"And two, I don't want to talk about James or Will. Whoever said that talking about stuff helped was wrong."

"So wrong," Emma agreed.

Neve sniffed again and wiped her eyes. The soggy tissue

in her hand turned black. "Oh, Lord, what a mess I am." She paused then looked to Emma. "If you don't want to talk about your...*thing*, and I don't want to think about James, that only leaves..."

They both looked to Flick.

"Oh, no!" She shook her head and waved her hands at them. "I don't want to talk about Seb and my marriage either."

Neve almost smiled. "I was going to suggest you fill us in on Zoe's latest wedding plans. I think we could all do with a little happy distraction right now. Don't you think?"

"Yes," Emma said. But as Flick started talking about an email she got from Zoe that morning about what flowers to choose for her bouquet, she couldn't help thinking that she might not be around to see Louise or Laura walk down the aisle. Everything came back to her stupid head. But blasted cancer had robbed her of a mother and her children of a grandmother. She was not going to let it take anything else from her family.

Whatever Dr. Radcliffe told her today, she would fight it.

"Do you want us to come help you choose a mother-of-the-bride outfit when we get back?"

Neve's question drew Emma back into the conversation. "You don't want to leave it too late. And you'd better show Beau's mom your choice. It would be a calamity if you both turned up in the same dress."

"A calamity," Flick said, her face straight, "would be if me and *Seb* turned up in the same dress."

Neve burst out laughing and Emma joined her, the buzz of giggling with her girlfriends sending a flood of endorphins through her body. Even if their lives *were* falling apart, at least they had each other to laugh and cry with.

With that thought, Emma glanced again at her watch. "I guess it's time we got going." She didn't need to say where.

Neve sprang from her seat. "Let me just fix my face. I'll be two minutes, max. Promise."

While Neve reapplied her makeup, the others put on their shoes and once again Emma found herself in a yellow cab on her way to the hospital. When Flick and Neve had sprung a surprise trip to New York on her, this was the last place she'd imagined visiting. But hospitals were something she'd better get used to.

As if they'd sensed her thoughts, she felt Flick's and Neve's hands close around hers and smiled gratefully. Talking might be overrated, but having friends like these two definitely was not.

"Good afternoon, ladies," Dr. Radcliffe greeted Emma and the others as they entered his office. The walls were lined with certificates of his qualifications and diagrams of body parts. "Please take a seat."

As Emma sat on one of the three chairs across from his desk, she studied his facial expression and the tone of his voice. Were they positive or negative? Did he sound kind and gentle because he was about to deliver the worst news of her life? Or was that his usual style? She couldn't remember how he'd acted the other day and neither could she breathe as she waited for him to speak again.

"Thanks for coming in, Mrs. McLoughlin. I imagine the last two days have felt like forever."

She smiled tightly.

"I'll cut to the chase. We have the results of your MRI. It confirmed that you do have a tumor, but I'm pleased to tell you that we believe it is benign."

Emma heard the release of air as each of her friends sighed in relief, yet also detected an unsaid *but* in Doctor Radcliffe's words. *Believe* wasn't enough for her to break out the champagne. She held her breath, waiting for his next sentence.

He clicked a few buttons on his computer and then angled the screen for her to see. A black-and-gray image appeared. She guessed it was her brain, but it could just have easily been a photograph of a head of broccoli for all she could interpret it. He pointed at an area of the image that was much brighter than the rest. "The MRI together with the CT scan has provided a good indication of the size and location of your mass. As I said, this information *indicates* the tumor is benign, but we won't know for certain until a biopsy is conducted."

"A biopsy?" Emma swallowed, her legs shaking even though she was sitting down. "Does that mean you have to stick a needle into my brain?"

Dr. Radcliffe ignored the question. "However, obviously things are complicated because you're away from home. If you were a US resident I would recommend we do the biopsy right away and work out a treatment plan, but due to the location of your tumor and the fact it isn't impinging on any important structures, I've been speaking to a specialist in Western Australia. We are both comfortable with you going home for the next stage of assessment and treatment. I won't lie. There are risks of flying with a brain tumor, such as an increase in intracranial pressure. I'll go through these properly with you in a moment so you can make an informed decision about whether or not to stay on in New York or go home as soon as possible."

"If it is benign like you think, will I still need to have it out? What are the risks? Could I still...*die*?"

Dr. Radcliffe folded his hands together on the desk and sighed. "Until we've done a biopsy and confirmed the type of tumor you have, I cannot give you an informed prognosis. Brain surgery is risky business—it might be that we simply monitor the tumor, but because you experienced a seizure, it's more than likely that we would go ahead and operate."

Emma blinked. He hadn't answered her question about death.

"Look," he continued, "I understand this is a lot to take in, especially when you're in a foreign country, so let's go through the risks and I'll help you make an informed decision about whether you want to travel home for the biopsy or stay here."

"Okay." Emma nodded and struggled to regulate her breathing as he listed the pros and cons of staying versus going.

In the end, neither option sounded appealing. It felt like a choice between running into a burning building or leaping off a cliff.

36

Felicity

"Seb?" It was early morning in Australia when Flick escaped the hotel room and found a quiet spot on the conference-floor level to call home.

"Hello, sweetheart. How are you?" He sounded drowsy but happy to hear her voice.

"We got the results of Emma's MRI. They're fairly certain her tumor is benign, but that still brings with it a whole load of complications and danger. She'll probably have to have brain surgery." In the cab on the way back to the hotel, Flick and Neve had forced Emma to focus on all the good news Dr. Radcliffe had given them, not allowing her to think negatively. But alone, all Flick could think about were the risks of surgery: bleeding, blood clots, strokes, comas, infection and all sorts of possible problems with speech, memory, coordination and other things. "Worst-case scenario, she could die."

"Fuck." At his heartfelt exclamation, Flick lost the battle she'd been waging to hold on to her composure while in Emma's company. She cried for her friend, the last person in the world who deserved more crap in her life. And she cried for herself

and Emma's children at the possibility of losing her. Seb joined her in tears and neither of them spoke for a full minute.

When the sobs finally began to subside, he asked, "Does that mean you guys are staying longer in New York? Do you want me to fly over there?"

She loved that he assumed if Emma needed to stay, Flick would stay as well. She loved that he'd support her in that decision and put aside everything to be with them.

"No, thank God." Although she'd been eager to escape her life, now she couldn't wait to get home and hug Seb and the kids. "The doctor here has given her permission to travel and is transferring her care over to a neurosurgeon in Perth."

"I can't believe this is happening."

"You and me both. It's certainly put a lot of things in perspective for me. We are so lucky to have our health, but we can't take anything, any day or anyone in our lives for granted."

The last forty-eight hours—trying to remain optimistic and strong for Emma—had clarified a lot of things for Flick. As had Neve talking about James and Will meaning more to her than anything. Flick understood that because Seb, Zoe, Toby, and now Beau, were her world. She didn't want to even try to imagine her life without any of them in it.

"No. Never."

"We've moved our flights forward to tomorrow," she told him. "We called Emma's boss, and even though it was the middle of the night, he organized everything for us." She gave Seb their flight details and the time they were due to land at Perth airport.

"I can't wait to see you," he said, his tone uncertain.

"I know," she breathed. "And I can't wait to see you. I'll need to be there for Emma over the next few weeks, months, but I know we need to talk, too. I was shocked when I found out about your wish to transition, and I'm not sure I reacted as I should have."

"You reacted better than I imagined, to be honest," Seb said. "I never meant for you to find out the way you did. I just didn't know how to tell you."

"That's in the past now. I want to discuss the future, *our* future, and I want to know everything about how you feel and what you want to do."

There was silence on the other end of the line, and after a few moments Flick wondered if they'd been disconnected. "Seb? Are you still there?"

"Yes." His voice was choked with emotion. *"Thank you."*

"I'm not making any promises yet. I haven't made any decisions, but I'm ready to talk."

"That's all I ask," Seb said. "How's Emma taking all of this?"

Flick sighed. "It's hard to tell. She's not one to speak openly about her feelings. Since Max betrayed her trust, she keeps a lot to herself, but here and there she lets things slip and I know she's worried about finances and the kids. About what will happen if she needs to be off work for an extended period and how Caleb and the twins will cope while she's in the hospital or if…" She couldn't bring herself to finish the sentence.

"Divorced or not," Seb said matter-of-factly, "Max will have to step up to the plate. They're his kids, too, and if he loves them, he'll make sure their mom is financially okay and they're looked after. And we'll be there for her as well."

They spoke for another few minutes and then Seb apologized about having to get up and ready for work.

"That's okay. I should get back so Neve can call James."

"Who's James?" Seb asked, and Flick remembered just how little they'd been talking when she decided to go to New York. Although she'd told Seb earlier about Neve's dilemma, she'd never told him that was the reason behind going to New York. As far as he and the kids were concerned, Flick and Emma were accompanying Neve on a work trip.

"It's a long story, but I promise to fill you in on everything when I get back home. Have a good day."

"You, too. Love you. Travel safe."

Flick tried to say "Love you, too" but the words caught in her throat.

37

Genevieve

Neve's fingers barely even shook as she dialed James's number from a couch downstairs in the hotel lobby. She'd been more nervous sitting in the doctor's office with Emma waiting for her diagnosis. Funny how tragedy had a way of making you see things more clearly. That and the fact that she was too tired to get overly worked up.

He answered after a few rings. "I told you I needed time to think and that *I'd* call *you* before you left."

"I know," she replied to his accusing tone, "but my situation has changed and I'm paying you the courtesy of telling you I'm going back to Australia tomorrow morning. So, if you want to meet again in person, it will have to be tonight."

"Courtesy?" James snorted. "Didn't think you knew the meaning of the word. You never paid me the *courtesy* of telling me about our son when you were pregnant with him eighteen *years* ago."

She closed her eyes and took a breath. Maybe she deserved his wrath, but he was the one who'd been married when they were sleeping together. He'd always made it clear where she stood—that as much as he cared for her, he wouldn't leave his wife and two daughters.

And after the day she'd had, she wasn't in the mood to put up with his self-righteousness. "Whatever, James. If you want to talk before I fly home, it'll have to be tonight."

"I'm at the theater tonight."

"Oh, well, guess we'll chat once I've spoken to Will, then." Ignoring the dread that welled in her stomach and relieved she wouldn't have to face James again today, Neve was about to disconnect when he spoke again.

"Hold your horses. I think it'll be easier to speak in person. There's a few things I want to discuss before I meet Will. Where are you?"

Neve swallowed. "At our hotel."

"I'll call in some favors at work and be there as soon as I can."

This time he disconnected before she had the chance to say anything. "Well." She looked at the phone in her hand. "It was lovely to speak to you, too, James. I'll await your arrival with eagerness and anticipation."

Another guest walked past and saw her talking to herself, but she rolled her eyes, starting to care less and less about what other people thought of her. When one of the two people in the world she truly loved hated her and the other soon would, what did it matter what anyone else believed? Emotionally exhausted, she sat there a few minutes unable to move, then just as she was heading back to the room, James rang.

She sucked in a breath as she answered him. "Yes."

"I'm on my way to your hotel. Meet me in the bar." It was a directive, not a request, and again he disconnected before she could reply. Her jaw tightened and her eyes narrowed as she shoved the phone into her handbag and stalked in the direction of the bar. How dare James treat her with such contempt!

She may have made a mistake in her life—okay, a fairly major one—but that didn't erase all the good things she'd done, and she wasn't going to let him make her feel any more worthless than she already did.

He wasn't in the bar when she arrived, so she positioned herself to one side of the entrance where he wouldn't immediately see her and stood back to watch. Call it petty, but he could wait for her rather than the other way around. He strode in a few minutes later, looking smoking hot in designer jeans and wearing a black business shirt pushed up to his elbows. His dark blond hair looked perfectly ruffled, as if he'd run a hand through it only a few moments earlier.

Neve caught her breath and placed a hand against her chest to try to calm the erratic beating of her heart. Good thing James couldn't see the irrational way her body reacted whenever she saw him. He didn't need that kind of advantage.

It was hard to believe only a few nights ago they'd been tearing up his sheets together and now they were meeting as hostile adversaries. How things could change.

James glanced at his watch and then looked around the bar, scanning for her. She jumped behind a pillar just in time and waited another few moments—telling her hormones they had no place in the conversation about to be had. Finally she came out of hiding and walked across to where James was now tapping his fingers on the tabletop.

She smiled in a manner that wasn't friendly at all. "Evening."

He looked up and then raked his gaze down over her body. No matter what he thought of her, he couldn't hide the appreciation that flared in his eyes. Neve threw him a look that told him he'd been caught. He scowled and gestured to the seat opposite him.

Neither of them suggested buying drinks. This wasn't a social conversation.

"Lost your voice?" she asked coolly as she pulled out the seat and sat. Probably not a good idea to rile him any further, but she wanted to make it clear where they stood. Sparks might fly whenever they were together and he might be the father of her son, but that didn't mean she would put up with him calling all the shots. James cleared his throat and shifted in his seat. She smiled at the knowledge that sitting in such close proximity was physically difficult for him. Or perhaps *hard* would be the more accurate term. He might not like her, but his body didn't much care for his opinions.

"Why are you leaving so soon?" he asked when he'd repositioned himself.

"Something's come up and my friends need to go home. I see no reason to hang around here without them."

He nodded and then got straight to the point. "I spoke to my boss today and I've arranged for some time off in a couple of weeks. I'll fly to Perth and spend a few days getting to know Will, if he's agreeable, and then I'll return again after *Mamma Mia!* closes and bring the girls for a visit."

"You've already told your daughters?" Hell, she'd only told *him* that morning.

"Of course. My kids are my life, and I don't keep secrets from them."

It was an obvious dig at her but she didn't take the bait; concern for Will overrode all else.

"What did they say?" She couldn't imagine anyone would be overjoyed to hear their father had cheated on their mother and had a secret baby, but if they took it out on Will...

"My daughters are no concern of yours. It's a good thing you're going home earlier—the sooner you'll be able to tell our son the truth the better. Will's almost an adult. Once you've told him, we won't have to have anything else to do with each other."

This morning when he'd said *son* it had sounded sweet; now it sounded almost threatening. A chill lifted the hairs on the back of her neck and she felt her resolve to be strong slipping. Thank God Will *was* nearly an adult and could make his own decisions. If he were younger, James could launch a custody battle and attempt to take him away from her. This had been one of her fears all those years ago, that somehow James and his wife would take her baby. In the end, it would be her word against his if he chose to play it that way. But if push came to shove, she was certain Will would choose her.

Neve tried to keep her voice steady as she stood. "In that case, I don't think we have anything further to say until I have told Will." She didn't know how much longer she could hold herself together. And the last person she wanted to fall apart in front of was him. "I'll be in touch."

"Don't take too long," he said, his tone threatening again.

Neve narrowed her eyes at him. "Don't push me, James. I'll call you when I'm well and ready."

Before he could argue, she turned and marched away. With her heels click-clacking against the floor, she held her chin high and her shoulders back, but inside her heart was quaking and she was *this close* to falling apart.

38

Emma

The flight home from a vacation was always worse than the trip there, and as Emma sat between her two best friends, a somber note drifted between them. In between trying to sleep, they all attempted to watch movies and read the cheap paperbacks they'd bought at JFK, but Emma didn't get past chapter one and she couldn't even recall the names of the films she'd started to watch but abandoned before the end of the first scene. On the way to New York, the three women had been like excited kids—even Neve, full of nerves about seeing James, had been looking forward to other parts of the vacation—but none of them had much to look forward to now.

Emma had an appointment with her neurosurgeon on Monday, Neve had an awful secret to deliver to Will, and Flick had serious decisions to make about her marriage. This vacation would definitely go down in history as Emma's worst ever—she only hoped it wouldn't be her last. Dammit, every thought came back to the tumor. Although the idea of brain surgery terrified her, in some ways she hoped her new doctor would suggest they go ahead with it as soon as possible. She hated the thought of this uninvited thing growing inside her head. Yes, there were risks—she shuddered just thinking about them—but letting the tumor stay and simply monitoring it didn't appeal to her either.

As long as it was there, it was like a storm cloud looming above her.

In keeping with their moods, Perth put on a lightning and thunderstorm as the plane came in to land, and the two babies on board wailed their disapproval. Emma almost joined them and, judging by the expressions on Flick's and Neve's faces, they wanted to as well. The three of them grabbed their carry-ons and filed out of the plane, looking and feeling like they'd been on a three-month trek in some remote corner of the globe. They shuffled through customs and emerged into the arrivals hall to see a hundred or so cheery faces staring back at them.

Emma wasn't surprised to see Seb waiting with Toby and Will, but she hadn't expected to see Patrick there with the welcome party. Was he a mirage? A very tall and sexy mirage at that. She blinked, shocked by the pleasant jolt brought on by seeing him.

How could she feel such carnal awareness at a time like this? And about Patrick of all people? The gods must be laughing. "Did you tell him?" she asked her friends, but they had already rushed ahead. It dawned on her that he'd have been the one to arrange their sudden change of flights and that they must have given him some kind of explanation. As Neve and Will embraced and Flick went to hug Toby and Seb, Patrick came toward Emma.

He stopped in front of her and brushed his lips against hers in a perfectly respectable greeting. "Hello, Emma."

Her cheek tingled and the shivers that shot through her body were anything but respectable. Heat rushed to her cheeks as she imagined how horrified he'd be if he knew the thoughts going through her mind. "Hi," she managed to say as he reached out to take her suitcase. "What are you doing here?"

His smile only made her temperature climb higher. "I guessed you'd be tired from your flight and that Neve and Flick would want to spend time with their families. Knowing yours was still away, I didn't want you to be alone if you didn't want to be. I've come to drive you home."

"Thank you" was all she could think of to say. Although he hadn't mentioned the big T, his reference to her not being alone made it clear Flick had told him everything. She didn't actually mind—he would need to know sooner rather than later anyway because of work. "That's very thoughtful of you and way beyond the requirements of a good boss, but I could have caught a cab."

He raised a thick, dark eyebrow. "A few days in the States and already you're using their lingo."

She bit her lip, her cheeks flaring again. There was something in the way he said these words that felt like flirting, but of course she knew how crazy that was. "I'm so sorry about the time I'm going to have to take off work."

"Shh," he whispered, lifting a finger to his lips but keeping his intense gaze on hers. "I don't want you to worry about any of that. All I want is for you to concentrate on getting better. That's all that matters."

Emma's heart sank. She didn't want Patrick to think of her as an invalid, someone who needed to be looked after. Truth was, however ridiculous it might be, she wanted him to look at her the way Max looked at Chanel. Not that she'd ever admit *that* to anyone.

"So I guess Flick told you, then?" Emma glanced sideways at her friend, lost in conversation with her two men. Despite Flick's revelation in New York, she couldn't wrap her head around thinking of Seb as anything but male. Not yet anyway.

"She gave me the basics." Patrick paused a moment. "I'm so sorry, Emma."

Her eyes prickled and her throat closed over. She shook her head and held up a finger, begging him not to look at her that way. She didn't want to cry in front of him. She didn't want to cry here. She didn't want to cry at all, because then she would have to admit weakness and the thing inside her head would win.

He nodded as if he understood, and then Flick turned to them and leaned over to peck Patrick on the cheek. "So nice to see you again. It's a lovely surprise. And thank you for all your help."

He shrugged a shoulder, and Emma swore his cheeks darkened a little. "Emma's a very important employee and I have a vested interest in making sure she gets home safely."

Flick smiled her approval at him, then spoke to Emma. "Do you want me to come back to your place? Seb can take my things home and I can stay with you tonight if you want."

"No." Emma loved Flick and Neve but she needed some time alone. Not that she could blame her friends for being overprotective; if one of them got gravely ill, she'd do everything she could to look after them as well. "I'll be fine. A good shower, a quick bite to eat and I think I'll crash the moment I hit the pillow."

"Me, too." Neve, her arm still wrapped tightly around Will, nodded. "Nothing like your own bed."

"Okay then, if you're sure." Flick still sounded a little hesitant.

Patrick stepped closer to Emma. "She'll be fine. I'll look after her. I promise."

While Emma wanted to argue that she could look after herself, thank you very much, she couldn't deny the rush that came with his words. Then a thought struck—did her weird feelings of attraction toward Patrick coincide with the beginning of her headaches? She'd read that brain tumors could affect a person's thinking. Without a doubt she hadn't been entirely herself for months—snapping at friends, colleagues and family for the slightest thing.

And now experiencing inappropriate feelings for her boss.

While she silently pondered this thought, the others exchanged goodbyes and promises to catch up the next day. Once again Emma found herself being embraced by Flick and then Neve—they'd hugged more in the last week than they had in five years of friendship.

Patrick had parked at the opposite end of the parking lot to Seb, so Emma bid her friends goodbye and then walked beside him out into the cool Perth evening.

"Last time I go on an unplanned vacation," she said, trying to make small talk.

He chuckled. "When Flick came to me with her proposition, I hoped you'd have a relaxing and fun time away. I've been worried about you lately."

"You have?" She slowed to look at him and he nodded. "I'm sorry if my work hasn't been up to snuff, I didn't—"

"Emma." His deep voice interrupted her as he reached sideways and took her hand in his. He caught her by surprise and her breath caught in her throat.

"Stop apologizing. You've never given any less than a hundred and ten percent at work. I was worried about *you*, not your work or the business. You haven't been yourself." He gave her hand a little squeeze, then dropped it again and crossed to the ticket machine.

While Patrick paid with his credit card, Emma glanced down at her hand, expecting to see evidence of the zap she'd felt at his touch. How long had it been since a man had held her hand? Such a simple thing that Max had stopped doing long before they'd separated. She curled her fingers around her palm, hoping to hold on to the feeling.

"Right, let's go," Patrick said, stepping back and smiling at her to follow him.

"Who have you got closing up the agency?" she asked, trying to distract herself from his touch as they arrived at his slick black sedan.

"Jenny and Mandy can handle it."

He beeped open his Audi. The trunk rose automatically and he lifted her suitcase into it. Then he ushered her around to the passenger door and held it open as she climbed inside. As the door shut and Patrick strode around to the driver's side, Emma clicked on her seat belt and took a deep breath, inhaling the clean leather scent of his relatively new car mixed with something sweet.

Patrick climbed into the car, and the moment he turned the key in the ignition, one of her favorite songs drifted out of the stereo.

"You like Kings of Leon as well?" she asked.

"Who doesn't like them?"

A smile crept onto her face as she relaxed back into the comfy leather seat. The first genuine smile since the meeting with Dr. Radcliffe.

Patrick drove out of the airport, his fingers tapping along to the beat on the steering wheel. Comfortable silence hung between them until they got onto the highway that would take them to her place, then Patrick turned down the music and spoke.

"I want you to know, Emma, I consider you a friend as well as a colleague."

The word *friend* had never sounded so appealing, and her smile grew. "Thank you. I feel the same."

"I'm not sure if you want to talk about your illness," he

continued, "but I want to be here for you *whatever* you need. Please don't worry about the security of your job or money. I'm going to pay you sick leave however long you're off work, and your position will be open for you whenever you want to return."

"You don't have to do that."

"I know I don't. But I want to. *Please*, Emma, let me look after you."

Again, she had that urge to argue that she didn't need looking after, but two little voices in her head niggled at her. One, sick pay would be a lifeline; she wouldn't be able to pay the mortgage or feed the kids without it. Two, if looking after her meant spending more time alone like this, she wasn't going to object. A woman with a tumor in her head needed some joy in her life, didn't she? If she didn't have long to live, what would it matter if her stupid little crush never led anywhere?

"Thank you," she said finally. "I'm not sure yet how long I'll need off or if I'll be able to work part-time for some of it, but I'm seeing a doctor on Monday, so hopefully I'll have more of an idea then."

"It's okay. Do you need someone to come with you on Monday? I'd be happy to."

"That's very kind, but I promised Flick and Neve they could." She half laughed. "They need to feel useful."

"I understand. But if you ever need anything, company or otherwise, you know my number."

This time she smiled her thanks.

"Does it hurt?" Patrick asked as they stopped at a traffic light.

She rubbed her lips together. "It's like a constant migraine, but without the nausea. At least now I know I'm not becoming a painkiller addict for no reason."

He didn't laugh. "How long have you been having the headaches?"

"I think a few months, but I'm not exactly sure. I just thought it was stress, trying to juggle the kids and work and everything."

"Have you told your children?"

"No. They're still with my ex in Hawaii. They get home in a few days." She sighed. "I'm not sure what or when I should tell them. Caleb has his final exams in a few months. I don't want him worrying about me on top of that."

"I might not have children, but if my mom had something serious like a tumor, I'd want to know about it. Flick mentioned it was benign? Surely that will reassure them."

"In the case of brain tumors, *benign* doesn't always mean *not dangerous*. There are huge risks with surgery. The neurosurgeon might even recommend leaving it in there and waiting to see if it gets worse."

"But if you do have surgery, you'll need to be in the hospital for a while, I imagine. The kids will know something is up then."

"Dammit, you're right." She bunched her fingers into fists. "See. This thing in my head is affecting my thinking. I've thought of nothing else except how to cope with this, but that never even crossed my mind. They'll have to stay with Max, I suppose." She didn't like that idea any more than Chanel would.

"Hey, it'll be all right," he said as he turned into her driveway. "Just take it one day at a time. I shouldn't have mentioned the kids. Here I am trying to help and I'm making it worse."

"No. You're not. I'm glad you're here. And I don't mind talking about this." In New York, she hadn't wanted to even utter the word *tumor* out loud, but something about Patrick made it easier for her to discuss. "Would you like to come inside for a drink?"

"Only if you're not too tired."

"Well, I am, but I won't be able to switch off right away anyway."

"In that case, I'd love to."

Emma opened the passenger door, and by the time she'd climbed out, Patrick was already at the trunk lifting out her suitcase. She dug her house keys out of her bag and started up the path with him following closely behind.

He'd never been to her house before and when she opened the door and welcomed him inside, she silently praised God she'd scrubbed it from top to bottom in anticipation of Max coming to get the kids. It even still smelled of her favorite vanilla cleaning spray, but it was hard to believe that day was only a week ago—so much had happened since then, it felt like a lifetime.

She dumped her keys on the hallway table and gestured to the floor beside it. "You can leave my suitcase there. Can I get you a drink?"

"How about that shower you mentioned first?"

"What?" Emma swallowed as her thoughts took a nose-dive toward the gutter—contemplating what it would be like showering *with* him.

The expression on her face must have given this away, for Patrick's eyes widened and he rushed to set her straight. "Oh. No! I didn't mean with…*me*. Just you said you needed a shower, food and bed, and I thought while you freshen up, I could make you something to eat."

"Of course you didn't. Sorry. Jet lag messing with my head." She felt so stupid. "Anyway, that's a good idea. I'll go freshen up. You make yourself at home."

"Okay. You take your time and I'll see what I can whip up."

Emma scurried toward her bedroom, mortified that she'd imagined he wanted to shower with her. Problem was, once an image of him naked entered her head, she didn't know how she was going to erase it. Only when she'd stripped and stepped into the shower did the thought of what Patrick may find in her kitchen eradicate the thought of him sans clothes. Or rather, what he would *not* find. Knowing the kids would be away for a week, she hadn't bothered to stock up her fridge or cupboards.

Her head started to throb again, so she washed and dressed quickly—choosing flannelette pajamas, a reminder to herself that Patrick wasn't here to be impressed. Then she popped two strong, supposedly fast-working painkillers and went to join him in her kitchen.

"Nice pj's," he said, glancing down at her outfit.

She raised an eyebrow and he grinned. "I didn't find much to work with, so I've planned a gourmet meal of Vegemite on toast and hot chocolate. Would you like to dine at the table or would you prefer the couch?" He spoke in a faux formal tone as if he was a waiter in some posh restaurant listing the expensive wine choices.

Relaxing a little, she laughed. "The couch wins every time. I hope you're feeding yourself as well."

"I didn't want to presume, but if you're offering, I'd love to join you."

"Please do. You have the very important task of keeping me awake long enough to eat."

He saluted her and then turned to the toaster. "I'll do my best."

Emma went into the living room, picked up the remote, switched on the TV and flopped down onto the couch, curling her feet up beside her. She'd never been happier to be home. And strangely, despite the misunderstanding when they'd first come inside, it didn't feel weird sitting in one room while her boss cooked toast for her in another. Perhaps that was a perk of having a brain tumor—you learned to embrace the unexpected.

A few minutes later Patrick joined her, carrying two plates of Vegemite toast and two steaming mugs of delicious-smelling hot chocolate on an old floral tray of her mother's.

"I haven't used that thing in years," she said as he placed it down on the coffee table.

"I hope you don't mind me digging it out."

"Not at all. It was my mom's. I love it, but the kids generally inhale whatever food is in the house as soon as it gets as far as a plate. Never mind a tray."

"I can imagine. My mom was always grumbling about my hollow legs when I was growing up."

Emma smiled and then gestured to the couch beside her. "Sit," she instructed.

He hesitated a moment and then did as he was told. She got another whiff of that sweet-smelling scent that had been in his car.

"Vanilla," she shrieked.

"Huh?"

"Your aftershave has vanilla undertones."

"Is that a bad thing?"

"No." She resisted the urge to lean in closer and inhale. "I love vanilla."

He seemed pleased by this confession, and they smiled at each other for a few long moments. Yes, this week would go down as one of the strangest in her life thus far.

"Eat up," he said, picking up one of the plates and handing it to her.

"Thanks." She took the plate, picked up a piece of toast and took a bite. "There really is nothing better than Vegemite on toast when you're not feeling great," she said when she'd finished the mouthful.

"Do you have another headache?"

"I always have a headache. At least now I know why."

He smiled sadly. "Anything I can do to help?"

She shook her head as she chewed another bite. Patrick may be sweeter than a lot of men she knew, but whatever his sexual orientation, he was still male, and men liked to fix things.

Emma attempted to distract him. "You can change the channel if you like."

"You don't want to give me control of the remote. You'll get whiplash. I've been told I have a bad habit of channel-hopping."

"Really? Who told you such a thing?"

He blushed again. "An old girlfriend."

Emma almost choked on her last mouthful. She coughed hard, tears springing to her eyes as she tried to dislodge the bit of toast stuck in her throat. Patrick rushed to her assistance, patting her on the back and then dashing off to fetch a glass of water. When he returned, she'd almost recovered, and she took a sip, a deep breath, and then looked sheepishly at him.

He raised one eyebrow. "What? Did you think I'd never had a girlfriend?" He sounded half amused, half horrified.

"Well, I…" The words tripped on her tongue. What could she say? That from the moment she'd started working at Donoghue's her fellow employees had led her to believe he was gay? That his good dress sense, his thoughtfulness and the fact that he worked in travel and annually sponsored a float at the Perth Pridefest had only reinforced this belief?

Patrick's lips quirked and his eyes widened—she saw the moment realization dawned. "Shit. You think I bat for the other team?"

She swallowed, her cheeks so hot she thought she must look

like a baboon's bum. Her embarrassment at believing such a cliché overrode the joy she felt upon discovering that perhaps he wasn't what she'd always assumed. "It's not that I... It's just... Well, you..."

He interrupted. "I'm not gay, Emma."

And the way he looked at her, the deepness of his words, the way he said her *name*, as if it was the most precious name in the world, sent shivers rolling through her.

Their gazes locked, and she found she couldn't look away, despite feeling all kinds of foolish. What else in her world would be turned upside down? Because right now it felt like nothing, no one, was as she'd imagined.

"You know, Patrick," she said, trying to sound normal when she felt like leaping off the couch and doing a celebratory jig around the living room. *He's not gay. He's not gay. He's not gay!* "You know all about my crazy kids and my ex's sordid affair, but I know very little about your past or your family. Why is that?"

He shrugged and leaned back into the couch. "There isn't much to tell. What do you want to know?"

"Everything." She put down her plate, lifted the mug and curled her fingers around the warmth. "Who is Patrick Donoghue when he's not working?"

"I don't want to bore you to sleep."

She tossed him a look similar to what she gave the twins when they were trying to get out of telling her something. "You won't. I'm interested. Besides, you'll keep my mind off... other things." It might not be fair to use her tumor to manipulate him into sharing, but if it helped him open up, she didn't care. She wanted to know more, and she wasn't going to waste this opportunity.

Fatigue ate at her insides, but she didn't want him to go home.

Not yet.

"Well, I was born on the fifteenth of January, 1968, in a little hospital in County Cork," he offered in a storytelling voice. Emma smiled and sat back to listen, taking a sip of hot chocolate. "My mom and dad were good Catholics and I was their eleventh child."

Hot chocolate spluttered most ungraciously from her mouth as she almost choked at his words. "Eleven?" She grabbed a tissue from the side table next to the couch and wiped her chin.

"Yes. Do you want the birth dates and names for all of them as well?" he asked, his expression poker-faced.

She punched him playfully on the arm. "Do you have any younger brothers and sisters?"

He shook his head. "My parents stopped when they finally got the perfect child."

Emma laughed and he continued, jumping forward to his early twenties and telling her about how he almost married a woman he met while traveling in the United States. "I'd always wanted to travel—we could never afford to when I was a kid—and I thought I'd found a like mind in Gemma. I couldn't wait to get married and start a family. We got engaged but she never turned up to the church."

"Oh, my God. Deserted at the altar. What a witch." She wanted to track down this Gemma woman and kill her. Her visceral reaction shocked her—she'd never considered violence before. The sooner she got this lump out of her head the better.

Patrick shrugged. "It was a long time ago now. It hurt like hell when it happened, but she didn't love me, so I guess in hindsight she did me a favor. There's not much to tell after that. I kept traveling, came to Western Australia and started working for a travel company." He paused. "Are you sure I'm not boring you?"

"No. Go on." She finished her drink as he talked, and although she was hanging on his every word, eventually tiredness overcame her. Patrick sharing about himself helped her focus on something else aside from the elephant in her head. It relaxed her, and somehow she ended up stretching out on the couch, her legs resting on his knees. It felt like the most natural thing in the world.

She must have drifted off, because the last thing she remembered was him telling her about his annual trip back to Ireland to visit his parents and the next thing, she felt a blanket being placed gently on top of her. Was this what being looked after felt like? All warm and snuggly. The thought of getting up and walking the short distance to her bed didn't appeal to her. She was about to open her eyes and thank Patrick for the evening when the air shifted above her and he leaned down and kissed her on the forehead.

Her heart stilled, along with every other part of her body. "Good night, sweetheart," he whispered, obviously thinking her to be zonked out. And then he stepped back and quietly left the room. A few moments later, Emma heard him turn the latch in her front door so that it locked when he pulled it shut.

She opened her eyes and touched a finger to her forehead. His kiss had sent a fresh burst of energy pulsing through her. If Patrick had kissed her like this before, she'd have assumed it was a platonic peck between good friends, but this evening had changed everything. And although this filled her heart with joy, her illness cast a shadow.

Even if she was lucky enough to find that Patrick had feelings for her, would it be fair to get close to him when her future was so uncertain? She'd felt his pain as he told her about his broken heart, and she didn't want to be the person to break it all over again.

But as she drifted back to sleep, she couldn't help replaying his kiss over and over again.

39

Genevieve

"It's so good to be home," Neve said as she and Will waved Flick, Seb and Toby down the road.

He dragged her suitcase two steps ahead of her as they headed toward the house. "You can say that again. Another few days with Nan and I'd have lost it."

"I thought you loved your grandmother."

"I do. In small doses." Will stopped at the front door and dug his key out of his pocket, so like the man of the house. "Was she such a slave driver when you were at school?"

"What do you mean?" Neve asked as they stepped inside.

"She wouldn't let me use my phone until I'd finished *all* my homework, and you know how much the teachers give us in grade twelve. Nan took it off me as soon as I got home every afternoon and put it in the cookie tin up on that shelf that she thinks I can't reach."

Neve smiled, reminiscing. "You never used to be able to."

"Whatever." Will looked down at her and rolled his eyes. "I'm glad you're home, Mom, and not just because of Nan. I ordered pizza for us—should be here any minute. I didn't want you to have to cook on your first night back."

Neve hadn't been planning to cook, but he didn't need to know that. She understood her mom fussing over Will. He'd grown up so fast, and they sometimes forgot he was almost an adult, legally at least; everyone knew boys didn't begin to mature until they were thirty. Possibly why she'd always had a thing for older men. Not only were they more her mental age, but they also had added experience in *other* areas.

"Thanks, hon," she said, toeing off her shoes. "That's very thoughtful of you."

He beamed, and that little boy who had craved the approval of others shone through. Her heart almost burst with love for him.

"What?" he asked, looking at her like she'd lost the plot.

"Nothing." She blinked back tears. "I missed you, that's all."

Discomfort crossed Will's face. "You're not going to get all sappy on me, are you?"

She laughed. "I was considering it, but—"

The doorbell rang before she could finish her sentence.

"Saved by the pizza." Will stepped past her and opened the door again, paid the delivery guy, took the two boxes and then stepped back inside, kicking the door shut behind him.

The house filled with the aroma of take-out pizza.

Neve rarely ate such unhealthy food, but tonight she couldn't wait to bite into a slice of Will's favorite, meat lover's supreme. She followed him into their tiny kitchen and he slapped the boxes down on the countertop, then grabbed a couple of plates, a jug of water from the fridge and two mismatched glasses. They didn't do formal dining at home. Will's homework was usually scattered over their dining table so they mostly ate at the breakfast bar or in front of the TV.

"How come you guys came home early?" Will asked, biting into a slice of pizza even before he sat on a stool.

Neve hesitated a moment—she couldn't tell him the truth

because Emma hadn't told her kids yet. Why hadn't they come up with a story? "Umm…well…my job finished earlier than they thought it would."

Will screwed up his beautiful face. "Why didn't you stay and shop? See a few plays on Broadway?" He shared her passion for the theater; he just didn't know he'd inherited it from *both* his parents.

"We shopped up big the first couple of days and didn't have any money left, but we saw *Mamma Mia!*" A knot formed in her stomach. "And then we got homesick."

He shook his head as if she was crazy and shoved the rest of his slice of pizza into his mouth.

"Tell me about your week," Neve said, picking up a slice. "How's Stacey?"

He shrugged. "Nan wouldn't let me see her—said I'm too young for girlfriends—and she had my phone most of the time."

"Poor baby." Neve reached over and ruffled his hair. It was slightly too long, just like his dad's. The knot in her stomach tightened as a little voice in her head reminded her James would be here in just over a week. She put her pizza down without taking a bite.

Will nodded toward her plate. "Aren't you hungry?"

She was ravenous but didn't think she could eat. "Not really," she lied.

Neve wanted to enjoy this moment with Will, but she couldn't enjoy anything with the dread of telling him about James hanging over her. And sleep would also be impossible until the deed was done.

She poured herself some water and took a sip, wishing it was wine. A dose of Dutch courage was exactly what the doctor ordered. "Sweetheart," she began, "you know how you want to meet your father?"

Will, previously more focused on devouring the pizza, stopped chewing and offered her his full attention. "Yeah?" He nodded expectantly.

"Well, the truth is…he was the real reason I went to New York."

There was a second's silence, then Will's angry shout echoed around the room. "What? You told me you were going for work! You lied to me."

If he sounded angry at this little falsehood, she could only imagine his rage when she told him what else she'd lied about. Her stomach rolled around inside her, but there was no point putting off the inevitable.

"I wanted to talk to James first, let him know you wanted to meet him." She swallowed. "Let him know you existed."

Her words lingered in the air for a few moments, and then Will shook his head. Part of her had been hoping he wouldn't register that last bit, but he ran a hand through his hair and glared at her. "What the hell? What do you mean, *let him know I existed*? Did he think you had an abortion or something?"

"No." The words came out barely more than a whisper. "Truth is, darling, as you know, I met your father when we were working in the theater in Melbourne. He was a director and I worked behind the scenes on makeup. We met one night at a cast party and hit it off immediately. Problem was your father was married."

"Married?" Will exclaimed, grimacing as if he'd never heard of the concept. "You fucked a married man?"

Neve flinched at his language. He'd sworn before—all teenage boys dropped the occasional F-bomb—but he'd never directed such curses at her. "Yes, but—"

"What did Nan think of that?" he asked before she could try to justify herself.

"I didn't tell her. I was young and ashamed of the relationship, but I loved your father. I couldn't help myself. Then, when I got pregnant, I was terrified about the ramifications of him already having a family. I didn't want to put James in the position of having to choose us over his wife and daughters, so I...*wrongly* decided that it would be better for everyone if I came home to Perth. I didn't tell him I was leaving and I didn't tell him why. I didn't tell anyone. The first Nan and Pop heard the truth was a few weeks ago, and the first James heard about you was a few days ago when I tracked him down in New York."

He stared at her a few moments, dumbfounded and furious. She wanted to say something else, to try to justify her actions, but she didn't know what or how. "What did Dad say when you told him?" Will asked eventually.

Her grip tightened on her water glass as an image of James's face when he'd learned about his son flashed into her head. "He said he wanted to meet you. He was angry," she confessed, her eyes watering. "At me, not at you. He wanted to see photos of you and to know everything about you. I'm sorry, Will, I'm so sorry."

"You're *sorry*?" He stood, his stool crashing onto the floor in his haste. He didn't pause to right it. "I can't believe you did that to us. What about those times I had to do a stupid family tree at school and you pretended you barely knew anything about my dad? I can't believe you went all the way to *New York* and met him without me. I thought you loved me."

He shook his head, looking at her with an expression of revulsion and shock.

"I *do* love you!" She tried to reach out for him but he shrugged her off. "Whether it was the right or wrong decision, I did what I did for you. I didn't think James would leave his wife, and I wanted to protect you from being his dirty secret."

"So instead you made me yours," Will spit.

"No!"

"Whatever you made yourself believe, your reasons sucked."

And with that eloquent declaration, he stormed out of the kitchen.

"Will!" Neve called, knowing her cry would be ignored. He needed time. Time to cool down. Time to digest the information she'd just given him. Lately life seemed to be one difficult conversation after another. She let her head fall into her hands as she listened for the slam of his bedroom door, but instead she heard the sound of keys being lifted from the hook in the hallway and the front door open and slam.

Her eyes widened as her head snapped up, confirmation of her worst fears coming moments later when her car started in the driveway. By the time she'd hurried down the hallway and flung open the front door, Will and her car had already disappeared into the night. Terror shot through her as she heard him screech around the corner.

This was *so* much worse than James's fury.

Will was a good, usually sensible driver, but he was still on his learner's permit, so it was illegal for him to be on the road without another licensed driver in the car. Her breathing quickened and she pressed her hand against her chest as she worried about whether he might do something to harm himself. Should she call the police?

Yeah, that would go down real well, Neve.

But Will already hated her, and she'd rather have him hate her than kill himself in a car accident.

"Oh, shit!" She kicked her foot against the doorjamb, forgetting she'd taken off her shoes. Pain rushed to her big toe and she hobbled back into the kitchen, swearing and cursing and biting back tears. Ignoring the throbbing pain in her foot, she plucked the cordless receiver off the wall but found she couldn't bring herself to dial the cops. If she reported her car stolen by a minor, they might launch a pursuit, and she didn't want Will to be another high-speed car-chase death statistic.

Instead, after a few desperate silent pleas to a God she wasn't sure she believed in and a few moments of deliberation, she called Stacey.

"Hi, Neve," she answered after a few rings. "How was New York?"

Stuff New York—she wished she'd never heard of the goddamn place. "Stacey, Will and I have just had a…a disagreement. I told him something upsetting and he didn't take it very well. He's taken my car and I think he might turn up at your place. If he does, can you please message me and let me know he's safe?"

"He's taken your car? Holy shit, what did you tell him?"

"I'm sure he'll let you know when he's ready, but please message me if he turns up."

"Okay. Of course."

"Thank you." Neve disconnected before Stacey could ask anything else. Next she called Flick's house, but no one answered. Flick didn't answer her cell either, so she tried Toby's.

"Toby?" she said desperately when he answered.

"Mrs. Turner? Is that you?" He sounded uncertain; while she had his number in case of an emergency, she didn't think she'd ever used it. She told him exactly what she'd told Stacey and made him promise to let her know if he heard from Will. Being a guy, he didn't ask questions like Stacey had, and for that she was grateful. She disconnected and slumped back against the kitchen counter, trying to think if there were any other friends he might go to.

Caleb was still in Hawaii, so he was out.

Dammit, she'd never felt so helpless in her life.

40

Felicity

"Wow, thanks, Mom!"

Flick smiled as Zoe stared down at the Tiffany's box holding two beautiful white-gold, heart-shaped, diamond-encrusted earrings that she'd bought. They'd cost a fortune, but she'd still been ripe with anger at Seb at the time and hell-bent on spending their savings as some kind of punishment. She should have returned them, and probably would have if Emma hadn't ended up in the hospital. But the grin on Zoe's face now made all the money worthwhile.

"You're welcome, sweetheart. Do you think they'll go well with your dress?"

"Are you kidding?" Seb answered for her. "They'll match perfectly. Can I have a look?"

Zoe passed the box over to her dad, then got up and went around to Flick. As she kissed her cheek, Flick couldn't help but see Seb's eyes gleam as he looked at the earrings glinting under the light above them.

She cleared her throat, looked away and reached down to the pile of shopping bags next to her on the floor. "I didn't forget you, boys," she said, pulling out a couple of caps. "I hope I got the right ones. Do you know how many types of snapbacks there are?"

"Wicked." Toby took his and popped it on his head.

"Thanks, Mom," Beau said, ripping the tag off. She smiled at him—loving the sound of *mom* coming from his lips.

"Why'd you come home early?" Zoe asked.

Flick glanced at Seb, who was still admiring the earrings. "Um…Neve's job finished early and we just…uh…"

Dammit, they should have come up with a cover story.

"She just missed us," Seb finished for her, closing the lid on the earrings and passing them back to Zoe.

Zoe grinned. "Well then, next time you'll have to take us with you."

Flick breathed a sigh of relief that the kids accepted this ridiculous excuse. Thank God Zoe and Toby still thought her world revolved around them.

"Yeah." Toby nodded. "Then Beau, Dad and I could go to a Yankees game."

They were sitting around the dining room table, remnants of the meal Zoe and Beau had prepared to welcome her home scattered around them. Flick couldn't think of anywhere else she'd rather be, but that didn't stop a yawn escaping.

"Sorry." She covered her mouth as another one threatened.

"You must be exhausted. It's a long flight." Seb pushed back his chair, stood, then looked to the kids. "I think I'd better get your mother to bed. You three are on cleaning duty."

"But Beau and I made dinner!" Zoe objected. "Toby can do it."

Toby shook his head. "No way. I'll help, but I'm not doing it all on my own. When you cook you use every bloody thing in the kitchen."

Zoe stuck out her tongue at her brother and Flick stifled a smile. For a teenage boy, Toby was very observant. And for an almost-married woman, Zoe still had a lot of growing up to do.

"I don't care who does it," Seb said, his voice raised. "But by the time your mother and I wake up in the morning, the kitchen better be sparkling or there'll be hell to pay."

Beau, still eager to please the future in-laws, stood and started clearing the table. "Come on, you two, the sooner we get started, the sooner it's done."

"Thanks, guys." Flick kissed her kids and then did the same to Beau. "I'm glad our girl found you," she told him.

He blushed. "Me, too."

As Toby and Zoe rose to help, Flick let Seb take her hand and lead her down the hallway to their bedroom. Holding his hand had always felt natural, safe and comforting, but tonight she had to try very hard not to yank her hand away and shove it into her jeans pocket.

You just need time, she told herself.

"I put the electric blanket on for you," Seb said as he closed the bedroom door behind them. "Can I run you a bath or would you rather just collapse into bed? You must be exhausted."

Seb had always been thoughtful, but tonight his words felt like awkward small talk. Flick knew she wouldn't be able to sleep until they'd talked about their future. As tired as she was, she had questions for him and didn't want to wait any longer for the answers. Before the bombshell, she'd have accepted the bath offer, he'd have sat on the toilet lid and they'd have talked while she soaked, but this was a conversation she didn't want to be naked for.

"I am, but I've been waiting for this opportunity to talk to you all night." She crossed to the other side of their room and sat in her beloved occasional chair, then gestured for Seb to sit on the bed.

He rubbed his lips together, nodded and took a seat. "Where do we start?"

"I want you to tell me about the first moment you knew you were in the wrong body." Flick so desperately wanted to understand, because maybe understanding was the first step toward acceptance and going forward.

Seb took a deep breath and began telling her how he'd always preferred girls' toys as a kid and how his mother put it down to having two older sisters. "Dad tried to buy me trucks and pretend tools and such, but they bored me senseless. I wanted dolls to dress up and tea sets, but I didn't realize this was an issue until I started school and my choices attracted bullies. I soon learned that the easiest way to get through life was to ignore these preferences—and definitely never admit to them.

"Luckily I wasn't bad at sports and I enjoyed them, although I always secretly preferred netball over football. I guess I always thought of myself as female inside, but I learned to be a good actor. It's not easy being different, and so I tried to deny it. I thought my feelings were a mortal sin and hated myself for being this way. And I knew what it would do to Mom and Dad if they ever found out what I was."

Flick tried to ignore the pain that filled her as he spoke—she couldn't tell if it was sympathy for him living this shameful life or guilt for herself, unwittingly becoming a pawn in his game of make-believe.

She just knew something hurt badly inside her.

When he got to the part about hating boys' school, she interrupted. "If you hated Dayton so much, why did we work our asses off to pay for Toby to go there? I thought it was an old boys' tradition you were desperate to keep up."

"He always wanted to go there, remember? He heard my dad waxing lyrical about the great time he had there, and I guess I always knew that Toby wasn't like me. If he was, I may have objected, but I knew he'd love it there and thrive, exactly as he has."

Her shoulders relaxed—she hadn't even realized they'd been tense. The worry that this *thing* could be hereditary had been niggling at her, but Seb seemed so sure about their son.

"So you say you've always been this way. You don't remember any incident that instigated it?" If he could pinpoint a moment in his past that had made him this way, maybe they could get help for it. Just like a victim of sexual abuse could. "Maybe you can get counseling?"

He glanced down at the carpet. "I've been having it for years."

Her eyes bulged. *"What?"*

"Do you think I want to be like this?" he asked, his voice rough, almost angry. "I want us to be a normal family as much as you do. I don't want to hurt you, but years of counseling have only made me realize that nothing can change me. I am the way I am and it's time to accept that. To embrace it. I've lived forty-five years in the wrong body. I don't want to live the next forty-five the same way, depressed and ashamed of who I am."

There were so many secrets between them. And yet she'd always imagined they had none. How had she never known how much he was struggling? "Have you ever considered suicide?"

He took a moment to reply, then said, "Yes. The possibility has crossed my mind. That's why I sought counseling in the first place. But I couldn't do that to you and the kids."

Tears filled her eyes—the shocking possibility of Seb killing himself getting the better of her resolve to stay strong. She ached inside at the thought of him living alone with all this turmoil all those years. How could she have been so blind?

"Oh, Flick. I'm so sorry." He got off the bed, crossed over to her and then knelt down in front of the chair and laid his head in her lap. "I never wanted to hurt you."

She sniffed, her fingers instinctively reaching out to rake through his hair. "So why did you marry me?"

He looked up at her as if she'd asked a ridiculous question. "Because I loved you. I still do. Always will. My gender doesn't affect that."

She frowned, unable to comprehend this. "So you're gay? A lesbian? Is that what you're saying?"

"No. Who I want to sleep with has nothing to do with gender."

Flick raised an eyebrow. "Are you sexually attracted to women or men?"

"Women. One woman—you."

"Which means if you go ahead with the gender transition, you'll be a lesbian." It was black-and-white to her.

"Technically I guess—if that's the way you want to look at it."

Flick frowned. How else was she supposed to look at it? "Despite everything, I love you, too, Seb, but I'm not a lesbian. I'm not and never have been attracted to women."

"I understand," Seb whispered, hurt and disappointment in his voice. He thought this was the end.

"In New York," she confessed, "I almost slept with someone else."

He sat bolt upright, jerking away from her. "What? Who?"

Flick sighed and explained all about Jeremy—how he'd been friendly and flirtatious and she'd been looking for a way to forget her pain. Seb looked close to tears but she continued, "I think I also wanted to prove to myself that you're not the way you are because I'm a dud in bed. And also maybe to prove that I'd be able to recover and move on from this."

"You're not a dud in bed."

She shrugged. "Truth is, I'm not sure I really care. The point is, I couldn't sleep with Jeremy. It didn't feel right. I didn't want to hurt you. And when everything went bad with poor Emma, all I wanted was to see you, to talk to you."

He reached out and squeezed her hand, a silent thank-you, and this time she didn't want to pull away. She looked right into his eyes. "If you do this, it's not going to be easy. Are you prepared for what might happen? For rejection, abuse... You might lose your job, your kids."

"What about you? Will I lose you?"

That was the million-dollar question. The one Flick had been asking herself over and over again since Seb had confessed. *Should I stay or should I go?* Whatever her choice, what would people say? What would they think? Where was the Magic 8 Ball to tell her what to do when she needed it?

It's no one else's damn business. Part of her had always cared too much about being "normal," but she hadn't let that stop her becoming a taxidermist, and she didn't regret that decision. Just like taxidermy was part of who she was, so was Seb. She couldn't imagine her life without him and she couldn't just switch off her love, no matter how much she might want to.

Maybe she just needed to move her goalposts—accept that their relationship was built on a strong friendship and a love that transcended sex and all that stuff. Everyone knew that sexual chemistry faded after years of marriage, and the divorce rates proved that when it did, many couples had nothing left in common. That wasn't the case for her and Seb.

"I'm so angry," she said. "I feel betrayed, and I feel like you've lied to me all these years. I wish you'd told me the truth from the start."

He simply nodded.

"But I'll be honest," she went on. "I might have walked

away back then, and if I had, we wouldn't have Zoe and Toby. We wouldn't have so many wonderful memories. Because of all that, part of me is glad you never told me. And that part of me wants to try to make this—us—work. We'll create a new us."

Hope flared in his eyes. "Are you...are you saying what I think you're saying?"

Her stomach churned at what she had to face ahead, but she nodded. "All the stuff in New York—with Emma, Neve and Jeremy—made me realize what's important to me. And that's you. I don't want to lose you, and so I'll stand by you while you go through the transition, if that's what you decide to do. But you've got to promise me no more secrets, no more lies. We're in this together."

"I do. Of course. Oh, Flick. I love you." He reached up and cupped her cheek in his palm as tears streamed down his cheeks. She leaned into him and smiled.

"And there's one other thing I want you to promise."

"Anything."

"You know how I asked you to wait before speaking to Zoe and Toby about your...cross-dressing?"

He nodded.

"Well, the same goes for this. I need you to wait a few more months till you start the process or tell anyone else what you plan to do. This year is paramount for Toby. He's worked for years toward getting the grades to do aviation, and his focus should be on study and exams. Not family drama. And Zoe's about to have the most important day of her life. If you come out before then, everyone will be watching *you*, whispering behind their hands when the wedding should be about Zoe and Beau. Nothing else."

He dropped his hand and his brows knit together—she could tell he was deliberating. She thought back a few weeks when she'd asked him *almost* this same question, and he hadn't given her a straight answer.

"This is a deal breaker, Seb. You've waited years to do this. If you can't wait another few months, I'll walk."

Finally, he nodded. "Okay, I promise." And then his lips stretched into a smile and he got up onto his knees, leaned forward and kissed her.

She'd made the right decision. She knew she had.

41

Genevieve

The call came in the early hours of the morning. Neve startled at the sound, snapping her head up off her arms, which were stiff from where she'd fallen asleep at the kitchen table. It took her a few seconds to work out what the noise was and then she sprang at her phone. No caller ID.

Her heart leaped into her throat as she nervously answered, "Hello?"

"Is that Genevieve Turner?" asked a deep male voice she didn't recognize.

"Yes. Who is this?"

"Senior Police Constable Baxter. I'm sorry to wake you in the middle of the night, but your car has been involved in an accident."

No! Her chest tightened, but she didn't give a damn about the car. "What about my son? Will? Is he okay?"

"You knew your son was driving your car without a license?" Disapproval rang in his tone.

"Yes. We had a disagreement. He stormed out angry and took my car." Oh, God, why hadn't she run after him? Why hadn't she stopped him? "Please, is he okay?"

"He was driving the vehicle when he failed to stop at a stop sign and clipped the tail end of another car. Luckily, the other car and its occupants were unharmed, but William lost control of the vehicle. It rolled and collided with a tree."

Neve gasped, her free hand rushing up to her chest. "Oh, my God! Is he…?" She couldn't bring herself to finish her question.

"He's in critical condition in the hospital. Is there someone who can drive you there? Is your husband at home? Or would you like me to send a patrol car to pick you up?"

Neve couldn't contemplate his offer; she was stuck on *critical*. How many times had she heard that awful word on news reports and felt momentary sympathy for the family before getting on with her day? She was chastised to admit she rarely gave another thought to such incidents, but everyone knew critical wasn't good. Critical was about as close to death as you got without actually dying.

"Ms. Turner, are you okay?"

What a stupid question! She was anything but okay. Her body felt as if it had filled with ice, her heart the only organ in her body not frozen. Instead it was beating so hard she could hear it.

"Ms. Turner?"

"Sorry," she said after a few moments. "This is a lot to take in."

"I understand. Do you need a ride to the hospital?"

She was about to say she could drive herself and then remembered that her car was no longer still sitting outside on the driveway. God only knew where they'd taken it after the accident.

Her mother would come; that was if she didn't have a heart attack when her phone rang in the middle of the night. Her next thought was to call Flick—Emma wasn't allowed to drive after the seizure—but maybe a police car would be quicker.

"Yes, please. I'd appreciate a ride."

"Right. I'll have a patrol car to you in the next few minutes."

"Thank you," she managed. "I'll be ready."

Ready consisted of grabbing her handbag and slipping on the first pair of shoes she could find. Though she never usually left the house without a full face of makeup and perfectly styled hair, Neve hurried out to wait by the road without even a glance in the hallway mirror. No doubt she looked terrible, but her appearance had suddenly dropped way down on her priority list. Nothing mattered except getting to Will as fast as possible.

It felt like forever, but finally a police car appeared. It had barely slid to a stop at the end of her driveway before she yanked open the back door and climbed inside. Two cops turned around to look at her, and the female one behind the wheel said, "I guess you must be Genevieve Turner?"

She nodded, unable to speak for the fear that had balled up in the back of her throat.

They introduced themselves but she didn't register their names. "Right then, let's get you to the hospital." Without another word, the female officer turned back to the wheel and started down the street. Neve feared they might ask her about what her son was doing driving her car late at night without a license, but they must have sensed she couldn't deal with such a conversation right now.

The journey was a blur and the police officers escorted her into the hospital and all the way to intensive care. They seemed to know where they were going, and she guessed this wasn't the first time they'd been in this situation. But everything was new to her. Will hadn't even had so much as a broken bone before now.

"ICU?" she whispered to no one in particular. She thought he'd still be in A&E and the fact that he wasn't sent the terror in her heart up another few levels.

The policewoman placed a supportive hand on Neve's arm and gave her a sympathetic smile as the other officer opened a door into the waiting room.

There was one other couple in there but she barely glanced at them. "Where's Will?"

"Wait here," the policeman instructed as he stepped away and made a phone call on his cell. Neve heard him tell someone they were there and then a few moments later, a more senior-looking officer appeared.

He sighed deeply and offered his hand. "Ms. Turner? We spoke on the phone. Senior Constable Baxter."

Without thought she shook his hand. "Can I see my son?"

"Soon. The doctors are just finishing doing their stuff."

Neve raised an eyebrow. *What the hell does "doing their stuff" mean?*

"Can I get you a tea or coffee?" The policewoman interrupted.

Neve didn't usually drink caffeine after eight o'clock at night—it affected her sleep—but these were extenuating circumstances and sleep wasn't on the agenda anymore. "Thank you. I'll have a coffee."

While the woman walked across to an ancient-looking coffee machine on the wall, Baxter led Neve to a row of plastic chairs and insisted she sit.

"Once you've seen Will, I'll need to get a statement from you regarding your stolen car."

She glared at him. "It wasn't stolen!"

"You're telling me you allowed an unlicensed driver to take your vehicle?" he asked, his tone stern.

"No... I..." She didn't know what she was supposed to say. "Can we please talk about this later? I just want to see my boy."

Baxter frowned but sat back in his seat. The policewoman delivered Neve's coffee and her partner tapped his feet against the linoleum floor as if he had better places to be. Neve's fingers curled around the polystyrene cup and she lifted it to her lips, then absently took a sip. Words were exchanged between the three officers but Neve couldn't take her eyes off the door that led into the ICU. What were they doing to Will in there? If someone didn't let her see him soon, she'd barge in without an invitation.

Finally, after what seemed like forever, the door did open and a tall, gray-haired man in scrubs wearing a stethoscope around his neck approached. He had a kind smile as he introduced himself.

"Evening, Ms. Turner," he said, his tone soothing yet professional. Neve didn't know what time it was but she guessed it was past midnight. "I'm Doctor Mortein and I've been looking after your son since he arrived."

She simply nodded, terrified of what he might be about to tell her.

"Is he going to...to make it?" It was almost impossible to speak past the lump in her throat.

"It's too early to give a long-term prognosis. The next twenty-four to forty-eight hours are critical. Your son suffered serious injuries in the accident—he has a number of broken bones, but it's the internal bleeding and possible swelling on the brain that concerns us most."

Internal bleeding? Brain swelling? Neve almost dropped her cup as the seriousness of Will's condition slammed into her like a physical blow. Dr. Mortein reached out to steady her hand.

"We've put William into an induced coma—"

Neve gasped at this news, her fingers loosening again, but this time as the cup slipped from her grasp, Dr. Mortein caught it. He passed it to Baxter and continued.

"I know the word *coma* sounds terrifying, but we've done this so we can monitor his intracranial pressure and keep his body temperature cool. I promise you we are doing everything we can to get him through this. Now I'm going to take you in to see him, and then if you have any further questions, we can talk some more."

Neve shot up. She didn't need to be asked twice. She wanted to see Will more than she wanted her next breath. Somehow, despite her trembling limbs, she managed to follow Dr. Mortein into the ICU, stopping only to disinfect her hands with the pump at the door. Her stomach twisted at the sight of rows of beds, high-tech machinery and the lights, which were dimmed due to the late hour and gave the place an almost-eerie feel. Nurses buzzed around like busy worker bees. It was surreal, a little like she'd stepped into some television medical drama, until her eyes found Will.

And then suddenly everything felt very, very real.

He was lying on a gurney, his body motionless, his face pale and all sorts of tubes and wires attached to him. A medical-type person stood beside him doing something with one of the wires. "My baby," Neve whispered as she took a step toward him. She looked to the woman beside him. "Can I touch him?"

She nodded. "Yes, but just be careful of the tubes. You're his mother?"

"Yes." Neve stopped beside Will's bed, touched her hand to his and stared down at her beautiful boy. A tear trickled down her cheek.

This was all her fault.

"I'm so sorry, darling," she said, as she brushed her thumb gently across his hand. "I love you and I'm so, so sorry."

Sorry didn't cut it, but she uttered these words over and over again.

As she sat there through the hours, watching the monitors near Will's bed and anxiously trying to read the expression on the nurse's face as she attended him, thoughts whirled inside Neve's head, but she couldn't seem to focus on any one of them.

She should phone her parents.

Baxter was probably still out there waiting to grill her about the "stolen" car.

She should call Flick and Emma. Would she have to give a statement?

Her parents would want to know, even if it *was* the middle of the night.

Maybe there was a way *she* could somehow take the blame rather than Will? It wouldn't be good to have this on his record for future employers and the like to see.

She would have to call James. He was going to kill her.

And then, the most terrifying thought of all.

None of this would matter if Will didn't make it through.

42

Emma

"I'm fine," Emma said to Flick when she opened the door to her on Sunday morning. She felt better than fine actually—after Patrick had kissed her good-night, she'd drifted into the best night's sleep she'd had in a long time and had woken with only a smidgeon of a headache. "You really didn't have to come and check up on me, but come on in, I'll make you a coffee."

Flick shook her head. "Can't. We have to go to the hospital." Then, before Emma could get her head around this statement, she added, "Will was in a car accident last night. He's in critical condition."

"Oh, my God." Emma's hand flew up to cover her mouth. "What happened?"

"I'll fill you in on the way." Flick glanced down at the flannelette pajamas Emma had pulled on after her shower the night before. "Go get changed. We'll wait in the car."

Toby was in the back of Flick's car when Emma climbed in a few minutes later, and Seb was in the driver's seat, his hands gripping the steering wheel. They both said hello and Seb glanced around and offered a solemn smile. Flick sat in the passenger seat beside him. If it weren't for their matching expressions of worry, they'd have looked as normal as they always did together. You'd never guess the demons that were tormenting their marriage. Then again, Emma would never have guessed that Seb thought himself a woman either.

Her cheeks flushed at this thought, and she was glad he was in front and couldn't see her. Knowing what she did, she wasn't sure she'd ever be able to look at him the same way again.

It wasn't that she had anything against transgender people per se, just that she'd never had anything to do with anyone like that *personally*. She'd read about them in glossy magazines and watched TV documentaries with a bemused fascination, but they were almost in the same realm as unicorns to her. But times were changing. The girls had come home from school only a couple of months ago and informed her about a discussion they'd had in health and PE on the whole trans issue. If she recalled rightly, they'd slipped the comment in between announcing dire hunger and then asking her why they had nothing good in the fridge. The casual way they'd spoken, you'd have almost thought they were talking about a new rock band.

Was that why Seb had always been so lovely, so helpful to her? And to Neve? Not as the husband of their friend but because he viewed himself as one of them? Now that she thought of it, he always complimented them on their outfits and never failed to notice if one of them had been for a haircut.

Bringing Emma's thoughts back to the most pressing issue, Flick turned around and explained what had happened to Will.

"So I guess Neve told him?" Emma said once Flick had finished telling her how they'd argued and he'd taken Neve's car and zoomed off into the night.

"Told Will what?" Toby asked and Emma realized Flick

hadn't actually mentioned what the argument had been about. "What's going on?"

Flick shook her head dismissively. "Never mind. It doesn't matter right now."

Toby crossed his arms and turned toward the window and once again Emma felt grateful her kids were out of the country, away from all this drama. Flick switched on the radio and none of them said anything else as Seb navigated the city streets toward the hospital.

Emma dug around in her handbag looking for one of her new extrastrength painkillers. News of Will's accident combined with being a back-seat passenger had turned the dull pain in her head into another shocking headache. With a bonus bout of nausea to go with it. She popped two pills and then sighed in relief as they arrived.

As they climbed out of the car, Emma said wearily to Flick, "How many hospital visits is this in a week?"

Seb shot them a sympathetic glance and Toby looked questioningly at her. "What do you mean?"

Flick gave Emma a look of reproof, and she closed her eyes a moment, cursing her lack of forethought. She'd made Flick and Neve swear they wouldn't tell the boys about her tumor until she'd had the chance to figure out how to break it to her family. But, dammit, there were so many secrets it was getting hard to keep track of who knew what.

Thinking quickly, she touched a finger to her forehead and drew back her bangs, which had been hiding the evidence of her fall. "I tripped and split my forehead in New York. Your mom and Neve insisted I go to the hospital to check it out."

As she suspected, Toby was more interested in her wound than what had happened at the hospital. "Wow, you're going to have an epic scar."

She chuckled. A scar on her forehead was the least of her worries right now.

The moment they entered the hospital, Toby's awe over her scar ended as they all looked to each other, wondering what was next. "Neve said to go through to the ICU waiting room," Flick said.

"I'll ask the receptionist for directions," Seb offered.

While he approached the main desk, Flick stepped close to Toby and put her arm around him. "He's gonna be okay, I'm sure. He's a fighter."

Toby nodded, but looked as close to tears as Emma had ever seen him. She silently prayed Flick was right.

Seb returned a few moments later and they followed him to an elevator, which took them to the ICU waiting room. Emma shivered as they stepped into the bare room, lined with horrible plastic chairs and a decrepit-looking coffee machine on one wall. A TV on mute flickered in the corner, but of the few occupants in the room, only one person was looking at it, and even he didn't seem to be taking anything in.

"There's Neve parents," Flick whispered, nodding toward a couple holding hands, sitting on two chairs in the corner. Emma had only met them a couple of times, but Neve's mother could almost pass as her older sister. Although in her sixties, she preserved herself well. It was easy to see where Neve's interest in hair, makeup and fashion had come from. Her father was nondescript and balding, your typical retiree.

"We should go talk to them?" Emma meant it as a statement but it came out as a question.

Flick nodded and they followed her the short distance across the room. Neve's parents looked up as they approached and recognition flashed in their eyes.

"Hello, Mr. and Mrs. Turner," Flick said. "We're Neve and Will's friends. I'm sorry we have to meet again like this."

Mr. Turner clasped his wife's hand, and she sniffed before burying her head in a pretty floral handkerchief. "Thank you for coming in for Neve," he said.

"How is she?" Emma asked. "How is Will?"

At that moment, a door off to the side opened and Neve emerged. She appeared to have aged ten years since the previous day. They watched as she approached, and Emma didn't dare breathe in case she was about to deliver bad news.

"Hey, guys," she whispered. "What a week, hey? Thanks for coming in."

Flick asked the question they were all thinking. "How is he?"

Neve took a quick breath as if she hadn't had time to worry about a simple thing like inhaling until now. "He's still critical but they're doing everything they can. Mom, Dad, do you want to go in for a bit? He's unconscious but…" Her voice drifted off and her parents stood.

Words weren't necessary. They exchanged looks and a long hug with Neve and then went through the door she'd come from.

Neve fell into the seat her mom had been warming only moments before. Emma and Flick sat on either side of her and Seb and Toby remained standing. "I'm sorry, but they'll only allow immediate family in the ICU."

"We're here for you," Flick said. "Is there anything we can get you? Or Will?"

"A change of clothes, some toiletries?" Emma suggested, hoping Neve wouldn't take this the wrong way.

"I need coffee. Proper coffee." She glared at the machine over on the wall that looked like something out of a 1970s' sitcom.

"Toby and I are on it," Seb said.

As the two of them walked off, Seb wrapped a comforting arm around his son and Emma's heart squeezed at the sight.

He'd always been such a great, hands-on dad, but what would happen to the strong bond he had with his children once he came out?

"This is such a mess," Neve said, rubbing her hand over her face. "He looks awful. All pale and battered."

"Have the doctors given you any further information?" Flick asked as Emma gripped Neve's hand.

Neve shook her head. "They put him in an induced coma. That's about as much as I understand. And that's apparently a good thing. I have no idea what half the big scary medical terms they use mean, but it sounds like they know what they're doing."

"Of course they do," Emma said. "What exactly happened last night?"

Neve sniffed. "We were having a lovely chat over pizza, and then I went and ruined it by telling him why we'd really gone to New York. He reacted worse that I imagined. Totally flipped, stormed out of the house and then took my car. I should have called the police then. I should have—"

"Stop!" Flick interrupted. "Should-haves are a waste of time. You need to focus on Will. There's no point going over how you could have done things differently."

"I can't stop thinking about what must have been going through his head when he rolled the car. How betrayed he must have felt. I just want to give him a big hug and never let go but he's got so many tubes attached to him that I'm scared I'll knock something out."

Emma and Flick didn't say anything. Emma had no idea what to say. If she were in Neve's position, if one of her three were lying in intensive care, there'd be nothing in the world that would make her feel better. She hoped that simply being here to listen was something.

"Would you like me to call James for you?" Flick offered.

James. Emma had almost forgotten about the poor man who had only just found out he had a son and now faced this, but Neve shook her head. "I already did it."

"Oh," Flick said.

"I called him straight after I called my parents," Neve explained. "It was the least I could do after what I've put Will through. He's catching the first flight he can get."

"Here?" Emma asked. Her eyes widened in shock. "He's coming here?"

Neve nodded. "He's a good man. I only hope he gets here in time." With those words, her whole face crumpled, her shoulders shuddering as she broke down.

Emma and Flick looked helplessly over the top of her at each other, before both leaning in and embracing their friend. Emma had lost count of the number of group hugs they'd shared in the past week.

It wasn't long before Seb and Toby returned with two cardboard carriers of take-out coffees. "I wasn't sure how your parents took their coffees," Seb said as he handed Neve hers, "but I bought them a couple of flat whites."

"Thanks," Neve whispered, her hand shaking as she took the drink.

At that moment, Neve's parents reappeared from the ICU ward and all eyes snapped to them. It was obvious they'd been crying. "Is there any change?" Neve leaped up, spilling coffee down the front of the sweater she'd been wearing on the plane.

Her father shook his head. "We've been thinking, though. Mom can sit with Will while you go home, freshen up and get a change of clothes. I'll drive you."

"No! I'm not going anywhere." Without another word,

she shoved her barely touched coffee into Emma's hands and rushed back into the ward.

Emma and the others, including Mr. and Mrs. Turner, sighed in unison.

"I wouldn't want to be anywhere but here if I was her either," Flick said. "Perhaps Seb and Toby can go to Neve's place and collect a few things instead?"

"We'd be happy to, wouldn't we?" Seb said, looking to Toby. He nodded.

Mrs. Turner looked skeptically at Seb. "Will you know what things to get? Neve's very particular about her clothes and makeup."

"I don't think she's worried about anything but Will right now," Emma said, but inside she wondered if Seb perhaps knew more about Neve's needs than anyone else.

"I'm sure we'll manage."

"Yes." Neve's mom sighed. "I'm sorry, you're right. Thank you."

"Not a problem." Seb smiled and once again he and Toby left.

The Turners retreated to the corner they'd been sitting in when everyone had arrived, and Flick and Emma sat back in their seats and each took a gulp of coffee.

"How are things with you and Seb?" Emma asked.

Flick took a moment to reply. "Good, actually. We had a big chat last night."

"And?" Emma prompted.

"And I've told him I'll stand by him."

Emma was about to take another sip, but her hand froze, the paper cup suspended halfway to her mouth. "What do you mean by that?"

"We're going to stay married."

"Oh!" Emma couldn't hide her surprise. Flick had been so

angry in New York, so determined that Seb's transitioning would be the end of their relationship. And quite frankly, neither Emma nor Neve could blame her. It would certainly be a deal breaker for her. It was one thing to be politically correct and agree that everyone should have the right to be whoever they wanted, but it was quite another when such a decision affected you personally. What had changed Flick's mind?

"I've given this a lot of thought," Flick said. "The last week has been hell in many ways, but it's also clarified a lot of things for me. And in the end, I love Seb. Always have and always will. It's as simple as that."

Emma forced her head to nod and tried to offer an understanding smile, but all she could think of was that love was never simple. And that marriage was one of the most complicated institutions ever invented.

"What about sex?" Lately she'd lost some of the ability to think before she spoke. She blamed the tumor. "I'm sorry, you don't have to—"

Flick smiled. "It's okay. To be honest, I'm not sure. We're going to go to counseling so I can understand more how Seb feels and what is ahead of us, but although we'll still be married, of course our relationship will change."

In other words, it would no longer include the exchange of bodily fluids.

As if reading her mind, Flick said, "Seb's my best friend, and that's the real foundation of marriage. Everything else fades after time anyway."

Emma thought that a pessimistic way to think, but then again, her own marriage hadn't exactly been the epitome of success. Even so, she worried about her friend's emotional well-being. It seemed the only person making any compromises in this scenario was Flick. Seb got his dreams fulfilled, but Flick had to readjust hers. She couldn't help but wonder if Flick would one day regret those sacrifices.

"Are you even allowed to stay married?" she asked. "Like, same-sex marriage isn't legal in Australia, but I guess you guys are already married, so…"

"I have no idea." Flick exhaled deeply. "That's a good question. One of many I hope will be answered when we talk to the counselor at the reassignment clinic."

How Flick could speak about this so matter-of-factly, Emma couldn't comprehend. Her decision to stay seemed like such a leap from their conversations of a few days ago. "You know I love you and will stand by you whatever you decide, but have you really given this enough thought?" she asked.

"Yes. I married for life. For good, for bad, for better, for worse."

Emma tried very hard not to raise her eyebrows. She was fairly certain the for-worse part of the marriage vows meant things like terminal illness or dire financial straits, but your husband wanting to be a woman?

That was on a whole other level.

"Enough about me. How are you feeling today? Do you want me to come with you to your biopsy tomorrow?"

"Patrick has offered to drive me."

Well, that part wasn't a lie, but she'd brushed him off with the promise that Neve and Flick were taking her. Truth was, she was happier this way. Her feelings for Patrick were too complicated to deal with right now and Neve needed Flick more than Emma did. Having a tumor in your head wasn't a walk in the park, but nothing could compare to the possibility of losing your child.

43

Felicity

Exhausted after another day hanging out in the waiting room of the ICU, all Flick wanted was to head home, fall into a warm bath and have a glass of wine, but first she had to check on Emma. She felt guilty for even thinking of things like warm, soothing water and alcohol when Will was still critical and Emma so sick. She'd been tempted to simply call Emma and ask how the biopsy had gone, but a little reprimanding voice in her head reminded her that a phone call could hide things. She needed to see her face when she asked.

Taking a sip of the Diet Coke she'd bought from the hospital vending machine, she turned the steering wheel with the other hand and pulled into Emma's driveway to find another vehicle already there. As she climbed out of her car, a tall man emerged holding a bunch of bright flowers, and it took Flick a couple of seconds to recognize Patrick.

"How'd it go today?" Flick called by way of a greeting. She guessed he'd popped out to get takeout for dinner or something. The flowers were a nice touch and made her wonder if there wasn't something more going on between him and Emma than she'd let on.

"We were quite busy for a Monday actually," he replied, and then lowered his voice as Flick got closer. "How did Emma's biopsy go? I wanted to call and wish her well but the day got away from me."

She frowned. "Hang on, didn't *you* take her to the hospital?"

"I thought you and Neve were going with her," he said, his tone uncertain.

Flick shook her head. "Neve's son was involved in a serious car accident on Saturday night. He's in intensive care. I've been with her at the hospital all day—not the same one Emma had her biopsy at, unfortunately."

As realization dawned on them, they turned to face Emma's house and then started toward it.

"She drives me crazy with her determination to be superwoman and her refusal to ask for or accept help," Flick said. "If she hadn't had the seizure in New York, she'd still be popping painkillers like they were candy and no closer to knowing why she had such shocking headaches."

"Hmm," Patrick murmured and then gave a solid rap on the front door.

They both folded their arms across their chests and waited for Emma to answer. Flick silently counted in her head. She'd give her thirty seconds—if Emma didn't come to the door by then, she was using her spare key.

At twenty-seven, the door opened and Emma appeared, dressed in dark jeans, a long-sleeved T-shirt and a puffer jacket as if she were ready to go out. She glanced from Flick to Patrick and bit her lip, knowing she'd been caught.

"Hi, guys," she said, her eyes not meeting either of theirs. "I thought you might be my taxi."

"What taxi?" Flick asked with a slight shake of her head.

"I'm not allowed to drive, so I called a taxi to take me to the hospital to see Neve. How is she? Any progress on Will?"

"He's still the same," Flick said, her heart hurting at the thought, a reminder of the helplessness she'd felt all day. She hadn't been allowed in to see Will, but fetching coffees and snacks when Neve or her parents needed them hadn't seemed enough.

Emma sighed and pursed her lips together. "I still can't believe it."

"I'm sorry to hear about Neve's son," Patrick said, offering Emma the flowers he'd bought. "These are for you, Emma."

She blinked and then took them, lifting them to her nose and inhaling. "Thank you. They smell lovely."

Patrick shoved his hands into his pockets and smiled, a slight red tinge flushing in his cheeks. Flick watched with interest.

"You're welcome," he said, then said, "Did you have your biopsy today?"

"Yes. It went well, I think. I'll get definite results tomorrow or the next day, and then an operation date will be set if that's what the specialist believes needs to be done." Emma spoke as if they'd asked her about a job interview, not something as serious as drilling a hole in her skull and taking a sample. Flick could tell she was pretending to be fine when inside she was probably terrified about what the results might show. "Would you guys like a coffee?"

As she asked this, a taxi pulled into the driveway behind Patrick's and Flick's cars and beeped its horn.

"I'll send him away," Patrick said. "If you want to visit Neve, I can drive you."

Emma nodded as if realizing it wouldn't be wise to refuse another offer of help. As Patrick turned and jogged toward the taxi, Flick glared at her friend. "How *did* you get to the hospital today?"

Emma gestured toward the taxi. "I called a cab. I was fine. Really. Neve needed you and I didn't want to inconvenience

Patrick. He's already going to be overworked with me need-ing time off."

Flick didn't have the energy to argue. "Okay, but promise me you'll stop trying to be so independent. We're your friends, we *want* to help."

"Promise," Emma said, although she didn't sound very con-vincing. "Now, coffee or wine? I'm not supposed to drink but don't let that stop you."

"I'll have a coffee but I won't stay long." She leaned closer to Emma. "Don't want to cramp your style."

Emma blushed. "Don't be ridiculous. Patrick is just a friend. A good friend."

"A good friend who brings you beautiful flowers? I *knew* he wasn't gay."

"*You've* given me flowers before."

"Yes, but in my experience, men don't bring flowers with-out an ulterior motive, and I reckon Patrick's is to get in your pants."

"Shh!" Emma pressed her finger against her lips, her cheeks turning crimson as Patrick's footsteps sounded behind them. "Come inside, you two."

She ushered them into the house and then headed down the corridor toward the kitchen.

"Your house is immaculate," Flick noted.

"It's easy to keep clean when the kids aren't here. And even easier when I've hardly been here either. Now, let me put the kettle on."

"Please sit and let me do that," Flick said, only just stop-ping herself from physically forcing Emma onto one of the stools at her breakfast bar. "You put those flowers into a vase."

"Anything I can do to help?" Patrick asked.

Emma smiled at him. "You can hold the flowers while I fetch a vase." She handed him the bouquet and Flick could practically see the spark that flashed between them as their fingers brushed against each other in the exchange.

When the coffee was made and the flowers organized, they all perched on stools at the breakfast bar nursing their mugs and staring into them.

Emma was the first to break the silence. "How's Neve coping?"

Flick sighed. "As well as can be expected. She's barely left the ICU, but her parents have made her take a few breaks while they sit with Will. She refuses to leave the waiting room, though, just in case something changes while she's gone. James is arriving tomorrow."

"Jeez. I hope he's not too harsh on her." Emma had changed her tune dramatically since first finding out about Neve's affair—but then again a lot of things had happened since then.

"He'd better not be." Flick tightened her grip on her mug. "Or he'll have me to deal with."

"What exactly happened to Neve's son?" Patrick asked. "And who's James?"

Emma started from the beginning, and the way she confided in Patrick, telling him the whole situation—including Neve's affair with James—proved to Flick she valued his friendship a lot, even if she wasn't yet prepared to admit this.

But despite the can of Diet Coke and the coffee she was drinking, she felt her eyelids getting heavy. "Sorry," Flick said, interrupting Patrick and Emma's conversation, "but I think I need to head home. I'm going back to the hospital tomorrow morning. Call me if you want me to pick you up on my way."

She slid off her stool and Emma went to do the same. "Don't go yet!" She sounded panicked.

Flick ignored Emma's protest. "I'll talk to you in the morning. Have a good night. I can see myself out."

Emma, her back turned to Patrick, narrowed her eyes, but

Flick pretended not to understand the silent plea. Emma might be nervous about being alone with a man, but it could be exactly what she needed right now.

"Okay." She let out a reluctant sigh. "Thanks for checking up on me."

"That's what friends are for." Flick put her mug in the sink and glanced at Patrick and Emma sitting beside each other. They looked good together.

She hoped if she left them alone, the wall Emma had built up around her heart after Max's betrayal might start to crumble. She deserved some happiness after everything she'd been through.

"Mom," called Zoe from the dining room the moment Flick walked through her front door fifteen minutes later. "Come in here, we need your advice."

Flick groaned as she shrugged out of her jacket and hung it on one of the hooks in the hall. "Coming."

She found her family—Zoe, Beau, Seb and even Toby—sitting at the table with a massive piece of cardboard in front of them and lots of tiny fluorescent-colored Post-it notes. Was it that time already? Zoe, eternally organized when it came to some things, had a dated to-do list of things that needed to be achieved before the big day. Working out the seating chart for the wedding reception was one of them. Flick remembered arguing when she'd first seen the list that you couldn't work out the seating arrangements before you'd sent out the invitations, but Zoe had been adamant.

"This way we don't invite people who are going to cause issues," she'd said matter-of-factly. Flick didn't think it worked that way—you couldn't not invite Seb's great-aunt just because *nobody* would want to sit with her—but she'd learned early in her daughter's life that Zoe had to work out these things for herself.

But tonight? The prospect made her want to burst into tears.

Seb took one look at her and stood. "Your mom's had an exhausting day. I think we can manage this without her." He took a few steps toward her and kissed her on the cheek. "Would you like me to run you a bath and pour you a glass of wine?"

He knew her so well, but Flick shook her head and went to sit down at the table. She didn't want to neglect her children—not when life had shown her that she shouldn't take them for granted. "No, it's fine. Let's do this." She tried to swallow her irritation and show some enthusiasm as she glanced at what decisions had already been made.

"Any news on Will?" Toby asked, his tone anxious as he ripped a bright pink Post-it in half.

Flick shook her head, wishing she could give him some good news about his friend. Toby's face fell. "But he's not any worse either," she said, reaching beside her to squeeze his hand. "Right, where have you decided to seat Great-aunt Glenda?"

A synchronized groan echoed around the table, which made Flick smile for the first time in forty-eight hours.

Zoe made a face. "We're kinda hoping she'll be sick that day." That was like hoping for a lottery win to get you out of debt. Aside from the quandary of what to do with Seb's great-aunt, they appeared to have made solid progress on the plan, except for a few tiny disagreements over a couple of family friends who'd divorced two years ago. Zoe was adamant they were still civil and would sit together for the sake of their adult children, but Seb wondered if it was wise to put their new partners at the same table. Flick tried to concentrate and add her thoughts, but her mind kept drifting to Will lying uncon-scious in the hospital.

Just the thought of Toby being in his place sent terror flooding through her body. Their boys might be tall, strapping men physically, but they were at critical stages in their emotional development, and if Neve's news about James had caused Will to react like he did, how would Toby react when he found out about his dad wanting to be a woman? And what about Zoe? She wasn't much older than Toby, and Seb had always been her hero.

A chill slid down Flick's spine and she pushed back from the table. "I'm sorry. I can't do this tonight."

She stood and just managed to flash Zoe an apologetic smile before hurrying down the hallway. But instead of going to her bedroom, she rushed outside, retreated to her studio and locked the door.

Hopefully Seb would take the hint that she needed to be alone.

44

Genevieve

After more than forty-eight hours sitting by Will's side in the ICU, Neve barely registered the sounds around her or the comings and goings of people anymore. It wasn't like the maternity ward, where visitors, medical staff and patients alike were all smiles, happy to chat and share in a stranger's joy. Here the solemn-faced visitors kept to themselves and the doctors and nurses went about their business, only occasionally offering sympathetic smiles to the people who sat in plastic chairs keeping vigil beside their loved ones' beds.

Will's bed wasn't far from the door that swung open on a regular basis, but Neve couldn't have given a description of any of the people that drifted in and out.

Until Tuesday afternoon, when the door opened again, footsteps approached and the hairs at the back of her neck tingled to life. Her insides froze and she turned slowly to find James standing at the end of Will's bed. She'd been expecting him, of course, but this knowledge hadn't prepared her for the almost physical impact she felt as she laid eyes on him. No man should look that good in a pinkish-colored shirt after Lord knew how many hours on a plane. But as usual, James defied such laws. Her body temperature skyrocketed and she had no control over her gaze as it slid down over his body, taking in his faded jeans and brown boots, and then skipping back up again to his sexy stubble and the dark sunglasses pushed up on top of his head.

The past few days she'd felt barely alive, but James's arrival sent her pulse racing again.

Immediately she remembered that she hadn't showered or changed her clothes—she hadn't wanted to take the time away from Will in case his condition changed while she wasn't there. She even begrudged the time it took to go to the bathroom. So she could only imagine what she must look like.

Guilt speared her. Who the hell cared what she looked like when Will was lying beside her, clinging to life by a thread?

This thought snapped Neve back to reality, and her grip tightened on Will's hand. *He's here, baby.* All her son had asked of her was to help him meet his dad, and she'd royally messed up in that department. She cleared her throat, ready to speak, and then realized she had no idea what to say. Her relationship with James had always been a roller coaster but nothing like the emotional whiplash of the last week.

He stood like a statue, staring at the bed, his expression unreadable as he saw Will for the first time in the flesh. This wasn't how it was supposed to be. Neither of them said a word, but then James emerged from his trancelike state. He shook his head, turning his gaze slightly to rest on Neve—as if he'd only just noticed her sitting there. Their eyes met and she swallowed, biting down on the impulse to apologize again.

But before she could say anything, he stepped around the bed and came toward her. Her heart shot to her throat as fear overwhelmed her. He was understandably furious but surely he wouldn't try anything in here?

"Gennie." His voice was barely a whisper.

She dropped Will's hand and stood, ready to protect herself if need be.

Then, taking her totally by surprise, he closed the distance between them and pulled her against him. Was this some kind of trick? She'd never been more shocked in her life.

"How are you doing?" His deep warm voice whispered against her cheek as her body relaxed against his. So much for being a strong, independent woman. Aside from when her parents and Flick and Emma had arrived at the hospital, Neve had barely shed a tear since being here, but now the barricades came crashing down and tears sprouted in her eyes. She wasn't sure whether she was crying at the comforting feeling of being wrapped in James's arms, at the shock of him actually being here or the kindness in his voice, which she totally didn't deserve.

Whatever the reason, she couldn't speak to answer him. They stood there, wrapped in each other's arms, for what felt like an eternity. Her tears soaked his shirt and when he finally pulled back, she realized her hair was wet from his tears. Again, she had to physically restrain herself from saying sorry.

James, one arm still holding her to his side, turned toward the bed and looked down at Will. "He looks like me."

His voice held such pride and emotion. All Neve could do was nod.

"It's okay to touch him?" he asked.

"Yes," she whispered. "The doctor said touch is good and that it's quite likely he can hear what is being said around him. We've been encouraged to talk to him, especially about things he loves, like rowing."

"We?" He looked into her eyes and her heart skipped a beat.

Neve licked her lips. "My parents. They're the only ones apart from me who have been allowed in here. It's immediate family only. They're outside in the waiting room—you probably passed them on your way in."

He nodded, dropped his hand from her side and reached out, hesitating a moment before placing it on top of Will's hand.

"Hello, son," James said, his voice choked.

Neve's heart turned over in her chest at the emotion in his tone. For the briefest second, she swore Will's eyes flickered, but the next moment they were still again, and she guessed desperate hope had fueled her imagination. For so long it had been she and Will against the world—when he was a toddler, she'd called them the Dynamite Duo—but suddenly she felt as if she was an intruder.

Perhaps she should leave James alone with Will for a little while. Not long enough to go home and fix her appearance—*let's not get carried away*—but long enough to have something to eat, down another coffee and go to the bathroom. Long enough to let James spend some one-on-one time with his son. He probably had things to say, private things.

She took a step back so that she could walk behind James, but his voice halted her.

"Stay!" he said, without even turning his head. "Stay and tell me more about our boy."

Neve let out a long sigh. "Are you sure?"

"Yes. I may have been angry at you for what you did, but this—" he gestured to Will lying on the bed "—is my fault as much as it is yours."

"What? How do you figure that?"

"If I hadn't put so much pressure on you, maybe you'd have had some more time to work out the best way to tell him, maybe—"

Neve held up a hand. "Stop, James. This is *not* your fault." There was no point in both of them beating themselves up.

"Either way, now isn't the time to hold grudges," he said.

"The past is past. All that matters now is our son getting well again."

A lump formed in her throat. She couldn't agree more. Will didn't deserve any of this, and neither did James. If she needed to be punished for living a lie, for keeping a terrible secret all these years, then it should be her life in jeopardy.

"Okay," she whispered as she lowered herself back into the plastic seat. Her knees were too shaky to hold her up any longer. She wasn't naive enough to think that James had forgiven her, but he was man enough to set aside his disgruntlement for the time being, and for that she was grateful.

She began to speak, telling James random anecdotes from Will's seventeen years—funny things he'd said as a child, hobbies he'd been passionate about, awards he'd received. She couldn't have kept the pride from her voice if she'd wanted to. Over the years, Neve had learned to curb her enthusiasm when speaking about her son's achievements, but James was an avid listener, wanting to know every tiny thing about Will, and the act of telling him calmed her in a way that nothing had been able to until now.

She hoped Will could hear her voice as she spoke and James's laughter as he listened. She hoped the knowledge that his much-longed-for father had finally arrived would help give their son the will to survive.

45

Emma

Emma desperately wanted to be at the airport to meet her kids as they came through Arrivals, but she'd been specifically told not to drive. Flick had made her promise to ask for help if she needed it, but she was dealing with enough of her own issues. She could ask Patrick, but that might raise suspicions from her kids. She wasn't yet sure what was going on there, but even if something was, the rules of single-parent dating clearly stated that children should not be introduced to boyfriends until the relationship was serious. Then there was the fact that Caleb and the girls would wonder why she hadn't just driven herself.

Sigh.

They would find out soon enough. That thought sent a shiver down her spine as if a spider had scuttled over her back. She still hadn't determined exactly how much to tell them about her illness. While she'd always been up-front and honest with them, the prospect of having her head sliced open terrified her, and she wanted to protect her children from the stress. With Will still in a coma and exams coming up, Caleb had enough to stress about without adding her problems to the equation.

Double sigh.

She glanced at her watch and paced to the other end of the veranda. According to her flight tracker, the plane had landed over an hour ago, and Laura had messaged her from the car when they were leaving the airport. Her family should be home at any second. Usually she'd be bouncing up and down like an excited child after not having seen her kids for two weeks, but today there was nothing in her heart but trepidation. Emma put a hand to her forehead, surprised there wasn't an indent by now from all the rubbing. Her doctor had given her a prescription for a stronger painkiller, so that had kept the ache tolerable, but the thought of telling Caleb, Laura and Louise about her tumor and imminent operation had brought with it the worst headache she'd had all week.

The sound of a car coming up the road halted her pacing, and a few moments later Max's flashy SUV rolled into the driveway. Emma forced an enthusiastic smile and lifted her hand to wave as the vehicle came to a stop. She hurried down the steps onto the grass as the back doors of the car were flung open in synchrony and her babies tumbled out. They looked a few shades darker than when they'd left and were wearing clothes she didn't recognize. Laura and Louise waved crazily and screamed, "Hello, Mom," as they rushed toward her, but Caleb approached more slowly. She opened her arms wide for the girls and looked over their heads at him, seeing pure fear in his eyes.

"Any more news on Will?" he asked.

She shook her head and he nodded solemnly. The girls stilled in her arms and looked up to her.

"But he's going to be okay, isn't he?" Laura's voice shook.

Although Will was primarily Caleb's friend, the close association of their families meant the twins looked upon him as another older, slightly less annoying brother.

Emma swallowed. She wanted to say yes to reassure them, but the latest news from the hospital hadn't been as good as they'd hoped.

"I want to see him," Caleb said, shoving his hands into his pockets. "Can we go now?"

Emma spoke softly, her voice barely more than a whisper. "I'm sorry, but you can't. It's only immediate family in the ICU."

Caleb cursed and kicked the grass beneath his feet. Then, without another word, he stormed up the steps and into the house, no doubt intending to take his anger out on his Xbox.

"Guess I'll grab all the luggage, shall I?" Max called from the car.

"Thanks, Dad," the girls shouted back. Oblivious to his sarcasm, they headed into the house after Caleb.

With a sigh, Emma trudged over to the SUV, greeted Max with as much civility as she could garner and helped him unload the kids' suitcases from the trunk. Chanel didn't look up from the front seat or acknowledge Emma, instead tapping away on her iPhone like the teenager she practically was.

Emma and Max dragged the three suitcases and extra carry-ons up the steps onto the veranda. It was an unspoken rule that Max no longer came inside the house that had once been their family home, but instead of dumping the luggage and leaving, he crossed his arms over his chest and sighed.

"This thing with Will?" he asked, keeping his voice low, presumably so as not to be overheard. "Is it serious?"

She nodded. "The doctors were expecting to bring him out of his coma by now, but the pressure on his brain hasn't abated as much as they'd hoped."

"Jesus."

"But that's not the only problem we have. Well, the other thing is my problem really, but because we share kids, it's gonna be your problem, too."

His brows knit together, highlighting the wrinkles on his forehead. Maybe *he* was the one that needed Botox. "What are you talking about?"

"I have a brain tumor." Before he had time to digest this news, she added, "I'm going under the knife to have it out this Monday, and I'll need you to take care of the kids while I'm in the hospital."

Max blinked, then shook his head slightly as if he couldn't believe what he'd heard. "Shit, Em! Are you serious?"

No, of course not, she almost snapped, *I find joking about brain tumors hilarious.* But his reaction wasn't far from what hers had been when the US doctors had landed the blow.

"I'm afraid so."

At the sound of Max's raised voice, Chanel poked her head out the window, obviously trying to listen in. Max didn't appear to notice. "Shit," he said again, and then stepped closer and pulled her into his arms.

Emma hadn't been this close to her ex-husband since long before their divorce, and his gesture caught her off guard. For a few seconds she stood like a wooden plank in his arms, but then the thought of how confused the kids might be if they stumbled upon this sight jolted her into action, and she extricated herself.

He rubbed his hand over his face and looked at her as if for the first time. "I don't know what to say. Is it…"

When it was clear he couldn't say what he wanted to, she rescued him. "It's benign. A biopsy earlier in the week confirmed this but due to its location and size and the fact that I'm getting serious headaches and have already had one seizure, my surgeon believes the best course of action is to operate."

"Shit." Emma wondered if he'd left the rest of his vocabulary behind in Hawaii. "Seizures? Why didn't you tell me you were having health issues?"

She raised an eyebrow—they hadn't exactly been the friendliest of ex-partners—and ignored his question. "I know it won't be ideal, and Chanel won't be stoked about it, but I think the kids should stay with you for a while."

It broke her heart to say this, but she didn't see any other alternative.

"Don't worry about Chanel," Max said with a dismissive wave of his hand. Normally such a gesture would give Emma a zap of victorious joy, but it didn't bring her any satisfaction right now.

"I'll be in the hospital most of next week and then, depending on how the surgery goes, I might be able to come home. But this is brain surgery, and apparently it could take months for me to return to normal."

In ordinary circumstances Max might make a joke about her *never* being normal, but the fact that he didn't showed he understood the seriousness of this situation. He appeared lost for words, and Emma felt the need to fill the silence.

"They gave me a never-ending list of things that might occur postsurgery, and I don't want the kids to suffer because of it."

"We'll do whatever it takes," Max promised, offering a warm smile that gave her a glimpse of the man she'd once fallen in love with. "What are you going to tell them?"

She rubbed her lips together. "Well…"

"Caleb's really worried about Will right now. Maybe we should make up some routine kind of surgery you're going in for? Or we can say the house has a termite infestation and needs to be fumigated so they have to stay with me for a bit?"

Until Max suggested this, Emma had been undecided on

how or what to tell the kids, but Patrick's words of a few nights ago came back. *I might not have children, but if my mom had something serious like a tumor, I'd want to know about it.*

For all his faults, Max had the best interests of the kids at heart when he'd suggested lying to them, but the fact was there was no perfect option in this shitty situation. Emma didn't like the idea of lying to her children. And how betrayed would Caleb and the girls feel if something did go wrong with her surgery? If they didn't know the truth, they couldn't be prepared for the worst. Emma didn't want to be pessimistic, but neither did she want them in the dark about something this big. They weren't babies anymore, however much she sometimes wished they were.

"No." She shook her head. "Haven't we always been open with the kids? I think they deserve to know the truth. They'll be upset if they learn it from someone else. There are risks with surgery but they'll likely only register the part about me not having cancer. Let's focus on that and tell them they need to stay with you while I recover."

"Okay." Max reached out and put his hand against her arm. "I'll support you in whatever decision you make."

"Thank you." It was weird having a conversation with her ex in which they were talking like a unit, let alone one where he was almost acting human. She wondered what Chanel would think of all this.

To hell with Chanel. She was the one who'd slept with, then married, a man with baggage. All that mattered was getting well and doing what was best for her family.

As if the other woman could read Emma's thoughts, a beep sounded from the SUV and Chanel called through the window, "Hate to interrupt the chitchat, but...*jet lag.*"

Her singsong voice grated on Emma's nerves, and even Max let out a grunt of annoyance. Without glancing at his wife, he said, "How about I take her home and then come back this evening? I'll bring takeout so you don't have to cook and we'll sit the kids down and tell them what's what."

"Okay." She nodded. "Yes. That sounds like a plan, if you're sure you can spare the time." However much he pissed her off, she couldn't deny that she liked the idea of having another adult there for support when she told the children.

"I'll see you then. And please look after yourself." With those words, Max leaned forward, kissed her on the cheek, then turned and walked back to his waiting wife. Emma watched him go, unsure of who was more stunned by this gesture—herself or Chanel, whose mouth was now hanging wide-open.

You could almost see the steam coming out of her ears.

"Is it Will?" Caleb asked when Emma and Max sat their three children down in the living room after dinner from the local Chinese restaurant. "Has something happened?"

Emma shook her head.

"Well, you can't be telling us you're getting a divorce," said Laura. "We've been there, done that conversation already."

"I know!" Louise exclaimed. "You're getting back together." Emma looked at Max in horror.

"Don't be stupid," Caleb snapped, then he looked to Emma, his expression far too serious for a seventeen-year-old boy. "It's those headaches you've been having, isn't it?"

Before Emma could say anything, the girls spoke together. "Are you sick, Mom?"

"Will you just let your mother get a word in?" Max said.

Emma took a deep breath and then reached out and took hold of the girls' hands—they were sitting on either side of her on the couch—and as much as they acted all grown-up, they suddenly seemed very young. Caleb and Max sat opposite in the matching armchairs.

"Yes, sweethearts, I am sick." She continued quickly before they could get carried away, "But you don't need to worry, because everything is going to be okay. When Neve, Flick and I were in New York, I had a seizure and had to go to the hospital. They discovered that the reason I've been having so many headaches is because I have a brain tumor."

Louise sobbed. "Oh, my God!"

"You're not going to die, are you?" Laura asked, her voice quivering.

Caleb remained silent but she could see the anxiousness in his eyes.

"I certainly hope not," Emma said. "The doctors tell me the tumor is benign."

"What's that mean?" asked the girls, once again speaking in unison.

"That she hasn't got cancer," Caleb told them.

Emma nodded. Did the girls' posh private school teach them anything?

"That's good news then, right?" Louise spoke through her tears.

"Very good," Emma said. "But I'm going to be honest with you. Surgery on the brain is risky, and although I have a good chance of a full recovery, it is not going to happen overnight. I'll be in the hospital at least a week, and recovery is going to take some time. I won't be up to looking after you three for a while afterward, so you're all going to go stay with Dad and Chanel for a bit."

It broke Emma's heart to say this, but if she'd learned any-thing over the last week or so, it was that when it came to her health she needed to be sensible. It was going to take ev-

erything she had to get better and Max was their father; he
would look after them.

"No," Laura said adamantly. "We're not leaving you on
your own when you need us the most."

"Definitely not," agreed her twin. "We can look after you."

"They're right," Caleb said. "I know we've been pretty crap
at helping around the house, but we can do our bit. We're not
babies, and we *want* to."

Emma opened her mouth to speak—to tell them they'd
been normal teenagers and shouldn't beat themselves up—but
found herself too choked with emotion.

Max spoke instead. "We know this is scary, and Mom ap-
preciates that you want to look after her, but the best way to
do that is to give her some time to recover without having to
worry about anything else. We'll come visit all the time and
check she's following doctor's orders, but as hard as it may be
to understand, staying with me while your mom is convalesc-
ing is really for the best."

"You and *Chanel*," Louise said, her distaste evident in the
way she said her father's wife's name.

"Oh, Mommy." Laura shuffled over on the couch and threw
her arms around Emma. "I love you so much."

Emma couldn't recall the last time any of her children had
called her "Mommy." As a tear slid down her own cheek, she
snuggled into Laura and drew Louise into her arms as well.
Caleb got off the couch and came to sit beside them, and she
reached out and took his hand. This was the closest she'd felt
to her babies in a long time.

Maybe she shouldn't have been so worried about the possibility that they might *choose* to leave her and go live with
Max and Chanel instead.

Max left not long after that, making Emma promise that
she would call him at any hour if she needed anything at all,

but the kids refused to leave her side. In the end, Laura and Louise climbed into bed beside her and Caleb sat in the chair in her bedroom until the twins had finally fallen asleep. They talked for hours about Hawaii, New York and school. He asked for more information about the tumor, his sensible questions showing his interest in medicine and proving he'd be good in the field. His bedside manner would be a lot better than some of the medical staff she'd dealt with over the last week.

Emma reckoned he'd have spent the whole night sitting vigil by her bed if she didn't convince him that she was okay and would rest better knowing he was comfortable in his bed.

He stood reluctantly and started toward the door, stopping and turning back just before he got to it. "I know life hasn't been easy for you over the last few years, Mom, and I'm sorry if I've contributed to that in any way. But I want you to know, you're the best, I appreciate everything you do for us and I love you."

"Oh, darling." Emma wished she could leap off the bed and go wrap her arms around him, but being squished between the girls made it impossible. "I love you, too, and you have done nothing at all to contribute to this. Don't ever think that. It's just one of life's sucky things, but we're going to get through this. I'm going to beat this, and I'm sure Will is going to be better again soon as well. Try to get some rest."

"I will. Good night."

"Good night, sweetheart. I love you."

Emma was almost asleep when her phone beeped on the bedside table, indicating a message. Feeling like a player in a game of Twister, she extracted her arm from underneath Laura and stretched across to retrieve the phone.

She read Patrick's message. I hope things went okay telling the kids tonight. I'm always here if you want to talk.

And she smiled.

46

Genevieve

Saturday brought the first bit of good news in what felt like forever. Dr. Mortein stood beside Will's bed and smiled down at Neve and James.

"The swelling on William's brain has gone down enough that we believe it is safe to bring him out of the coma. It's taken us a little longer to get here than we'd hoped, but the prognosis is good. Will should make a full recovery."

As goose bumps erupted across her skin, Neve gasped, and James, sitting beside her on a plastic chair, gripped her hand. It felt like the most natural thing in the world, and she squeezed back, thankful to have had his support these past few days.

"That's fantastic," James said, an optimistic smile sprouting on his face and smoothing out the worry lines. Neve couldn't speak past the lump in her throat but she nodded in agreement.

Since his arrival, the two of them had barely spent half an hour apart during daylight hours. He'd insisted she take some time out to go home and freshen up at least once a day, and they'd taken turns retreating to her house for a few hours' nap in every twenty-four. The hotel he'd booked seemed like a waste of money when he was spending most of his time at the hospital, so he'd canceled that and dumped his stuff at Neve's place. Offering him basic hospitality felt like the least she could do, although nothing would ever make up for her transgressions.

They'd barely spoken about those transgressions—James had stayed true to his declaration that he wanted to focus on the future and Will getting well again. During those hours where they'd kept joint vigil in the ICU, there'd been periods of comfortable quiet and other times where James and Neve had talked almost as if the last eighteen years had never happened. It was all too easy to remember why she'd fallen under his charms the first time, yet the way he held Will's hand and spoke to him in a gentle fatherly tone warmed the cockles of her heart in a manner far more lethal than physical attraction. She knew she was falling in love with him all over again and that her heart was destined to be broken.

But as long as Will made a full recovery, she could deal with the pain of a permanently broken heart.

Dr. Mortein explained the procedure for reviving Will from the coma and asked them to step into the waiting room while the medical team did what they needed to do. He promised he'd call them back the moment Will was conscious. Reluctantly, Neve and James did as they were told, standing as one and traipsing out into the waiting room to join her parents, who'd set up camp there during daylight hours.

Only when her mom's eyes dropped did Neve realize she and James were still holding hands. They'd been introduced but had spent little time chatting or getting to know each other. She didn't want to let go but nor did she want her mother to go getting any ideas, so she extracted her hand.

"News?" her father asked, his anxious tone matching his expression.

"Wonderful news." She nodded, speaking for the first time

since the doctor had delivered it. Her eyes watered with happy relief. "They're bringing Will out of the coma. They're happy with his progress."

"Oh, praise the Lord." Neve's mother—who had never been in any way religious—made the sign of the cross and then pulled Neve in for a hug. "Hallelujah."

Although they'd been told they'd have time to go for a coffee or grab a bite to eat, no one wanted to venture far, so they all got coffee from the vile machine on the wall and sat down to wait. While James repeated to her parents exactly what Dr. Mortein had said, Neve leaned back in her plastic seat and pulled her cell phone out of her pocket. She took what felt like the first breath in days and then shot off text messages to Flick and Emma telling them the good news. Jubilant replies came almost immediately, and Neve smiled before tucking the phone back into her pocket.

Both she and Will were extremely blessed in the friends department.

It had been almost a week since the accident—a week that felt like forever—and in that time Flick, Seb, Toby and Emma had also spent many hours in the ICU waiting room. Stacey, Will's girlfriend, had been there every day after school, and yesterday Emma's children had come, freshly arrived back from Hawaii. Although they weren't allowed in to see Will, they'd all wanted to be close to him, and Neve and James had made sure to tell him that his friends were all out there hoping for his recovery.

And finally he had turned a corner. Neve had never felt so light-headed in her life. After days of feeling as if she were trapped beneath a semitrailer, she now felt as if she'd been filled with helium and could float right up into the sky.

After forty-five minutes—yes, they'd all been watching

the clock like hawks—the door to the ICU opened and Dr. Mortein strode out looking pretty damn pleased with himself.

He grinned from Neve to James and back to Neve again. "There's a young man in there who wants to see his mom."

Tears of happiness and relief spilled from Neve's eyes as James grabbed her hand. "Come on," he said, tugging her as he followed Dr. Mortein. She loved that he didn't appear nervous whatsoever about meeting Will—instead, he couldn't get there fast enough.

At the door, James let her hand go to clean his with disinfectant and Neve did the same. Over the past week, this act had become so ingrained that she barely registered doing it anymore. But today it felt like an unwanted delay.

Their hands clean, they stepped through into the ICU and Neve almost tripped over her own feet in her rush to get to Will. In many ways he didn't look very different—he was still lying on a hospital gurney, all pale and listless—but his eyes were open, and the moment they met hers, he let out a childish sob.

"Oh, baby." Tears streaming down her cheeks, she rushed at him and hugged him without the carefulness and trepidation of late. "I love you."

He tried to speak, and she pulled back to make it easier for him. "What is it, darling?" she asked, gently squeezing his hand and running her other one over the beautiful golden curls on his head.

"I'm...sorry." It was obvious that speaking even two words was hard for him.

"Hush." She pressed a finger against his lips. The doctor had explained that Will might not be able to remember how he'd got into this situation, but his eyes told her otherwise. "You have nothing to apologize for. I'm just glad you're going to be okay. You had us all so worried."

He tried to smile and she could tell even that was an effort. She simply stared at him a few long moments, unable to take her eyes off his, and then she remembered James. Her heart stilled. Part of her wanted to ignore him. She had her boy back now and she didn't want anything to come between them again, but Will was in this situation because she'd kept him from his dad. If that hadn't taught her anything, nothing ever would.

She stepped back a little and then glanced over at James, who was watching them with a look of trepidation on his face.

"Will, there's someone I'd like you to meet," she said, looking down at him again and hoping the shock of meeting his dad wouldn't be too much on his fragile body. "Somebody you've wanted to meet for a long time."

She nodded to James and he stepped closer so that Will could finally see him. "This is James, your dad. He's come all the way from New York to see you."

Reluctant to let Will go, she clung to his hand but shuffled sideways a little so that James and Will could get a proper look at each other. Neither of them said anything for a few long moments, not with words anyway. But as Neve watched her son and the only man she'd ever truly loved make their acquaintance, a feeling of rightness clicked into place inside her.

"Hello, son," James said eventually, emotion dripping from every syllable. "You gave us quite a fright there."

Will opened his mouth but no words came out.

"Hey, relax." James spoke soothingly, so that even Neve felt the tenseness in her body easing. "We've got all the time in the world to talk. Right now you need to concentrate on getting better. You've got quite a posse of people rooting for you." He leaned in closer and winked. "And as for Stacey, well, let's just say you have good taste in women. Must get that from me."

Neve's insides twisted at James's words as a flicker of a smile appeared on Will's face. Did *good taste* mean her?

She silently scolded herself the moment the thought appeared in her head. Even if he'd once felt something for her, after what she'd done, the only hope she had was that they could go forward together as coparents, and that in time both James and Will would forgive her.

As if he could read her mind, Will's hand moved in hers and she met his eyes. "Yes, honey?"

"Thanks, Mom." Those two words, the first clear ones Will had managed since coming out of the coma, warmed her heart like nothing ever had before.

She smiled back at him. "Better late than never, hey?"

"Will is likely to tire very quickly over the next few days," Dr. Mortein said, interrupting the moment; Neve had all but forgotten he was there. "I suggest one-on-one visits for the next twenty-four hours and ask that you don't overexcite him."

Oh, dear. Perhaps they should have waited to introduce James. But it was too late, and Neve felt certain that meeting his dad would give Will added incentive to get better. Still, Dr. Mortein knew best, so as reluctant as she was to leave her boy, she stood.

"I'll go and tell Nan and Pop how you're doing," she said, giving Will's hand another squeeze before letting it go. Unspoken was the acknowledgment that she was giving him and James some long-awaited time to get to know each other.

Still, James looked at her questioningly. *Are you sure?* he silently asked, showing that he knew how hard it was for her to leave Will after being so close to losing him.

She nodded and offered a grateful smile. "I'll be back soon."

With those words, she strode the few meters to the exit and into the waiting room to find Flick and Emma there with Seb and their children. Even Zoe appeared to have taken time out from her wedding planning to come share the good news.

"He's awake," she told them, unable to keep her voice down despite her consciousness of the strangers in the waiting room. Her friends applauded.

Then Flick and Emma opened their arms wide and Neve launched herself into them.

47

Emma

They say when you are near death that your life flashes before your eyes, and as that felt like what was happening to Emma now, she feared the operation was not going according to plan. She hovered outside her own body and watched, like a fly on the wall—as if anyone would ever let a pesky insect get as far as a hospital operating room—as the team of people in aqua scrubs surrounding her grew frantic.

One of them swore. Machines and monitors beeped. All hell broke loose.

Yet, feeling astonishingly calm, Emma peered past the doctors and nurses to look down on herself. She was mildly appalled to be able to see right into her head. Someone had shaved off a huge patch of her beautiful long hair, but she could barely bring herself to care. The gaping hole in the side of her head where the surgeon had sawed into her skull should have hurt like hell, but it didn't.

Instead a strange force was tugging at her. The medical staff spoke frantically to each other, talking about her as if she wasn't even there, but it wasn't their voices she heard calling. Was that her mother? Her grandmother, who had also died of breast cancer when Emma was just a child? She hadn't heard either of their voices in so long.

As their voices grew stronger, clearer, louder, a blinding white light appeared above, drawing her to it like a magnet. She felt her soul being sucked up as the sensation of whooshing down a tunnel at great speed took over. The light at the end flickered—getting stronger and then fainter, over and over and over again.

Being in the tunnel made her think of Caleb—and how as a little boy, he'd begged her and Max so many times to drive through the tunnel in the city. This and a hundred other strange thoughts entered her head. Like had she remembered to put the trash out yesterday?

Max appeared at the edge of her vision, looking exactly the way he had when she'd first met him all those years ago. As Emma traveled closer to the light, pretty much every person that had ever had the slightest impact on her life made an appearance. Her friends, people she'd worked with, children of her friends and then finally, her own children.

This could only mean one thing.

Who would be the one to break the news to them? Who would comfort them? She'd never see them graduate. Choose careers. Get married.

She thought of Caleb, so tall, so strong, so grown-up in some ways, but always a little boy to her, and she sent him a silent message, hoping that somehow he'd hear it.

I love you, sweetheart. Look after the girls. Work hard, be honest and kind. I know someday you'll make a wonderful doctor.

And then she thought of the twins—physically alike in every possible way, but as different as chalk and cheese in personality.

Yet in spite of their differences, they'd always been the

best of friends and she hoped their closeness would get them through the struggles ahead.

Stay strong, my lovelies. Continue to grow into independent women and never let anyone walk over you. Only give your heart to men who deserve it.

That advice made her think of Patrick. Wonderful, lovely, sexy Patrick, who she now had to admit meant much, much more to her than a boss ever should.

The light grew closer and her mom's silhouette at the end of the tunnel became sharper. Now she could see her properly—waiting there, arms outstretched, a smile on her face and her body free of the cancer that had taken her from them.

"Mom!" Emma desperately wanted to reach out, to once again take comfort in her mother's arms. But another equally strong part of her wanted to resist. She wasn't ready to go yet.

Two invisible forces yanked at her from opposite directions. Then a voice called distantly from the entrance of the tunnel.

Patrick's voice, begging her to come back. And she wanted to—oh, boy, did she want to—but tiredness overwhelmed her. Was she strong enough to fight it?

Suddenly, a shock jolted her body; she felt as if she'd been plunged into a pool of ice. And then everything went black again.

48

Felicity

"If I never see another hospital waiting room as long as I live, it will be too soon," Flick whispered to Neve, who was sitting beside her on yet another hard plastic chair, nursing yet another cup of wannabe coffee.

"Tell me about it," Neve replied, tapping her high heels on the floor.

Today was the first time she'd left Will's bedside for longer than it took to go home and shower, but she appeared relaxed in the knowledge that James would be with their son. Between all their different dramas, the two friends hadn't had a lot of time to talk, but from what Flick gathered, things with James had gone a lot better than expected.

She had met him at the hospital and already liked him a lot. Quite aside from his looks, it was easy to see how someone could fall in love with his personality. Privately she worried that Neve was halfway to falling in love with him all over again, and that once Will was fully recovered and out of the hospital, James's fury over what she'd done might return.

Neve wasn't the only one trying to burn up nervous energy while they waited for Emma to come out of brain surgery. On the other side of Flick, Toby and Caleb were playing games on their phones, occasionally grunting at each other in the way that teenage boys do. Next to Neve were Laura and Louise, leaning against each other as they listened to music from the same phone, one earbud for each of them. They were tapping their shoes to the beat, which Flick could also hear due to how loud they had it playing. Under normal circumstances, she'd have told them to turn it down, but today she kept her mouth shut.

It was Monday, and even though Emma's children had already had two weeks off school in Hawaii, they'd begged their parents for another day so they could be close while Emma went under the knife. That the kids could have one more day might have been the first thing Max and Emma had agreed on since they'd split.

When Toby asked if he could come to support Caleb and the girls, Flick and Seb hadn't argued either. Truth was, after the emotional upheaval of the last few days, Flick wanted the kids close—and it was unlikely any lessons learned at school would register today anyway. Flick wouldn't have been able to stay home in her studio and try to create, so how could she expect Toby to go to school? Zoe had a class at university she couldn't miss but had already texted Flick five times asking if there was any news. On another row of plastic chairs, only a few feet away, staring aimlessly up at some midday movie on the TV, were Seb, Max and Patrick.

Flick wasn't sure who she'd been more surprised to see—Max or Patrick. According to Emma, her ex-husband had been very supportive and sympathetic when she'd told him about the tumor, but it was still a little weird to have him here after so many years of him being the bad guy. Thank God Chanel hadn't decided to join the waiting party. Although Patrick had introduced himself to Max as Emma's boss, it had been impossible to miss the flash of wariness in Max's eyes when they'd shaken hands. She guessed he suspected as much as she did that Patrick wasn't quite this attentive with all his employees. Was he jealous of a possible relationship between Emma and Patrick? Whatever the reason, an undeniable friction buzzed between the two men, so Seb had landed the unofficial role of peacekeeper.

When a tall figure in scrubs appeared in the doorway and surveyed the waiting crowd, Flick's eyes jolted away from Patrick and Max. Every head in the room snapped up, hoping this man would bring good news of their loved one, but when he strode past Flick over to a couple of strangers, she slumped back into her seat and surreptitiously glanced at her watch. News of Emma's surgery should be imminent; according to the surgeon's words that morning, she should have been in recovery for a few hours already. Ice crept into Flick's heart at the possibility that maybe the operation hadn't gone as smoothly as hoped.

When Neve nudged her, Flick looked sideways to see her friend biting her lip and offering a questioning glance. They exchanged a whole conversation with their eyes, neither wanting to alert the kids to the fact that they were starting to worry.

Then Max stood, stretched his arms wide and turned around to face them. "Shouldn't Em be in recovery by now?" he boomed, his voice loud enough for all and sundry to hear. He sounded more annoyed that he was having to wait longer than anticipated than worried about his ex.

Flick clenched her jaw tightly. *So much for protecting the children.* Seb and Patrick stood and also turned to the group. Caleb and Toby looked up from their phones, the twins tugged the buds out of their ears and all four kids stood to join the adults.

"Do you think something's gone wrong?" Laura asked. She and Louise clung to each other, twin expressions of worry on

their faces and their lower lips quivering. They were both trying very hard not to cry.

"Who knows?" Max shrugged one shoulder and Flick resisted the urge to rip off her shoe and throw it at him. "Maybe
I could ask someone." He looked around but there was no
one in the waiting room but other families in the same situation as them.

Thank God Emma had refused him the honor of being
listed as her next of kin. As her children were underage and
she didn't want Caleb, Louise or Laura to be the ones to receive any bad news directly, she'd named Flick and Neve instead. The hospital had *their* phone numbers, and they would
be the first to hear any news of Emma—whether it be good *or*
bad. Before she'd headed into surgery, Emma had also made
her friends promise that if she didn't come out, they'd look
out for Caleb, Laura and Louise, and make sure Max didn't
make a mess of parenting them.

They'd told her to stop being so pessimistic, but deep down
they knew they'd do whatever it took. Did that give them
the right to tell Max to take a hike? Only for the benefit of
Emma's children did Flick swallow her desire to do exactly
that. He might be a total dick sometimes—okay, most of the
time—but he was still their dad, and for that reason alone
she'd put up with him.

"Let's not get carried away," Seb said, his voice calm and
his smile reassuring as he walked around the row of chairs
to the girls. He pulled them into a group hug and they clung
to him, taking some of the support their own father should
have been offering. "Hospitals aren't train stations. They don't
always run according to schedule. No news is good news."

Although Flick wasn't sure if that was the case when it came
to brain surgery, the girls perked up at Seb's theory and she
flashed him a grateful smile. He always knew the right things

to say and truly would be the perfect guy…if he didn't actually think himself a woman. Her stomach contorted at this thought, and that made her angry.

Her head had accepted the program; why couldn't her body keep up?

Before she could contemplate this question, another doctor appeared and this time she recognized him as the surgeon in charge of Emma's operation. One look at the smile on his face and relief flooded her body. That wasn't the grin of a man about to be the bearer of bad news.

"Good afternoon," he said, coming over and addressing the group. This added to Flick's good feeling, because if what he had to say wasn't good, he'd take her and Neve aside to speak privately, wouldn't he? Still, she held her breath as she waited for the news.

"I'm pleased to report that Emma is in recovery and should return to the ward within the next few hours."

Flick puffed out a breath in perfect time with the others. They all looked at each other, their grins positively bursting.

The doctor looked pleased at this response. "I'm sorry things took a little longer than we expected. I'll be honest, it was touch and go there for a moment, but Emma is a fighter."

"Touch and go?" Flick didn't mean to say the words out loud.

The doctor's expression turned solemn. He nodded. "Yes, there was a difficult moment on the operating table."

Difficult moment? Did that mean they'd almost *lost her*? A chill descended over Flick's body, goose bumps sprouting on her arms and at the back of her neck. Jumping to the same conclusion she had, the twins sobbed.

"But she's okay now, right?" Flick asked, wanting reassurance for herself as much as for the girls.

Again the doctor smiled. "Yes. We got her back. We managed to remove the tumor, and although her journey to a full recovery will take a while, I'm pleased with the outcome of today's surgery. Now, unless you have any further questions, I must go. It'll be a good few hours before Emma is up to visitors, and even then, the nurses on the ward will limit it to one or two people for small periods of time. Emma will be very tired and will need her rest."

The last line sounded like a reprimand, and they all nodded like chastised children.

When the surgeon left, the small circle of friends broke into hugs. Toby slapped Caleb on the back in an adolescent male show of support, and then Caleb yanked his twin sisters into a hug, something he rarely did for fear of appearing *uncool*. Seb and Patrick even hugged but Max looked a little uncomfortable at all this emotion.

Flick wiped happy tears from her eyes as she pulled back from Neve's embrace and then lost herself in Seb's a moment later. "She's okay, she's okay, she's okay," she whispered over and over again, feeling as if a huge weight had been lifted.

Will and Emma were both on the road to recovery. What more could any of them ask for?

When the hug frenzy finally died down, Patrick made his excuses.

"I'd better be getting back to work. Jenny and Mandy will be wanting to know how Emma is. Tell her I've been thinking of her and I'm pleased the operation went well." He shoved his hands into his pockets, and although he'd spoken about leaving, he made no attempt to do so.

"We'll tell her." Flick smiled encouragingly at Patrick. "Thanks for being here. I'll call you later and let you know how she's doing."

Patrick gave a nod. "Thanks. That would be great." And then he left.

Neve was the next to make a move, slightly apologetic about wanting to get back to Will. "Can you tell Emma that I'll visit her tomorrow?"

"Of course. She'd want you to be with Will," Flick reassured her. "And anyway, you heard the doctor. We don't want to tire her with too many visitors today."

Neve nodded, then hugged Caleb and the twins before following in the direction Patrick had gone a few moments earlier.

Max, to his credit, summoned the kids—including Toby—and took them down the street to get takeout for lunch while they waited for Emma to be up to visitors. This left Flick and Seb alone in the hospital waiting room.

"Do you want to go get some lunch?" he asked.

Flick shook her head. She was too full with relief to be hungry.

"Been a crazy couple of weeks, hasn't it?" he said, reaching out to take her hand.

"You can say that again," she said, collapsing back into one of the plastic chairs and trying to resist the urge to pull her hand from Seb's.

Although the worst might be over for Emma and Neve, Flick suspected that her craziness was only just beginning. Her gut still rolled and her palms went clammy every time she thought about the day Toby and Zoe would discover the truth about their dad. Thank God she had a few months' reprieve now to focus on Zoe's wedding. A few months to get her head around the future and to garner the courage necessary to face the drama that undoubtedly lay ahead.

49

Emma

Emma awoke to a room full of flowers and a middle-aged motherly-looking nurse standing beside her bed.

"Hello, love," said the nurse, all cheery smiles.

It took a second for her to orientate herself, to remember where she was and why.

The damn tumor.

There'd been lights and voices. A tunnel.

"Am I alive?" she whispered to the nurse, her throat parched.

The woman chuckled. "Of course you are. Unless this is heaven and I'm an angel, but my husband will tell you I'm definitely not one of those. And if *this* is heaven, I'll be extremely disappointed. I was hoping for a place with long, white sandy beaches and lots of clear blue ocean." She leaned in closer to Emma. "Populated by tall, dark, sexy cabana boys that answer to my every beck and call. You know what I'm talking about, right?"

It was Emma's turn to chuckle, but that only exacerbated her dry throat.

"Here, let me get you some ice chips to suck on," said the nurse, who was apparently a mind reader as well as a comedian.

She retreated and Emma found herself all alone in the small private hospital room. She couldn't remember waking up in recovery but guessed she must have for them to have brought her up to the ward. How long had she been here? Had she seen her kids yet? Patrick? She racked her brain, trying to remember, but that only made her head hurt. Wanting to check said head, she tried to lift her arm but a tube coming out of her hand hindered her efforts. Dammit. She moaned a little in frustration as the nurse returned to the room.

"There now," she said, rushing over and dumping a plastic container on the adjustable table. "Don't overexert yourself."

With the push of a few buttons, the back of the bed rose a little, drawing Emma almost into a sitting position and enabling her to read the name on the nurse's badge. "Daisy" suited her down to a T. Daisy spooned a few ice chips from the container into a plastic cup and handed it to Emma.

She took one out and popped it into her mouth. Nothing had *ever* tasted so good. After a few moments, she felt able to talk again. "What time is it?"

Daisy glanced down at her cute little fob watch. "It's almost seven p.m. You woke briefly in recovery but you've been asleep ever since. Totally normal after the kind of surgery you've just been through. You've got quite the fan club waiting out there to see you, though. Do you think you're up for a quick visit?"

Emma's heart leaped at the thought of seeing her kids. "Yes. Definitely. I don't look too scary, do I?" After surviving brain surgery, *she* didn't care what she looked like but scaring her kids wasn't something she wanted to do.

Daisy smiled warmly and then conjured two tiny mirrors from one of her pockets. "I don't think your family will give two hoots how you look right now, but I understand you wanting to present your best for that spunky hubby of yours.

Here you go." She held the mirrors up in a way that gave Emma a full view of the wound site.

"Husband?" She screwed up her nose. The side of her head looked more like a medieval dungeon—all dried blood and metal staples—than a human body part.

Daisy put the mirrors back into her pocket. "Tall, dark, broad shouldered...looks a little like Russell Crowe. Ring any bells?" She chuckled. "I like that rugged look, a man that looks like a man, if you know what I mean."

Emma smiled—Daisy's description of Max couldn't have been more perfect. And he had the celebrity arrogance to go with it. "That's my ex. You're welcome to him. Although his new child bride might have something to say about that."

"Oh, I'm sorry." Daisy's eyes popped wide. "He's been demanding to know when he could see you... I just assumed."

"It's fine." She supposed she should be grateful that Max had come to the party to look after and support the kids, and then she thought otherwise. They were his children as well after all. This was half her problem, she realized suddenly— even before they were divorced, she made excuses for him being a workaholic, mostly absent dad and had taken it upon herself to be both parents. She'd taken it upon herself to be everything for everyone. *No more.*

With near death came a clarity of mind she'd never had before. "Do you want to see him, then?" Daisy asked.

Emma sighed. Four people had been on her mind as she'd drifted in and out of consciousness these past few hours, and Max wasn't one of them. She didn't have the energy or inclination to deal with him right now. "Would it cause you a huge problem if I said no?"

"Not at all. You are my patient, and keeping you healthy and happy is my priority," Daisy said, but then she frowned. "Only problem is I'm only supposed to allow you two visitors at a time and you have three children desperate to see you. If I let them all in at the same time, you have to promise not to tell a soul."

Emma smiled. She liked this woman immensely. "The secret's safe with me."

"In that case, I'll be right back."

As Daisy left the room, Emma sucked on another ice cube and tried to position her head so that her wound wouldn't be the first thing the kids laid eyes on. She was quite proud of the battle scar—it was proof she'd had brain surgery and lived to tell the tale! No doubt Caleb would delight in the gruesomeness of it all, but neither of the girls liked blood and gore. However, covering the monstrosity was impossible. They'd had to cut and shave off half her hair for the operation. Strangely, this didn't cause her the pain and anguish she'd imagined it would.

"Mom!" The moment the door opened again, her three most favorite voices in the world spoke her favorite word in unison. She grinned as her children rushed at her, not hesitant about all the tubes and stuff as an adult might have been.

Happy tears streamed down Laura's face as she practically climbed onto the bed and snuggled in beside Emma. Louise, also tearful, took a position on the other side and Emma didn't care one iota about feeling squashed. Caleb's eyes were red, indicating he'd been through all the emotions today, but he wasn't crying now. He stood right next to the bed and grasped her hand.

"Hello, my darlings," she said, emotion pooling in the back of her throat. When she'd gone under earlier that day, her greatest fear had not been getting her skull cut open but that something might go wrong and she might never see these three special people grow up.

"It's good to see ya, Mom." Caleb grinned, then nodded to her head. "You're going to have an awesome scar."

"Ew." Laura pulled back slightly as if she'd only just noticed her mom's head.

Louise gasped. "They've taken all your beautiful hair."

"Not all of it," Emma said, loving the feel of her daughters' warm bodies pressed against her. "And it'll grow back, although maybe it's time for a change. This tumor thing could have taken a lot more from me. From us."

"I know," Laura whispered. "Apparently you died for a few moments today."

Caleb rolled his eyes. His tone condescending, he said, "That is *not* what the doctor said."

"I'm pretty sure that's what he meant," Louise added, sticking up for her twin and glaring at her older brother.

Emma smiled; usually their bickering drove her crazy but tonight it was just another beautiful sound she was grateful to be alive to listen to. And she was pretty certain Laura was right. A part of her had died today—it was the only explanation for the light and the voices she could recall with absolute clarity—but it was a part of herself she could do without. The part that lived in constant stress and fear, constant worry that she wasn't doing enough for her loved ones, constant anxiety over insignificant things such as paying bills and dealing with the day-to-day rigmarole, which left little room for the things that mattered.

Things like spending quality time with family. Things like friendship and love. The latter made her think of Patrick and warmth filled her fluttering heart.

"The important thing," Emma said, "is that I'm here now and so are you three. So, no more long faces. Tell me something exciting!"

The girls giggled. Caleb rolled his eyes again but grinned

nonetheless. This was something the four of them had shared since the children were very little. A conversation starter to take their minds off whatever was bothering them and to focus on the positive. Emma hadn't asked this question of them or herself for a long time; another indicator of how lost she'd got.

"Chanel and Dad have been bickering like cats and dogs since we got back from Hawaii," Laura announced. "I overheard them arguing about having a baby—she wants one and he doesn't."

"Is that right?" Emma tried to sound interested when in fact she couldn't care less about what went on between her ex and his new wife anymore.

"It's disgusting, if you ask me," said Louise. "He's too old to have a baby."

Emma laughed, but then winced because the action made her head hurt.

A frown creased Caleb's forehead. "Are you okay?"

"I'm fine," she told him. "More than fine."

At that moment the door opened again and Daisy bustled in carrying a small tray of food. "In my experience you're either famished or not feeling up to food just yet but I brought you a little selection of things just in case. Sorry—nothing exciting. Jelly and watery soup are all they'll allow until we've seen a bowel movement."

"Gross," Louise exclaimed.

"Nothing gross about bodily functions," Daisy said, placing the tray on the adjustable table.

Emma's stomach rumbled as she looked down at the meal but a yawn escaped her mouth at the same time. Fatigue overcame her again and she wasn't sure she had the energy to eat.

Daisy checked her pocket watch. "All right, kids, time to give Mom some more rest."

The girls groaned but Caleb nodded, a glimpse of maturity shining through in his understanding eyes.

"I'll see you all tomorrow. After school," Emma clarified, in case they thought they could use her as an excuse to solicit more absentee days. "Love you all."

"Love you, too," Caleb said, leaning over to kiss her on the cheek.

"Yes, love you, Mom." As usual the twins spoke as one and then the three of them trudged reluctantly out of the room. The door swung shut behind them and Daisy smiled.

"Lovely three you have there. You must be very proud."

Emma simply nodded as she attempted to lift a spoon and scoop some jelly.

"I know I just said you need rest but there's a friend of yours out there who has also been here all day and wonders if she could just pop in for a quick good-night before you go to sleep again."

A rush of excitement gave Emma a boost of energy at the mention of a friend, but her pulse slowed again as she registered the word *she*. Some crazy part of her had assumed the friend in question was Patrick. She wanted to see him more than she'd ever wanted anything in her life, but she guessed the friend was Flick, and despite the exhaustion, she'd like to see her as well.

"Yes. Please. Send her in," Emma said, and then managed a mouthful of jelly.

Daisy retreated again and returned a few moments later with one very harried-looking Flick. Honestly, Emma felt more relaxed than her friend looked.

"We've been so worried about you," Flick said, bypassing the formalities. "I just had to see you for myself before I went home."

"I'm fine."

"You're not in pain?" Flick asked, taking the seat beside the bed.

Emma shrugged. "A little. Tired more than anything. I'm hungry but…" She sighed as she struggled to lift another spoonful to her mouth.

"Here, let me." Flick leaned over and took the spoon from Emma's hand, proceeding to feed her as if she were a toddler. The old Emma would have refused such help, but the new Emma happily let her friend look after her. She finished the jelly and devoured almost every mouthful of the entirely horrible soup.

"Neve was here during your operation," Flick said as she put the spoon and empty bowl back on the table. "She wanted me to give you her love and said she'll visit tomorrow, but she had to get back to Will."

Emma nodded. "Thank God he's going to be okay."

Flick smiled. "Thank God you both are. I don't think I've ever been so worried in my life as I have been this past week or so."

"You and me both." But she didn't want worry to occupy so much of her time and energy from now on. "Do you believe in near-death experiences?"

Flick frowned. "I've never really thought about it. Why? Do you think you had one?"

"Something like that. I saw bright lights and then I saw Mom and Grandma and I felt this strange sense of slipping away, but something pulled me back at the last moment."

"Good Lord! Really?"

"Yep. It was exactly as they say. My life flashed before me—all the good times and the bad, all the people that mattered and some of those that don't. Suddenly everything made perfect sense. I want to see Patrick."

Flick's lips turned upward in victory. "I knew something was going on between you two. I guess he isn't gay after all?"

Emma shook her head, unable to stop herself from grinning wildly.

"He was here most of the day as well," Flick said, "but he left once we heard you were in recovery. I don't think he wanted to go, but Max wasn't particularly welcoming. He made it clear that Patrick should leave this time to your family."

But Patrick *was* her family. At least she now knew she wanted him to be.

"I want to see Patrick," she said again.

"Now?" Flick frowned and glanced at her watch. "But it's almost the end of visiting hours."

"I don't care. I need to see him," she insisted. "Please call him and ask him to come in. If this whole ordeal has taught me anything, it's that life is for living and I don't want to waste a second more. I don't want to live with any regrets. You were right, there is more going on between us. At least I want there to be."

"Wow." Flick blinked. "When you have a near-death experience, you don't mess around, do you?"

She shook her head and smiled up at her friend.

A few hours later, Emma awoke again, this time to a dimly lit room and a shadowy figure sitting beside her bed. For two seconds fear leaped into her throat, and then she remembered the request she'd given Flick before saying goodbye.

"Hello, Emma," came the shadow's deep voice—the same voice that had brought her back from the brink earlier that day.

"You came?" she whispered.

"Of course I did," Patrick replied. "When Flick called me I drove right in, but you were already asleep when I arrived.

The nurse on duty refused me entrance to your room at first, but I can be very persuasive when I want to be."

A lump swelled in her throat. Oh, how she loved the comforting lilt of his deep voice. Patrick had softer edges than Max, but that didn't make him any less masculine. Any less attractive. She didn't know how she'd ever convinced herself he was gay; for purely selfish reasons, she was *so* glad he wasn't. Despite the fact that she had only half a head of hair and was lying on a hospital bed in the unsexiest night wear she could possibly imagine, tingles shivered all over her body.

She reached out toward him, a courage she'd never had before springing from deep inside her. "I'm glad you came. The only thing that could make me happier would be if you kissed me."

Patrick let out what sounded like a choked groan. "Are you sure?"

"I've never been more certain of anything in my life. I've been scared until now, scared of getting hurt or betrayed or rejected again, but I don't want to live in fear anymore. I'd rather tell you what I want—which is *you*—and risk rejection than continue to live the half-life I've been living these past few years. So, if you don't want to kiss me, if you're appalled by the idea of kissing Frankenstein's sister, if you don't have the feelings inside you for me that I have inside me for you, then I'll—"

Emma didn't get to finish her sentence.

Patrick leaned toward her and ever so gently pressed his lovely warm mouth against hers. Her breathing hitched, and her whole body filled with warm liquidy goodness. It wasn't the raunchiest of kisses—there'd be plenty of time for those later, when she was completely well again—but it was a kiss full of promise and, most important, love.

When Patrick finally pulled back, Emma smiled so hard

she thought her face might snap. He enveloped her hand with his and said, "I hope that wasn't the anesthetic speaking because I've been wanting to do that for a very, very long time."

"Why didn't you?" she asked, grinning from the inside out.

"You're not the only one who was scared," he admitted. "When we first met you were married and off-limits, then when Max broke up with you, you were so brokenhearted, I didn't think I could ever compete. There was also the tiny thing about you being my employee and me not wanting to take advantage. Not to mention you thinking I was gay."

Emma's cheeks flushed at the thought. "Thank God you set me right on that. After that kiss, I'm hoping you'll start taking a lot more advantage."

He laughed, a lovely deep chuckle that echoed around the small room and rippled right through her body. "It's a promise."

With that knowledge, Emma fell asleep again, Patrick by her side and a warm contentedness in her heart that had been missing for far too long.

50

Felicity

"Hello, Sofia, Felicity, so lovely to meet you."

Flick forced a smile at the bohemian-dressed woman called Learna and then, following Seb's lead, accepted a handshake as they were ushered into her office. They'd only had a short wait at the gender support clinic, but Flick would have waited all day. She wasn't sure she would ever be ready for this meeting, but…here they were.

"Please, take a seat." Learna gestured to a funky multi-colored couch in her very chill office. Some kind of herbal incense wafted from a burner in the corner—Flick got the impression it was supposed to be relaxing, but it didn't have that effect on her at all.

Flick and Seb took the couch as they were told, and Learna sat in the armchair opposite them, smiling a few long moments before speaking.

"Now, I don't want to overwhelm either of you with too much information on our first session together, but I want to start by commending you for taking this first step." She positively beamed at Seb. "Sofia, it shows a great deal of courage to make this decision. And Felicity, it shows true strength of character to be able to support your partner along this journey. You obviously have a very special and very strong relationship."

"We do." Seb squeezed her hand. Flick tried to smile, but quite frankly she felt like throwing up.

"One of the most important parts of the transition process," continued the woman who would be their contact at the gender clinic going forward, "is a strong support network of family and friends, but also of nonbiased parties, which is why we insist on psychological counseling for the transgender candidate and strongly recommend couples counseling. Felicity, I'll suggest a counselor just for you as well. It's important for you both to remember that you are not alone in this situation and you will not be alone on your journey. Sofia, there are group sessions you can attend with other transition candidates and, Felicity, I'm going to put you in touch with other partners on this same journey. We should never underestimate the power of conversation."

Flick nodded, wishing this woman would stop calling Seb Sofia and stop referring to whatever this was as their journey—as if they were about to embark on some expedition or safari.

"So do either of you have any questions before I start asking a few of my own?"

Flick raised an eyebrow and summoned up her mental notebook. It was bursting with so many damn questions she didn't even know where to start. But maybe her questions would be better asked in couples counseling or when she talked to someone on her own.

As if Learna were a mind reader, she gave Flick a sympathetic smile. "I know this is a lot to take in. Although you've made this decision to stand by Sofia, you should give yourself time and permission to process your thoughts and feelings. The good news is, you will have plenty of time. Whatever route Sofia chooses to take in her transition, it won't happen overnight. Hormone-replacement therapy won't begin immediately, and it can be months, sometimes years before physical changes start to become apparent."

Out of the corner of her eye, Flick saw Seb physically deflate at this news, but inwardly it felt like a victory.

"Surgery, if it happens," Learna continued, "will be even further down the road. What we ask of you, Felicity, is to try to learn more about what it means to be transgender so that you can help Sofia on the journey. I won't lie—it's not always going to be an easy and straightforward one. And Sofia won't be the only one who could be ostracized from friends and family, but learning and understanding what transition involves and talking to others in your same situation will help you to navigate this road. It will also help you support your children. I understand you have two?"

Seb nodded. "Yes, that's right. Zoe is twenty and Toby seventeen."

Zoe and Toby. Flick didn't know how Seb planned on telling them his secret but the mere thought of sitting down for that chat twisted her up inside. Never mind how it would make them feel about Seb. Would it also change their views on *her*? She sniffed, not wanting to show any sign of weakness in front of Learna, and tried to focus on the rest of the session, which was more of an overview of what meetings going forward would entail. There was so much to think about, to discuss and to plan—from the actual physical transition to the financial implications and everything in between.

They left an hour later, armed with brochures containing everything she could possibly want to know—or not, if she was honest—about gender transitioning, including hormone therapy options, breast augmentation and even electrolysis. Flick had never even considered the latter herself so it was hard to wrap her head around Seb's excitement.

She felt like she was on a scary roller coaster at some theme park—she didn't want to stop and get off, she just wanted it to slow down a bit.

"Well, that went well," Seb said brightly as they emerged into the clinic's parking lot. It wasn't too far from his office and she couldn't understand how he couldn't be concerned about the possibility of being seen by a colleague—or worse, a client. "Thank you for coming with me."

"You're welcome." She dug her car keys out of her handbag, itching to escape.

"I told the boss I wasn't sure how long my medical appointment would last," Seb said, seemingly unaware of her anxiety, "so do you want to go get some lunch before I head back to work?"

Lunch? As if she could eat right now.

"I'm not really hungry," she confessed, hoping Seb would take that at face value. "And I have a lot of work to catch up on after the New York trip and then everything with Emma and Will. Do you mind if we take a rain check?"

"Not at all." Seb half smiled. "But are you sure that's it? Are you sure you're okay with everything… You know?"

"*Okay* is a broad term, Seb, but I wouldn't be here if I didn't want to be. We'll talk later." Then before he could argue or ask any more questions, she leaned forward and kissed him on the cheek. "I'll see you at home."

As she stalked off toward her car, Flick closed her eyes briefly and endeavored to swallow the lump in her throat. The last thing she really wanted was to go home and spend time alone with her own thoughts.

She got into her car, started it on autopilot and found herself driving toward Emma's place instead of her own. As she slowed in front of the house, she saw Neve's little hatchback approaching from the other direction. They parked one behind the other on the driveway, then climbed out of their respective cars and greeted each other with a hug.

"Great minds think alike," Neve said as she pulled back from Flick's embrace. "How are you today?"

"Fine," Flick lied. "And you?"

"Going slowly crazy," Neve admitted, "but Will is alive and out of the hospital, so who am I to complain? I decided to give him and James some alone time, but to be honest, I couldn't stay under my own roof with both of them a moment longer."

"I can imagine this must be hard," Flick said as they started up the path toward Emma's front door.

Neve rang the bell and they waited a few moments for Emma to answer.

"Hello," she said as she peeled back the door. A massive grin sat in pride of place on her face, and despite her half-shaved head and pajama-clad body, she looked way too good for someone who had been through life-threatening surgery just over a week ago. "Come in."

They followed Emma into the kitchen and sat down on stools at the breakfast bar. Although Emma had a perfectly good living room with a perfectly good couch, they rarely made it out of the kitchen.

"Coffee?" Emma asked.

"Let me," Flick insisted, standing and forcing her friend to sit on one of the stools. "You're supposed to be taking it easy."

Emma smiled. "Thanks. Honestly, I'm feeling much better than I imagined."

"You look good, too," Flick said as she picked up the kettle to fill it.

"Do I smell curry?" Neve asked, sniffing the air.

Emma's smile grew. "You do indeed." Her cheeks flushed as she confessed, "Patrick made it for dinner last night."

"Ooh," Neve said, that one word weighted with speculation.

Flick grinned. "I think you have some explaining to do, young lady."

Emma actually giggled as if she was the young girl Flick accused her of being.

"Yes." Neve nodded as Flick started making the drinks. "We want details. What's going on with you and Patrick?"

"Well...we're together, I guess."

"You guess?" Flick smiled at Emma's coyness.

"Does *together* mean what I think it does?" Neve asked.

The blush in Emma's cheeks spread all over her face and down her neck; if anything, her smile grew even wider. "You were right about sex, Neve. It can be mind-blowing with the right person."

Neve squealed as she reached across and wrapped an arm around Emma. "Oh, my God, I'm so happy for you."

Flick frowned. "Should you be...you know, *doing it* so soon after surgery?"

"Oh, don't be a spoilsport," Neve said, laughing. "Let the girl enjoy the ride." She laughed some more at her double entendre.

"Sorry." Feeling chastised, Flick blinked and summoned an enthusiastic smile as she placed a steaming mug of coffee in front of each of them. "This is truly wonderful news."

"So has Patrick been staying while the kids are at Max's?" Neve asked, picking up her mug.

"Yep. I'm making up for all those lost child-free weekends wallowing in self-pity. I feel like I've been given a new lease on life and I'm gonna live it to the fullest. But enough about me. I know things aren't easy for either of you right now."

"I'd rather talk about you," Neve said, but then promptly admitted, "Right now I feel like an unwanted guest in my own house."

"Oh, I'm sorry." Emma reached out and patted Neve's hand.

"I know I wasn't very supportive when you first told us about James and I'm sorry about that, but I can't imagine how difficult it must be having to share your home with him."

"He's not being cruel, is he?" Flick asked. James had been nothing but polite and friendly at the hospital but she knew looks could be deceiving.

"No. Definitely not. He's being a perfect gentleman actually and he's so great with Will—they've been playing the Xbox together and watching guy movies. It's lovely to see them bonding and I'm so happy and relieved for Will, but it hurts like hell, you know. I still love him, and living under the same roof is all kinds of torture when I can't tell him."

"If that's the truth, then I think you *should* tell him," Emma said.

Flick looked to Neve and they exchanged a glance. Although they were happy about Emma's new romance, that didn't mean life always had happy endings. "When does he leave again?" she asked, filling the silence that Emma's suggestion had made.

"In a few days." Neve looked close to tears. "But the thought of him not being there doesn't make me feel any better either."

Flick honestly didn't know what to say to help her friend. Maybe Emma was right and she should throw caution to the wind and confess her feelings to James. Then again, maybe that would make everything even worse—they had to think of Will's feelings. "If only life came with a handbook on how to deal with all the obstacles it deals out," she said.

As Neve nodded her agreement, Flick thought again about the first session at the clinic. It was never going to be easy but she'd jumped the first hurdle and she would manage the rest as well.

"You're quiet this afternoon," Emma said, jolting her from her thoughts.

"Am I?" She tightened her grip on her mug. "I just had a session at the gender support clinic with Seb. Or should I say Sofia?"

Silence hung between them for a few moments.

"Wow," Emma said eventually. "I can't begin to imagine how tough that must have been."

"You want to talk about it?" Neve asked.

Flick sighed. "I wouldn't know where to start. There's so much to consider as we *navigate the journey ahead*."

Neve and Emma frowned at the way she mimicked Learna's words.

She explained how the counselor had grated on her nerves. "There's just a lot to take in," she concluded.

"No kidding," Neve said. "But you're handling this a whole lot better than most would."

Emma nodded. "I'd be a total mess." Was that what she was inside?

"You know," Emma began, "we respect your decision to stand by Seb and in turn we'll stand by you, but are you sure this is the right thing for you, Flick? Have you really thought this all through?"

"With all due respect, Emma," Flick snapped, "I've barely thought about anything else in weeks. And a little like you feel about Patrick and Neve feels about James, I can't imagine my life without Seb in it, so yes, it might take some time, but this *is* what I want to do."

"In that case," Emma said, reaching over and taking Flick's hand in hers, "I support your decision one hundred percent and I promise to be here for you in any way I can."

"And so do I," Neve added.

Flick tried to swallow the lump in her throat long enough to thank her friends; instead she burst into tears.

51

Genevieve

James pushed Will in the wheelchair and Neve walked beside them as they headed toward the airport for his flight back to New York. Neither of them wanted him to go—at least Neve didn't, and she got the feeling James was dragging his feet as well, but perhaps for different reasons. He'd been in Perth for just over a week, and what a highly charged, emotional week it had been.

It felt like forever; it felt like less than a second.

In that time, Will had been transferred from the ICU into a ward and then a couple of days later he'd been given the all clear to come home. Two broken legs meant he still needed a lot of care and assistance. Neve and James had fallen into this role as easily as if they'd been a team of two their whole lives, overlooking the tension between them to focus on their son. Part of her was thankful that Will wasn't completely recovered—it meant she could fuss over her baby without him being able to object too much but it also meant that while he and James got to know each other, she was never too far away.

James had accepted her offer to stay in their spare room and this was both a blessing and a curse. She loved watching the way he doted on Will and the relationship that had blossomed quickly between the two of them, but seeing this made her feelings for James even harder to ignore. For Will's sake, he treated her with respect and politeness; occasionally she even thought she saw a flash of something more when his eyes met with hers, but it was probably her overactive imagination. James might be civil because of Will, he might be back in her life for the same reason, but after what she'd done, she had no illusions that anything besides joint parenthood would ever happen between them. And she couldn't help the ache in her heart whenever she thought about it, which was *all the bloody time.*

Once inside the international terminal, James stopped pushing the wheelchair and took the small suitcase Neve had been dragging along behind them. Their fingers brushed against each other in the exchange but she'd learned to school her facial features this last week so that she didn't react to accidental touches.

"I'll check in, and then do you want to head up and get a drink before I go through customs?" he asked, addressing the both of them.

Neve would rather not prolong the agony of being in his company, but she nodded and took the handles on the wheelchair. Will wanted to stay with James until the last possible moment; father and son wanted to spend every second they could together, but due to Will's temporary handicap, she had to tag along as well. If it weren't for being confined to the wheelchair, Will might have held on to his anger toward her longer—perhaps indefinitely—but the crash had shocked him as much as it had his parents, and his brush with death had, like Emma's, made him realize what truly mattered in life.

He hadn't forgotten what Neve had done—he might never completely forgive her—but he didn't want to gain a dad only to lose a mom. He'd made that clear in the hospital, making her prouder than ever of the son she'd raised. Surely if she'd created a boy like him, she'd done some things right, and she hoped in time James might come to this conclusion as well.

Even if they'd never be lovers again, maybe they could be friends.

"I can't believe he's going already," Will said as they watched James join the check-in line at Emirates. He was flying to New York via Dubai.

Neve had no idea what to say to that, but she tried. "You've made the connection now. I'm sure you'll see him again before too long."

At this thought fear wrapped itself around her heart like barbed wire—Will was a couple of months from finishing school. Only a few months after that he'd be eighteen and free to do as he pleased. The possibility that he might decide to head to the United States and spend some more time getting to know his dad terrified her, and the awful thing was that she completely understood. She'd miss him like crazy, but who wouldn't want to get to know James better? He was such a wonderful person—the fact that he'd overlooked his own issues with her for the sake of Will proved this. And only made her feel guiltier that she'd kept them apart for so long.

"He's a great guy, isn't he?" Will looked up at her. "I can see why you fell for him."

She smiled. "Yes, he's a very good guy. You're a lot like him, you know that?"

"Thanks." Pride shone in Will's face at her words. "I wonder what Hannah and Jolie will think of me."

"They'll love you," Neve said with absolute conviction. James's daughters sounded close to him and he'd said they were excited at the prospect of having a little brother. She liked them already; not that she'd probably have much to do with them. They might embrace Will, but that didn't mean they would want to get all friendly with the woman their dad betrayed their mom with.

Will went quiet again and Neve sneaked a look at James as he shuffled forward in the line toward the check-in desk. For a man of fifty, he looked good. Better than good, and her mouth went dry as she stared at the way his faded denim jeans hugged his butt. It seemed such a long time since they'd been up close and personal, but in reality it was less than two weeks, and her body craved more of him like she'd never craved anything in her life.

"Did you love him, Mom?"

Again Will's words snapped her out of her fantasy. "What, honey?"

"Dad. Did you love him when you guys were together or was it just…you know…sex?"

She blushed at Will's words, despite his embarrassed hesitation. Yet this was one question she didn't need to think about at all. "Yes," she told him honestly. "I loved James more than I've ever loved anyone before or since—aside from you, of course."

Will grinned up at her, his smile so boyish in comparison to his almost fully grown body. "That's what he said, too."

Her grip tightened on the wheelchair's handles. "What?"

"He said he loved you more than his wife, even though it was wrong, and that even after you left, he never stopped thinking about you."

"Really?" She couldn't keep the joy from her voice. She wanted to sob loudly and messily but somehow managed to restrain herself. A little voice inside her head told her that perhaps James had said this purely for the sake of their son, but she ignored it and took comfort from Will's words as if they were a warm blanket wrapped around her.

If James had loved her once, was there a possibility that he could one day love her again?

James strode over a few minutes later. "Right, I'm all checked in." He may have spent the last few years living in America but he still had an Aussie swagger that made her pulse skip. Hell, who was she kidding? Every tiny thing about him made her pulse go crazy. Even during the height of his anger toward her, she'd wanted to jump his bones.

"Excellent." She swallowed. "Let's go get a drink."

He took the handles of the wheelchair again and they took the elevator up to the next level of the airport. They bypassed the duty-free shop, news agency and tourist boutique and went straight for the bar.

James positioned the wheelchair next to a table. "Drinks are on me."

He'd whipped his wallet out of his pocket and was halfway to the bar before Neve could object. She pulled out a chair and sat down beside Will, her heart squeezing at the glum expression on his face. She wanted to comfort him, to remind him that it wouldn't be long before they saw each other again, but the fact that it was her fault they'd been apart Will's whole life kept her mouth shut.

They sat in silence until James returned a few minutes later. He handed her a flute of pink bubbles and she smiled her thanks, amazed he still remembered it was her favorite. Dammit, why couldn't he have brought her something she didn't like? He gave Will a can of Coke and then sat and lifted the beer he'd bought for himself to his mouth.

Neve lifted her glass to her lips and focused on the lovely feel of the bubbles on her tongue, rather than the sexy column of his neck as he drank.

After another mouthful, James put down his bottle and looked from Will to Neve and back again. "I have some news."

Will's eyes widened in expectation and Neve lifted an eyebrow, her pulse once again pausing in its business.

"As you both know, *Mamma Mia!* is closing soon and I've been on the lookout for a new job. Well, I've got one." James paused and Neve's stomach twisted in anticipation. "I'm going to be working on *The Lion King*." He grinned from ear to ear at this declaration.

Will frowned and Neve could see their son didn't understand what this meant. But she did. As a lover of all things theater, she kept up-to-date with the musicals that were coming to Perth, and *The Lion King* was one of them. If her memory served her right, it opened at the Crown Theatre in November. Just a few months away.

"I'm moving to Perth," James proclaimed, and Will's mouth dropped open in surprise.

"Seriously?" he asked a few seconds later. "*The Lion King* is in Perth?"

"Seriously." James nodded, a smug expression on his face at the excited surprise in Will's voice. "I'll get you and Stacey opening-night tickets if you like. Girls dig that kind of stuff."

Will beamed, seemingly speechless. Moisture glistened in his eyes and Neve's stomach flipped. It was one thing James being in Will's life, their lives, while he was on the other side of the globe, but how could she cope with him in the same damn city? She should be happy that Will would no longer have reason to move away, but how was she supposed to protect her heart in this scenario?

"That's wonderful," she managed. "I bet your daughters will be happy to have you closer to home again, especially Hannah, since she's going to be here, too."

James shrugged. "I don't know. She might be scared I'll cramp her style, but she'll get over it." He reached across and ruffled Will's hair. "And I couldn't pass this opportunity by."

If anyone else had ruffled his hair in such a manner, Will would have been furious, but instead he grinned, that same superwide smile that matched his father's. "Awesome."

"I'm just going to pop to the ladies'," Neve said, pushing back her seat and shooting to her feet. She turned and fled before Will or James could say anything, but no doubt they barely noticed her go, too ensconced in their future plans.

She tottered toward the restrooms on her too-high heels and had almost made it to the door when a heavy hand landed on her shoulder and spun her around. She came face-to-face with James, in all his beautiful two-day-stubble glory. His steel blue eyes searched hers as if asking her a question but she had no idea what it was. She blinked twice, hoping to stop the silly rush of tears that threatened.

"I was hoping you'd be happy about my news," James said, his voice deep and his expression serious.

"I am," she lied. "It will be good for Will to have you around."

"I didn't just accept the job because of Will."

She nodded. "I know. It's awesome that Hannah will also be living here," she said.

He shook his head. "Hannah being here will be another bonus, but I had other reasons for accepting the position. Entirely selfish ones."

The way he looked at her sent ripples of awareness all through her body, but it had to be her imagination. She wished he'd stop talking in cryptic sentences. "I don't understand."

He leaned toward her and grabbed hold of her hands. "As much as I've tried to hate you for what you did—for keeping Will a secret—it's futile. Living with you this past week has only proved one thing—everything we shared eighteen years ago is still as strong and alive as it was then. I want *you*, Gennie. I want you now as much as I ever wanted you back then, and so much more."

Neve couldn't believe her ears. If James hadn't been holding her hands, she'd have pinched herself to check this wasn't another torturous dream. She frowned up at him. "Is this some kind of joke?"

"No," he whispered with the slightest shake of his head. "And something tells me that you feel exactly the same way. Fighting the chemistry between us is impossible." And with that, he dipped his head, captured her face in the palms of his hands and kissed her.

As her body relaxed into his, Neve's mouth opened to welcome him and endorphins danced through her veins. The tears she'd been fighting broke free, salt water sliding down her cheeks and in between their fused lips. James pulled back, his hands still cupping her face. "I hope those are happy tears," he said, licking them from his own lips.

All Neve could do was nod.

She didn't deserve James's forgiveness, she didn't deserve his love or his body, but, by God, she wanted it. She'd made some terrible mistakes in her life, but turning down his offer of love was not going to be one of them.

52

Felicity

"How do I look, Mom?"

Zoe stood in front of the floor-to-ceiling mirrors in her parents' bedroom and looked to her mom for her approval. Emotion caught in Flick's throat at the vision of her stunning daughter, sparkling almost as much as the Tiffany earrings she wore, dressed in the classic white gown they'd chosen all those months ago. Months that had gone by far too quickly.

She summoned a smile and stepped toward Zoe. "You look… You are…the prettiest thing on the entire planet and I'm so damn incredibly proud of the woman you've grown into."

Not usually one for too much sentiment, today Zoe beamed, the love shining brightly from her face. "Thanks, Mom, I can't wait for Beau to see me."

"Me neither. I just know he'll burst into tears."

Zoe laughed, then her expression turned serious. "While we're alone—" her bridesmaids, brother and father had left the room to let her finish getting dressed "—there's something I've been wanting to say."

"Oh?"

Zoe nodded. "I wanted to thank you for the wonderful example you and Dad have given to me over the years. And to Toby, although he's probably too stupid to realize it yet. We're so lucky to have parents who are not only still together, but are still blissfully in love. I only hope that Beau and I will have the kind of marriage you and Dad do."

Oh, God! It was all Flick could do to stop from gasping as Zoe closed the short distance between them and pulled her into a hug.

As she held her beautiful daughter close, her heart hammered in her chest.

Did Seb realize exactly what he wanted to do?

How would Zoe react if she knew the marriage she wanted to shape her own on was actually a big fat lie? Yes, she and Seb loved each other, but not in the way the world assumed when they saw the perfect couple. Since Will's car accident, Flick's worries about how Toby would react to Seb's news had never been far from her mind, yet every time she'd tried to raise her misgivings, the words had caught in her throat. But she hadn't given enough thought to how his coming out might affect Zoe and Beau as well.

Luckily, years of being married to Seb had made her into a pretty damn good actor, so instead of falling apart in her daughter's arms, Flick donned her metaphorical big-girl panties.

"That's lovely of you to say. We've all been very blessed," she said, although the words she spoke didn't at all match the feelings of turmoil that simmered within her—feelings that had been growing with every day they came closer to Seb's deadline.

Truthfully, Flick had hoped that the time she'd made him wait—till after Toby's graduation and Zoe's wedding—might have caused him to rethink his situation, even change his mind, but no fairy godmother had appeared to grant her wishes.

Only last night, he'd showed her the outfit he planned to wear when he first went out in public, and the joy on his face had been indescribable. Seb had kept his part of the bargain; now it was Flick's turn to keep hers.

A knock sounded on the door and seconds later it opened. Seb strode into the room, looking illegally handsome in a near-black tuxedo and a magenta-colored tie that matched Zoe's bridesmaids' dresses. The groomsmen, Beau's young friends and Toby, had refused to wear pink waistcoats, so Seb had valiantly stepped in and offered to add a little fuchsia flair to his father-of-the-bride outfit. Of course Zoe thought the world of *daddy dearest* for doing this for her, but secretly Flick knew Seb wore pink as much for himself as he did for his daughter.

Pink was one of the colors most featured in his secret wardrobe. The knot that had taken up permanent residence in Flick's belly twisted again.

"There're my gorgeous girls," Seb said now as he smiled from Flick to Zoe and back to Flick again. "The photographer has just arrived. Are you ready to be snapped silly?"

Zoe went over to kiss Seb on the cheek. "I'm so ready."

Seb offered her his arm and she linked hers through his. Flick followed closely behind as he led their girl through the house and out into the front garden, where the photographer and bridesmaids were waiting. Dog rushed over from where he'd been rolling in the grass.

"No!" Everyone shrieked in unison as he launched himself at Zoe.

Luckily Toby had quick reflexes. He grabbed hold of Dog's collar and reined him in before walking him over to his kennel on the front porch. "Sit," he said firmly, and Dog flopped his head onto his paws in chastised disappointment. "Stay."

The mutt put in its place, all eyes turned back to focus on Zoe. Her bridesmaids shrieked oohs and aahs of approval. Toby and the photographer even wolf whistled. Zoe positively beamed. Flick tried to focus on the moment—on the absolute joy of her daughter's big day—and push her anxieties aside. There'd be plenty of time to deal with them later.

The photographer snapped away—taking photos of Zoe with her bridesmaids, then Zoe with her dad, Zoe with Flick, Zoe with both parents and finally a family shot of the four of them. As Flick smiled at the camera she couldn't help the heavy feeling in her heart. This would be the last photo like this ever taken of them. From now on Beau would be an official part of their family. And more significantly, from tomorrow Seb would become Sofia. Suddenly Flick wondered if they'd been wrong to wait until after the wedding to tell the kids. Would there ever be a right time to drop this bombshell? Before she could give this any more thought, one of the bridesmaids, Zoe's best friend Clare, appeared with a tray full of champagne flutes. Flick couldn't down hers fast enough.

"Mom, I think you're supposed to wait for the toast," Toby said, smirking.

"Whoops. Sorry." She smiled nervously as everyone around her lifted their glasses.

"To my baby girl. To her being the happiest married woman that ever walked the earth." Seb smiled warmly at Zoe but his words left Flick cold.

"Besides Mom, you mean." Zoe grinned and then lifted the flute to her mouth.

"Yes, besides your gorgeous mother," Seb said, briefly meeting Flick's gaze before taking a sip of his champagne.

Flick could barely remember what it felt like to be truly

happy, and she silently prayed her daughter would never forget. That Beau would never compromise their marriage and Zoe's sense of self as Seb had hers.

Before their glasses were all empty, a black London taxicab pulled up in the driveway.

"The cars are here," Zoe squealed, shoving her empty glass at Toby. "Oh, my God, I'm so excited I could wet myself."

"Please don't," her brother replied drily.

A smartly dressed chauffeur got out the driver's side and started toward them. "I'm really sorry," he said, and Flick's heart jumped into her throat, "but our second car broke down on the way over." He offered a sheepish look of apology.

"What do you mean?" Zoe asked. "Can you fix it? We can't fit all of us in one car." She gestured around her to Flick, Seb, Toby and her three bridesmaids.

The man shook his head. "Not on a Saturday I'm afraid. Parts for these cars aren't easy to come by. We can call a taxi, though, and obviously we'll cover the costs."

"A taxi?" Zoe's mouth hung open as if the driver had offered them a tandem bicycle. She'd been calm and collected all morning, but the first signs of panic crept into her voice. "Are you kidding me? You want me to wear *this* in a taxi? I don't want the remnants of some drunk's vomit all over my beautiful gown."

"I… We… Of course not. I'd take you and whoever else we could fit in my vehicle," the man said, glancing down at his shiny, polished black shoes.

"This is a nightmare." Zoe lifted her hand to her head as if to run it through her hair, something she did whenever she was nervous or angry, but caught herself just before she ruined her hairstyle.

Flick let out a quick breath of relief. "Calm down, honey," she said, snapping back into mom mode. "I know this isn't ideal, but how about you and Dad go in the main car and I'll bring Toby and the girls in our car. It was valet cleaned only a couple of days ago."

"But you won't be able to drink," Zoe exclaimed.

"It's fine." Flick rubbed her lips together. "I can have another taste of bubbly when we do the speeches, but I don't need to drink to have fun."

"Are you sure, Mom?"

Flick nodded. She'd do anything to make Zoe and Beau's day run smoothly, and in some ways having to focus on driving would keep her mind from other less desirable thoughts. "Come on, let's get this show on the road."

Placated slightly, Zoe climbed into the black taxicab with her father, while her bridesmaids and Toby tumbled into Flick's car.

"Can I drive?" Toby asked. He was on his learner's license, and while Flick wanted him to get as much experience as possible on the road, her nerves couldn't handle much more right now.

"No," she said firmly as she turned the key in the ignition. "Not today."

When they arrived at the church, Flick slipped the car keys into her clutch and then walked over to join Zoe, Seb and the bridesmaids, who'd escaped her vehicle almost before she'd stopped it.

She kissed Zoe lightly on the cheek so as not to spoil her makeup. "You look gorgeous, my darling. I'm so happy for you. See you on the other side."

And then, without so much as a glance at Seb, Flick grabbed Toby's hand and dragged him inside the church. Soft classical music wafted over them as they made their way down the aisle to the front pew, waving and smiling at the gathered guests.

"You look hot," Neve mouthed as Flick and Toby passed her, Will and James.

Flick smiled at her friend, grateful for the compliment. She tried to ignore the tug of jealousy as she noticed James's and Neve's hands linked like two teenagers who'd just discovered sex and couldn't stop touching each other. James had landed back in town just in time for Will's high school graduation last week and was about to start working on *The Lion King*. And Flick was happy for Neve, truly she was.

Two rows in front was Emma, looking equally as radiant with Patrick and her three children by her side. She smiled up at Flick and wiggled her fingers in an excited wave. The last few months hadn't been easy for Emma—it turned out that recovering from brain surgery wasn't a walk in the park. She'd had mood swings and hormonal, rage-filled tantrums that the doctors had warned her about, but Patrick had stood by her through every moment, proving himself to be ten times the man Max was or had ever been.

Flick blew Emma a kiss and hurried on down the aisle to take her seat beside her dad and Seb's parents. She kissed them all on their cheeks and glanced across the aisle to Beau's family and waved. When she finally faced the front of the church, her breath whooshed out of her lungs at the sight of Beau standing up at the altar waiting for her girl. For *his* girl. She waved at him as happy tears welled in her eyes. Whatever the consequences of Seb's announcement, at least she had faith and confidence that Beau would make it all okay for Zoe.

Before she had any more time for contemplation, the organist launched into the "Wedding March." For a couple so young, Zoe and Beau were very conventional. An excited buzz hummed around her and Flick joined the rest of the guests as they stood to welcome the bride. Shivers littered her skin as she watched her daughter and Seb slowly come toward her, both of them beaming happiness from every pore.

A spike of envy hit her heart that Seb got to have this special moment with Zoe. She couldn't help but wonder if things would have played out differently if she hadn't made him wait these past few months. Would Zoe be happy for *Sofia* to walk her down the aisle or would she have been appalled and asked Flick to do the honor instead? Would the wedding even be going ahead if that bomb had been detonated before it?

Unable to watch Seb a moment longer, Flick turned to focus on Beau. There was nothing more special than watching a groom see his bride walking toward him, and Beau didn't let her down. As she predicted, tears streamed down his face and he tried to blot them away with the hankie his mom had insisted he tuck into his pocket. She remembered Seb on their wedding day and the way he'd howled like a baby as she'd floated down the aisle toward him. At the time, she'd thought it sweet and had fallen even more in love with him, but now she questioned every shared memory they owned.

And she hated him for that.

She hated that Seb had gone and ruined her perfect existence and that the knowledge of what he would soon be doing meant she couldn't even enjoy this special day the way she deserved to.

As they came to the end of the aisle, Zoe stepped up to join Beau at the altar. When Seb kissed his daughter's cheek and then retreated to the seat beside Flick, she dug her nails into her thighs, uncaring if she drew blood.

The ceremony was beautiful—a true reflection of the gorgeous young couple. Although Flick had initially had her reservations about them marrying so young, Zoe and Beau being together was the only thing in her life that felt right at this moment. Both she and Seb cried through the personal-ized vows and Toby shook his head, seemingly embarrassed by both of them.

When the priest gave Beau permission to kiss his bride, Seb's sobs eased and he smiled his approval, but Flick had to try a lot harder to stop from bawling.

The rest of the day passed in a blur. Flick stood with Seb, Toby and Beau's family beside the bride and groom, offering their best wishes as the guests filed out of the church. When Neve and Emma heard that she was playing second chauffeur to the bridal party, they both volunteered to take her place, but she refused their offers, happy to have a steering wheel to take her frustrations out on as she drove around the city.

At the reception, which was held at a beautiful winery in Swan Valley, Flick enjoyed her one glass of champagne with the speeches. As Seb spoke about his love for his family, his pride in his daughter and the joy of being her father, Flick thought it good she had to limit herself to one drink. If she drank any more, she might not be able to control her tongue or her stomach.

Once the speeches were over and the cake was cut, Zoe and Beau took to the dance floor, starting with a sweet love song by Shania Twain, which quickly segued into "Macarena" and had not only the bridal party but most of the other guests joining them in craziness.

Flick watched on as Seb, entirely in his element, shook his tush along with the best of them.

"Great wedding," Neve said, plonking herself down in the seat next to her.

Emma landed on the other side. "Are you going to dance?"

"Maybe later," Flick replied, trying not to sound so melancholy.

"You okay?" Neve and Emma asked at the same time.

"Of course," she lied. "Why wouldn't I be?"

Emma gave her a look. "Your little girl has just tied the knot. You're allowed to be emotional."

Any eavesdroppers would assume that the emotion they spoke about was down to Zoe leaving the nest, but Flick knew that her dearest friends were not referring to that. She'd confided in them about the agreement she'd made with Seb—they knew that tomorrow everything would change. When they smiled at her, it was pity Flick saw in their eyes. Although Emma and Neve supported her and had promised to stand by whatever decision she made, they'd made it clear they didn't think they'd be strong enough to stay with Seb if they had been in her shoes.

Sometimes she wondered if she'd made the right choice herself, but it was her bed and she had to lie in it.

"I'm fine," Flick said, tossing them a full-faced grin as she pushed back her chair and stood. "Come on, let's dance."

And dance they all did.

The tunes alternated between fun and boppy songs like The Monkees' "I'm a Believer," and much more romantic numbers like "(I've Had) The Time of my Life" from *Dirty Dancing*. During this last song, Seb pulled Flick into his arms and held her close, whispering sweet words that made her nauseous as they danced alongside the other "happy" couples.

"It's been a wonderful day, hasn't it?" he said, his deep voice tickling her ear. "I can't believe our little girl is a Mrs."

She made a murmur of agreement.

"I want to thank you for everything," he continued. "I'm so lucky to have you in my life. I can't thank you enough for…" His voice drifted off but he didn't need to say the words aloud. She had agreed to do what she guessed few wives would, and that, in Seb's eyes, made her some kind of angel.

But if she were an angel, would she be feeling the gut-wrenching pain she was right now as she danced with her husband for the final time? This might be the beginning of Zoe and Beau's marriage and she hoped against hope it would be a fabulous one, but she couldn't help mourning the end of her own as she knew it. She glanced sideways to see Emma cocooned in Patrick's arms. Neve and James were only a few steps away in an almost-identical embrace.

A silent tear trickled down her cheek.

It had been a long day, and after waving the new Mr. and Mrs. off into the night, Flick couldn't wait to get home. Seb acted as if he could have partied all night, but Flick feigned a headache and they made their excuses to escape not long after the bride and groom. Beau's parents—fueled by the alcohol they'd paid for—were happy to stay on and host any lingering guests, and as Toby had gone back to Neve's house to play Xbox into the early hours of the morning with Will and Caleb, Flick didn't have to put on a brave face for him either.

She drove solemnly home, although Seb, lost in his own happiness, didn't seem to notice. At the sound of their car's approach, Dog raised his head from where he was asleep on the front porch, but the moment he recognized them, he slumped back down to rest, obviously thinking this far too ungodly an hour to do his usual hyperactive greeting ritual.

Seb chuckled. "Some guard dog he is. I'll get the gate." And then he put his hand on the door, opened it and climbed out, shutting it behind him.

Flick watched as he jogged in front of the car toward the gate. He peeled it open and waved her through with a theatrical swirl of his hand. She summoned a smile, unable to mean it, hating the fact that he could act so lighthearted and devil-may-care when *her* heart felt as if it were full of lead. He'd kept his side of the bargain; he'd been patient and waited until Toby had graduated and Zoe was married. Now it was her turn to keep hers.

With a sigh, she drove forward and then stopped to wait for Seb to close the gate again. Not that she needed to—although he'd had an excessive amount to drink at the reception, he could manage the short walk up the rest of the driveway to the house—but something made her pause. She glanced in the rearview mirror as he started to pull one gate over to meet the other and she suddenly saw a woman standing behind the car instead.

Sofia.

Her heart went cold and her breath hitched as her future flashed before her eyes, much like the near-death experience Emma had relayed, except Flick was looking ahead, not behind.

And what she saw horrified her. She'd had months to get used to this, counseling session after counseling session and yet...

Could she really go through with it?

For one brief second something snapped inside her.

She looked away, thought how easy it would be to put the car into Reverse and slam her foot down hard on the accelerator. She'd claim it was an accident. Seb's secret would still be safe from the world, and no one would ever know she'd had an incentive to end his life. Everyone thought they were the perfect couple. Except Neve and Emma, but they were her friends; they'd believe her story. It would be so easy—such a simple solution to her problems. The kids wouldn't suffer any from Seb's coming out; instead they'd mourn the loss of a great father. And she'd be a widow, rather than...

Her heart galloping, she put her hand on the gearshift. She closed her eyes and sucked in a quick breath. The vision of Seb/Sofia lying lifeless on the concrete behind the car—his/her limbs at all angles and blood pouring from his/her head appeared large as life. Or rather death. Her hands began to shake.

What the hell am I thinking?

She couldn't *kill* her husband. She couldn't kill her friend. But neither could she continue living this lie. This *wasn't* okay with her. It was making her crazy.

The gate clicked shut behind the car and a few seconds later, Seb climbed back inside. *"Flick?"* His tone was anxious. "What's the matter? Are you okay?"

She opened her eyes and turned her head to face him. "No, Seb, I'm not."

His eyes brimming with unshed tears, he reached out to hold her hand and his voice cracked as he spoke. "It's okay, sweetheart. I love you. I'll always love you, but I can see what this is doing to you. I wish I could change, but I can't, and it's been unfair of me to hope that you could either."

"I wanted to," she whispered as tears flowed down her own cheeks. "I wanted *us* so bad that I thought I could accept you however you are, but I can't. In trying to accept you for who you are, in trying to wrap my head around a new kind of us, I've been living as big a lie as you have."

Seb squeezed her hand and nodded.

Although Flick could forgive him for what he'd put her through to get to this point, although she could even support his choice going forward and help him to navigate the rocky path ahead, she could not stay as his wife.

The time for secrets and lies was over.

★ ★ ★ ★ ★

Acknowledgments

A massive thanks must go to my faithful and devoted readers, who buy my books, read my books and then go out of their way to send me personal messages. When one of you tells me you have forgone sleep to finish one of my books or that the joy of reading has helped you through a particularly tough time in your life, it makes all the long hours at the keyboard worthwhile and gives me motivation to keep writing.

I've been overwhelmed by the response to my books, but especially my last book, *The Patterson Girls*, which won the General Fiction category in the 2015 Australian Book Industry Awards. It was such an honor to accept this prestigious award, but I have to acknowledge that the success of *The Patterson Girls* was a team effort. Not only by the wonderful team at Harlequin Australia, but also the wider group of enthusiastic booksellers who got behind the book, and also the bloggers and journalists who wrote thoughtful reviews to help spread the word. You all rock, and I can't thank you enough for your support. Thanks also to the team of wonderful industry professionals who judge the ABIAs.

As always, I'm indebted to the wonderful team at Harlequin in both the New York and Sydney offices for working so hard on my books. It's truly a team effort, but I thank Ann Leslie Tuttle, Nicole Brebner and Sue Brockhoff for directing it all.

I'm so privileged to work with Lachlan Jobbins, who edits my books, and also lucky to have my agent, Helen Breitweiser, always at the end of an email offering her wisdom and support. Thank you—I would not be without either of you.

Thanks to Emily Madden for being my travel buddy and, in particular, my New York partner in crime. Thank God you know your way around Google Maps; let's not mention your mishap on the subway. And also to Sofia Tate, who took us out into the *real* New York and also happily answered my stupid questions while writing about her fabulous home town.

My friend L-A deserves *massive* thanks for helping me with the medical jargon, offering information and wisdom, and for gladly reading the medical scenes in this book. Any mistakes are mine, not hers, *or* creative license.

Mention must also go to my book-club friends for the hilarious conversations we share over wine, which often spark ideas. A part of this story—no spoilers—was inspired by one such discussion.

And thanks to my writing buddies, who over time have also become some of my best friends. There are now too many of you to mention, but you know who you are! And a special shout-out to reader Bree, who has also become a good friend on this journey and helps keep me sane—or almost sane—with her Twitter messages.

Always last but never least, thank you to my family. My long-suffering husband, Craig, who puts up with all sorts of things in the name of my books. To my mom, Barbara, my first reader, biggest supporter and chauffeur of my kids to school in the mornings so I can work when the muse is fresh. And to said kids, who also contribute thoughts and ideas to stories/characters, despite the fact my books are a little old for them and they'd much prefer I wrote about zombie dinosaurs or fart machines. Maybe one day. Love you all!